Half-Breed

Trudie Collins

ISBN-13: **978-0-6485051-5-0**

DEDICATION

This book is dedicated to all of the doctors, nurses and other medical personnel around the world who risked their lives treating others during the 2020 Covid-19 pandemic. You arc all true heroes.

ACKNOWLEDGMENTS

Thank you to Pete, Julie, Terry, Wendy, Michelle, Marcia and Connie for their feedback.

Contents

Garrick

Garrick watched his target closely, as he had for the last two weeks. So far, the werewolf had done nothing to indicate that he had attacked a human, but that didn't mean he wouldn't.

The werewolf's registration had lapsed over a month ago and the final reminder had been delivered, by hand, so there was no doubt in Garrick's mind that the man seated a few rows in front of him was aware that his registration needed to be renewed. He had been given until the end of the previous day to contact the Agency and had failed to do so. Garrick was now free to act.

He dragged his eyes away from his quarry and surveyed the other bus passengers. He wasn't worried that the werewolf would escape; he had been following him long enough to know his routine. It would be another three stops before he reached his destination and disembarked the bus. Garrick would be right behind him.

As Garrick scanned the other people onboard, including the driver, he wasn't looking at their faces. Instead he was checking their auras, something the werewolf blood that he regularly injected into his veins allowed him to see. Most were pale blue, identifying the person as human. One was orange, indicating a registered werewolf. His target's aura was glowing bright red, showing that he was a werewolf who had either failed to register or had missed their re-registration date. His own, if he could see it, was green, due to the regular injections of serum he received.

Garrick was about to return his attention to the man he was there to arrest, when he noticed the woman sitting two rows behind him, on the opposite side of the bus. What he saw surprised him. He quickly looked away before she noticed him staring at her.

Her aura was light purple. He had never seen one that colour before and had no idea what it meant.

Taking his phone out of his pocket, he switched it to camera mode, making sure the front camera was being used, not the back. He then positioned it next to him, angling it so he could see the screen, and moved it until it clearly showed the woman's face. Anyone watching would think he was trying to see his screen without it being affected by the glare of the lights in the bus. At least they always had in the past, based on the comments he had overheard, and the one person who questioned his actions had believed his story.

He took a quick photo and texted it to Carl Weston, head of the division of the Agency he worked for, along with a question about who she was. He neglected to mention the reason for his enquiry. That was something that needed to be discussed in person.

He turned to look at her once more, noting that her attention was on the book she was reading: The Status Debt by Edie Baylis. He had read it himself and thought it was an interesting choice, not one he would expect someone who looked so sweet and innocent to be reading. Then again, looks could be deceiving, as he himself was testament to. Nobody looking at him would suspect he worked for a secret worldwide agency or that he had werewolf blood running through his body.

He took in her overall appearance, her long brown hair pulled back in a ponytail, her pale complexion and the way her rimless glasses rested on a nose which looked a little too big for her face.

Her eyes flicked up from her book as she turned the page and he quickly looked away. When he turned his head back again, she was once more focused on her novel.

Dressed in a smart skirt with a matching jacket, over a pale cream blouse, she looked professional, but he had no idea what that profession might be. Definitely office based, he decided.

He let his gaze travel down her legs, which were devoid of tights or stockings, to her shoes. The deck shoes didn't match the rest of her outfit, so he assumed that it was a pair she only wore for travelling to and from work, with a pair of high heels under her desk or in her locker for her to change into upon arrival.

Her hazel eyes flicked over to him once more and he couldn't help noticing how long and thick her lashes were. There was no sign that she was wearing any makeup so he thought they must be natural rather than enhanced by mascara. She intrigued him. What was she?

That was a question that would have to wait for another day. He had a job to do and he forced himself to turn his attention back to his target, who was busy playing with his phone, oblivious to the fact that Garrick was even on the bus, let alone what he was there to do.

The journey continued and somehow Garrick resisted the urge to turn toward the woman once more. He put her in her mid-twenties, but he had never been good at guessing someone's age. He wanted to check his assumption, but managed to stop himself looking at her again.

He saw the werewolf rise, so he put his phone back in his pocket and stood up, ready to disembark at the next stop. As he and his prey were the only ones getting off, he managed to stand directly behind him. He momentarily thought about confronting him there and then, but he didn't want too many witnesses.

The werewolf, who appeared to be nothing more than an ordinary human male in his early twenties, didn't look behind him as the bus came to a stop and he stepped off. Garrick followed him as he crossed the road and entered an alley. The streetlamp was broken so it was dark, the perfect place for Garrick to make his arrest. Of course, it was also the perfect place for an ambush if the werewolf wasn't as oblivious to Garrick's presence as he believed him to be.

Peering into the darkness with his werewolf-blood-assisted eyes, Garrick could see clearly, almost as if the entire alley was being illuminated by the moon, even though it was currently hidden behind clouds.

Seeing no sign of another presence, he stepped into the alley and walked after his target, moving at a faster pace so that he would catch him before he reached the end.

He made little noise as he walked, but he knew that the werewolf would still be able to hear him, though he made no indication that he was bothered by someone following him.

As soon as he was close enough, Garrick placed a firm hand on the young man's shoulder. "Thomas Bradly, you are under arrest for failing to visit the Agency for re-registration."

The speed with which Thomas moved would have surprised someone else, but Garrick was ready for it. As Thomas spun around, pulling out of Garrick's grip and raising an arm, ready to punch him, Garrick pulled a pair of handcuffs from the inside of his jacket and forced them onto the werewolf's wrist. Before Thomas had time to react, Garrick had his cuffed arm behind his back and quickly grabbed the other arm, cuffing it in position.

That was one reason Garrick never did up his jacket: ease of access.

Garrick then stepped back. Had he used normal handcuffs, the werewolf would have been able to easily break them apart, but these were Agency cuffs, specially made to not only withstand werewolf strength, but also to drain their power and prevent them transforming. While he was still wearing them, Thomas wouldn't be able to walk at speed, let alone run or jump. He was now as helpless as any human and would stay that way until Garrick took off the handcuffs.

"Now would you like to explain to me why you have failed to attend one of the Agency's clinics to re-register despite having multiple reminders?" Garrick kept his tone casual, rather than demanding. It made no difference. The response had so many expletives in it that the entire speech would have been bleeped out had it been on television.

"I'll take that as a no, shall I?" Garrick was aware that sarcasm was supposed to be the lowest form of wit, but sometimes it was called for and this was one of those times.

Thomas spat at him. Garrick moved out of the way and shook his head as he looked at the globule of sputum that lay on the ground.

"Now we can do this the easy way or the hard way. The easy way is that I walk you to my car and we take a drive to the Agency, where you will be given the choice between registration or imprisonment. Or, if you prefer, I can just execute you now."

Garrick was bluffing; he would never execute a defenceless werewolf, but the werewolf didn't know that.

With his head hung low, Thomas said, "I'll go with you."

"Wise decision," Garrick told him and gave him a shove to make him start walking down the alley.

Knowing that Thomas would be heading home, Garrick had parked his car opposite the werewolf's apartment block. As soon as he had his prey locked in the back, Garrick called his headquarters to let them know he was bringing another one in.

It would take them a while to reach their destination, so Garrick turned the radio on. It was tuned to a station which played sixties, seventies and eighties music. He had no idea why, but he loved the old stuff. Thomas grumbled about the choice of music, but Garrick ignored him.

A little over an hour later, he pulled off the main road and stopped at the gates to an industrial estate. He pulled up in front of a building with a sign stating it was the Smithson Health Clinic and got out of the car.

When he opened the car door for his passenger, the werewolf reluctantly got out. Garrick escorted him through the doors, which opened automatically as he approached.

The inside of the building looked like any other medical practice, with uncomfortable-looking plastic chairs, a small table filled with old magazines and a reception desk. Due to the late hour, it was currently unmanned, but two security guards approached as Garrick and his prisoner entered.

"Hey Garrick," one said. "We've been expecting you." He was a tall man with a full beard covering most of his face. The way his uniform stretched over his muscular arms suggested he regularly worked out.

"Hey Jim, Frank," Garrick replied, nodding his head to each man in turn. He then placed his hand on Thomas's shoulder. "Thomas Bradly to see the registrar."

"Come with me," Jim said as he took hold of Thomas's elbow. As he was led away by the two guards, Garrick wondered what decision he would make. Until recently, the werewolf had kept his registration up to date, so he was curious as to what would make him skip it this time.

Then he shook his head. It was none of his business. He had done his job and was ready to move onto the next one. Before he got his next assignment, however, he wanted to know more about the woman he had seen on the bus.

Walking up to a door on his left, he used his ID tag to gain entry. He followed the corridor to the end and called for a lift. When it arrived and the doors opened, he used his badge once more to select the lowest level.

When the lift reached its destination, he found himself looking down a long corridor, with numerous doors on either side. This was the heart of his branch of the Agency, the place only those of high rank were permitted.

Without looking at any of the doors he passed, he made his way to the end of the corridor and turned left. Stopping in front of a door to his right, he knocked and waited for permission to enter. He didn't have to read the text on the nameplate to know he was in the right place; he had been to the room enough times he could have gotten there with his eyes closed.

"Enter," a deep voice sounded from within so he opened the door.

Carl was seated behind his desk and looked up as Garrick walked in, signalling with his hand that he should take a seat. As he did so, he studied his boss. In his late fifties, Carl was old enough to be Garrick's father, though he never came across as the fatherly type. Married with no kids, Carl was a no-nonsense guy who expected his orders to be carried out, but was willing to listen to other opinions when the situation allowed.

His moustache and hair were both turning grey, to match his eyes, but he still looked younger than he was. Years of working in the armed forces before taking up his position in the Agency had indoctrinated into him the need for physical fitness and he still exercised every day.

Carl turned one of his monitors around so Garrick could see it. The photo Garrick had sent through was on it.

"I presume you're here to ask about her," Carl said, then continued without waiting for Garrick to respond. "She's not in our database, so she's never registered with the Agency. Facial rec also came up blank so she isn't known to the CIA, FBI, MI5, Interpol etcetera. Basically we have no idea who she is."

"What about her aura?" Garrick asked. "Why is it purple?"

"We have no idea."

One of the things Garrick liked about his boss was his openness. If he didn't know something, he freely admitted it.

"Have you checked with the wolves?" he asked, using his pet name for the family of werewolves who lived in an Agency facility and willingly provided the werewolf blood the Agency required.

He had known them for a long time, since his army days. It was Lawrence who had recruited him into the Agency. Garrick had become good friends with his son while they served together, before he had been killed in action. He still felt his loss. Lawrence and his wife and daughter felt like family to him, not just friends.

Carl nodded. "They have no idea either. I've also checked with all other branches. There is no record anywhere of anyone having a purple aura. It could indicate a half-breed, half human and half werewolf, a mix of blue and red, but we all know that's impossible."

"What are my orders?" Garrick didn't say Sir. The first time they had met, Carl had said his name was Carl not Sir and until he received a knighthood, nobody was ever to call him that.

That was another thing Garrick liked about him.

"Follow her. Find out where she lives, where she works, what she does in her free time, who her friends are. I want to know everything about that woman. Once we have an address we can get a name. As of now, she is your only priority unless you hear different directly from me."

"Got it." Garrick stood up to leave. He didn't need to provide a report on his previous mission. Carl was aware that he had brought in Thomas Bradly and didn't need to know the details. He was only interested in knowing when there were complications.

Without saying another word, Garrick headed to the door. Just as he was about to leave, Carl called out to him.

"Garrick, I want to know who that woman is and, more importantly, what she is. I'll leave it to your discretion as to how you obtain that information. Good luck."

Garrick nodded and left the room, closing the door behind him. Finding out who she was would be easy, discovering what she was, was a completely different matter. It was a challenge, but he loved challenges. 'I'm in for a few interesting weeks,' he thought as he made his way to the lift. 'Some interesting weeks indeed.'

Amy

Amy glanced up from her book and noticed the man was in what had become his usual seat. She had no idea who he was or where he worked, but over the last few days she had noticed he had been on her bus when she got on. Not that she minded. He kept to himself and gave no indication that he even noticed her. Unfortunately. He was an attractive man and she would have liked him to introduce himself.

He was in his early thirties, she guessed, and from the way he held himself, he was probably ex-military, though she could be wrong about that.

She found herself looking at his left hand as he held up his phone, playing some game. She told herself she wasn't looking for a wedding ring, but she knew she was lying. She couldn't help smiling to herself when she noticed his fingers were ring-free. Not that it made any difference these days. He might be living with someone, married in every way except for the official ceremony.

The first time she noticed him, he had disembarked a few stops before hers. It had also been much later in the evening on one of the days she had to work late. The second time, he got off at the same stop as her. She initially thought he was going to speak to her, maybe ask her out on a date, and was disappointed when he walked straight past, not even looking in her direction as she left the path and opened her garden gate. Since then he had remained on the bus after she got off.

Only once had she seen him in the morning, which was a shame. Knowing he would be on her bus would give her something to look forward to when she got up.

Dragging her eyes away from the stranger and back to her book, she tried to continue reading, but found she couldn't focus. Should she introduce herself? She had to pass him to get to the exit so it would be easy enough to do. She shook her head. No, she didn't have the confidence to go up to a complete stranger and ask him on a date. Besides, why would he be interested in her? She wasn't exactly model material.

Unable to stop herself, she returned her gaze to the man, hoping he wouldn't turn around and catch her checking him out. Her eyes travelled from his short, neatly trimmed, dark hair, down his neck to his impressively wide shoulders. She was glad that the jacket he wore was never done up. It gave her a nice view of his body as she walked past him when she got on the bus, making her wonder what great abs the tight-fitting black t-shirt was hiding. The chain he wore intrigued her. He didn't seem the sort of man to wear a necklace.

From where she was seated, she couldn't see his captivating dark eyes. The only time they had made eye contact, she felt like they were drilling through her, down to her soul. Given the chance, she could lose herself looking into them.

On top of everything else he had going for him, he was also tall. She, herself, was well over average height for a woman and was conscious of how ridiculous she would look standing next to a shorter man.

She was so busy watching him, she almost missed her stop. If it hadn't been for the man sitting next to her politely asking her to let him out, she wouldn't have noticed that she needed to get off.

Just before she stepped off, she looked behind her. The man was looking at her. At least she hoped he was looking at her; he could just as easily be looking past her, but she could dream couldn't she?

It didn't take her long to walk from the bus stop to her small townhouse. As she walked up her garden path, she searched her bag for her keys. Finding them in the usual place, she retrieved them and opened her front door. She didn't have time to close it before the sound of the dog flap being used reached her ears and Ainin, her border collie, came bounding toward her.

Dropping her bag on the ground, she knelt down so he could put his paws on her shoulders and lick her face. Some people thought her allowing him to do that was disgusting, but she didn't care; she loved the way he greeted her every time she walked through the door.

"Hey boy," she said, rubbing his head with one hand. "Have you missed me?"

He barked his response, making her smile. She was sure he understood every word she said to him. Border collies were one of the smartest breeds of dogs, which was one of the reasons she got one, but she wouldn't be surprised if Ainin's intelligence surpassed those of his brethren. She had named him Ainin, after Ainin Cawley who reportedly, at the time, had the highest ever recorded IQ.

"Would you like a walk before dinner?" she asked. He barked once more and ran to retrieve his lead from where it hung from a hook near the back door.

She raced up the stairs; she didn't have long to get changed before he hunted her down. She was still pulling up her jeans when he sauntered into her bedroom, his lead in his mouth.

She finished getting dressed, laughing when Ainin dropped his lead and brought one of her walking shoes from the shoe rack to her.

"I need the other one," she said as she slipped her foot in and started to lace it up. He raced back down the stairs and soon returned with the second shoe in his mouth.

As soon as she was dressed, he picked up the lead once more and ran out of the room and down the stairs. He was patiently sitting by the front door by the time she got there.

"Come on then boy," she said and opened the door. The dog bounded out of the house and waited by the front gate for Amy to take the lead from his mouth and attach it to his collar.

Like the obedient dog he was, Ainin walked calmly ahead of her as they strode down the footpath. He didn't pull at the lead and other than the occasional sniff at some interesting smells, kept his focus on their destination. The dog park was just around the corner.

Two dogs and their owners were already there, one of which they knew. Amy greeted the owner and the dog, making sure she said the dog's name prior to her owner's. As soon as she was inside the enclosure, she released Ainin and he ran off to join his friend.

Amy hadn't seen the other man there before and couldn't help smiling as she watched Ainin introduce himself to his husky before turning his back on it and offering it his butt to sniff.

The owner, a man in his fifties with thinning hair and middle aged spread, turned and smiled at her. As he approached, he held out his hand.

Instantly Ainin was by Amy's side, his playtime forgotten as his protection instincts kicked in. He growled, making the man stop, his arm still outstretched.

"It's okay, Ainin," Amy said. "Go play with your new friend."

The canine glanced once at her then was off to join the other two dogs.

"I'm Amy. Sorry about that," Amy said as she walked up to the stranger and shook his hand. "He's a little over-protective sometimes. He wouldn't actually bite someone, but he does like to demonstrate who's in charge."

"John, nice to meet you," the man said. "And no apology necessary. Snow was just the same with my daughters when they lived at home. Any young man who came to the door had to be thoroughly sniffed before he would let them in the house."

"I haven't seen you here before. Are you new to the area?"

"Sort of," John said. "My wife and I moved into our new house last week but we used to live not too far away. I've only just discovered this place exists."

After a short while, both John and the other dog owner left, so Ainin was put back on his lead. The only reason Amy brought him to the park was to play with other dogs so there was no point in staying once they were alone.

The two went for a long walk and Amy was tired by the time they returned. And hungry, but that would have to wait. First she had to feed Ainin and then shower.

While Ainin made his way through his bowl of biscuits, Amy went up to her bedroom and removed her clothing. Catching sight of herself in the mirror, she noticed she had another bruise, this one on the front of her left thigh, near the top.

12

Looking at it closely, she saw that it had rows of dark purple spots, almost uniformly placed. She had seen this before and had wondered what it was. It was probably something to do with the pores in her skin, but she had never bothered to look it up. It made it look like she had been hit with a meat tenderiser.

Like many of her bruises, she had no idea how she got it. She had always bruised easily, the deep red or purple marks appearing on her skin in situations where most people would only show a slight reddening of the flesh. Her habit of walking into things didn't help; chairs, tables, even walls. She claimed they jumped out at her, but that wasn't true. Most of her bruises were the right height for her desk at work or her kitchen counter. She still had yellow marks on her hip from where she walked into the bin when she went into her back garden last week. Though she couldn't remember hitting her leg on anything recently, it didn't mean she hadn't.

Putting it from her mind, she took her shower and put on a loose fitting pair of trousers and a t-shirt before preparing her evening meal. Smelling the aromas of cooking meat, Ainin ran into the kitchen and jumped up at her, his paws directly hitting the middle of her bruise, making her wince. Then his claws dragged down her thigh as he slid down to place his paws on the ground. Well that answered that question. His claws weren't sharp, but she could still feel them through her clothes. Maybe it was time to visit the vet to have them trimmed.

As soon as her food was ready, she sat on the sofa and switched on the TV. There was a drama series on Netflix that she enjoyed and she pressed play on the next episode. She didn't watch much television, usually only while she ate. Soon her plate was clear, with a little help from Ainin, as usual, and she sat back to enjoy the rest of the show.

A while later, she stacked the dishwasher before pulling out her law books. She could fit in an hour or two of study before going to bed. When she eventually turned in for the night, she took her novel to bed with her and read for an hour or so, with Ainin curled up on the bed beside her. When she first got him, she had put a bed in the corner of the room for him to sleep in.

That had lasted until he had grown big enough to jump on the bed. Usually an obedient dog, that was the one time he refused to obey her and from then on the bed was no longer hers alone.

She awoke just before her alarm went off and quickly put on her walking clothes. Ainin was nowhere to be seen, which was unusual. She called out to him and the sound of him climbing through the dog-flap reverberated through the house.

An hour later, the dog had been walked, both of them had eaten breakfast and she was dressed ready for work.

As soon as she opened the front door, she realised it had started to rain and swore under her breath. Going back inside, she grabbed her umbrella and called out to Ainin, instructing him to stay in the house until the rain stopped.

It was an unpleasant walk to the bus, which was late, and the good looking stranger wasn't on it. Not that she expected him to be. She would just have to wait for the journey home.

It was a long and tiring day and didn't get any better when she got onto her bus to go home. She looked around, but there was no sign of him. Taking one of the few spare seats, she sighed and got out her book. She had finished book one in the series and was onto book two, which was even better than the first. She began reading and soon lost herself in the lives of fictional characters.

Surveillance

"What do you mean she has a pet dog?" Carl asked. "Dogs hate werewolves."

Garrick couldn't help smiling at his boss. He was reacting the same way Garrick himself had when he had watched his target taking her dog for a walk.

"Not only does she have a dog, but it protected her when a stranger approached."

"That makes no sense," Carl said.

"Tell me about it." Garrick was in Carl's office, giving him an update on all he had discovered about the strange woman with the purple aura. "I snuck into her back garden this morning, before she got up, and her dog came right up to me as though I was a friend. It was almost as if he could sense that I'm the same as his mistress, assuming she does actually have werewolf blood in her."

"So tell me everything you know," Carl instructed.

Having followed her home, he had obtained her address and from there was able to get her name. Amelia Ritchie, no middle name, had purchased the property a few years previous. She was the only registered tenant and it seemed she preferred to be called Amy.

Tailing her to her place of work allowed him to ascertain that she worked full time as a legal secretary in one of the big name law firms in the city. She appeared to have no social life; at least she hadn't gone out any of the days he had followed her, other than to the local university where he discovered she was studying part time for her law degree. It had been easy enough, after the first few days, for him to get off at a different stop and drive to near where she lived so he could pick up her route again without being seen.

So far he had seen nothing to suggest she was anything other than a normal human being. He seemed to have attracted her attention on the bus journeys, but he wasn't worried about that; a lot of women eyed him up when they thought he wasn't looking. Part of him hoped she would approach him, but the one time he thought she would, she seemed to change her mind at the last minute.

"So other than her aura," Carl said once Garrick had finished his account, "there's nothing to indicate she is someone worth investigating."

It wasn't a question, but Garrick answered anyway. "No, absolutely nothing." He knew where this conversation was leading and wasn't happy about it. The Agency didn't have enough resources to spend any more time on someone who didn't appear to be a werewolf, but he wanted answers; he didn't want to have to give up his investigation until he knew exactly what she was.

"Go to her house," Carl said, taking him by surprise. "Break in when you know she's at work. Set up shields, but don't activate them until she's in the house. Interrogate her. Bring her in for questioning if you have to. I want to know exactly what she is and I want to know sooner rather than later."

"Yes Sir," Garrick said in a mocking tone, earning himself a glare from Carl.

He got up and walked to the door, but before he could leave the office, Carl called out to him. "Garrick, be careful. We don't know what we're dealing with here."

Garrick grinned at him. "Aren't I always?"

"No, you're bloody well not," he heard Carl mutter as he closed the door.

The smile left Garrick's face as he strode down the corridor. Carl was right; he didn't know what he was dealing with. He knew what werewolves were capable of and how to handle them, even after they had transformed into wolf form, but Amy was an unknown. He would have to be careful, take extra precautions and go into the mission assuming nothing.

He had plenty of time to reach her house before she was due back from work, so before leaving the building, he took a detour to the armoury.

He grabbed two shields, one for the front door and one for the back, as well as an additional pair of special handcuffs, just in case, and a high voltage taser. Despite it being a well-known fact, in books and on TV at least, that silver bullets were needed to kill werewolves, nothing could be further from the truth. Normal bullets worked just fine and werewolves didn't possess special regenerative powers. Shoot dead a lycanthrope and they stay dead. But Garrick didn't want his target dead, hence the taser. Before leaving the armoury, however, he grabbed additional bullets for his gun. You couldn't be too careful.

He would have requested backup, but he preferred to work alone. Taking someone with him meant one more person he had to protect. He'd never had a permanent partner; he didn't trust anyone enough, not even his own sister. Tabitha was a great Agent and was more than capable of looking after herself, but having her with him would be a distraction he couldn't afford.

Satisfied he had all he needed, he left the Agency building and drove straight to Amy's house, parking almost in front of it. To the best of his knowledge, she had never seen his car so wouldn't recognise it and wonder why it was there.

Without looking around to see if he was being watched, he opened the front gate and walked up her path. Rule one of breaking and entering: always look like you are supposed to be there.

The path led up to her front door, but that wasn't his destination. The gravel pathway also wound around to the side of the house, where a gate separated the front from the back. This one was locked, but it was easy enough for him to climb over.

Barking and growling came from the back of the house and he stood his ground, waiting for the canine to appear. The moment the dog saw him, he went down on one knee and said, "Come here Ainin." The tag on the dog's collar had let him know its name when he read it earlier that morning. It also contained Amy's phone number, which he now had stored in his own device.

Ainin ran up to him, tongue hanging out of the side of his open mouth, and gave him a wet lick up his cheek as soon as he was in reach.

"Good boy," Garrick said as he fussed the animal. "Now I need to get into the house. You're not going to stop me are you?"

Ainin barked once before running toward the back door. By the time Garrick got there, the dog was in the house, having entered through the dog flap.

Garrick looked at it, deliberating whether he would fit through or not. He shook his head. It was big, but not that big. He would have to pick the lock. It was something he was proficient at and it didn't take him long to gain entry into the house. The dog didn't seem to mind him being there, despite his unorthodox method of entry.

The first thing he did was take a good look around the house, making a mental note of where the exits were and the location of anything Amy would be able to use as a weapon; the block of knives in the kitchen, for example.

Next he checked that all the windows were locked. He needed to ensure the only means of escape from the house were the front and back doors. Once satisfied, he put the miniature shield generators in place and switched them to stand-by. He would activate them the minute Amy entered the house. They were specially designed to affect werewolves only. Inaudible to the human or werewolf ear, they emitted a high frequency pulse that rendered a werewolf unconscious if they got too close. If Amy tried to run from him through either of the doors, she would be on the floor before she knew what hit her.

He then took a more casual look around the house, closely followed by Ainin. It was a small but neat dwelling, with no signs of anyone else living with her on either a permanent or temporary basis. The spare room contained a single bed, which had bed linen folded neatly on it, ready to be used, and an empty wardrobe. Obviously Amy wasn't expecting visitors anytime soon.

He next went into Amy's bedroom and glanced around. It looked no different to any other bedroom of an unattached female. Nothing seemed out of the ordinary and no alarm bells rang in his head. There was a chest of drawers against one wall and when he started to open a drawer, Ainin growled at him, indicating his welcomed presence had limits.

"Okay, boy," he said, smiling at the animal while trying to ignore the bared teeth. "I get the message." He closed the drawer once more and took one more quick look around the room before leaving.

The only other room upstairs was the bathroom, which contained the usual toilet, sink and bath, with a shower in it. Garrick took a quick look in the bathroom cupboard, after asking the dog's permission, but there was nothing unexpected in there.

Returning downstairs, Garrick went to the living room first. A photo on the wall showed a middle-aged couple, who he assumed were Amy's parents. He took a photo of it and sent it to headquarters for comparison to their werewolf database. If one, or both, of her parents were registered werewolves, he wanted to know.

Other than a black and white painting of a forest, the rest of the walls were bare. There was little in the way of personal items on display, but enough to make it feel homey.

He returned to the kitchen, which was large for such a small house. It contained a 4-seat dining table, which appeared to be used as a substitute desk rather than a place to eat meals.

Garrick took a quick look at his watch. There was still another hour before Amy was due home and he debated whether he should take Ainin for a walk or not. It was unlikely Amy would be able to, given he was probably going to arrest her, but he decided it would be a bad idea, just in case someone saw him and called Amy. He needed his presence in her house to be a complete surprise.

Coffee, however, was a good idea. She had a Nespresso machine in the corner, near the sink, and he found clean mugs in the cupboard above it.

While he drank, he browsed through one of Amy's law books, placing one about taxation to the side and selecting the one on criminal law below it.

His coffee was almost finished when his phone rang. He glanced at the caller ID. It was one of the land lines at headquarters so he answered it. "What have you got for me?"

"Not as much as I hoped I'm afraid," a voice he recognised but couldn't put a name to said. "The man is in our database. Frederick Ritchie, more commonly known as Fred, was a registered werewolf. He kept his registration up to date and caused no problems until he died a few years ago. We have no idea who the woman is I'm afraid. She's either human or a werewolf who never registered with the Agency."

"Thanks," Garrick said. "Keep looking for the woman and let me know if you find her. Try the national database of registers. See if he was married and who the parents are on Amelia's birth certificate." He hung up without waiting for a reply.

He was part way through his second cup of coffee when he heard someone at the front door. Ainin's ears pricked up, but he remained where he was, watching Garrick, as though making sure he didn't do anything the dog didn't like. Garrick couldn't help smiling.

He waited until he heard the door close before activating both shields. Amy wasn't leaving the house without his permission. The smile dropped from his face as he said, "Show time."

Werewolves

Amy sighed. It felt strange that she missed someone she had only ever seen and not spoken to. It had been a tiring day and she was glad to be home.

She was surprised that she heard no sound from Ainin when she opened the door and entered the house. She was even more surprised when he didn't come running to her when she called out his name.

Puzzled, but not concerned, she went straight to the kitchen. The sight that greeted her made her freeze. Ainin was there, staring up at the stranger from the bus, as though guarding him. 'What is he doing in my house?' was her first thought. 'Run,' was her second.

Instinct kicked in and her hand dived into her bag. As soon as her fingers closed around her can of pepper spray, she pulled it out and aimed it at the man. He wasn't close enough to hit him with the contents, but that didn't stop her pressing down and filling the air with the foul smelling substance.

She then dropped the can, turned around and ran to the front door. Then everything went black.

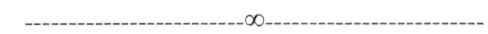

Amy wasn't unconscious for long and when she came around she found she was in the kitchen, slumped on a chair at the table. Her hands had been handcuffed in front of her and the strange man sat opposite, an amused smile on his face. Ainin was seated next to him, looking like he was ready to attack if he made a wrong move.

"Pepper spray?" he asked, his voiced filled with laughter. "What good did you think pepper spray would do?"

Amy should have felt scared, but for some reason she didn't. Why wasn't her heart pounding? Why had adrenaline not kicked in? Why wasn't she panicking? Maybe it was because if the man

21

wanted her dead, she probably would be. If he wanted to sexually attack her, she wouldn't be sitting in the kitchen, fully clothed. Or maybe she was in shock.

"Hopefully blinded you long enough for me to escape," she said.

"Why not just attack me? Use your strength to overpower me? Or shift into your other form?"

Amy looked at the man, then herself, comparing their physiques. How on Earth did he think she would ever be able to overpower him? Then she realised what he had said.

"What other form?" she asked.

The man smiled. "Your wolf, of course."

Amy shook her head. She was being held hostage by a mad man.

"Don't pretend you don't know what I'm talking about," he continued.

"I don't," she replied.

The man didn't show any indication that he believed her. "What are you? I know you're not a normal werewolf."

Amy sighed in exasperation. She was getting nowhere with this lunatic and she had no experience dealing with mentally ill people. "I'm not any sort of werewolf. Or any other mythical monster, for that matter. Now let me have my phone so I can call whatever mental hospital you have obviously escaped from." She couldn't believe she was staying calm instead of having hysterics. Surely this wasn't normal behaviour.

A look of incredulity crossed the man's face. "You're serious, aren't you? You really don't know what I'm talking about."

Amy rolled her eyes. "Finally."

For the first time since she had seen him on the bus, he looked unsure of himself. "I'm Garrick. And I really don't know what I'm going to do with you."

Amy held up her arms, showing the handcuffs on her wrists. "You can start by removing these. I'm Amy by the way." She saw no harm in telling him her name. Maybe building up a personal rapport would get him to release her, enabling her to call the proper authorities. This man needed help.

"I know," he said. "I know everything about you. Well, almost everything. And there is no way in hell I am removing those cuffs. They're the only thing stopping you transforming and while you appear not to know what I'm talking about, it doesn't mean you won't do it without realising. They stay in place until we establish exactly what you are. Coffee?"

"Sure," Amy said. "White with two."

While Garrick made the drinks, his back was to her, so she looked closely at the handcuffs, seeing if there was a way out of them. She had no idea what they were made of, but they didn't appear to be the usual metal, based on the colour of those she had seen on TV. There was no keyhole for her to pick, not that she had any idea how to do that. It looked like they would be staying in place, at least until she could persuade the lunatic to release her.

Once the coffee was ready, he placed a mug in front of her and sat down again. He took a sip from his own cup before continuing where he left off.

"Amelia Ritchie, daughter of Frederick and Mary Ritchie; at least that's the official version. No siblings. Works as a legal secretary while studying law. I would say your friends like to call you Amy, but it doesn't appear that you have any."

"I have plenty of friends," she snapped at him. She didn't like him suggesting he knew things about her that he obviously didn't. "Just because I'm not out partying every night, doesn't mean I'm some sort of loner."

He shrugged. "I'll take your word for that. Now let's get back to your parents shall we?"

Before she could reply, he stood up and left the kitchen. She heard him enter her front room and was annoyed when he returned with a photo frame in his hand. It felt like he was invading her privacy. He placed it on the table in front of her, turned so she could see it was of her parents. He pointed to her father.

"We know this is Frederick Ritchie, a registered werewolf, and that he is on your birth certificate as your father." He then pointed to the woman in the picture. "Who is this? I had a call while you were unconscious from someone in my Agency saying that you are registered as being the daughter of Frederick and Mary, yet we have no knowledge of this Mary in our database. How come?"

None of what this Garrick person was saying made any sense to her, but she decided playing along might be her best bet, at least for the time being.

"They are Fred and Mary and, as you have already stated, they are my parents. My father is not, and has never been, a werewolf."

Garrick smiled at her. She didn't like his smile, at least not this one. She had a feeling she wasn't going to like what he said next.

"Oh, but he is, or should I say, was. Our records indicate that he died a few years ago. Cancer, I believe. I guess even werewolves aren't immune."

Anger surged through Amy. She had heard enough. "My father was a good and decent man. How dare you try to corrupt his memory by accusing him of being some sort of evil fictional creature. I've had enough of this. I'm leaving."

She stood up and moved toward the back door, but Garrick calling out to her made her freeze.

"I wouldn't do that if I were you."

She turned around to look at him. "Is that a threat?"

He shrugged. "No, just a warning. The werewolf shield that I have on the front door knocked you unconscious. The one on the back door will do the same."

"Yeah, right."

She turned around once more but hadn't taken more than two steps before he spoke again. "Do you want me to demonstrate?"

"Sure," she said. Maybe if he went through the door she would be able to lock him out.

Smiling at her once more, he walked over to the back door and called Ainin to him. The dog looked at Amy, waiting for her to nod her approval before he walked over to Garrick. Garrick opened the door and together they walked through.

Amy ran over, hoping to close and lock the door. She had no idea how Garrick had entered her house in the first place and she hoped that her actions would give her enough time to call the police.

She didn't make it to the door before blackness claimed her once more.

------------------------∞------------------------

When she awoke, she was lying on her sofa. Ainin was sitting in front of her, staring at her intently as though checking she was still breathing.

She sat up, which wasn't easy with her hands still cuffed in front of her.

Garrick was sitting in a chair, watching her almost as closely as Ainin was.

"Do you believe me now?" he asked.

Amy shook her head. She had no idea what had knocked her out, but she was sure it wasn't some invisible shield designed to affect only werewolves. For starters, werewolves didn't exist. Secondly, even if they did, she sure as hell wasn't one.

Garrick leaned forward, but in a relaxed rather than threatening manner. "You're either a good actress or you genuinely don't know what you are. Why don't I tell you everything. You can stop and ask questions at any time."

He relaxed back and began to talk.

"My name is Garrick Barton. I'm a senior Agent for the W.A.R. agency – Werewolf Activity Regulation, more commonly known as just 'the Agency'. They recruited me when I left the army. We're an international organisation and have branches in almost every country. Most governments don't know we exist. Interpol does, and we get our funding through them, but that's about it. Can you imagine if politicians found out that werewolves were real?"

It was a rhetorical question so Amy didn't answer it. She knew what he meant though. Word would get out, there would be mass hysteria and anyone accused of being a werewolf would be hunted down and killed. If, of course, he was telling the truth, which, she reminded herself, he wasn't.

"We keep a register of werewolves," Garrick continued. "They have to re-register each year and receive an annual injection which will prevent them transforming against their will. It will still allow them to take on their wolf form, but it gives them control; they have to want to change into a wolf, they have to will it to happen."

"Why?" Amy asked. "Why not just kill them?"

Garrick frowned. "Why would we do that? The vast majority live relatively normal lives, are not a threat to anyone and contribute to society. Would you destroy all dogs just because some attack humans? And we're not talking about animals here. Werewolves are human beings, with just a few extra abilities."

Amy huffed. She would hardly call being able to turn into a wolf an ability.

Garrick smiled at her reaction. "They're stronger, faster, have more endurance and their senses are enhanced. If it wasn't for the transforming into a wolf thing, you could argue that they're superior humans, nothing more. Of course, they are banned from taking part in any sporting competitions, for obvious reasons."

"You say they have to register," Amy interrupted. "What if they don't?"

"Then people like me are sent to hunt them down."

"And kill them."

"No, we take them to headquarters, where they are given the option of registering."

"And if they refuse?"

"Then we lock them up."

There was no remorse in his voice, no guilt that people were being imprisoned because of him. Then again, were they really people? Amy shook her head. What was she thinking? None of what this Garrick person was saying could possibly be the truth.

"So how do you know who's a werewolf and who isn't? How do you know who's registered and who hasn't?" Amy was trying to trip him up, trying to find a flaw in what he was saying. She didn't succeed. He had obviously spent a lot of time thinking up and memorising his tale.

"By their auras. Humans have blue, registered werewolves have orange and unregistered ones, the ones we call rogue, have red."

"You can see auras?" She couldn't hide her scepticism.

"Yes. All Agents in the Agency can. Each branch has a werewolf, or a family of werewolves, working with them. The werewolves provide us with a supply of blood which our scientists use to make a serum. When injected into our veins, it gives us some of the powers of a werewolf, including the ability to see auras."

"Really." Amy's voice dripped with sarcasm. "So what colour is my aura then?"

Garrick leaned forward again. "That is why I'm here. Your aura is purple. I've never seen that before, nor has anyone in the Agency, in any branch, in any country."

"So what does that mean?"

"I have absolutely no idea. Which is why I'm here."

"This is all bullshit." It was the closest Amy ever got to swearing in public. "If you inject werewolf blood into you, why did your so called werewolf shield have no effect on you?"

"I don't have enough werewolf blood. Unlike you."

Amy said nothing. He seemed so sure of what he was saying that she was beginning to think he might be telling the truth.

"So what do we do now?" she eventually asked.

Garrick smiled once more. "You and me are going to go for a little drive."

"Where to?"

"To visit your mother, of course."

Mother

Before leaving the house, Garrick phoned Carl to give him an update. He, too, couldn't believe that Amy had used pepper spray. It made no sense to either of them. Garrick informed Carl of his plans and was told to be careful. If the mother was a werewolf, he would need to be prepared.

Garrick smiled at his boss's concern. Like a boy scout, he was always prepared. He had an extra set of cuffs on him, just in case, and had brought along the shields from Amy's house.

He still couldn't work her out. She hadn't resisted when he said he was taking her to see her mother, which was strange, but she seemed far from convinced that he was telling her the truth. She had, however, insisted that her dog come along. Or had it been the dog who had insisted? When they went to leave, he had growled and looked ready to attack until Amy had told him to come.

Why was a dog protecting a werewolf? It was another mystery he would have to solve.

"Why does Ainin seem to like you?" Amy asked as Garrick drove. She had wanted to take her own car, but Garrick wasn't sure where she would really go so made her get in his. He was now regretting the decision. Ainin was securely tied up on the back seat by his travelling harness attached to the seatbelt, but it would take him ages to get all the fur out of his car.

"I'm not sure," Garrick replied. "Maybe it's because we both have werewolf blood in us."

"I don't have werewolf blood," came the predictable reply. Garrick could have pointed out, again, that the shields wouldn't have worked on her if she didn't, but he knew he would be wasting his time.

"It's rather ironic that your surname is Ritchie," Garrick said. "The first werewolf novel was a book called 'The Man-Wolf' by Leitch Ritchie. Maybe he was a werewolf. Maybe you're a descendant. You should look into your family tree."

28

The look Amy gave him told him she wasn't amused.

"I don't believe for a moment that werewolves really do exist," she said after a few minutes. "But if they did, where did they come from?"

"Good question. It's not one I can answer, I'm afraid. We think they have been around for a long time. Back in the Viking days there were people known as berserkers. Our experts think they were actually werewolves. Throughout history, there have been tales and legends of people who may have been lycanthropes. A lot of reported animal attacks we believe are caused by rogue werewolves. It's one of the reasons the Agency was formed. We investigate all such occurrences and if we believe the supernatural was involved, we try to track the culprit down. Any werewolf found attacking a human without justification is executed."

"Justification?" Amy asked. "How do you justify attacking someone?"

Garrick glanced at her, trying to read her face. She didn't look like she was being sarcastic so he treated it as a genuine question.

"Self-defence is the usual one. Or defence of others. Most werewolves I have met are decent people who like to protect humans as well as each other. A lot go into professions like medicine or the police."

He paused before adding, "Of course there are those who like to act as vigilantes. We tend to turn a blind eye if they can prove the person they attacked is guilty of a serious crime, but we try to discourage such behaviour."

The rest of the journey was made in silence. Garrick's mind was filled with how he was going to explain to Mrs. Ritchie who he was, why he was visiting her and why her daughter was in handcuffs.

He had allowed Amy to use her phone to call her mother, to make sure she was at home before he had confiscated it. He couldn't risk her trying to contact anyone else. Now all he had to do was work out how to introduce himself, but that would all depend on the colour of Mary's aura.

As they turned into the right street, Amy gave instructions regarding where to park. She held her arms out in front of her.

"You're going to have to take these off you know," she said, raising her wrists to direct his gaze to the handcuffs.

Garrick snorted. "You must be joking."

Amy raised an eyebrow. "Do you really think I'm going to do anything with my supposed enhanced abilities? We both know I don't have any."

Nobody could be that good an actress, could they? He decided to take the risk.

"Thank you," she said as she rubbed her wrists once the cuffs had been removed.

"Were they hurting?" Garrick asked. He didn't see how they could have been as he hadn't put them on tight.

Amy seemed surprised by the question. Then she looked down at her hands and immediately stopped what she was doing.

"No," she said. "I have no idea why I'm doing that. Instinct I guess."

'Or your skin is tingling as your powers surge through you again,' Garrick thought, but didn't voice his observation.

"Let's go," he said instead.

He got out of the car and glanced into the back seat. "You too," he said as he opened the door for Ainin. For a moment he wondered why the dog didn't get out, then he remembered he was strapped in.

He could feel the canine breathing down his neck as he leaned into the car to unhook him. He was not impressed when the dog said thank you by licking his face.

Amy walked up the garden path and knocked on the door, the dog on her heels. Garrick was tense. He had no idea what to expect.

He instantly relaxed when Amy's mother opened the door; her aura was a pale shade of blue. She was human.

"You must be Mary Ritchie," he said before Amy could speak. He held out his hand to her. "I'm delighted to meet you."

He regarded her as she shook his hand. She was tall, taller than Amy, and a little on the plump side. Looking from one to the other, he could see the family resemblance. There was visually no doubt that they were mother and daughter. That posed more questions than answers.

"My name is Doctor Barton," he continued. "May we come in?"

Mary seemed a little perplexed at finding a stranger on her doorstep, standing beside her daughter, but she stood aside so they could enter. She led them into the lounge, indicating with her hand that he could take a seat.

"May I get you some tea?" Mary asked. "Or coffee?"

"That would be great. Coffee, black, no sugar."

Amy asked for her usual. Just before leaving the room, Mary turned around and pointed at the dog. "You, keep off the furniture."

Ainin's tail dropped between his legs and his ears went flat against his head. Mary rolled her eyes.

"No need for the theatrics," she said. "I'll get you a biscuit if you promise to behave."

At the word 'biscuit', his ears pricked up and his tail started wagging. That animal sure knew how to manipulate humans.

While Mary was gone, Garrick looked around the room. There were photos of Amy, placed so that as you scanned left to right you could see her growing up. There were also family photos of her with Mary and the man who everyone claimed was Amy's father, though Garrick knew he couldn't be, not if he was a werewolf and Mary was human.

On one wall was a large picture of a younger Mary, dressed in a wedding dress, standing next to the werewolf she was marrying. Garrick wondered if she knew.

His thoughts were interrupted by Mary returning, carrying a tray. He instantly got up. "Let me help you."

He took the tray from her hands and placed it on the coffee table before returning to his seat. Mary took a bone shaped biscuit from her pocket and Ainin instantly sat back on his haunches.

"You are such a good boy," she said as she handed it over.

She sat down next to her daughter, took a mug from the tray and looked directly at Garrick. "Now why are you here?"

Garrick couldn't help smiling. He liked a woman who spoke her mind. He could see where Amy got it from.

"As I already said, my name is Doctor Barton. I'm your daughter's physician. I'm sorry to tell you that she is showing signs of a rare genetic disorder. I'm here to find out all I can about her family."

Mary went pale.

"Don't worry," Garrick said hastily. "It's nothing too serious. It will make life uncomfortable for Amy, nothing more."

Mary looked at her daughter. "Why didn't you tell me?"

"I didn't want to worry you," she said, as though her illness wasn't new information for her. "I've been feeling 'under the weather', as you like to put it, for a while. I didn't see much point in mentioning it to you until I knew exactly what the problem was."

Accepting her daughter's lie, Mary returned her attention to Garrick.

"How may I help? What do you want to know?"

"I may have to ask some really personal questions I'm afraid. I apologise in advance, but some may be a little insulting. That is not my intention, I assure you."

Mary placed her hands in her lap. "Ask your questions, doctor. I'll answer everything."

Garrick wasn't comfortable with what he was about to do, but he had to determine, beyond a shadow of a doubt, that this woman really was Amy's mother.

"Are you Amy's biological mother? Did you give birth to her?"

Mary appeared unphased by the question. "Of course. I have medical records to prove it, if you wish to see them."

Garrick shook his head. "That won't be necessary. I can see the family resemblance. I hope you understand that I had to ask, to make sure she wasn't your niece or a more distant relative. I need to confirm who her parents are and then ascertain if they are also carriers, in order to work out the next step in her treatment."

"I understand," Mary said. "What else do you need to know?"

"Who is Amy's father? All records show that it is your late husband, Frederick. Is there any possibility that it is someone else?"

Mary snorted with indignation and sat up straighter. "Just what are you implying?"

"Nothing," Garrick said immediately. "I swear. I'm just confirming the records are correct."

"Of course they are," Mary snapped at him. "Fred is the only man I have ever been with. It's impossible for him not to be Amy's father."

Nothing about Mary's demeanour made Garrick think she was lying. If she had, in fact, had an affair, of course she would deny it, but he didn't believe she was being anything other than truthful. He would, however, have to use DNA to prove it.

He then asked many questions about Mary's background, and Fred's. He asked about Amy's life to date, childhood illnesses that sort of thing. Nothing was really relevant but he was trying to see if Mary knew the truth about her husband. If she did, she hid it well.

He wanted to ask, 'did you know that Fred was a werewolf', but it was the one question he couldn't ask out loud.

Eventually he ran out of questions and thanked Mary for her time. Amy had remained silent during the entire interrogation.

"One more thing before I leave," Garrick said as he stood up. "May I have a sample of your blood, so I can have it checked for the genetic mutation your daughter has?"

"Of course. What do I need to do?"

Garrick extracted a kit from his jacket pocket. He always carried one on him; you never knew when a blood sample would be needed in his line of work.

He unwrapped it and held it out to her. "This will give your finger a little prick and extract a small amount of blood. It may sting."

Mary held out her hand, wincing when Garrick pressed the button. Once finished, he sealed everything away and returned it to his pocket.

"Thank you for this," he told her. "And I'm sorry I had to disturb you. I hope you enjoy the rest of your evening."

Amy hugged her mother goodbye and kissed her on the cheek before promising to visit her soon.

Once Ainin was strapped into the back of the car and Amy was in the passenger seat, she said, "Now do you believe me? I'm nothing different. I'm just a normal human."

Garrick looked at her. "I believe you believe that. I believe your mother also doesn't suspect you are part werewolf. I also believe that she has no idea your father was a lycanthrope. However, I can assure you he was. I just have no idea how he fathered a child with a human."

Amy rolled her eyes. She was obviously still unconvinced about her father.

Garrick turned his attention to the road and started the car.

"Where are we going?" Amy asked after a while. She must have realised that he wasn't heading back to her house.

"My headquarters," he told her. "We are going to get to the bottom of exactly what you are. That I can assure you."

Agency

They hadn't travelled far when Ainin started to whine.

"He probably needs to go to the bathroom," Amy said. "There's a park nearby I can take him to."

Garrick followed the provided directions and took the opportunity to phone his boss while Ainin took care of business. He told Carl everything and the older man agreed that bringing Amy to headquarters was the right thing to do.

Garrick neglected to mention the dog. Carl was not a dog person and would insist that the mutt be taken home first, but Garrick wanted to see how Ainin reacted to others, both those who had werewolf blood injected into them and those that didn't. He had a theory and he needed to take the dog with him to prove it.

The fact he didn't want an argument with Amy about it had nothing to do with it, or so he told himself.

"He's hungry," Amy said as she got back into the car. "It's way past his usual mealtime."

"We can get something at headquarters. I'm sure there'll be something there he'll eat. Hopefully it won't be one of my colleagues."

He noticed the trace of a smile forming on Amy's face and couldn't help smirking.

Amy asked a lot of questions about the organisation and its headquarters on the journey, all of which Garrick answered truthfully. He saw no point in holding anything back. As a result, she showed no sign of surprise when he pulled up outside what looked like a medical centre.

He led her inside, with Ainin following. Nobody was in sight, but as he made his way to the door on his left, a security guard appeared. As he approached, the dog sat back on his haunches, watching the man closely. When he got closer, Ainin drew back his top lip, revealing his fangs in a threatening manner.

"Hey Garrick. What's with the dog?"

The guard must have been too close to Amy for Ainin's liking because he started to growl. The guard immediately stopped walking and placed one hand on his gun.

"It's alright Mack," Garrick said. "He's with me."

"Shouldn't he be muzzled or something?"

"He'll be fine," Amy said. "He's just a bit overprotective sometimes."

Garrick noticed that Mack was backing away. He couldn't help smiling. It partly confirmed his theory about the dog.

"You have to admit," Garrick said, turning his grin to the guard. "You do look threatening."

"Whatever," was the surly reply. "He's your responsibility. If he bites anyone, I'll make damn sure you get the blame."

"No problem," Garrick replied and turned around so he could swipe his card. He held the door open for Amy and Ainin and winked at Mack before following after them.

"He's not a dog person," he said to Amy once the door had closed. "He's also not an Agent."

"What difference does that make?"

"He doesn't have werewolf blood in him."

"So?"

"I believe that your dog can detect werewolf blood and only sees those without it as a threat."

"He has never seen me as a threat."

"I rest my case."

He expected her to comment, to contradict what he was saying, but she didn't bother. Whether it was because she was starting to accept the truth about herself or whether she had just given up arguing with him, he wasn't sure.

He went to the lift and the doors opened. He selected the floor the medical unit was on once everyone was in. He wanted to get a DNA sample from Amy and have the techs compare it to her mother's and the one they would have on file for her alleged father.

"Hi, Garrick," a pretty young scientist said as soon as he entered the lab. "To what do we owe this honour? You don't come in here very often."

'Maybe because every time I do you try to flirt with me,' he thought. What he said was, "I need you to run some tests for me." He deliberately didn't say her name, though he knew it.

"Sure," she replied. "What sort?"

He took the kit containing Mary Ritchie's blood out of his jacket pocket and handed it over.

"I want you to take a sample from this lady here and compare it to this one and the one we have on file for Frederick Ritchie. I want to know if she really is their daughter."

"No problem. I'll get the results to you in a few days. If you want it quicker, it'll cost you dinner."

He gave her a serious look. "It's important. The boss wants the results as soon as possible." It wasn't quite true, but close enough.

She pouted at him. It was not a good look for her. "Fine. I'll get it done as soon as I can. It'll still take a few hours though."

She stood up from her stool and went to a nearby cupboard to retrieve a DNA kit. She opened the packet and approached Amy.

"A cheek swab will be good enough," she said, addressing Garrick rather than Amy.

As she approached Amy, Ainin growled. The young lady stopped, looked down at the dog, then up at Amy.

"Here," she said, holding the kit out. "I think you'd better do this. Just put it in your mouth and rub it on the inside of your cheek. Avoid the gums and don't get it too wet."

Amy obeyed and handed the implement back to the scientist, who didn't thank her. She placed it in a sealed container and took both samples away into another room.

"We should get out of here before she comes back," Garrick said. "Hungry?" Amy nodded. "Canteen it is, then."

"You're wasting your time," Amy said as he led her back to the lift area. "Do whatever tests you want. They're only going to confirm what I already know. My mum and dad are really my mum and dad."

"You may be right, but I have to confirm it."

"Why?"

37

"Because you are claiming that your mother is a human and your father is a werewolf and that just isn't possible."

"I'm not claiming anything. You are."

Garrick growled in frustration. He said no more until they were on the correct floor for the canteen. He was hoping other Agents would be present and was pleased to see his sister when he opened the door. He was even more pleased to see she was with her boyfriend, who worked for the Agency as an analyst. He made a bee-line for them.

"Tab, let me introduce you to Amy. Amy, this is my sister, Tabitha, but don't ever call her that, she hates it."

"Not as much as I hate being called Tabby. I'm not some god damn cat," Tabitha said, holding out her hand.

Garrick purposely let Tabitha shake Amy's hand first, before introducing Tom. He noted that Ainin, who was close enough to sniff his sister, didn't react.

"And this is Tom, Tab's better half."

The moment Tom stepped closer to Amy, as if on cue, the dog started to growl.

"Stop it," Amy hissed at him. "He's not going to hurt me." She then looked at Tom. "Are you?"

"Of course not," he said and made a show of shaking her hand so that Ainin could see. Garrick couldn't help smiling at the indignation in his voice. Tom was one of the nicest people he had ever met. He couldn't imagine him ever hurting anyone, or anything. He imagined he even avoided stepping on ants. It was one of the reasons he was an analyst not an Agent; he just wasn't ruthless enough.

Garrick couldn't understand why Tom and Tabitha were together; their personalities were so different. And they looked ridiculous when standing together, not that he was brave enough to say so. While Tom was small, for a man, and looked like he needed to put on a bit of weight, Garrick usually described Tabitha as 'a bit butch'. Though never to her face.

Still, they seemed happy together and that was all that Garrick cared about.

Garrick continued the introductions. "Amy is something of an enigma. Her aura is purple."

That got both of their attentions.

"Did you say purple?" Tom asked. Garrick nodded.

"What does that mean?" Tabitha asked as she looked at Amy closely, seeing for herself that Garrick was telling the truth.

"That's what I'm hoping to find out. On top of that, it seems that her mother is human and her father is a werewolf."

"That's not possible," Tabitha immediately said.

"Why do I keep hearing that?" Amy asked, her exasperation evident not only in her voice but also in the way she held her body and her facial expression.

"Because it's not," Tom said. "Werewolves can't father children with humans. Or vice versa. Many have tried. All have failed."

"My father is NOT a werewolf," Amy grumbled and crossed her arms. Garrick ignored her.

"What's even more interesting is her dog, Ainin. He protects her. He won't let anyone he doesn't know near her, unless they have werewolf blood in them."

"Now that's interesting," Tabitha said.

"What do you mean?" Amy said at the same time.

"He growled at both Mack and Tom and I saw him growl at that man you'd never met before in the dog park. However, he didn't react to Tab and he didn't react to me letting myself into your house. Tab and I are both Agents, so we have werewolf blood in our bodies. Tom and Mack aren't, so they don't. He can probably sense werewolf blood and is used to it, seeing as you have it."

He could have predicted her response.

"I do not."

"I'd love to stop and chat," Tabitha said, "but I've been given a rogue wolf to hunt down." She turned her attention to her brother. "Let me know what you find out."

With a wave goodbye, she and Tom left the canteen.

"Food," Garrick said as soon as they were gone.

He led Amy to the front of the room, where a server was taking orders, and pointed to the menu up on the wall. While Amy perused it, he placed his order and requested a plate of extra-rare steak with vegetables for Ainin.

Once Amy had told the server what she wanted, Garrick took her to an empty table. They got a few questioning looks, mainly directed at Ainin, but nobody approached them to ask why a dog was in the canteen.

While they waited for their food, Garrick made a call. He didn't tell Amy who he was speaking to and she didn't ask why he was asking the person to send one of the wolves to headquarters.

Amy had more questions about the Agency and the building they were in. Garrick could see she was feeling uncomfortable and could guess the reason why. She hadn't believed anything he had told her. Now that she was here, it was obvious he hadn't been making everything up.

Their food was steaming when it arrived, but instead of diving straight in, Garrick took the time to cut up the steak before placing the plate on the floor. Ainin just looked at it until he was given permission to eat.

"Jesus, dog," Garrick said as he watched the animal demolish the meal. "Anyone would think you hadn't been fed in weeks. Did you even chew it or just inhale it?"

"He does like to wolf his food down," Amy said.

"A fitting expression," Garrick said, "given where we are."

Before Amy could respond, Garrick's phone rang. He looked to see who it was before answering.

"Hi, Carl," he said as soon as he hit the green button.

"Where the hell are you?" the voice on the other end said. "You should have been here ages ago."

"I'm in the canteen," Garrick said, doing his best not to smile at his boss's impatience. "Amy needed food before facing a grilling from you."

He was glad he didn't have the phone on speaker so Amy couldn't hear the reply he received. Then again, if she was part werewolf, her hearing would be enhanced so she might still be able to do so. She showed no reaction though so either she wasn't listening in or she had perfected the art of eavesdropping without appearing to be doing so.

"We'll be down in twenty minutes or so," Garrick said into his phone before hanging up. He then turned his attention to Amy. "Eat up. The boss is eager to meet you. We won't have time for dessert I'm afraid."

Amy paled and placed her fork back on the plate. She had hardly touched her food.

"There's nothing to be worried about," he told her. "Carl is a good guy. He just wants to ask you a few questions. You will be perfectly alright."

"What about the wolf you asked to meet you here?"

"That's one of our friendly werewolves. I want to see how Ainin reacts to a full blooded werewolf, nothing more. You are in no danger, I promise you. Now eat up."

Reluctantly, it seemed, Amy picked up her fork again. Her plate was still half full when she gave up again. Garrick could understand why her appetite had been killed. He could remember how he had reacted when he joined the Agency and found out that, not only were werewolves real, but that his best friend in the army was one. He couldn't even begin to imagine how he would have felt if he had been told he was a werewolf.

"Come on," he said. "If you've had enough, I suppose we had better get this over with."

Garrick took Amy directly to Carl's office. The door was closed so he knocked and waited for permission to enter.

"Amy, this is Carl Weston, my boss and head of this division of the Agency. Carl, this is the woman I have been investigating."

Carl looked from Garrick to Amy and jumped back in his chair. "Good God. You were right."

Carl was no longer an Agent, but he kept up to date with his injections of the serum made from werewolf blood, just in case he was ever called into the field. Garrick knew he was seeing the purple aura.

Another man was in the office, seated in front of Carl's desk, and he turned around when Garrick entered. Even if he hadn't,

Garrick would have known who he was. His dark hair, turning to grey, indicated his age, but his piercing green eyes showed the wisdom he had gained over the years.

"Lawrence," Garrick said, smiling at his friend. "You made good time. Come and meet Amy. We are hoping you can tell us what she is."

The man in question rose from his seat and approached Amy. Ainin moved to intercept, but didn't growl. Instead he sniffed at the strange man. If Garrick didn't know better, he would have said the dog was confused.

"Now that's interesting," he said, before remembering his manners. "Amy, this is Lawrence Gervase. He's a werewolf."

"Yeah, right," Amy said as she shook his outstretched hand.

"Ah, an unbeliever," Lawrence said. He didn't sound insulted or surprised. "Let me show you."

He removed his shoes and socks. When he started to undo the buttons on his shirt, Amy stepped away from him.

"What the hell do you think you are doing?"

"Isn't it obvious? I'm getting undressed."

"And why the hell are you doing that?"

Garrick did his best not to smirk.

"My dear lady, I have spent a fortune on replacing clothes. I learned a long time ago that it is much cheaper to get undressed prior to transforming."

Amy looked away as Lawrence took off his shirt, trousers and underwear.

"You really need to see this," Garrick said.

"I've seen naked men before, thank you. I don't need to see another one."

Garrick couldn't suppress his chuckle. He then nodded to Lawrence and watched as the man's body began to undulate. He had seen transformations many times, but it still fascinated him. Soon the human body had been replaced by a large grey wolf.

"You can turn around now," he said to Amy.

He was watching her closely as she did. He saw the moment her brain worked out what had happened. The blood drained from her face and he ran to catch her fainting body just before it hit the ground.

Father

Amy woke to find herself in what appeared to be a hospital room. She was lying on top of a bed, fully clothed, and Ainin was curled up at the bottom. What sort of hospital allowed dogs?

Then she remembered her evening and how she had turned around to see a large grey wolf standing where a man had been only moments before. It wasn't possible. There was no way a man could turn into a wolf. It must have been a trick of some sort, an optical illusion.

Yet she had seen movement out of the corner of her eyes. Not movement away from her or toward her, just movement, like the man's body was convulsing.

She shook her head. Maybe her food had been drugged or something.

"How are you feeling?"

The deep masculine voice made her jump. She turned toward it and found the man who had 'transformed' sitting in a chair in the corner of the room, looking at her. Thankfully he was fully dressed.

"What happened?" she asked, ignoring his question.

"You saw me turn into a wolf and fainted." Was it her imagination or was he trying not to laugh? "It's been a while since I had that sort of effect on a young lady."

She couldn't help herself; she smiled at him. Despite what he had just said, he didn't frighten her. Just the opposite, in fact. He seemed to be a calming influence. There was something about his tone of voice, or maybe it was the fact that he made fun of himself, even in front of someone he had only just been introduced to.

"Seriously," she said, "how did you do that? Misdirection? Mirrors?"

He leaned forward. The look on his face when he spoke told her he was being deadly serious. "Amy, I really am a werewolf. My wife, daughter and I supply this division of the Agency with the blood they need to make the serum the Agents inject into themselves. In exchange, we are treated as part of the family."

Before Amy could respond, the door opened and Garrick walked in, carrying a laptop.

"Ah, you're conscious again. How are you feeling?"

"A little bewildered. I have no idea what's happening anymore."

Garrick smiled. "I can understand that. And what I'm about to show you is really going to make the bottom drop out of your world."

As he approached the bed, Ainin raised his head and quickly looked him up and down before then tucking his head against his body and closing his eyes once more.

'Well you obviously don't think I'm in any danger from these men,' Amy thought to herself as she watched her dog.

Garrick sat on the bed next to her and passed her the laptop he was carrying. "We record every visit from every werewolf who comes here. These are all the recordings we have of your father. You just need to press play."

Using the touchpad, she positioned the cursor on the play button, but didn't select it. Did she want to see this?

Knowing she had no choice, she clicked the button. Instantly an image of two men sitting at a desk appeared. One she didn't recognise, but the other looked so much like her father did in his wedding photo that she couldn't doubt who she was watching. She was too stunned to speak as the two men discussed the fact that her father, the man who had been by her side until his death, the man who she thought she knew everything about, was a werewolf.

"This has to be a fake," she said as tears formed in her eyes. She wasn't sure who she was talking to. Herself, maybe. She didn't want to believe what she was hearing.

The two men talked about what registration meant and what the annual inoculation would do. She clearly heard her father say, "So I will still be able to transform, but it will be when I want to, not when my body decides to." He sounded so serious, as though they were discussing some business deal not the fact that he was a supernatural creature.

"Turn it off," she said. "I've seen enough."

"Sorry," Garrick said, sounding like he actually meant it, "but you need to see more."

Unable to take her eyes off the screen, she watched as a nurse, or someone dressed to look like one, entered the room. She was holding a large syringe. She waited for both men to nod before injecting her father in the neck, making him grimace. The man who had done all the explaining, thanked the woman, who left without saying another word.

"How long before it takes effect?" Fred Ritchie asked.

"It's immediate," came the reply. "Would you like to try transforming now or later?"

Amy wanted to look away as her father began to remove his clothing, but she couldn't. The table the two men were sitting at was in just the right spot to maintain his modesty when he stood up and removed his underwear.

Then he began to transform. His body looked like it was bubbling as it changed shape and began to grow hair. Less than a minute later, a wolf stood where Fred Ritchie should have been.

Amy began to shake uncontrollably.

It took a while, but eventually Garrick and Lawrence managed to calm her down enough to watch the rest of the videos. None of them were as graphic. They were set at roughly yearly intervals, if the timestamp on them could be believed, and showed her father slowly aging as he received his annual injections.

Amy didn't watch them all; there was no need. She pushed the laptop away from her. She felt numb and drained of all energy.

"Does my mother know?" she asked, her voice so small she was surprised anyone heard her. Then she remembered that one of the men in the room with her was a werewolf and the other had a serum made from werewolf blood regularly injected into him, so they might have enhanced hearing.

"I don't believe so," Garrick said. "We think he managed to keep his secret from everyone."

"How? Why?" Amy didn't know what she wanted to ask. "What does this mean I am?"

It was Lawrence who answered. "We think you are the first ever half-breed, half human and half werewolf. I wish your father was still alive. I would love to find out how he managed to impregnate a human."

"I feel sick," Amy said.

"Do you want some water?" Garrick asked. She could hear concern in his voice, but she wasn't sure if it was for her or the possibility of her puking on him.

She shook her head. "Where's the bathroom?"

"I'll show you." Garrick stood up, holding out his hand so he could help her off the bed.

She was surprised that her legs didn't give way when she put weight on them. She managed to walk out of the room and down the corridor without assistance. Ainin went with her.

She barely heard Garrick say he would wait outside as she entered the bathroom. She walked up to the mirror and looked into it.

"I look like shit," she said to her reflection. Ainin whined. "There's no need to agree with me," she said as she looked down at him.

She splashed cold water on her face. It didn't help. She then went into a cubical and took care of business, praying she didn't vomit while she was sitting on the throne, as her mother liked to call it.

She looked at herself again as she washed her hands. Her eyes were still red, but at least some colour was returning to her cheeks. And she no longer felt like she was going to see her dinner again.

Taking a deep breath, she let it out slowly. Her entire world had just turned upside down and she had no idea what would happen next.

"How are you feeling?" Garrick asked as soon as she exited the bathroom. She was getting fed up with being asked that question.

"I've been better." She tried to smile, but couldn't. "I want to go home."

Actually she wanted to curl up in her bed, go to sleep and wake up in a world where she wasn't the offspring of a mythical creature, but she couldn't see that happening.

"Of course," Garrick said. "We discussed your situation while you were unconscious. If you were a full werewolf, we would require you to take the injection and register, but as you're not, we're not sure what effect it will have on you. With your permission, we would like to keep in contact, study you, learn exactly what abilities you have."

Amy snorted. 'With my permission my arse,' she thought. What she said out loud was, "Yeah, right. Like I really get a say in it. If I say no, you'll just arrest me and bring me here against my will."

"Do you really think your dog will allow that?" Garrick asked.

Amy looked at him sharply, trying to assess whether he was being sarcastic or not. He didn't appear to be.

"From his reaction to you so far, probably. He did, after all, let you break into my house, knock me out and handcuff me."

"To be fair, you knocked yourself out. Both times."

"Whatever. Please, just take me home."

"As you wish," Garrick said and led her to the lifts.

By the time they reached Garrick's car, an uncomfortable silence had developed between them, creating an unpleasant atmosphere once they were alone in the enclosed space. Ainin must have picked up on it, as he began to whine before Garrick even pulled out onto the main road. Amy ignored him as she stared out of the passenger window, though her eyes weren't focused on anything.

"Do you want to talk about it?" Garrick finally asked.

"What's there to talk about?" Amy said. To her own ears, she sounded petulant, but she couldn't help it. All her life she had known who she was and who her parents were, as people. Now

48

she felt like her entire upbringing had been a lie. She had no idea what she was, let alone who. She wished she had never found out the truth, a truth she could no longer deny.

"There's no shame in admitting you're freaked out by what you've discovered. Any sane person would be."

Amy turned to face Garrick, who had his eyes on the road, not her. "I'm not freaked out, I'm pissed. At my father, for lying to me. At you, for forcing me to face the truth. Even at Ainin for not protecting me from you."

Amy expected Garrick to grin, but lucky for him, he didn't. If she had seen even a trace of a smile on his face, she would have hit him.

"Firstly," he said, "your father didn't lie to you. He just neglected to tell you everything about himself. He was probably trying to protect you. Secondly, I'm sorry you found out the way you did, but I didn't know how else to prove to you I wasn't making everything up. Thirdly, Ainin knew I meant you no harm. Had I been a threat, I'm sure he would have reacted differently toward me."

"No harm?" Amy said incredulously. "How can you sit there and say you've done me no harm? How am I supposed to get on with my life now? Knowing I'm some sort of half-breed freak."

Garrick said nothing. Then again, what could he have said? He didn't know what she was any better than she did.

The rest of the journey was made in silence. Garrick put the radio on, but it did nothing to ease the tension.

As soon as he pulled up outside Amy's house, he took her phone out of his pocket and asked for her security number to unlock it. She gave it to him. What would have been the point in refusing? She was too tired to have an argument she was eventually going to lose.

He played about with it for a moment before handing it to her. "I've put my number in. Call me if you need anything, even if it's just someone to yell and scream at. If I don't hear from you, I'll be in touch soon anyway."

She got out of the car and went into her house. She grabbed a can of soda from the fridge and took it into the lounge, putting it untouched on the table. She sat down on the sofa and put her head in her hands. For a long time she just sat there, wondering what the hell she was going to do about Garrick, the Agency and the fact she appeared to be not completely human. She ended up having to admit to herself that she didn't have the faintest idea.

Lia

As Lia watched Garrick drive away from Amy's house, anger boiled inside her. From the moment she laid eyes on him, she knew exactly what he was. She may have hated Amy, but that didn't mean she wanted her handed over to the Agency.

Maybe hate wasn't the right word. Despised sounded better. She had known Amy for a long time and despised her for being a weak half-breed who didn't even know she had a werewolf side, let alone embrace it. As far as Lia was concerned, Amy was an embarrassment to everything lycanthrope. If she thought it worth her while, she would have disposed of her ages ago, but you never knew when someone might be of benefit to you.

She disliked everything about Amy. She found her pathetic. In her eyes, she wasn't worthy to be classed as even a part werewolf. She was almost as bad as those traitors who registered with the Agency and received their annual injections. At least Amy had the excuse that she didn't know what she was. Those losers knew exactly what being a werewolf meant, yet did everything they could to deny who they really were. She would slaughter them all, if she could.

She wished, not for the first time, that she could get hold of that register. She could then use the information to hunt down and assassinate everyone on it. Especially whichever werewolf provided the Agency with the blood needed to create their serum. That was the ultimate betrayal. It was bad enough surrendering yourself to humans, but to aid them in subjugating others was worse than treasonous.

Lia often found herself lying awake at night, imagining what she would do to everyone who worked at the Agency, human and werewolf alike. Sometimes she could almost taste their blood in her mouth.

But that was still just a fantasy. She had no way of getting into the Agency's headquarters, let alone being able to access their computer system. She could probably gather together enough wolves to attack the place, but what good would that do? She wouldn't be able to force anyone to give up their passwords, not someone with the right access for what she needed, anyway.

No. An all-out assault on the building was not the answer, but what was? She had yet to think of something. She had tried capturing an Agent, but the damn chain he wore prevented her from accessing his mind, as she should have been able to, given all Agents had werewolf blood in them and all werewolves could read the minds of other werewolves. She would love to find out who was making the werewolf-proof chains. Then she would rip them to pieces. Cut off their access to protection and their supply of what gave them the ability to see who was a rogue werewolf, as they liked to put it, and they would be unable to do their job.

Of course, every sector in every country had their own traitors working for the Agency, but if she could somehow get access to their computers, she would be able to track down them all. And the Agency wasn't the only network which was global in this war between humans and werewolves, a war most people didn't know was going on.

She decided to speak to her contact, to see if anyone had any ideas on how she could use the Agency's interest in Amy to her advantage.

She needed a spy in the Agency. Could Amy be it? Lia shook her head. No. That little weakling would never agree and there was no way to force her. She could threaten her mother, or her dog, but Amy would probably go crying to the Agency and they would provide protection.

Garrick was now out of sight, so she went into her house and poured herself a drink.

She had been watching Amy for a long time, though the half-werewolf didn't even know she existed. There had been times when she had been tempted to reveal herself, to see how Amy would react and if she could be persuaded to join the cause, but each time she had backed down. She had no faith that Amy would be able to do anything, let alone agree to do it.

She made a call to the man she reported to in the resistance and he agreed that there was nothing to be done for the moment other than monitor the situation. After all, she couldn't be certain Amy would have anything more to do with the W.A.R. Agency.

The acronym made Lia laugh. It felt like they had decided on the name before deciding what it stood for. Then again, it was appropriate, seeing as they had declared war on werewolves, while making out they were helping them.

Thinking about the Agency and what they were doing to innocent werewolves made her angry again. The injections they forced those who had registered to take, reduced their strength and their improved senses. It was only by a small amount, but that wasn't the point. It made them weaker. It made them less in the eyes of other werewolves, herself included.

What they were doing to her kind should never have been made legal. Yes, after taking the injection their victims were still able to transform, but it wasn't as easy and the urge to do so had been removed. So what if occasionally they turned into wolves against their will; it was part of their nature and nobody should be given the power to take away or limit someone's abilities.

Some of the members of her resistance group had agreed to be registered and provided detailed accounts of what happened and how the injection affected them. Of course, they had only ever done it once, never going back for their annual re-registration. This put them in danger as the Agency was aware of them and could track them down when they failed to attend a clinic on schedule, but it was a danger they were prepared to face.

They had also managed to recruit a few werewolves who had been re-registering for a number of years and persuaded them to stop.

Her thoughts went to Thomas. He had been due to re-register a few months ago and nobody had seen him for a few weeks. He had failed to attend their last meeting. And the one before that. His home had been checked, as had his place of work, but his employer said he hadn't turned up for work or called in with an explanation as to why and the mail piling up at his house suggested he hadn't been there for a while either.

Lia couldn't help wondering if he had been captured and killed for refusing to take another dose of the injection, but she had no way of finding out. She needed a spy in the Agency.

She had even tried to use an Agency worker who wasn't an Agent, but they were insanely loyal and, as they had no werewolf blood in them, she couldn't access their minds. She had yet to find one who would be prepared to betray their employer. Whenever she had one of her people approach someone, the werewolf was hunted down and disappeared within the following few days. It wasn't a risk she wanted to expose any of her team to again.

Her irritation was beginning to make her skin crawl, so she took a shower. It didn't help. She knew what she had to do, but could find no way of doing it. She was still thinking about it when she went to bed.

Assignment

Garrick was whistling as he walked down the corridor to his boss's office. He had slept well, better than usual, and was ready to face whatever his next assignment was. Part of him hoped it was Amy still. She intrigued him. Everyone, including herself, was now convinced she was the offspring of a werewolf and a human, but he wanted to know more. What abilities did she have? Could she transform into a wolf? Could she have children with a werewolf? Or a human?

The last thought made him smile. If she wanted to experiment, he might enjoy volunteering. After all, she was an attractive woman and fooling around with her for a while might be enjoyable.

Garrick wasn't the only one interested in finding out more about her history and abilities. Lawrence had also voiced his desire to know more as soon as Garrick had returned to headquarters. He had requested Garrick provide her address so he could visit her the next day, but the younger man had managed to persuade the werewolf to give her a few days to get used to knowing what she was.

Garrick wasn't sure what the Agency's approach to Amy would be. He didn't want her to become a lab experiment. Though he doubted Carl would give permission for the scientists to experiment on her, he couldn't be sure that those higher up the chain of command wouldn't overrule him.

"You sound cheerful," Carl said as Garrick strode through the open office door, still whistling.

Garrick shrugged. "I'm just eager to get on with the day. I've already swam fifty laps and jogged around the park twice. So what have you got for me?"

Carl turned his laptop around so that Garrick could see what he had been looking at. The photo of a man dressed in a worn out Iron Maiden tour t-shirt filled the screen. It hadn't been taken at the clinic so Garrick assumed he was looking at a rogue werewolf.

"Your sister sent this to me last night," Carl said. "He has a red aura, but Tabitha was on another mission so she couldn't track him down."

Garrick grinned. "You're brave, calling her Tabitha. She'll be pissed if she finds out."

"She won't," Carl said in a serious voice, "because we're the only two here and you aren't going to tell her."

Garrick could have wound Carl up by saying he would, but they both knew he wouldn't. "Do we know who he is?"

"Yes," Carl told him. "He has a criminal record. Nothing serious. Petty theft, shoplifting. Nothing violent, at least nothing he has been caught for."

"Do you have an address?"

Carl nodded. "I'll email you everything we know. Go pick him up and bring him back here."

Garrick nodded and turned to leave the room. Carl called out to him just as he reached the door. It was a habit he had that Garrick had grown used to over the years.

"You should really take a partner with you. There's nothing to indicate he is dangerous, but you never know."

Garrick turned back to look at him. "You know I work better alone."

"It's your call. But one of these days you're going to need backup and you won't know until it's too late."

"I'll be fine," Garrick said over his shoulder as he walked out of the office.

A few minutes later, he was drinking coffee in the canteen when his phone pinged, indicating he had received an email. He opened it up and scrolled through its contents.

Arthur, more commonly known as Art, Greenfield was in his mid-twenties but had already served time twice for short periods. He last got out a few months ago and was living with a friend. He had never registered with the Agency and until Tabitha had spotted him, had never been on their radar.

Nothing else was known about him, no next of kin or girlfriend. Garrick decided to pay him a visit to test the waters before letting him know who he was or that he worked for the Agency. It was possible that he didn't know about the Agency, or that Agents had green auras. As Art had recently been released from prison, he could pretend to be a parole officer.

Garrick finished his coffee and returned the empty cup to the counter before leaving the building and heading to his car. He entered the address he had been given into his Sat Nav then headed off. It would take him a while to reach his destination so he put on some music and turned on the aircon. It wasn't an especially hot day, but he liked the car to be cool when he was driving.

The neighbourhood he pulled up in wasn't the sort of place he liked to leave his car, but he didn't really have much choice. He clicked the button on his keys twice to make doubly certain it was locked before walking up to the apartment block he had parked outside.

Number 23 didn't have a name against it, but he pressed the buzzer anyway, confident that the research people at the Agency had provided the correct address; the only time they got it wrong was when the target had recently moved.

It took a while, but eventually it was answered.

"Who is it?"

"My name is Garrick Barton. I'm looking for Arthur Greenfield."

"Never heard of him." The voice sounded slurry as though its owner had just woken up. Or was drunk or high on drugs. Garrick thought it was the latter.

"He goes by Art."

"Why do you want him?" At least Garrick now knew he was at the right place.

"Parole office." He wasn't sure if it was illegal to pretend to be a parole officer, but, technically, he hadn't just claimed he was one. He could argue that he meant he had been sent by Art's parole office, not that he was an officer.

Grunting sounded from the intercom. "You'd better come up then."

A buzzer sounded and when Garrick pushed on the door, it opened. The lift had an 'out of order' sign on it, so he had to take the stairs.

Guessing that apartment 23 was on the second floor, he climbed two flights of stairs, which smelled of urine.

The corridor was dingy, the one lightbulb far from adequate. He made his way to the end of the corridor and stopped in front of a door which had no number on it. It was between 22 and 24 so it had to be the right one.

He paused before knocking, realising that he had no idea what he was walking into. He didn't know how many people would be in the apartment and whether they would be human or werewolf. He hadn't thought to ask about the friend Carl said Art was staying with. If there were any werewolves inside, they would be able to see his aura so would know what he was.

He had recently injected himself with the werewolf serum, so he knew his aura would be bright green. The brightness was one of the ways they monitored when they were due for a renewal. Nobody was allowed on a mission if their aura had gone pale or was turning back to blue.

He tapped his jacket, making sure his guns were readily available. He also had a spare down the back of his jeans, but, so far, he had never had to use it.

Taking a deep breath, he knocked on the door.

The man who answered was human and looked like he was having trouble focusing.

"Who are you?" he asked.

Garrick smiled. The voice sounded so much like the one in the intercom it had to be the same person.

"Garrick. You buzzed me up a moment ago."

"I did? I guess you had better come in then."

The man was dressed in faded jeans and a t-shirt that looked like it should have been washed weeks ago. He stepped aside and as Garrick entered the room, the smell of unwashed bodies and smoke hit him. At least one person in the apartment had been smoking illegal substances.

"Is Art in?" Garrick asked.

The man, who had yet to introduce himself, signalled behind him with his head.

Garrick looked over and saw another man sitting on a sofa, drinking from a can of beer. A child, who looked no more than four, was playing with a doll at his feet. Both had red auras.

Garrick swore under his breath. Carl should have warned him that a child might be present. It made his job much harder. Then again, if the child wasn't Art's, Carl might not have known about her.

"Arthur Greenfield?" Garrick asked, even though the man looked exactly like the photo his sister had taken. "I've been sent to speak with you."

He didn't mention who had sent him or why. He avoided lying when he could. Saying as little as possible and letting people jump to their own conclusions was usually the best tactic, he had found.

Art looked up and locked eyes with Garrick. Instantly he began to transform. Garrick barely had time to pull one of his guns before a large grey wolf was launching itself at him.

It hit him in the chest, knocking him backward. He landed on his back, hard, and he felt the air being forced from his lungs by the impact.

Before he had chance to breath in once more, a heavy weight landed on his chest and a large paw pushed down on his neck, preventing him from breathing. He got his arm up just in time to stop strong jaws closing around his throat.

The wolf bit down on his arm, but didn't reach his flesh. All agents wore reinforced jackets, specially designed to withstand wolf bites. It hurt a hell of a lot though and if the animal decided to yank back or throw its head about, his shoulder could be dislocated.

His gun had been knocked out of his hand, but he managed to retrieve another one with his other hand. He placed it against the wolf's head, but didn't pull the trigger.

"Get off me," he somehow managed to say, using the last of the air in his lungs. If he didn't get a breath soon, the wolf would suffocate him.

His mind was so focused on staying alive, he forgot about the child, until he felt razor sharp incisors biting into his leg.

Instinct kicked in and he pulled the trigger, sending a bullet directly into Art's brain. Blood splattered the room as it exited his skull. He was glad he had an Agency gun, which were quieter than most, or his ears would be ringing.

Ignoring the pain in his leg, Garrick pushed the dead body off him and took a deep breath. He looked around and spied the human cowering in the corner. He had pissed in his pants. Garrick wasn't surprised. If he hadn't known that Art was a werewolf, seeing him transform would have been terrifying.

The small wolf, who had been a little girl when Garrick walked in, still had her jaws attached to his leg and when he looked down, he could see blood seeping through his trousers.

Cursing loudly, he bent down and grabbed the scruff of the wolf's neck. "Let go," he hissed, "or I will break your neck."

He was lying, but the wolf didn't know that. Even though the young werewolf was no longer in human form, she was able to understand him. She opened her mouth and released her hold on his leg.

He placed her gently on the sofa and told her to stay, as if she was a dog. She was visibly trembling.

Ignoring the blood flowing down his leg, he returned his guns to his jacket pockets before taking his phone and calling Carl.

"It didn't go quite as planned," he said as soon as his boss answered. He could picture Carl rolling his eyes. He didn't give him time to comment. "Arthur transformed as soon as he saw me. Pinned me to the ground before I had chance to do more than draw my gun. I had to blow his brains out to get him off me so I could breathe. I wish I hadn't had to."

He was serious about the last sentence. He rarely killed those he was sent to arrest and hated it when he was forced to do so. The names, dates and places were etched in his brain. This was another one he would never forget. Training and experience had taught him not to react, but once he was alone, his emotions would kick in. He was in for a long, sleepless night.

"Need a clean-up squad?" Carl asked.

"Yes. It was also witnessed by a human, but he's so off his brain with drugs he might not be a problem."

"I'll have the cleaners bring him in anyway. Anything else I should know?"

"There's a kid here. Somewhere between four and five, I think. Unregistered werewolf. Bit a hole in my damn leg. I don't know who she is."

"Will the human know?"

"No idea. I can ask him but I'm not expecting to get anything coherent out of him."

"Alright. Bring her in if you have to. We'll do a DNA test in case she has relatives in our database."

"Will do."

Garrick hung up then went into the bathroom and cleaned himself up as best he could. He removed his jacket and was pleased to see his t-shirt was stain free. He then found another cloth that looked clean so he rolled up his trouser leg and used it to wash his wound. The bite wasn't too deep so he wasn't worried about seeking medical attention.

He wrapped the cloth around his leg then returned to the lounge, where the child was still sitting on the sofa. She hadn't turned back into her human form.

The man who was huddled in the corner flinched when he approached.

"I'm not going to hurt you," he said as he crouched down beside him. "I just want to know who the little girl is."

He pointed to the wolf on the sofa and instantly regretted his action. The man's eyes followed his finger, fell on the lupine and widened. He started mumbling incoherently to himself. Garrick rolled his eyes.

"Is Art her father?" he asked. He didn't expect an answer and was surprised when the man nodded. "Where's the mother?" The man shrugged. His eyes were still fixed on the small wolf.

"Do you know who the mother is?" Garrick continued. Again the man shrugged.

Garrick gave up and walked over to the corpse. Taking a kit from his pocket, he extracted a DNA sample then went to the sofa. He sat down next to the wolf, who backed away from him. He could hardly blame her. After all, she had just watched him kill her father.

He reached out and scratched her behind the ear, but she cowered away from him. "Do you think you can transform back into a human little one?"

Whether she didn't hear him, didn't understand him, didn't want to do it or wasn't able to, he had no idea, but she stayed as a wolf.

He continued talking to her until the clean-up crew arrived, but his words had no effect on her.

"It's not often you call us out," a middle aged woman said as she walked up to him. He recognised her, but couldn't remember her name. He'd only met her once or twice and wasn't sure if he had ever actually been introduced.

"Sorry about the mess," he said as he looked around the room. "We also have a witness that needs to be taken in."

"So we were told," she said. She looked down at the wolf, who had fallen asleep, probably through nervous exhaustion. "Who's your new friend?"

"That is what I need the investigators to find out."

"Want me to take it with us when we've finished here?" Her tone had changed to be more gentle, more motherly. Little furry animals often had that effect on people, even those who knew the creature was a werewolf.

Garrick shook his head. "No, I'll take her."

The woman smiled at him. "Get yourself out of here then and let us do our job."

He thanked her then left the apartment, cradling the small wolf in his arms. When he got to his car, he placed her on the passenger seat. Somehow, he had managed to not wake her.

Garrick decided to take a detour on the way back to headquarters. Amy didn't live far from the main road he had to take and he wanted to check up on her. It was a weekday, so she was likely to be at work, but he saw no harm in trying. Also, he had no idea if the young werewolf would need to pee before he reached his headquarters and he didn't want to risk her making a mess in his car.

He recognised her car as he pulled up behind it, but she usually caught the bus, so its presence didn't mean she was home. Not wanting to leave the pup alone in the car, in case she woke up and made a mess, he carried her to Amy's front door.

He knocked on the door and heard barking from the back of the house. The sound woke the young wolf and she started to whine and struggle.

He was trying to quieten her down when the door opened. Amy took one look at him and said, "What the hell are you doing here?"

Gemma

Garrick winced as Amy dabbed antiseptic on the wound on his leg. He didn't like the way she was smiling at his discomfort.

"Stop being a baby." He glared at her. He wasn't being a baby. It wasn't as if he was crying out in pain or blubbering.

She continued to smile as she finished cleaning the bites and wrapped a bandage around his leg.

He had told her the truth when he said he was only there to check she was alright, but the moment she saw blood on his trousers she insisted on dressing his wound.

"So what happened?" she asked as she pinned the bandage in place.

He looked over to where the little wolf had curled up in Ainin's dog bed. "The little werewolf down there bit me."

He must have been imagining things but he could have sworn he saw Ainin look at the young animal, then back at him. If dogs could smirk, he would have done so.

The smile dropped from Amy's face. "You got bitten by a werewolf? Doesn't that mean you're going to turn into one?"

Garrick shook his head. "That's just myth and urban legend. Werewolf bites are no more harmful than those of a normal wolf. It's impossible to turn a human into a werewolf. You should think of them as a different species of man, like an ape, almost. Werewolves reproduce the normal way, not by converting other creatures."

"So why exactly did the cute little thing bite you?"

Garrick paused before answering. He didn't want to tell Amy the truth, but he also didn't want to lie to her.

"I got into a fight with her father." He silently prayed that she wouldn't ask for further information. His prayers weren't answered.

"So who won?"

He looked her right in the eyes when he answered. "I did. I was forced to shoot him in the head. I didn't want to, but it was his life or mine."

Amy looked horrified. "You killed her father in front of her? What sort of bastard are you?"

"I had no choice. He had me pinned to the ground, trying to rip my head off with his teeth. He was pressing down on my neck so I couldn't breathe. I had to get him off me or I would have suffocated. Shooting him was the only way. I wish it could have been a non-lethal shot but I couldn't shoot him anywhere else."

"Are you trying to convince me or yourself?" Amy asked.

Garrick shrugged. "Maybe both. I don't like killing, even when it is in self-defence."

Did Amy believe him? He had no idea. Did he care? Yes, he decided, he did. He wanted her to trust him. It was the only way to find out more about her and what werewolf abilities she had.

"Coffee?" she asked.

Garrick looked across at the sleeping wolf before nodding his head. He should get her back to headquarters, but he didn't want to wake her.

"What are you going to do with her?" Amy asked as she waited for the coffee machine to finish.

"I'm not sure yet. We think the werewolf I killed was her father, but he may not have been. We have no idea who her mother is. I'm hoping a DNA test will help us track her down, but I'm not holding my breath. If her father never registered with us, it's highly likely her mother didn't either."

Amy placed a steaming mug in front of him. "So what will happen to her if her mother can't be traced?"

"I'm hoping Lawrence will take her in."

Amy took a drink from her mug before saying, "Tell me more about him. I can't work him out. Why would he work with an agency that imprisons and kills his kindred?"

Garrick smiled. He could understand why it would be confusing for someone who had only just found out that werewolves exist.

"Lawrence came to the Agency when he was still a young man. This was before I joined. He served his country in the armed forces and when it was time for him to leave, he was approached by the Agency, which was just getting off the ground. Nobody knew he was a werewolf and when he heard that a serum had been invented to help control the transformation, he volunteered to be a donor. He hated not being able to control his own body, but he was prepared to continue to suffer if it meant helping others of his kind. He donates blood to make that serum, as well as the one Agents use."

"Suffer?' Amy asked. "Is it painful to transform then? It didn't appear to be when I saw the video of my father doing it."

"You'll have to speak to him about that. My understanding is that it isn't the transformation itself, but resisting the need to do so when you don't want to."

"So he's never taken the serum, even just to see what it's like?"

Garrick shook his head. "No. His wife has though. They met at the clinic when she came in for her annual injection. After they were married, she made the decision to stop taking it in order to help others. Their daughter made the same decision when she finished university."

"So do they supply the blood needed for the serum for all werewolves, everywhere in the world?"

Again Garrick shook his head. He was pleased that she was so curious. It was a good sign that she was embracing what she was rather than trying to hide from it.

"No, only for this area. The Agency has local headquarters all over the country, and most others. Each has its own werewolf or group of werewolves who help out. Some even have werewolf Agents, who help to track down their rogue kindred."

Amy looked stunned. "Why would they do that?"

"To help them. Not all of them know about the Agency and the fact that we have the serum. They find those who don't know about it and educate them, giving them the chance to register and improve their control."

"And if they don't register?"

"They are imprisoned. An uncontrolled werewolf is just too dangerous to be allowed to stay on the streets." Garrick hated saying the words and, though they were true, he wished they weren't.

Amy didn't look convinced. "How are they dangerous? Surely if there were werewolves going around killing people it would be all over the news."

"It is. You just don't know it. The Agency covers it up well. Most of the animal attacks you hear about were actually werewolves. A lot of the murders that make the headlines aren't caused by humans. And, of course, werewolves are very good at hiding their victims if they want to."

Amy went pale. Garrick thought he should change the topic of conversation. There was a lot that Amy still needed to know, but it would wait until another day. Amy, however, beat him to it.

"So if werewolves exist, do vampires as well?"

Garrick somehow managed not to burst out laughing. It was the question he had been waiting for. He even had a bet on with his sister about whether Amy would ask it or not. He was pleased to have been right.

"No, they are purely fictional, as far as the Agency knows, along with most of what is said about werewolves."

He was going to say more, but at that moment the little wolf woke up and whined.

"Time to get her to the Agency," he said and stood up.

The small creature seemed pleased when Garrick picked her up. "Are you ready to become human again?" he asked, but she just closed her eyes and settled down in his arms. "I guess not."

Amy and Ainin both showed him out. Before she could close the door, Garrick turned back around to face her.

"If you're free on Saturday, can I come back? I want to test you to see what werewolf abilities you have."

He was expecting her to laugh in his face at the suggestion, but instead she agreed and told him to be there any time after ten.

Garrick drove directly to the clinic at the Agency's local headquarters and took the little bundle of fur directly to the lab. The young scientist who seemed to have a crush on him wasn't there, much to his relief. He explained to the man in a lab coat who approached him what had happened and what was needed.

"I'll see what I can do," the man said. "It's better if we have the mother's DNA, but I may be able to tell you if the father is who you think it is, based on the number of points of match. At the very least I'll be able to give you a likelihood of the sample you provided being from a parent. I won't be able to track the mother down though, even if she is in our system."

Garrick thanked the man then told the wolf she had to behave and that he would be back to see her soon.

"Be gentle with her," Garrick said to the scientist before he left the lab. "I haven't managed to persuade her to change back yet."

"That won't be a problem," the man said. Then he turned to the creature whose ear he was scratching. "Come on little one. Shall we see if we have any food for you?"

Confident that the wolf was in good hands, Garrick left them to it and headed to his boss's office.

Carl was on the phone when he arrived, but he waved him in anyway.

"See you soon," he said into the phone before hitting the disconnect button and turning his attention to Garrick.

"That was Lawrence. He'll head straight here. Rosemary is coming with him. They're both happy to become adoptive parents if we need them to."

Garrick nodded. "Good. I've got the lab running DNA tests at the moment. At least we'll know if the guy I killed was really her father."

"What took you so long to get here?" Carl asked. "I was expecting you a while ago."

Seeing no reason to hide his detour, Garrick took a seat and explained where he had been. "I'm going back there tomorrow. I want to test her."

"Fair enough. Just don't let it interfere with your next assignment. Speaking of which, I need you to track this one down."

Garrick read what was on Carl's screen. Raising his eyebrows, he said, "Why are you investigating her so soon? She's only two days overdue."

"She's never been late before," Carl said. "She's one of the first werewolves I brought to headquarters when I was an Agent and she's been back every year since. Never so much as a day late. I want you to check on her, make sure she is alright."

"Sure," Garrick replied. "Do you know if this address is still accurate?"

"It should be. She has always let us know in the past when she moves."

Garrick stood up. "I'll give you a call as soon as I know anything," he said as he left the room.

It took a while for him to drive to the location and when he arrived, the first thing he noticed was the amount of mail sticking out of the mailbox. It obviously hadn't been emptied in a few days. Either that or the woman was popular.

He walked up to the front door of the one storey duplex and rang the bell. He could hear it ringing inside, but when he looked through the opaque glass, he could see no signs of movement.

He was about to ring again when a voice said, "You're wasting your time young man. I've been trying for the last few days."

Garrick looked around. An elderly gentleman was leaning over the short hedge that separated the front lawns of the two conjoined houses.

"Do you know if she's gone away?" Garrick asked as he walked over to him.

The man shook his head. "Not that I know of. She usually tells me when she goes anywhere. Asks me to collect her mail and water her plants for her. I was debating whether to call the police, but they would probably think I'm just a senile old codger."

Garrick smiled. "Well I don't think that. Let me take a look around the back. See if I can see anything."

Before the man could protest, Garrick walked around the house, opening the side gate so he could enter the back garden. Looking through the kitchen window, he couldn't see anything out of place.

The back door was locked, but that didn't pose much of a problem for him. It creaked as he opened it, making him wince. If there was a werewolf inside, he had just announced his presence.

"Gemma?" he called out. "Gemma Carstairs?"

He listened carefully, but didn't hear anything. He continued to call out as he searched the house. He thought he heard a sound from the bedroom, so he knocked on the door before opening it.

The smell hit him before he entered the room. Human excrement and urine. He quickly scanned the room for the source and his eyes fell on a body on the bed. He rushed over to check if the person was alive or not.

As soon as he placed his hand on the clammy forehead, eyes shot open and stared at him.

"Are you Gemma Carstairs?" he asked the old woman. She struggled to move her head, but didn't appear to have the strength to do so.

Taking her movement as affirmation, he explained that Carl Weston had sent him. The woman seemed to recognise the name, making Garrick assume she was the missing Gemma.

"I'll get you some water," he said and left the room, returning as quickly as he could with a glass of water from the tap.

From the smell, it was obvious Gemma hadn't left her bed in a few days, but Garrick forced himself to ignore her odour and help her sit up. He held the glass to her lips and tipped it back so it trickled into her mouth.

"Thank you," she said when he removed it. Her voice was so weak he had trouble hearing it.

"Can I get you to a doctor?" Garrick asked, but Gemma didn't reply.

He gave her some more water then phoned headquarters, requesting they send over a medical team. He took a chair from the kitchen and moved it beside her bed so he could talk to her while he waited for help to arrive. He had no idea what was wrong with her, but he hoped it wasn't serious.

She drifted in and out of sleep as he spoke, telling her a little about himself and that her neighbour was worried about her. He tried to get more water down her, but she wasn't responsive enough for him to risk her choking on it.

When the doorbell rang, it almost made him jump. It was too soon for it to be the medical team. Deciding he had better see who it was, he opened the door to find the elderly neighbour standing on the doorstep.

"Is she here?" he asked. Garrick had been expecting his first question to be about how Garrick got into the house and was pleased that the old man's first thought was about Gemma.

"Come in," Garrick said and stepped aside so the man could enter. "She's sick. I've phoned for an ambulance." It was almost the truth.

The moment he saw Gemma, the man sat in the seat Garrick had vacated and took one of Gemma's frail hands in his. Her eyes fluttered open and Garrick was sure she tried to smile.

Garrick left them to it and went to the kitchen. He found the kettle and put it on. He located mugs and instant coffee and made a drink for himself and the neighbour.

"Do you want milk or sugar?" he asked as he placed a mug on the bedside table.

The man shook his head. "I'm Bob, by the way."

"Garrick." He didn't offer an explanation about who he was or why he was there and Bob didn't ask for one. He simply returned his attention to the prone form of Gemma. It was obvious he cared a lot for this woman.

Eventually the medical team sent from the Agency arrived and promptly threw both Garrick and Bob out of the room so they could examine Gemma in private.

Both men sat in the kitchen, waiting to hear what the medical professionals had to say. After what felt like hours, but in reality was less than thirty minutes, the door to the bedroom opened and a doctor walked out.

"She has the flu," she announced. "Nothing more serious than that. However, she hasn't been able to get out of bed for a few days so is severely dehydrated and very hungry."

"I'll make her some soup," Bob said and jumped from his chair and went to the cupboard. He moved around the kitchen as though he had been in there often. Garrick wouldn't have been surprised to find that he had.

"Will she be alright?" Bob asked as he opened a can and poured the contents into a saucepan.

"Yes, she just needs rest and plenty of fluids. The nurses are getting her cleaned up at the moment and will move her to the spare bedroom."

"I'll take care of her," Bob announced. "It would be easier if she was moved to my house. I live next door."

"I'll speak with her," the doctor said. "Make sure she is okay with that."

She returned a moment later to say that Gemma had agreed to the temporary move. Garrick couldn't help wondering how temporary it would be.

As soon as she had eaten all the soup Bob had prepared, Garrick carried her out of the house and into Bob's. The doctor handed Bob a container of cold-and-flu tablets with instructions on how often Gemma should take them and Garrick gave him his phone number, in case of emergencies.

As the doctor walked down the garden path beside Garrick, she said, "You saved her life. Another day without water and she wouldn't have made it."

Garrick shook her head. "Bob was just about to phone for help anyway."

"Still, you did a good thing today. I've given her her injection so that's one less thing for her to worry about. I'll complete the register as soon as I get back to base."

"Thanks, Doc," he said then phoned Carl to give him an update before he headed home.

Resistance

Lia watched Garrick leave Amy's house. That was twice in two days he had been there. She wasn't happy about the useless half-breed associating with an Agent, but there was little she could do about it, so she put her mind to how she could use it to her advantage.

To make matters worse, she could see that he was holding a small wolf and couldn't help wondering what would become of it. It was unlikely that it would be killed, but being brought up by werewolves who helped produce the serum which stopped other wolves being what they were truly meant to be was almost as bad. It was just something else she could do nothing about. She would have to wait until it got older so she could talk to it, convince it that the brainwashing it was likely to receive was just that, that it was better to not take the serum.

She spent a good deal of her time talking to other werewolves. Some she persuaded to abandon their annual trips to the Agency, but not many.

As soon as Garrick drove off, she called her second in command to arrange a meeting. He would contact the other members of the resistance group and they would meet in the usual place.

She changed clothes, then drove to the address. It was an abandoned warehouse, but it still had running water and electricity and was in good condition, so it was an ideal place to meet. The For Sale sign had been in front of it for almost a year, along with the For Lease one, so Lia assumed that the owner was keeping it in a decent condition in the hope that, one day, someone would be interested in it.

Other cars were in the parking lot as she pulled in. She often wondered why nobody had investigated why there were sometimes a large number of cars in front of an empty warehouse, but it wasn't close to any housing and the few firms that were in neighbouring buildings kept to themselves.

Lia did a quick count of cars. There weren't as many as there should have been, but, though it was late evening, it was a workday so some of the group may not have been able to make it. While she often wished her summons would take priority over everything else, she understood the need to maintain the cover of leading a normal human life. After all, she herself had to do so.

She entered the building and took the stairs to the first floor, where the offices and meeting rooms were located. A few men and women had taken seats in the largest one and turned around as she entered. The previous tenant had left without cleaning out the warehouse and the owner hadn't removed the office furniture.

"Are we expecting anyone else?" she asked as she walked to the front of the room.

"Two more are on their way," Warwick said. "And a few have dialled in."

Lia looked at her second in command. He was a short, stocky man who thought himself attractive. Lia didn't agree; though in wolf form he was an impressive sight. He regularly tried to persuade her to make their relationship less professional, but she rejected him every time. It wasn't that she disliked him; she just didn't mix business with pleasure. He was a good number two and if things became personal between them he might start to challenge her authority and that she couldn't have.

Two people hurried into the room and quickly took seats, muttering their apologies for being late.

The meeting had been called on short notice, so Lia wasn't angry. She looked at the men and women in the room, part of the resistance, as she liked to call it. After all, they were living in an oppressive state, if you were a werewolf, that is. All countries were the same. Nowhere in the world did werewolves enjoy the same freedom as humans. They were locked up for committing no crime other than being what they were. Some were even executed.

"Thank you for coming," she said, loud enough for those listening via the phones to hear her. "You all know about the half-breed. Now it seems the Agency has taken an interest in her."

Grumbling began. Lia let it continue for a moment before hushing them all. The word 'Agency' was a swear word for all those present.

"What we need to do, is decide how we can use this to our advantage."

"Has she been taken to their headquarters?" someone asked.

"Yes. The Agent who approached her took her there."

"Did she go willingly?" a voice on the phone asked.

"No, I don't think she did. However, we must assume that she now knows that werewolves exist. I would be surprised if both she and the Agency don't both now know exactly what she is."

"Any idea what they plan to do with her?" Warwick asked.

Lia shook her head. "You're asking the wrong question. What you should be asking is what should we be doing with her. Now that the Agency knows about her, can we use it to our advantage somehow?"

"She's part werewolf," someone from the back of the room said. "That means we can read her mind. Is there a way to do so without her knowing? She could reveal everything she finds out about the Agency without realising what she's doing."

"It's a good suggestion," Lia said. "But it's unlikely the Agency will reveal anything to her that we would be interested in knowing."

"Then let's use her as a weapon," Warwick said. "Let the Agent take her to their headquarters then once she's inside, we get her to kill everyone."

Though Lia liked the idea, she knew it wouldn't work. "She's not strong enough or skilled enough for that."

Warwick grinned at her. "Not yet," he said. "Not yet."

Lia gave him a challenging look. If he expected her to ask what he was talking about, he was in for a long wait.

It took longer than it should have, but eventually he continued.

"I'd rather discuss this in private."

She could hardly complain about that, so she dismissed everyone else and said she would be in touch about the next meeting. Until then, they were to continuing recruiting, but subtly. They were not to put themselves at risk of being discovered by the Agency.

Once they were alone, Lia addressed Warwick.

"Well?"

"I've been working on something that will make Amy tap into her inner werewolf, with me in control."

"Why you?" Lia immediately asked.

"We both know the answer to that. You can't reveal yourself. Not yet."

She didn't like the idea of him being in control, but couldn't argue against his logic.

"Alright. How are you planning on doing this?"

Warwick smiled at her. "I won't tell you that. Not yet. Not until it's ready."

Lia wanted to turn into a wolf and rip his head off, but managed to restrain herself. She needed to know what he was working on and if it would work.

With a patience she didn't often show, she said, "Keep me informed," then turned her back on him and walked out the door.

Tests

Garrick knocked tentatively on Amy's door. He felt a little nervous, though he had no idea why. He was there to test her, to see what werewolf abilities she had, nothing more.

"You look like shit," he said when Amy answered his knock.

"Thanks," she said sarcastically. "I greatly appreciate your appraisal of me."

"Sorry, what I meant to ask was 'are you okay'? You look like you haven't slept in a week."

"I feel like I haven't, though I don't remember waking up at all last night."

She stepped aside to allow him to enter the house then closed the door behind him. Ainin came bounding up and Garrick dropped down on one knee so he could fuss the dog without him having to jump up.

"Do you want to do this another day?" he asked as he was led into the kitchen, where Amy had put the coffee machine on.

"No, I'll be fine. I just need to get another coffee inside me."

"Is it alright if Lawrence comes over later? He wants to do some testing of his own."

"Whatever," Amy said. She sounded resigned instead of agreeable.

"You know you don't have to do any of this," Garrick said in a serious tone. He wanted her to understand that it was completely her choice. She would have to be monitored by the Agency, but they could do that discretely, at a distance, if that's what she wanted.

"Don't I?" she asked. Then she smiled. It was only a small one, but it was definitely there. "What I mean is, if I don't let you guys find out all you want to know about me, how will I find out anything about myself?"

At least she had accepted that she wasn't completely human.

She slid a mug across the kitchen bench to Garrick before filling her own.

"So what are you planning on doing?"

Garrick quickly outlined his plan. He wanted to test her hearing, eyesight, sense of smell, strength and speed, then compare the results to those of an average human, an Agent and a full werewolf. Nothing would be invasive and she could stop whenever she wanted.

While she got changed into something she could comfortably exercise in, Garrick called Lawrence and provided Amy's address.

It was not a productive morning. Amy willingly took part in all the activities and tests, giving them everything she had, but all results came back as human, nothing more.

She couldn't see better than he had been able to before he became an Agent and began to receive regular injections of the serum, even with her glasses on, which he checked to make sure were prescription rather than for show.

When he pulled out a device that emitted high pitched sounds which would have made him wince if he hadn't been wearing special headphones, Ainin ran away but Amy showed no sign of being able to hear them.

She also couldn't hear him when he spoke softly, though he was sure she should have been able to. Some of the things he said would have earned him a slap around the face, so he was confident that she wasn't lying about not being able to hear him.

Smell had the same result. She couldn't smell things a normal human wouldn't be able to, though both Garrick and Ainin could.

Strength wise, she couldn't lift things that she would have been able to if she did weight training regularly. Garrick was getting more and more frustrated.

"I give up," he said, throwing his arms in the air.

"I'm sorry," Amy said. "I'm doing my best, I swear."

There was sadness in her voice. "I know you are," he said softly. "I'm annoyed at the results, not at you. We've got one more test to do, then I'll leave you in peace until Lawrence arrives. Do you know if there is a running track somewhere near here?"

Amy nodded. "About fifteen minutes drive away there's a walking track you can take dogs to, but a lot of people use it for running. Ainin likes going there."

Garrick grinned. "Then we're taking your car."

After a heated 'discussion', which Garrick refused to call an argument, about who would drive, Amy got her way. He hated being a passenger, but agreed to put up with it. Garrick watched her closely as she chauffeured him and the dog to the park. She drove to the speed limit. Exactly to the speed limit. Without cruise control set, he had never seen anyone manage to keep a car at the same speed. Whenever the limit changed down, she hit the lower speed just as she went past the sign. She never even slowed down on corners most drivers would have done, taking the bends like a professional driver. When pulling away from traffic lights, she was moving as soon as the lights changed.

"You should have been a drag racer," he said.

"I've done this route a lot. I know this road well."

That didn't explain it. Maybe he was seeing some sign of werewolf ability. Then again, maybe he was only seeing what he wanted to see.

Suddenly she swerved, forcing him into the door.

"What was that for?" he asked.

"There was a frog in the road."

"A frog?"

"Well it might have been a toad."

"And you hate them so much you have to swerve to run them over?" He had known werewolves who would do that. Many had no concern for other creatures, especially small and insignificant ones, while others loved and cared for them. Much like humans.

Amy sounded horrified when she replied. "Of course not. I was swerving to avoid it."

Of course she was. Why Garrick had thought any different, he had no idea. Amy was nothing like he had been expecting. For someone with werewolf blood in her, she was acting far too human. He was beginning to doubt the evidence of her parentage, despite the DNA results.

The speed test did nothing to suppress his doubts. While she was faster than average over a short distance, it wasn't anything impressive. She'd never make it to the Olympics. And she had absolutely no stamina for long distance.

"Let's go home," Amy said, as she scratched Ainin behind the ear. The dog had enjoyed the outing, but he was the only one.

"I'm off to get some lunch," Garrick said as Amy pulled up outside her house. "Lawrence will be here in a couple of hours, so I'll be back before then."

"You could always stay," Amy said.

An idea formed in Garrick's head. He wanted to see her in other surroundings. "Let me take you out instead," he said.

"Sure, but I'll have to shower first."

"I think I can allow that." Garrick almost jokingly asked if he could join her, but stopped himself just in time. What was he thinking? He was there on a mission and taking her out to lunch was just part of that mission; it wasn't a date.

To emphasise, to himself, that it wasn't a date, he took her to a local café instead of a restaurant. They talked about anything and everything. He found Amy to be open and honest; she didn't hold anything back or shy away from any topic. He tried to be the same, but there were some things he couldn't talk about, especially not in public.

He was enjoying her company so much, he almost swore when his phone rang.

"Lawrence," he said as soon as he hit the answer button. "What can I do for you?"

"Where are you?" the voice on the other end of the line asked. "I'm at the address you gave me, but nobody's here."

Garrick looked at his watch and this time he did swear.

"Sorry, we haven't made it back from lunch yet. We'll get there as soon as we can."

He hung up the phone and looked at Amy. "Sorry, we have to rush back. Lawrence is waiting at your house."

Amy looked at her watch then she also swore. Garrick was glad it wasn't just him who had lost track of time.

They rushed back to the house, where they found Lawrence sitting on a chair in the back garden. Ainin kept walking up to him, sniffing him, then walking away with an almost puzzled expression on his face. He bounded over to Amy as soon as he saw her.

"I think he can't work out what I am," Lawrence said. "He's so used to smelling a half-werewolf that he can't comprehend that he's smelling a full one." Garrick saw the look on Amy's face and assumed Lawrence had also seen it as he quickly added, "Not that I'm saying you smell, of course."

"Of course," Amy said with a smile.

It was at that moment that Garrick noticed another person at the far end of the garden, studying the roses. She was holding the hand of a young girl, who was on her knees on the ground with her back to them.

"Rosemary," he called out and the woman straightened up and turned around.

As soon as she saw Garrick, she smiled and said something to the girl. The girl jumped to her feet and ran at Garrick, throwing her arms around his legs as soon as she reached him. Garrick gave Lawrence a puzzled look.

"Can we go inside so I can explain?" Lawrence asked, turning his attention to Amy.

"Sure," she said, though she didn't seem happy about it. Garrick wasn't sure if she didn't want a full werewolf in her house or if it was the two strangers who were bothering her.

"I'll go in through the front then open the backdoor for you," she continued. Garrick thought about going with her, but decided not to. She might want a few moments to herself.

The backdoor opened quicker than he expected. He was still trying to extract the girl's arms from around his lower thighs.

Everyone entered the house, even Ainin, who acted like he didn't want to leave his mistress alone with strangers. Once they were seated in the lounge, with the girl sitting on Garrick's lap, Lawrence did the introductions.

"Amy, my dear, allow me to introduce you to my wife, Rosemary."

The plump woman held out her hand to Amy, who was much taller than her. Amy shook it apprehensively.

"You must be the half-werewolf I have heard so much about," Rosemary said. "I'm delighted to meet you. Lawrence won't stop talking about you."

This seemed to make Amy uncomfortable, so Garrick took control of the conversation by asking about the young girl.

"This is Emily," Lawrence informed him. "It seems that her father didn't treat her well. She sees you as her rescuer not her father's executioner. The only reason she attacked you was because she was scared. She wasn't trying to defend her father. We've spoken to a psychologist and this sort of hero worship isn't common, but does sometimes happen. It helps the young mind deal with a traumatic situation. In this case he thinks she has completely blanked witnessing you killing her father from her mind."

Garrick was stunned. This was Art Greenfield's daughter? But she looked so different. Even now he knew who she was, he still didn't recognise her.

"How did you change her hair colour?" he asked.

It was Rosemary who answered. "I washed it."

"Wait a minute," Amy said. "Are you telling me that this is the cute little wolf that Garrick brought here?"

Lawrence and Rosemary both nodded.

"I need to sit down," Amy said and collapsed into a chair.

"So what's her story?" Garrick asked. "Where's her mother?"

"We don't know. She doesn't know who her mother is. She can only remember living with her father, then some of his friends when he went away. I'm assuming she means to jail. She liked the friends, they treated her much better than her father did. She didn't want to go back to him when he collected her, but she wasn't given a choice."

"What will happen to her now?" Garrick didn't like talking about her when she was able to hear. He found it rude, but she was curled up in his lap and didn't appear to be taking any notice, so he didn't have much of a choice.

"We'll adopt her," Rosemary said. "Carl is already arranging the paperwork. Unless you want to," she added, giving him a cheeky smile.

"I don't really think my line of work makes me a suitable candidate for adoptive father, but I'm happy to visit often."

As though she had suddenly remembered that there was a child in the house, Amy said, "Would she like a biscuit or something? Do werewolves even eat biscuits?"

"Do you?" Lawrence asked, earning himself a glare from both Garrick and Amy.

"Why don't you ask her?" Rosemary suggested.

Amy did so and Emily raised her head for the first time since entering the house. "Yes please," she said in a timid voice.

Amy held out her hand. "Come with me to the kitchen and we'll see what we can find."

Garrick couldn't help smiling as the girl took Amy's hand and left the room with her.

"How's the testing going?" Lawrence asked as soon as they were out of sight.

Garrick snorted. "It's not. She has absolutely no werewolf abilities, unless you count good driving skills."

"What did you expect?" Rosemary asked.

"I don't know. Something. Anything to indicate she isn't completely human."

"She might not have inherited anything from her father, you know."

Garrick didn't bother to reply. He didn't know why he wanted her to show some abilities, but he did and was deeply disappointed that, so far, she hadn't.

Amy led Emily back into the room. The young girl was carrying a box of chocolate chip cookies and a glass of milk. A smile was plastered on her face. As soon as she sat down on the floor, Ainin went over to join her. While he didn't attempt to take any of the biscuits from her, he soon demonstrated that he made a good vacuum cleaner, especially where crumbs were concerned.

"What exactly is it you are here to do?" Amy asked as she sat back down on the sofa. She was looking pointedly at Lawrence.

Lawrence leaned forward. "I want to test your mental abilities. As I'm sure you already know, werewolves can read the minds of those with werewolf blood, including Agents. I want to know if you can read mine or if I can read yours. I also want to see if I can get you to transform."

"I'm not stripping off in front of you," Amy immediately said, making Garrick chuckle.

Lawrence laid a calming hand on her knee. "I wouldn't dream of asking you to my dear. Let's try mind reading first, shall we?"

He then put his hand down the front of his shirt and withdrew a chain with an oblong pendant attached. He held it out for her to see.

"This is a blocker. I'm not sure exactly how it works, but it stops other werewolves from reading my mind."

"It emits a high pitched signal which blocks brainwaves," Garrick said. "If you want to know more, speak to the scientists. They love talking about that sort of thing."

"I won't," Amy said, making Garrick smile again.

"It runs on batteries, which is why you have to change it when its light turns green. That's the early warning indicator that it's running out of power."

"So what's to prevent a werewolf just taking it off you then reading your mind?" Amy asked.

"A nifty trick by the makers," Garrick said. He pulled something out from under his t-shirt then held it out, showing Amy that he, too, wore a blocker. "Touch the chain," he instructed.

She did as he requested, noting that it looked different from any other chain she had ever seen. It was smooth, with no sign of links.

"What's it made of?"

"A metal so strong it's impossible for anyone to cut this off me. It also has no clasp. One side of the chain is fused to the blocker, the other is locked inside it and only the owner of the chain can open it. It's fingerprint locked and each one has a

84

unique way of being released. I can't take Lawrence's off him and he can't take mine off me, not unless I tell him how to and he places my thumb on it, in the right place, while he's doing it."

"The reason I'm showing you this, Amy, is because I want you to try to read my mind and in order for you to do that, I have to take this off."

He turned his back on everyone so that nobody could see how he opened his blocker and when he turned around again, he had it in his hand.

Garrick wasn't sure why Lawrence had revealed the blockers to Amy, as he could have removed his chain without giving an explanation, but he was all for being completely open and honest with her, so he said nothing.

Lawrence handed his chain to his wife, then knelt down on the floor in front of Amy.

"I want you to place your hands on each side of my head and close your eyes. You need to picture your mind going into mine. You'll feel a barrier. Push against it."

Amy nodded, then did as he had told her to do. A look of intense concentration filled her face. "Nothing," she said after a few moments. "I can feel nothing. Maybe I'm just doing it wrong."

"Maybe," Lawrence agreed. "Or maybe you don't have the ability. May I try on you?"

Amy nodded and Lawrence placed his hands on her head, but he didn't close his eyes. Garrick had seen him do this before and knew he was so adept at it he no longer had to shut out everything else. Garrick grew a little concerned when a few moments later he did so.

A frown formed on Lawrence's face as he continued to try to access Amy's mind. Eventually he dropped his hands.

"There's a block," he said. "I'm not sure what exactly it is, but it could be her human side interfering. It took me a while to get past it. When I did, I couldn't find anything of interest. It seemed as though an impenetrable veil is hiding part of her mind."

"What are you saying?" Garrick asked.

"I may be wrong, but I think Amy has all the same abilities as a full-blooded werewolf, but something is preventing her from using them."

Nadia

Amy was tense. She had been meeting with both Garrick and Lawrence on a regular basis over the last month or so as they tried to find out what was causing her block, but this was the first time she was going to Lawrence's house.

She was wearing a blindfold, not because Garrick didn't trust her, but because only a select few were allowed to know where Lawrence and his family lived. It was just too risky. There were a number of werewolves who would love to get their hands on them and Lawrence had already proven that Amy's mind could be read. Well most of it, at least.

Amy didn't object. She could understand the reasons and while she had never been approached by a werewolf, that didn't mean she never would be.

It took a while for Garrick to drive from Amy's house to Lawrence's, but not as long as she had feared. If she had taken note of the turns he made and the feel of the roads, she might have been able to work out roughly where they were, but she didn't even try. She had no intention of putting Lawrence in any danger. Over the last few weeks, she had gotten close to him, looking on him as almost some sort of father figure.

"You can take off the blindfold now," Garrick said.

It was a bright sunny day and Amy blinked at the sudden incursion of light when she removed the material and opened her eyes.

She didn't ask where they were. She knew she wouldn't get an answer and she didn't really care.

Looking around her as Garrick drove down the dirt track, all she could see was trees.

"Lawrence and his family own nearly a hundred acres," Garrick said. "Mostly woodland. It gives them the freedom to run when they are in their wolf forms. They also have access to an Agency supplied house, which is nearer the city, but they prefer being here."

Amy could understand why. She gazed out of the window as Garrick drove. Wherever they were, it was in the middle of nowhere.

Eventually they reached the house and Garrick pulled up in front of it. He was driving Amy's car, again, as she had insisted on bringing Ainin and he didn't want dog hair in his car. It had taken ages to get it clean after the first time.

As soon as Ainin was out of the car, he went racing from tree to tree, having a good sniff before leaving his scent on them. Amy shook her head. She had never been able to work out how dogs could pee so much when they wanted to.

As Garrick led her up to the front door, Amy took in the house. It was two storeys, with a window in the roof, indicating an attic, and appeared to be made entirely of wood and glass. And it was massive. The front visage was so wide she couldn't help envisioning it eating her small abode for breakfast.

The door opened before they got there and Emily ran out. She leaped into Garrick's outstretched arms and he picked her up.

"Have you been a good girl for your mum and dad and Nadia?" he asked her and she immediately nodded her head.

"There's cookies inside," she said, beaming at him.

"Is there now? Then maybe we should go and get some."

Amy couldn't help smiling. Garrick was so good with the little girl. He would make a great father someday.

Now where had that thought come from? She shook her head as she tried to dispel the image of Garrick holding a newborn baby. He was a career man. A wife and family weren't on his agenda.

Rosemary stood in the doorway and held the door open wide so Garrick and Emily could enter. Amy followed them. Garrick gave Rosemary a quick peck on the cheek as he passed her.

"Welcome to my humble abode," Rosemary said to Amy, making her smile once more. She needed to get the woman a dictionary if she thought her home was humble.

"Thanks for inviting me over."

"It's an absolute pleasure. Please come in and make yourself comfortable."

Amy went to remove her shoes, but Rosemary shook her head, indicating it wasn't necessary. Before closing the door, Rosemary called to Ainin, who went racing into the house, following his mistress.

The inside was just as impressive as the outside and Amy couldn't help marvelling at the exposed beams and polished oak floorboards.

"This place is stunning," she said.

"We did a lot of the work ourselves," Rosemary told her. "Only getting in experts when they were really needed. It took us quite a few years."

"I can imagine."

"Would you like a tour?"

"I'd love one, but it was a long drive. May I use your bathroom first?"

"Of course. The nearest one is down the hallway. I'll show you." Then she looked down at Ainin. "The others are probably in the kitchen. I'm sure there'll be something there for you."

The dog didn't need telling twice. He raced off down the corridor, not letting the fact that he was slipping on the floor slow him down.

"Thanks for letting me bring him."

"No problem," Rosemary said. "It's not as if I could complain about the fur."

Amy snorted. "Garrick does. He won't let Ainin in his car, which is why we always take mine now."

"Well Garrick doesn't have a young girl living with him who keeps turning into a wolf on a regular basis. For some reason she likes to run around the house in her non-human form. And while the rest of the family try to stay outside when we are wolves, we prefer the privacy of our bedrooms for the transformation."

Amy took care of her bathroom needs then Rosemary showed her around the house. It had half a dozen bedrooms, all ensuite, a billiard room, a sauna, a gym, both indoor and outdoor pools, a formal lounge, a family room and a huge kitchen. It was better equipped than a lot of hotels were.

"The Agency makes sure we are taken care of," Rosemary told her when Amy asked how they could afford it. "As well as providing our blood, my husband, daughter and I also work for them in various roles."

After grabbing drinks from the fridge, Rosemary led Amy into the back garden, where Ainin was playing with Emily, who was in her wolf form. They were playing tug-of-war with some rope. As he was much bigger, Ainin could easily have taken it off the young wolf, but chose to play instead.

Garrick and Lawrence were sitting on chairs around a table, as were Garrick's sister and a young woman Amy didn't recognise. As soon as she spotted her, Tabitha (who doesn't like to be called Tabitha, Amy quickly reminded herself) stood up and walked over to her. She then surprised her by giving her a hug. They had met a few times, but Amy hadn't realised they had become that close.

"It's great to see you again," Tabitha said.

"You too," Amy said, with genuine feeling.

"Let me introduce you to Lawrence and Rosemary's daughter. She's also my best friend." She turned around to look at the woman Amy hadn't recognised, who was busy speaking to Garrick. Amy couldn't help noticing the way she held his arm.

"Nadia, come and meet Amy," Tabitha called out.

Amy noticed how Nadia seemed reluctant to leave Garrick and couldn't help wondering if there was something going on between them.

It was all Amy could do not to let her jaw drop as she watched Nadia approach. The woman was stunning. No wonder Garrick was interested in her. Her long hair, which she had tied behind her so that it flowed down her back, was so dark it made Amy's look pale by comparison. Her dark brown eyes matched it perfectly and she had the longest lashes Amy had ever seen.

Every feature on her face was perfectly formed and placed. It was like the best parts had been taken from several top models and rolled into one perfect human. Well, werewolf, Amy quickly corrected.

She was slim, not thin, and her figure-hugging jeans showed she had perfectly shaped legs. She looked fit, but not an exercise addict. She walked with a grace Amy couldn't even attempt and when she spoke, it was like an angel singing. Amy felt intimidated just being near her, though Nadia had done nothing to make her feel unwelcome or uncomfortable.

"You must be Amy," she said. Amy did her best not to image cartoon birds flying around her head. "I've heard a lot about you."

"I'm sure only half of it is true."

Nadia smiled at her. "We'll see. I would just like to thank you for bringing your dog with you. It's the first time I've been able to touch one. They usually avoid werewolves."

"I like to think Ainin is special," Amy said, unable to keep a smile from forming on her face. She liked it when people spoke kindly about her beloved pet.

"I hand reared him," she continued. "His heavily pregnant mother was rushed to the vet, having been the victim of a hit and run. The vet operated but the mother didn't make it. Nor did the owner. The vet was left with seven healthy puppies who would die without their mother. My friend worked at the veterinary practice and gave me a call. They found volunteers for all seven pups and they all survived."

"That must have been hard work," Tabitha said.

"It was. Especially the first few weeks. I got so little sleep, having to get up and feed him every few hours, that I felt like a zombie half the time. Still, it was worth it."

"Well that explains why he's able to tolerate werewolves," Tabitha said.

"Please, come and sit down," Nadia said, gesturing toward the table.

Amy chose a chair next to Garrick. For some reason, Nadia made her a little nervous and Garrick was a reassuring presence.

"I hear you're having problems tapping into your werewolf side," Nadia said, taking the seat opposite Garrick.

"That's one way of putting it," Amy said. "Though 'having problems' doesn't even begin to tell the whole story. Basically, I just can't do it. I'm not even sure there is a werewolf side to me."

"There is," Lawrence said. "It's just hidden away behind that block of yours. All we have to do is find it."

"Then you'll be able to transform into your true form," Nadia said.

Amy shuddered. "Doesn't it hurt?"

Lawrence shook his head. "Transforming doesn't. And being a wolf is amazing. The feeling of freedom it gives you when you are running wild is indescribable."

He looked wistful as he spoke. Then he turned serious. "Feeling the need to change, however, is another matter. It can be quite painful, becoming almost unbearable if you resist it for too long. I can understand why so many of my kind take the annual injections."

"You've never been tempted to give up helping the Agency so that you can stop yourself going through it?" Amy asked.

"No. The Agency needs all the werewolf blood it can get. Until there are many more werewolves willing to help them out, my family and I will continue to do so. The Agency would be a lot more efficient if more werewolves would agree to be Agents, but unfortunately, very few are prepared to do so."

"Speaking of which," Garrick said. "The scientists want to take some of your blood to see if it can be used. If that's alright with you."

"Sure," Amy said. "I'll make sure I go and see them next time you take me to your headquarters."

The conversation flowed for a few more minutes, then it was time to work on getting Amy to tap into her powers. Lawrence was determined to get past her block.

Lawrence, Rosemary and Nadia did everything they could think of, both mentally and physically, but nothing worked. Frustration began to set in.

"I give up," Lawrence said, throwing his arms in the air. "I just don't know what else to try."

"Maybe I just don't have any werewolf powers," Amy said. She didn't like upsetting people and felt it was her fault that Lawrence was annoyed.

"You do," Rosemary said. "I can feel them. There's just something stopping you accessing them."

"Why don't I bring Amy back next weekend?" Garrick said, placing a hand on her shoulder and giving it a slight squeeze. "That will give you plenty of time to think of something else to try."

Amy could have been imagining things, but she was sure she saw Nadia scowl.

"Are you ready to go?" Garrick asked. Amy wasn't sure if he was talking to her or her dog, who was laying at her feet, pretending to be sleep.

"Can I use the bathroom first?" Amy asked, not that she was expecting someone to say no.

"Sure. I need to go and say goodbye to Emily anyway. I'll meet you at the car."

Emily, much to the young girl's annoyance, had been sent into the house to play while the family worked on Amy. She had wanted to stay with Garrick. It was obvious she idolised him.

Amy took care of her business and as she exited the bathroom, someone grabbed her arm and pushed her against the wall.

"Keep away from him," Nadia hissed in her ear.

"What are you talking about?" Amy asked. Nadia's grip on her arm was hurting. She could almost feel the bruises forming.

"I've seen the way you look at him. Keep your hands and your eyes off him. He's mine."

"Who? Garrick? I'm not interested in Garrick." Amy hoped Nadia believed her. The werewolf was beginning to scare her.

"Good," she said in a low, menacing voice. "Make sure it stays that way, or you will regret it."

Nadia then released Amy's arm and walked away, leaving Amy shaking.

She made her way to the car. "What took you so long?" Garrick asked. She could see that he already had Ainin strapped in the back.

"Nothing," she lied. She wasn't ready to tell Garrick what had happened. She wasn't sure he would believe her.

He gave her a suspicious look, as though he knew she was lying to him, but he didn't push her. She breathed a small sigh of relief when he let the matter drop.

Subconsciously rubbing her arm, she got into the car and Garrick blindfolded her once more.

As they headed down the driveway, Amy said, "Are you and Nadia dating?"

She couldn't see the look on Garrick's face, but she could hear amusement in his voice. "Of course not. I've known her so long she's like a sister to me. Why do you ask? Making sure I'm single?"

"No," Amy snapped at him. He was just teasing her, but she hadn't recovered from Nadia scaring her so she didn't like it.

"Hey, calm down. I was just joking." The amusement had gone and concern replaced it. "What's wrong?"

"Nothing," she lied again.

They lapsed into silence. After a while Amy asked, "If I go back there next weekend, will Nadia be there?"

"Probably. Why? Is that a problem?"

"I just don't think she likes me very much." That was the understatement of the century.

"She'll come around when she gets to know you. But if you prefer, I can have Lawrence and Rosemary come to your place. Or we could meet at headquarters."

"Thank you." Knowing she wouldn't have to face Nadia again made her feel better.

When they were close to her home, Garrick said she could remove her blindfold. She blinked as her eyes adjusted to the sudden light.

A short while later he pulled up outside of her house and switched the engine off. He asked if he could take her to dinner, but she declined. She didn't want to risk Nadia seeing them together. It was highly unlikely that she would have followed them, but she didn't want to take any chances.

She watched Garrick switch to his own car and drive off before she headed into her house. As she closed the front door, she couldn't help wishing she had never found out about werewolves or the Agency or what she really was.

Implant

Lia tapped her foot as she waited for Warwick to arrive. It was he who had called the meeting so she was surprised that he hadn't been at the abandoned warehouse when she arrived. She was about to give him a call when she heard movement below her.

"Sorry I'm late," Warwick said as soon as he entered the office she had chosen to use. He looked like he had run up the stairs. "I got caught in traffic. An accident I think, though it could have just been roadworks."

Lia said nothing. She was well aware that half the roads in the area seemed to be being dug up or widened or whatever else you did to roads. Well, it wasn't really half, but it felt like it sometimes. And she was sure the diversions they put in place made the unsuspecting drivers go much further out of their way than was necessary.

"Do you want to sit down?" Warwick asked, gesturing toward a chair.

"If I wanted to sit down, I would already be sitting," Lia snapped at him. Then she took a deep breath to calm herself. "Sorry, it's been a long day. And that annoying Agent was visiting Amy again. I don't like having him so close so often. It hampers my movements. Still, I shouldn't be taking my bad temper out on you. So what have you brought to show me?"

Warwick grinned like a schoolboy as he put his bag on the ground and unzipped it. He withdrew a small black case and opened it toward Lia, so she could see what was inside.

"It looks like an implant of some sort," she said unenthusiastically.

"It is."

Lia was not pleased that he had brought her all the way to the warehouse on short notice just to show her some piece of electronic equipment.

"And what good is that to me?" She didn't even try to keep her annoyance out of her voice.

Warwick appeared unperturbed and he kept the smile on his face as he said, "Let me explain."

He picked the device up out of its case and looked closely at it. "This little baby will get you what you need from Amy."

That comment peaked Lia's interest. "How?"

"Implant this in the back of her neck here." He demonstrated on himself, indicating the base of his neck. "Attach it neat her central nervous system and it will give me control of her."

Lia took the implant out of Warwick's hand and examined it, though she had no idea what she was looking at.

"How?" she asked, hoping she would understand the answer.

"It's coded to emit a signal triggered by my voice. If I give her an order while she has this imbedded in the right place under her skin, she has to obey it. Kind of like hypnosis only much more effective."

Lia snorted. "Well it could hardly be less effective. Hypnosis is a load of bull."

"Not always," Warwick said. "Used correctly and on the right kind of mind, it can really help people. It can't, however, be used to make them do something they don't want to do."

"And this can?" Lia was sceptical.

"In the right person, I believe it can."

Warwick sounded sure of himself, but Lia picked up on a word she didn't like. "You 'believe' it can?" She mimed quotation marks as she said 'believe'. "You mean you don't know?"

Warwick grimaced. "That's the problem. I haven't been able to test it."

Lia wanted to snap 'why the hell not', but getting angry at Warwick wouldn't accomplish anything. Instead she forced herself to remain calm. "Why not?"

"Because it will only work on half-breeds."

It was a reasonable answer, but Lia wanted to know more. "Why?"

"It reacts with werewolf blood. Too much and the person will be able to fight against it. Too little and it will have no effect whatsoever."

'You're sure?" Lia asked, still holding the implant between her fingers.

"Positive," Warwick said. "I've tried it on humans and none of them did anything I ordered them to do."

Lia raised her eyebrow. Warwick had been experimenting on humans without her approval. She wasn't sure if she should be annoyed at him for not seeking permission or admire him for taking the initiative and not bothering her until he was sure he knew what he was talking about.

"And werewolves?"

"They could feel the compulsion to obey me but managed to resist. For some it was harder than others, but all managed to do so."

"And you don't believe little miss half-breed will be able to resist."

It wasn't a question, but Warwick answered it anyway. "No, I don't."

Lia tapped her finger against her lips, a habit she had whenever she was thinking. "Is there anything else I should know?"

"I think it will also overcome the block on her powers."

That was a big claim and she hoped Warwick could back it up. She was aware that Amy possessed all the abilities that a full werewolf had, but that a block prevented her from using them. She also knew what was causing the block, but had no intention of letting Amy or the Agency know. At least not until it was in her own best interests to do so.

"How?" she asked.

"Think about it. If she had to obey all orders and someone ordered her to use her werewolf powers, she would have to."

It was a bit of a leap in logic, but it was worth pursuing.

"Alright," she said. "I'm listening. What are your plans?"

She knew her second-in-command well enough to know that he wouldn't be showing her his device now if he hadn't already thought through how to use it. It would be a suggestion, of course, not a demand and he would be open to discussion. He knew what would happen if he wasn't.

Warwick smiled at her, a sure sign he was confident she would be pleased with what he had to say.

"I first thought we could use her to bring that Agent to us so we could extract information from him, make her get him to remove his chain first, but I don't believe that would work. There's nothing to indicate that his visits to her are anything other than professional."

Lia nodded her head, pleased he had thought things through instead of jumping to easy ways to use the half-breed. She agreed with his assessment of her relationship with the Agent.

"Then I thought about where she might have access to. We know she has been taken to their headquarters a few times. Would she be permitted entry if she turned up on her own?"

It was a good question, one Lia didn't know the answer to. "Carry on," she said, knowing that Warwick would have more to say.

"She might know where to find the head of that particular branch of the Agency. She might get close enough to transform and kill him. It wouldn't stop their relentless pursuit of us, but it might put a temporary halt to it, giving us a little bit of freedom to plan and act without the worry of being discovered."

While Lia didn't agree with his assessment, she remained silent. She didn't want to contradict him yet. Over the many years she had known him, she had learnt that he was sometimes worth listening to.

"Even if she can't get in there alone, we can program her to do it next time she is taken there," Warwick continued.

"Your idea has potential, but maybe she should do more than just kill the man in charge. Maybe she should kill everyone she can."

Warwick grinned. "I like your thinking, but killing one man would probably only get her detained, killing many would make them shoot first and ask questions later."

Lia grinned back at him. "I think that's a risk we are prepared to take. When can we get it implanted into her?"

Warwick shrugged his shoulders. "I'd like to do a few more tests on both werewolves and humans first. A week, maybe two."

Lia bent down and picked her bag up from where she had placed it on the floor, letting Warwick know that the meeting was over.

"Let me know as soon as it's ready and I will make sure you have access to that bitch Amy when you want her."

Self-defence

It had been a long day and Amy was struggling to read her book on her ride home from work. She took off her glasses and rubbed her eyes, but it didn't help; the words continued to swim on the page.

She sighed and put her book back into her bag. She would be on the bus for a while longer, so she leaned back into the seat and closed her eyes.

A short while later, she was disturbed by a raised voice coming from closer to the front of the bus.

"People like you make me sick," a male voice said. The hate in it made her shiver. "Why do you think you have the right to associate with your betters? If you want to ride on the bus with us, you should take that rag off your face and dress like a normal woman."

Amy's eyes fell on a woman who was cowering in her seat while a tall, muscular man, was leaning over her. The hijab she was wearing had made her a target for the man's anger.

The man didn't touch her, but he came close as he stabbed his finger toward her while continuing his tirade.

Amy looked around. People were either hiding their heads, pretending not to see what was happening, or were watching intently, eager to see what would happen next. Some had even taken their phones out and were filming it.

Amy felt nothing but disgust for her fellow passengers. She yelled out, at the top of her voice, "Hey you. Leave her alone. She has as much right to ride this bus as you do."

Silence filled the bus as all eyes shifted to her. The man slowly straightened up and turned around to look at her. His face showed his incredulity that someone had dared to confront him.

When his eyes fell on her, he sneered. "Mind your own business. It's got nothing to do with you."

Now that he had stood up straight, Amy could see how tall he was. And muscular. His biceps were bulging as they strained against his t-shirt. His weight must have been at least twice that of the woman he had been harassing. She found herself looking for tattoos. She mentally chastised herself for using an unfair and incorrect stereotype.

"Just like her using public transport is none of yours, you mean." She regretted the words as soon as they were out of her mouth.

Growling, the man started toward her. She looked around, but quickly realised that nobody would be coming to her defence, just like they hadn't for the poor woman being racially abused.

Gathering her courage, she stood up. She had no idea what would happen to her, but she wasn't going to remain seated; it made her an easy target.

"I was born in this country," the man sneered at her. "That gives me the right to defend my country against the likes of her."

Amy forced herself to laugh. It was the only thing stopping her whimpering.

"Defend against what? What harm is she doing? She's just sitting there, minding her own business, not bothering anyone, unlike you. Besides, how do you know she wasn't born here? You're just a racist bully."

"You bitch," the man screamed, his face going red with anger as he rapidly moved up the aisle in her direction.

He pulled his arm back and time seemed to slow down. Amy could see his fist flying toward her face. It was going to hit her and it was going to hurt. A lot. She would be lucky if he didn't break anything.

The next thing she knew, the man was lying prone on the floor and she was standing over him, her hand still clenched into a fist. She had no idea what had happened. She looked around her. Everyone was looking at her, some with their mouths hanging open. Most were clapping their hands.

"That was unbelievable," someone said. "The way you blocked his punch and then knocked him out was amazing."

Amy had no idea what the young man was talking about. She focused on her fist and willed herself to unclench it. Only then did she realise that her hand hurt. Had she really hit that man? She couldn't have. She didn't have the strength or skill to hit someone hard enough to knock them down. And he wasn't getting up. He must have hit his head on something as he tripped over. There was no way she could be responsible for him lying prone on the floor.

But the other bus passengers seemed to think she was.

She collapsed back into her seat.

"Are you alright, love?" the elderly woman seated next to her asked. "You look like you are in shock."

'I am,' Amy thought, but said nothing.

"Here," the woman sitting on the seat across from her said as she handed a plastic water bottle to her. "This might help."

Amy forced herself to smile at the woman and gratefully accepted the bottle. She drank deeply, but it didn't help.

"That was very brave of you," the woman continued. "Sticking up for that woman when nobody else would. You deserve a medal."

'Why?' Amy wanted to ask. 'Why should I be awarded for doing something that everyone else should have been prepared to do? Why was nobody else prepared to do it?'

But she didn't ask the questions out loud. She didn't want to embarrass anyone.

She took another mouthful of the water before handing the bottle back, along with her thanks. Only then did she realise that the bus wasn't moving and that the driver wasn't in his seat.

"What's going on?" she asked. "Why have we stopped?"

Even before she had finished speaking, she realised what a stupid question it was. There was an unconscious man on the floor. An ambulance would have to be called, probably the police as well.

A feeling of guilt flowed through her. If she had just kept her mouth shut, all these people would be on their way home now. Who knew how long they would now be stuck on the bus.

She opened her mouth to apologise, then realised she had nothing to apologise for. It was the bully's fault that everyone would be delayed, not hers. He was the one who started it. She just ended it. At least that was what she was being told. She just wished she could remember how she had defended herself.

The paramedics arrived, quickly followed by the police. The man was revived and assessed before being taken away in case he had a concussion. Her hand was looked at, but nothing appeared to be broken. They put an ice pack on it and told her to take it easy for a few days.

The police took witness statements from everyone, leaving Amy to last. Instead of being interviewed on the bus, she was escorted from it. After all, she might be arrested and charged with assault.

As she passed the woman in the hijab, she felt someone grab her hand. She looked down to find the woman holding it.

"Thank you," she said. "If you hadn't defended me, I don't know what would have happened."

Amy nodded her head, unable to force her face to smile. Forming words was beyond her.

"Am I under arrest?" she managed to ask as she was put into a patrol vehicle.

"Not at the moment ma'am," a middle aged man in uniform said. It wasn't a reassuring comment. He must have realised that as he added, "Everyone I spoke to said the victim attacked you and you just acted in self-defence. I'm sure everything will be fine."

Amy almost laughed when they called the brute she supposedly hit a victim. The victim was the woman he was abusing.

"Can I call someone?" she asked.

"Of course. As soon as we get to the station you can call your lawyer."

"I need a lawyer?"

"That's up to you."

The journey to the police station seemed to take forever. As soon as she was allowed to use her phone, she called Garrick. She had no idea why, but he was the first person she could think of. Maybe because he worked for a government Agency. Well, sort of.

She was placed in an interview room and given a coffee. She waved away the suggestion that she wait for a lawyer to be present and told the constable and sergeant, who sat themselves opposite her, to just get on with it. She wanted it over and done with so she could get home to her dog.

They were gentle with their questioning, treating her as a witness rather than a suspect. She answered all their questions as honestly and thoroughly as she could. They told her that everything she told them confirmed what everyone else had said. Their only confusion was how she managed to knock out someone who was obviously more powerful than her.

They weren't the only ones confused.

"I have no idea what happened," she said. "One minute I can see a fist flying toward me, the next the man's on the floor in front of me. I've been told I hit him, but I can't remember doing so."

They questioned her over and over again, asking in different ways, but no matter what they said, she wasn't able to tell them anything more.

Eventually they let her go. "You won't be facing any charges," the sergeant told her. "You didn't start the altercation. You verbally defended someone who was being racially attacked, nothing more, until you found yourself in a position where you had to defend yourself. It sounds like you got off a lucky punch. Don't make a habit of this sort of thing as next time you might not be so lucky. Having said that, don't let it stop you standing up for those who can't stand up for themselves. Not enough people do that these days."

Amy nodded her head. All she wanted was to get home and have a hot bath.

Garrick was in the waiting room when she was shown to it. He hadn't been allowed in to see her until her interview was over and he couldn't have revealed he worked for the Agency, as most police didn't know it even existed, he later explained to her.

"Are you alright?" he asked as soon as he saw her. She nodded her head and he pulled her into a hug. "Liar," he whispered into her ear.

"Come on," he said, loud enough for the policeman to hear. "Let's get you home."

He waited until he had Amy on the sofa with a blanket on her and a steaming cup of coffee in her hand before asking any questions. Ainin was curled up beside her.

"Want to talk about it?" he asked.

She didn't, but she knew she had to, and who better to talk to than someone who might understand what she was talking about.

"I've been told I blocked a punch then hit someone hard enough to knock them unconscious, but I don't remember doing it."

Garrick's reply took her completely by surprise.

"Want to see?"

He took his phone out of his pocket and unlocked the screen.

"Someone recorded it and it's already on social media," he said. "The tech guys managed to find it quite quickly as soon as I told them what had happened."

Amy groaned. If it was on social media, then anyone she knew might have seen it. Including her boss. How was she going to explain that to him?

He positioned his phone so she could easily see it and pressed play on the video he had selected. Amy watched in amazement as she saw herself defend against the blow aimed at her face and hit the culprit so hard he flew off his feet. It was so fast it was almost a blur.

"How?" she asked. She didn't know how to finish the sentence, but she didn't need to.

"I may be wrong," Garrick said, "but I think that you can tap into your werewolf powers in an emergency."

Kidnap

Amy groaned. Her head hurt. It didn't feel like a hangover, but it probably was. Not only had her boss seen the video, but all the employees of the law firm where she worked had. Instead of being angry at her display of violence, the main partners were so impressed with how she handled herself, they took her out to dinner. Whoever had posted the video had told the full story, so they knew the reason for her actions. Dinner had involved lots of alcohol, so much that they gave her the next day off to recover.

Amy groaned again. She was glad her bedroom was dark. She could clearly remember everything that had happened during the evening and she was grateful that she hadn't said or done anything to make a fool of herself.

She was extremely thirsty and recalled that she had placed a glass of water by the bed just before she crept into it.

She reached out for it, but it wasn't there. Nor was her bedside table. On top of that, her bed felt really uncomfortable. Solid, but not in a good way.

She sat up and instantly regretted it. The base of her head was pounding and the sudden movement made her feel dizzy.

She looked around, but her room was so dark she couldn't see her hand in front of her face. She frowned. Her room was never that dark, even on completely starless nights. Her curtains did a good job of keeping out the light, but the streetlamp across the road always managed to get around the edges.

She pulled back the covers and swung her legs around. Her bed was low, so she should have been able to feel her carpet under her feet, but she couldn't reach the floor.

She lowered herself down and her bare feet came into contact with cold tiles.

She certainly wasn't in her bedroom. Or any other room in her house. So where was she? She had absolutely no idea.

With her arms out in front of her so she wouldn't, hopefully, walk into anything, she managed to find the wall and followed it around until she came to a door. Feeling the wall all over next to it, she managed to find a light switch and pulled it down.

Bright light illuminated the room, making her wince and screw her eyes shut. She opened them a little and as soon as they had adjusted, she opened them fully and looked around.

She was standing in a room containing nothing but the table she had been laying on, with a blanket on it. There wasn't even a window. Looking down, she found she was dressed in what appeared to be a hospital gown.

"Where the hell am I?" she said out loud. She received no reply, not that she was expecting to. She tried to open the door, but it was locked.

Taking deep breaths, in order to stop herself panicking, she returned to the table and sat down. She ran through the events of the previous night, searching for a clue as to where she was and how she got there.

She came up blank. Nothing unusual had happened and she couldn't remember anything between her going to bed and waking up in an unknown location.

The base of her skull was itching, so she reached under her hair to scratch it. The moment her fingers encountered her skin, she pulled them back. Then she tentatively returned them to the same position and gently probed. It was very sore there.

Her hand was still on her head when she heard a key turn in the lock and the door opened. "I'd leave that alone if I were you," a man said as he walked into the room. "It needs time to heal."

The man was short and stocky, with a few days worth of stubble on his face.

"Who are you?" Amy asked. "What have you done to me?" She was too terrified to be scared. She wanted to run for the open door but doubted she would be able to get past the man. She wanted to hide under the blanket and hope he would go away, but that wouldn't help her in any way. If he was there to hurt her, there was nothing she would be able to do about it. Then she remembered the incident on the bus. Maybe she would be able to defend herself again. Then again, maybe she wouldn't.

The man walked up to her, but stopped before he got too close. "My name is Warwick and I'm a werewolf. And you, my dear Amy, are going to do everything I say."

She had never felt so scared, not even when Garrick had taken her prisoner. There was something about this man that terrified her. She had no idea what he wanted to do with her and her mind immediately went to the most gruesome things she had seen in horror movies. She was unable to prevent a scream escaping her lips.

"Stop that right now," he shouted and she instantly went silent.

"That's better," he continued. "Now I'm sure you have lots of questions."

She nodded her head, too shocked to speak. She had no idea how he had made her stop screaming.

"My friends and I have been watching you for a while. We know exactly what you are and that you have been fraternising with that Agent. Any werewolf, even a disgusting half-breed like you, who has anything to do with the Agency is a traitor to their own kind and now you are going to atone for your disloyalty."

Amy remained silent. She wasn't sure if this Warwick person was sane.

Warwick waited for her to speak, shrugging his shoulders when she didn't. "We know you have been taken to their headquarters. You are going to go there today and you are going to kill everyone in there, starting with whoever is in charge."

Amy laughed; she couldn't help herself. What he was suggesting was ludicrous. How he expected her to be able to kill anyone, she had no idea. Even if the very thought of it didn't make her sick, she didn't have the power; she didn't have the strength or the know-how and technique. If she even attempted to do as he was demanding, she would be overpowered by security before she had even hurt anyone. She thought back to the incident on the bus, but that had been different. It had been in defence, not attack. And she still had no idea how she did it.

"You think this is funny?" Warwick sneered at her. "You won't be smiling when I give you a knife and tell you to cut your hand off."

"You're insane," she said. "Tell me to kill as many people as you want. It won't happen. Even if you can control me, as you claim. I'm not physically capable of doing it."

Amy didn't like the smile that appeared on his face.

"Oh but you are."

The coldness in his voice made her shiver.

"We both know," he continued, "that you have the same talents as full werewolves, even if you haven't used them yet. You are more than able to do as I demand. It's in your nature. You want to kill. You want to slaughter all those people. And you are going to do it. You have werewolf strength and speed; you don't need anything more."

Amy couldn't believe what she was hearing. This man genuinely believed everything he was saying. He wasn't insane; he was delusional.

"I can't access my werewolf side," Amy said in a small voice. She couldn't do what he believed she could and she had no idea what he would do to her once he figured that out.

He continued to smile at her. "You may not be able to, but I can. Transform into your inner wolf. Now."

Amy felt her body convulsing. She looked at her arm in horror as fur began to grow. She could feel her jawbone elongating and heard the sound of her gown ripping.

Despite what Lawrence had told her, she was surprised to find it didn't hurt. It also didn't take long. Soon she was on all fours, staring at Warwick. She felt an overwhelming desire to rip his throat out.

Almost as if he could read her mind, he took a step back. "Don't even think about it. I can see your hate in your eyes. The position of your hind legs and tail tell me you're preparing to attack. I wouldn't advise it. Now sit."

Like a well-trained dog, she obeyed.

"Now I could send you to the Agency like this, but I don't think it will do much good. You don't need to be in your wolf form to access your speed or strength. And access them you will. I order you to use all your werewolf abilities to kill as many members of the Agency as you can. Now transform back."

Once again Amy found her body changing shape. She could feel her whiskers withdrawing into her, along with all her fur. Her tail shortened before disappearing. Soon she was human again and stood up. Only then did she realise she was naked. She ran to the bed and pulled off the blanket, wrapping it around herself to hide her nakedness. She blushed a bright shade of red.

Warwick rolled his eyes. "Trust me, I have no interest in looking at your naked body. I've seen much better. I've had much better." The look in his eyes when they returned to her body betrayed his lie. "I'll have some new clothes delivered to you, then you have a mission to accomplish, don't you?"

Amy found herself nodding her head. She did everything she could to stop it, but she no longer had control of her own body.

All too soon, clothes were delivered and she was ordered to get dressed. Warwick didn't bother to turn his back to give her the illusion of privacy but, as he had ordered her to put on the clothes, she did so. She tried to say no, to tell him to leave the room first, but she couldn't form the words. Instead, like a slave, she did as she was told.

Warwick then took hold of her arm and dragged her from the room. She looked around her, taking in as much detail as she could. If she was going to have a chance to speak to anyone at the Agency before they killed her, she wanted to be able to tell them as much as possible.

Warwick watched her and laughed. "Look as much as you like. I'm going to order you to forget everything as soon as I drop you off."

Amy believed him, but that didn't stop her taking in everything around her. She appeared to be in an empty warehouse of some kind. Once outside, she scanned her surroundings, but didn't recognise anything. She had no idea where she was. She took in street names and signs as Warwick drove and eventually she began to recognise landmarks they passed. They were getting close to the Agency's headquarters.

111

Warwick pulled up by the pavement when they were just around the corner from their destination. He put on the handbrake and switched off the engine.

"Look at me," he demanded and Amy felt herself doing so.

"You will forget my name," he said in a flat, monotonous voice. "You will forget my face. You will forget where you were. All you will remember is your mission and that you will do everything you can to accomplish it. Do you understand?"

Amy nodded, unable to speak.

"Good." He then leaned over and opened the glove box. Amy gasped when he took out a pistol. "Ever shot a gun before?"

Amy had, once, at a shooting range. She hadn't enjoyed it, so she never went back. Warwick quickly ran through how to use it and how to reload before handing it to her, along with a box containing extra bullets.

He put his arm behind Amy's seat and picked up her handbag. "Put everything in here," he said as he handed it to her.

Once she had done so, he told her to get out of the car. "We won't be seeing each other again," were his parting words before he drove off.

Amy stared after the car until it turned a corner and was out of sight. She then quickly checked her bag. Her house keys and purse were still inside, as was her mobile. All she had to do was call for a taxi, go home, and forget everything that had happened.

She pulled out her phone, but was unable to even switch it on. No matter how hard she tried, she couldn't get her fingers to obey her. Instead, her hand dropped it back into her bag and her legs began walking in the direction of the medical centre where the Agency's headquarters was located.

Outwardly, she looked calm, but inside she was screaming.

She entered the building and looked around, her eyes falling on Mack, the security guard she often saw on her visits. Smiling, she headed over to him.

'Help me,' she silently shouted, but her mouth said, "Hey Mack. Do you know if Garrick is in?"

"Hi Amy," came the reply. "I think so. Do you want me to get him to come up?"

"No," she heard herself say. "That won't be necessary."

Her body felt like it was no longer hers to control. She acted out of instinct, without rational thought. She tried to fight against herself, but could do nothing to stop herself punching Mack so hard in the stomach he doubled over. Before he had chance to react, she ripped his ID badge from his uniform and punched him in the jaw, sending him flying across the room.

She couldn't believe the power behind the strike. If she hadn't been so shocked by her own actions, she would have been amazed at her strength.

Then she took the gun out of her bag and shot Mack in the chest.

People were screaming as she used Mack's ID to let herself into the main part of the building. She wanted to turn and run, but her legs kept her walking forward, toward the lifts.

Before she reached them, alarms started to ring. She didn't have much time before they would start hunting her. She needed to get to the right floor and she needed to do it fast.

She called the lift and tapped her foot impatiently as she waited for it to arrive. When the doors opened, she entered, swiped Mack's ID, pressed the button for the floor she wanted and got out again. If the Agents present had any sense they would be monitoring the lifts and would know what floor she selected. They would be waiting there for her. She, however, would be taking the stairs.

She had never used the stairs before, but she knew where they were. They were for emergencies only and couldn't be used to gain access to other floors. The emergency doors opened into the stairwell and couldn't be opened from inside. She wasn't going to let that stop her. At least the part of her which was obeying Warwick's command wasn't.

She ran down the stairs, barely breaking a sweat by the time she reached the floor she wanted. She tried the door, but it wouldn't move and there was no handle on the inside. Bracing herself, she gave it a hard kick once, twice, thrice, before the hinges gave way and it crashed into the corridor.

Someone dressed in a lab coat jumped out of the way. Before the young man could even cry out, she grabbed him and threw him against the wall. The sickening crunch of broken bones reached her ears, making her want to vomit. The crumpled body lay on the floor, but instead of checking if he was breathing, she just stepped over it.

"Hold it right there," a voice called out from behind her. She turned around to see a lone guard pointing a gun at her. She smiled at him and started walking toward him.

"Don't come any closer," he warned. She ignored him. "I will shoot." Again she ignored him. She didn't know how, but she knew she was fast enough to get out of the way if he did fire.

Then he pulled the trigger. A bullet came flying toward her. Time seemed to slow down as she watched the projectile approach with fascination. Then with a flick of her hand, she changed its trajectory. She had no idea how, but without even touching it, she had moved it.

The guard's jaw was still open when she hit him in the face hard enough to knock him unconscious.

The instructions she had been given were repeating themselves over and over in her head. She had a mission and she had to accomplish it. Whistling to herself, she turned back the way she had been going, shooting randomly through all the open doors she passed.

Attack

Garrick was in Carl's office when the alarm sounded. "What the hell is that going off for?" he asked. He knew what it was; he just couldn't believe he was hearing it. The alarm never went off at headquarters. "What's going on?"

"I don't know," Carl said and began tapping on his keyboard. He brought up on the screen the program that allowed him to see all the security cameras, both inside and outside, and began switching between them, trying to find where the problem was.

The main lobby showed nurses surrounding a body on the floor. It was dressed as a security guard. Carl and Garrick couldn't see what was happening, but it was clear he was injured.

The office door burst open and a young trainee Agent ran in. Ignoring all protocol, she burst out, "We're under attack. Lone female. Suspected werewolf."

Carl didn't reprimand her for not knocking and waiting for permission to speak. The situation required urgency not procedure. "Where is she?"

"In the lift. Coming down to this floor."

Carl switched to the camera that would provide the best view of the lift while Garrick took out his gun and checked it was loaded. All three of them watched the screen as the light above the lift indicated that it had arrived. Five agents had their weapons drawn and were pointing them at the doors.

With bated breath, the three observers watched the doors slowly open.

Nothing happened. Nobody stepped out of the lift. Shots didn't start firing into the guards. The guards didn't rush forward to subdue the intruder.

The lift was empty.

"Stairs," Garrick said.

"You can't get out of the stairwell except on the main floor," the young woman said.

"A werewolf could."

Carl quickly scanned through the cameras until he found the one that showed one of the emergency fire doors on the floor they were on. It was in pieces on the floor and the body of a scientist could be seen close by.

Carl quickly flicked between cameras until he picked up the intruder. Garrick watched as she casually walked down the corridor, gun in hand. She emptied it into one room before reloading. Something about her seemed familiar.

When she turned so her face could be seen on the screen, Garrick gasped.

"Is that—" Carl started to ask.

"Amy," Garrick finished for him.

He couldn't understand what was going on. He thought he had gotten to know her well and nothing in her personality indicated that she was able to do what he was witnessing.

All three Agency members looked at the screen in shock as they saw Amy stop bullets in mid-air and attack the person who had fired them with inhuman speed and strength.

"How the hell is she doing that?" Garrick exclaimed.

"I guess she found out how to tap into her werewolf side," Carl said. "It's rather ironic that after all we have done to help her, she not only manages it on her own, but then turns it against us."

"I meant how is she stopping those bullets. Werewolves can't control objects with their minds. I've never heard of one having telekinesis."

"Nor I," Carl said. Then he turned serious. "We're going to have to kill her, you know that."

"Not yet," Garrick said. "Something doesn't feel right. Let's try to take her alive. I want to question her. I want to know how she is doing what she is doing, if nothing else."

"Alright," Carl said, "I'll give the order, but if someone has to kill her in order to save their own or another's life, then that's what they will do."

"Understood." Garrick returned his gun to his pocket and took an earpiece out of another and put it in his ear. "Keep me informed of her movements. I need to take a detour to the infirmary, then I'm going to talk to her, if I can."

"Don't do anything stupid," Carl said.

Garrick smiled at him. "When do I ever do anything stupid?" He then turned to the young Agent. "Stay here. Protect Carl. Not that he can't protect himself," he quickly added when he saw the look on Carl's face.

Garrick made his way to the infirmary and quickly found what he was looking for. He took a syringe out of the box and removed a needle from its protective packaging and attached it to the syringe. Finding the bottle he was looking for in a cupboard, he filled the syringe with the clear liquid and put a protective cover over the needle before placing it in his pocket. He momentarily considered making up a few more, but decided against it. He was only going to get one shot at what he was planning so there was no point in wasting time.

"Where is she?" Garrick asked and Carl's reply came through his earpiece.

"It sounds like you might be the target," Garrick said. "I'll head straight to your office. Lock the door and don't open it for anyone except me."

"Are you giving me orders?"

"Yes, now do as I say."

"Yes, Boss." Carl was chuckling as he responded.

Garrick rolled his eyes. And Carl accused him of not taking things seriously enough. Talk about the kettle calling the pot black.

Though Carl's orders about detaining rather than killing Amy had been sent out, Garrick didn't have much confidence that they would be obeyed. When facing a rogue werewolf, Agents acted on instinct. And that's what Amy had become; a rogue werewolf.

Forcing his thoughts aside, Garrick ran back to Carl's office. He arrived just in time; Amy turned the corner just as he took up a guarding position outside the office door.

"Put the gun down, Amy," he said, making his voice firm, but calm. The tone sometimes worked, but this wasn't one of those times.

Amy's hand wavered, as though she was trying to do as he said, but then she raised her arm and pointed the gun at his chest.

"I don't want to kill you Garrick."

"Then don't."

"I don't have a choice."

"There are always choices."

"Not this time."

As she spoke, Amy was slowly moving closer and closer. 'Just a few more steps,' Garrick thought to himself.

"I have to kill Carl and as many people who work for the Agency as I can."

"Why?" Garrick asked. If he kept her talking, he might be able to accomplish what he intended. He just needed her to take one more step.

"I've been ordered to," she said as she put her left foot forward, followed by her right.

"Who by?"

Before she could answer, Garrick made his move. He took the syringe out of his pocket, stepped closer to her and injected the contents into her bloodstream so fast she didn't have time to react.

Instinct told him to step away, to prepare himself for a fight. He had no idea how fast acting the chemical was on humans, let alone werewolves. But he didn't move back. Instead he grabbed hold of her and pulled her closer, praying that it would take effect quickly.

His prayers were answered and her entire body crumbled as though she was a marionette whose strings had been cut.

He caught her before she hit the ground, using his body to protect her from making contact with the cold tiles. Then he gently eased her down.

"Thank you," he was sure he heard her whisper before her eyes closed.

Amy opened her eyes and raised her head. Looking around, she found she was in some sort of medical room. She was sitting in a chair, with her arms and legs handcuffed to it. It took her a moment to remember where she was and why she was there.

Sitting opposite her was Carl, her target. She smiled at him. "How nice to see you again Carl." To her own ears, her voice sounded dull and lifeless.

"I would say the same, but it appears that you are here to kill me. Why?"

Amy wanted to tell him everything, but she wasn't sure if her body was going to allow her to.

"I've been ordered to."

"Who by?"

"I don't know. He wiped the memory from my mind. I know it was a man, but I don't know who he was or what he looked like."

As she spoke, she looked around the room, rather than at Carl. She didn't know what she was looking for, but she had a desire to find something which would be of use to her.

"Let's say I believe you. Do you know why you have been sent to kill me?"

"You're the head of this branch of the Agency. Whoever sent me wants the Agency destroyed. Killing you, and anyone who gets in my way, would be a step in the right direction."

Her eyes fell on a pair of scissors which had been left on the bench instead of being put away. Her eyes went wide when she realised what she was about to do.

'No,' she silently screamed at herself. 'Don't do it.' The part of herself which was in control ignored her.

She turned her attention back to Carl, but her mind was on the scissors. She mentally pulled them toward her, turning them at the last moment so they flew at Carl's unprotected torso.

Whether it was instinct or someone shouted out a warning through the earpiece she could see in his ear, she didn't know, but just in time, Carl tipped his chair backward and the scissors embedded themselves harmlessly in the base as he landed on the ground.

Carl picked himself off the floor and brushed dirt that Amy couldn't see off his shirt before straightening the sleeves.

"That wasn't very nice," he said. He didn't appear shaken by her attack on him. He then looked off to one side, as though he was listening to something.

"Alright," he said, then left the room.

Amy was left alone and looked around the room. There were no windows and the walls were bare.

A few moments later, the door opened once more and Garrick walked in, locking the door behind him. Instead of speaking to her, he set about putting everything that could be picked up into drawers and cupboards. Amy would be able to open them with her mind and retrieve the objects, but it would take her longer than if they had been left on display.

"I learn from other people's mistakes," Garrick said when he had finished.

He straightened up the chair that Carl had been using and sat down on it. Amy noticed that he had done up his jacket, something she had never seen him do before. She knew where he kept his weapons, so it was a wise precaution. She couldn't imagine him entering the room without them.

Garrick leaned forward. "How are you?"

The question took her by surprise and she found she was able to answer before her body stopped her.

"I've been better."

"Will you behave while we have a little chat? I want to know how you are moving objects without touching them."

She nodded. The need to kill Carl and everyone else still flowed through her, but it was warring with a different desire. Garrick continued speaking, but she only half listened to him; she was concentrating on her handcuffs. How she mentally manipulated the internal locking mechanism in each she didn't know, but somehow she managed to undo them. She left them in place, ready to move when the time was right.

"So how long have you had the ability to move things?" Garrick asked.

Amy returned her attention to what he was saying long enough to answer the question.

"I don't know. I don't know whether I could do it before today and just couldn't tap into it until now or whether it's something new."

"Why now? What's changed?"

"I don't know," Amy said. She was looking Garrick in the eyes, but her mind was on his jacket. As she spoke, the zip slowly began to descend.

"I know," Garrick said. It took Amy a moment to realise that he wasn't speaking to her. He put his hand up to his ear and removed his earpiece. He put it in his pocket then said, "We won't be disturbed now. Why are you undoing my jacket? Enjoying showing off your new-found talent?"

Amy ignored the question, choosing instead to ask one of her own. "What do you plan on doing with me?"

"That depends on you."

The zip was now down as far as it would go. The sound of it releasing from one side made Garrick look down. Amy took that moment to free her hands from the undone restraints and launch herself at him.

He moved out of the way just in time, jumping to his feet and spinning out of her reach. If he hadn't recently had a new dose of the werewolf serum, he would have been too slow.

Amy heard herself snarl as she turned back to face him. He stood his ground as she walked up to him. She then shoved him with enough force to push him back into the wall. The impact forced the air out of his lungs.

She didn't want to hurt him, but she was unable to control herself. Fearing the worst was about to happen, she braced herself to deliver the fatal blow.

Instead she grabbed hold of his arms and moved them above his head.

"Stay there," she heard herself say and watched as he struggled to move his arms. She was pinning them in place with her mind.

She watched herself reach inside his jacket and extract a knife from one if his inner pockets.

'No, no, no, no, no,' she said to herself in her mind. 'Don't do it.'

Garrick didn't look scared. "You won't kill me," he said, though whether he was trying to convince her or himself she didn't know.

"I have no intention of killing you," she replied. "At least, not yet." She smiled as she held up the knife.

Surgery

The moment Amy launched herself at him, Garrick knew he was in trouble. Locking the door had been a mistake, but he hadn't trusted Carl not to enter the room again. Cameras were monitoring everything, but if Amy decided to kill him, help would not arrive in time.

Somehow he managed to avoid her, but he wasn't optimistic he could keep away from her for long. She was faster than he was, and probably stronger.

His fears were confirmed when he felt himself slammed against the wall with enough force to wind him. The next thing he knew, his arms were above his head and he was unable to move them.

He should have been terrified as he saw her take one of his knives from a pocket inside his jacket, but he wasn't. Even though she was holding a weapon and he was in no position to defend himself if she decided to use it, he couldn't bring himself to believe that she would hurt him.

She held up the knife, letting him know that she was going to use it on him. He swallowed, wondering what she was going to do with it. She took hold of his t-shirt and sliced it from top to bottom before throwing the knife on the floor.

Then her hands were on him. As she began to caress his chest, he wished that he had turned off the cameras.

He did nothing to resist as she pulled his head toward her. He had no idea what she had planned, but he intended to go along with it. For a while, at least.

When he felt her lips on his, all he could think about was how good it felt. He opened his mouth and she took the hint.

As their kiss deepened, he felt the hold on his arms release, allowing him to move them to her body. If he had wanted to, he might have been able to pull her off him, but he had no intention of doing so. Until that moment, he hadn't realised how much he wanted her.

He ran his hands through her hair, pulling her closer to him, deepening the kiss. Then he felt something on the back of her neck, at the base of her skull. It was a small lump as though something had been surgically implanted in her. Was that what was causing her to act so violently? There was only one way to find out.

Realising that he had stopped kissing her, he quickly resumed. Slowly, so she hopefully wouldn't feel what he was doing, he moved one hand away from her body, while making sure the other remained in contact. He moved one arm so he could reach into his pocket. If she suspected he was up to something, she didn't show it.

He was enjoying kissing her more than he would admit to Carl and anyone else who asked, but not to himself. He planned on making the most of it. If it was the implant affecting her personality instead of it being what she really wanted, then it might be the only chance he got.

He took out one of the syringes he had prepared while she had been unconscious and without pausing what else he was doing, stuck it into her neck.

"Time to go back to sleep," he whispered.

She immediately pulled back. Her legs gave way and her eyes rolled up into her head. She was unconscious before she reached the floor, which only his arms prevented her from hitting. He moved her into a chair before going to the door and unlocking it.

He retrieved his earpiece and returned it to his ear. Carl must have been watching because he started yelling at him as soon as it was in position. He quickly took it out again and looked at the camera, one eyebrow raised.

When he returned it to his ear, he was greeted with silence. Carl had got the message.

"I need a doctor," Garrick said. "Something has been implanted in her and we need to remove it."

"Understood," Carl said, then began issuing orders. A few moments later, two people in white coats arrived, along with a hospital bed. They picked up Amy's unconscious form and put her on it before wheeling her away.

Garrick made to go after them, but Carl, who had followed them into the room, grabbed his arm.

"Debrief first," he said as he handed him a new t-shirt.

Garrick opened his mouth to argue, then closed it again. There would be no point. Now that there was no longer someone trying to kill him, Carl was back in charge.

"She's in good hands," Carl added and Garrick nodded. He waited until he had removed his ruined t-shirt and was fully dressed once more before speaking.

"There's a recent wound on the back of her neck. It still has the stitches in and I'm sure I could feel something underneath. If something has been implanted in her, could it explain what's going on?"

Carl shrugged. "I have no idea. We'll have to wait for expert opinions on that. Now why didn't she attack you?"

Garrick couldn't help grinning. "She did, just in a different way." Then he let the smile drop. "I don't know. It's one of the things I'm hoping she will tell us when she wakes up."

He really hoped that she kissed him because she wanted to, not because some implant was making her, not that he was going to tell Carl that.

"Why did you lock the door?"

Garrick grimaced. Carl was not going to like his answer. "I needed to speak to her alone and I didn't trust you not to interfere."

"Fair enough." That was not the reaction Garrick had been expecting. "But don't do it again. If you needed backup, they wouldn't have been able to get to you in time."

"If I needed backup, leaving the door unlocked wouldn't have made any difference. You saw her speed. She's as fast as any full werewolf. And as strong. If she wanted me dead, I would be."

It was a sobering thought. Until that moment, neither man realised how much of a risk Garrick had taken locking himself in the room with Amy.

Carl put his hand on Garrick's shoulder and squeezed it. "Come on. Let's go watch the procedure."

They took the lift up two floors to the medical level and headed to the theatre. There was a viewing room which allowed them to watch without disturbing the doctors.

They arrived in time to see one of them extract something small and metal from Amy's neck and place it in a metal container being held out by a nurse.

Carl pressed a button and his voice sounded in the operating theatre. "I want that taken straight to the experts. I want to know what it is and how it works."

The nurse looked up at him, nodded once and left the room, holding the metal container in front of her as though it contained something explosive.

"What is it?" Carl asked.

One of the doctors moved away from Amy and took off her mask. Looking up at the observation window she said, "Some sort of implant. That's all I can tell you. It was close to her spine, but not attached to her central nervous system so removing it was easy."

While the woman was speaking, Garrick was watching the other doctor sew up Amy's neck.

"How long until she wakes up?" he asked. Carl passed on the question.

"If you gave her the full dose, another hour or so."

Garrick nodded. If there was no chance of her regaining consciousness during the surgery, why were armed guards present in the theatre? He answered his own question before he could ask it. She had just attacked and maybe killed many members of the Agency; the guards weren't going to take any chances.

Despite wanting to stay by Amy's side, Garrick had a job to do. He needed to find out how many were injured and how many phone calls Carl was going to have to make to grieving family members.

He informed his boss of his intentions and was told it was already in hand. A list was in the process of being compiled and Garrick would be allowed to see it as soon as it was complete.

126

"This isn't your fault," Carl told him. "And if you are right about that implant, then it isn't Amy's either."

Was Garrick blaming himself? He didn't think so, but that would probably change when he saw the list of casualties. After all, if he hadn't kept bringing Amy to headquarters, she wouldn't have known where to go. He couldn't fool himself into believing he did that purely for Agency purposes. He liked spending time with her and monitoring her; trying to get her to access her werewolf side was just an excuse to see her.

"I wouldn't have done anything different," Carl said.

'Maybe not,' Garrick thought, 'but your reasons would have been different.'

"Come on," Carl said when Garrick didn't respond. "Let's go to my office and see just how bad that list is."

When they arrived, the young Agent who Garrick had ordered to protect Carl was there. She looked up as they entered.

"You're not going to believe this," she said. "So far, there are no serious injuries. A few broken bones, a concussion or two, the odd bullet wound in a limb, but nothing that won't completely heal. Somehow she managed to do minimal damage, despite the number of people she attacked. Whether that was intentional or not, I have no idea."

"You mean she could have shot people in the head, but didn't?" Carl asked.

"It looks that way. Even someone who had never shot a gun before would statistically hit someone somewhere vital, given the number of bullets fired. Mack was hit in the chest, but he was wearing his bullet-proof vest so, other than being a little bruised, he'll be fine."

"That's good to hear," Garrick said. "Where is he? I'd like to talk to him."

The young woman smiled. "You know Mack. He's back on duty already."

Garrick thanked her. He then took the lift all the way to the top floor. Sure enough, Mack was in his usual place.

"Garrick," he said and nodded to him in welcome as he approached.

"How are you?" Garrick asked.

"Fine. I'll be a little stiff and uncomfortable for a while, but I'll live. How's Amy? Nobody knows what happened. You didn't kill her I hope."

Garrick told him everything. "You were the first to see her," he said when he was done. "How did she seem?"

"Fine. Her usual self." Then Mack paused. "But now I think about it, there was something in her eyes. It was almost as if she was scared, terrified even. I don't know why I didn't notice it earlier."

Garrick clapped him on his shoulder. "Don't worry about it. I don't think there would have been anything you could have done, even if you had noticed. I'm glad you're okay, but you should really consider going home and resting."

Mack just grunted at him.

Garrick returned to Carl's office, where the injury total had just finished being collated. By some miracle, there had been no deaths.

"What are my orders?" he asked.

"I'm planning on staying here until that device which was extracted from Amy has been analysed. At least preliminarily. I want to know if it can be used on anyone else. You can go and guard Amy if you like. She's been moved to a private room in the infirmary."

Garrick didn't like the way Carl was grinning at him as he left the room.

Blacksmith

Amy opened her eyes, then closed them again as bright light assaulted her. Her head hurt, as did her neck. She tried to move her hand to it, but found she couldn't. Looking down, she saw she was handcuffed to the rail of the bed.

"Just a precaution," a familiar voice said. Garrick. Just hearing his voice made her feel better; safe and protected.

"Where am I?" she asked. Her throat was dry and her voice sounded gravelly.

"Headquarters. Infirmary. Do you know why you are here?"

She shook her head. "Can I have some water please?"

She felt Garrick release her hand. She hadn't even realised he had been holding it. She felt cold and strangely empty without the warmth of his skin against hers.

He moved away, returning a moment later with a plastic cup with clear liquid in it. He helped her sit up and held it to her lips, tipping it just enough for her to drink without spilling it down her.

Once it was empty, he put it on the floor before pointing to the handcuffs.

"If I undo these, do you promise not to attack?"

Amy frowned. What on Earth was he talking about? Why would she attack?

Then her memories came flooding back and she cried out in horror. She saw herself attacking people, shooting them, throwing them against walls like ragdolls.

"All those people? Oh my god. I'm a monster."

She couldn't breathe. How many people had she killed?

Then Garrick was sitting on the bed beside her, removing one of the handcuffs before pulling her close to him and rubbing her back as he whispered in her ear.

"It's okay. It wasn't you. Someone made you do it."

His words didn't help. What difference did it make? People were still dead because of her.

"Breathe Amy. Everything is alright. You didn't kill anyone. Even Mack is okay. Somehow you managed to not shoot anyone in any place important."

She tried to focus on his words, but what he was saying wasn't possible. He had to be lying to her.

She cried out in horror. It was the only way to get her lungs working again. She took a breath, then another, and another. She knew she was breathing too fast and too shallowly, but couldn't stop herself hyperventilating. She had never had a panic attack and she wondered if this was what it felt like.

"Deep breaths," Garrick said. He pulled away from her, but didn't let her go. "With me. In. Out. In. Out."

Amy obeyed and soon she was breathing normally again. "I really didn't kill anyone?" she asked. She didn't want to hear the answer. Garrick had never lied to her before and now that she had calmed down, she knew he would tell her the truth, no matter how bad it was.

"Really. I know you weren't in control of yourself, but somehow you managed to do as little damage as possible."

"What happened to me?" Before he could answer, another memory returned. "I was moving things with my mind. How was I doing that?"

"That is one of the things we are hoping you can tell us."

An image filled her mind and her hand flew to mouth as she inhaled sharply in shock. "I sent a pair of scissors flying at Carl."

"I'm sure he'll forgive you."

She frowned again. More images came into her head. "And then I..." She didn't finish the sentence. The colour drained from her face as she remembered throwing herself at Garrick, literally. She recalled how she had cut his t-shirt so she could have her hands on his bare flesh and how she had kissed him. She felt mortified by her actions. Never before had she behaved like that with someone. She didn't dare contemplate what he must have thought of her.

She wanted to run and hide, but one of her arms was still handcuffed to the bed. Instead, she pushed Garrick away from her and laid down, grabbing the blanket as she did so and pulling

130

it over her head. She curled up into the foetal position. Maybe if she hid under the blanket for long enough, he would go away. She couldn't face him. Not now. Not ever.

She felt the blanket being pulled off her head and closed her eyes as tightly as she could.

"Look at me, Amy," Garrick said softly.

"I can't," she said and screwed her eyes shut so tight it hurt.

"Please, Amy."

He didn't sound angry, or amused, or embarrassed. If she didn't know better, she would say he was concerned.

She felt a hand softly stroke her cheek. "Please. I have to know. Was it the implant making you do everything or did it, in some cases, just suppress your inhibitions? Did you want to kiss me or were you forced to?"

How could she answer that? She had wanted to kiss him for a long time, but there was no way she was going to tell him that. Not now. Not after what she had done. But she also couldn't lie to him.

Stuck between a rock and a hard place, she didn't respond. She had ruined everything by her actions. She thought Garrick liked her, at least a little, but that was all gone now. How could he like someone who tried to kill his boss and had attacked his friends and co-workers?

She thought about them kissing and how good it had felt. She was sure he had been participating, had been kissing her back, but she had just been fooling herself. He had just been going along with it in order to inject her with a tranquiliser. After she had so shamelessly thrown herself at him, he would want nothing more to do with her.

A tear trickled from her eye and ran down her cheek. Garrick wiped it away with his hand. For someone so strong, he certainly knew how to be gentle.

"Please go away and leave me alone."

"Not until you have answered my question."

"Why do you want to know?"

"Because right now I want to take you in my arms and kiss you until you forget everything that has happened and I want to know if you are going to let me or slap me round the face."

Amy's eyes sprung open. She turned her head to look at him, unsure what she would see in his expression. She didn't have time to register it before his lips were on hers and she felt his tongue probing, asking to be let in.

She obliged and rolled onto her back so she could throw her arms around him. Well, one arm anyway; the other was still handcuffed to the bed.

The kiss told her everything she wanted to know. Either he was an accomplished actor who was used to faking things with women, or he wanted her as much as she wanted him.

One of his arms caressed her side as they kissed, but he suddenly pulled away.

"This won't do," he said and uncuffed her wrist. "That's better," he continued as he laid down beside her. "Now where was I?"

He didn't need her to answer, as his mouth immediately found hers once more. Without breaking the kiss, he pulled his body away just enough so he could remove the blanket which was covering her and pulled her up against him. His arms were strong and reassuring. His hand ran up her back. She had no idea what she was wearing, but it felt silky against her skin.

"You have no idea how much I want to take this off you," he said when they broke apart.

"Then do it." She had never gone to bed with a man the same day they went to first base and didn't plan to start now, but right then she wanted nothing more than to feel her naked body rubbing against his.

"Can't," he said. "Cameras."

She immediately froze. "You mean people are watching us?"

"Probably not, but I don't want to take the chance."

She gave him a shove. "This isn't the sort of thing I want to be doing in front of an audience. Get off me before someone sees us."

He grinned at her. "Not a chance."

132

He started kissing her again and she gave up her half-hearted attempt to stop him.

The sound of someone clearing their throat behind them made them both jump.

"When you've quite finished, we have some questions for Amy."

Amy almost said 'we aren't finished', but decided it wouldn't be a wise move. After all, Carl was Garrick's boss.

Garrick got off the bed, somewhat reluctantly if the look on his face was anything to go by. Amy sat up and immediately pulled the blanket over her. She was wearing some sort of thin nightdress with almost non-existent straps; not the sort of thing she wanted someone other than a lover to see her in.

Carl placed a bundle of clothes on the bed. "The nurse thought you might be more comfortable sleeping in that after your operation," he said, pointing toward what she hoped was fully hidden by the blanket. "But you might want to get dressed. These should fit you."

He then turned to Garrick. "Out."

"But—" Garrick started to say, but Carl didn't let him finish.

"If I leave you in here alone with her, you'll never let her get dressed."

Amy could see he was doing his best not to laugh. She didn't see what was so funny.

Carl grabbed Garrick's arm and dragged him from the room, shutting the door firmly behind them.

Taking this as her cue to get dressed, she got off the bed. Then she remembered what Garrick had said about cameras and looked around for them. Spotting two, she used the blanket and pillowcase to cover them. She then prayed that there weren't any more as she slipped out of the nightdress and put on the clothes she had been provided with. They weren't too bad a fit, even the bra. Whoever had undressed her had left her panties on, so she didn't have to worry about anyone seeing her completely naked.

Garrick was waiting for her outside the room and took hold of her hand as soon as she joined him.

"What happened to my clothes?" she asked.

133

Garrick grimaced. "Covered in blood I'm afraid. You split one man's lip and broke another's nose. They weren't badly injured, but they managed to gush blood well."

Amy nodded. She couldn't recall what she had been wearing so had no idea if she had just lost anything she really liked. Even if the clothes could be cleaned, she didn't think she would want them back.

"Are you sure you are up to speaking with Carl?" Garrick asked her. The concern in his voice made her feel warm inside.

Once again, she nodded.

He squeezed her hand. "Come on then."

Garrick took her directly to Carl's office, where he was waiting for them. A pot of coffee sat on his desk, along with two mugs. He had another one in his hand and was drinking from it.

"Please sit down," he said. He looked at Garrick. "Should she be restrained?"

Garrick shook his head. "What would be the point? If it wasn't the implant helping her tap into her werewolf strength, then we both know she will be able to free herself."

Amy wasn't sure she liked being talked about as though she wasn't there, but was too nervous to complain. She had no idea what questions Carl was going to ask her, or if she was going to be able to answer them.

Garrick poured them both coffee as Carl began the interrogation.

"What's the last thing you remember before arriving at headquarters?"

Amy told him everything she could, truthfully and honestly. She described how she went to bed and the next thing she knew she was on a street near the building she was currently in and she had an overwhelming desire to go inside and kill everyone, especially Carl. She had no idea how she got there, who was controlling her, or how, or when, or where she had the implant inserted into her.

A sudden panic set in, making her sit forward in her chair. "What day is it?"

"Wednesday. Why?"

She sat back in relief. "I was worried I had a few days missing from my memory, not a few hours, and that Ainin would need feeding."

Then she shot forward in her seat again. "What about work?"

"Don't worry," Garrick told her. "I've already called them. I said I was from the hospital and you had been in an accident, but would hopefully be able to return to work in a few days."

"Thank you."

The questions continued and she ended up describing how she felt when she shot Mack, how she tried to stop herself doing it, but was unable to do so. Then she went on to her entering the main part of the building, not stopping until she got to the part where Garrick knocked her unconscious for the first time. By the time she stopped talking, she was shaking.

"Are you sure Mack's okay?" she asked.

"He's fine," Garrick assured her. "I went to see him personally. He doesn't even blame you for what happened. He knows you weren't in control of yourself."

Carl then made her talk about when she regained consciousness. He was particularly interested in how she managed to get out of the handcuffs and attack him with the scissors, but she couldn't help; she had no idea how she had done it.

She wasn't forced to speak about what happened between her and Garrick, for which she was grateful.

"It sounds like that implant allowed someone to control you, but I have no idea how," Carl said when he had run out of questions. "I hope the tech boys can come up with an explanation."

"Does that mean it can happen again?" Amy asked.

Carl looked at Garrick. "Get her a chain. It might not help, but it would be a good idea. We should have given her one ages ago."

Garrick nodded. "But we didn't know that werewolves were a danger to her until now. Or that they even knew about her. Have you finished with her?"

"For now. But I may want to speak to her again. I would say keep an eye on her, but somehow I think that is more or less guaranteed."

Garrick grinned at him and Amy felt herself blush.

Garrick then took hold of her hand. "Come on, let's go see the blacksmith."

"Blacksmith?" Amy asked.

"Well, he's not really a blacksmith, but jeweller just doesn't sound manly enough."

Amy shook her head. She had no idea what Garrick was talking about and didn't feel like asking.

Garrick took her to a part of the building she had never been in before. He knocked on a door and entered when a voice inside gave permission. The sole occupant of the room was short enough to be classified as a dwarf. He stood on a chair, leaning over a table which was covered in metal objects, chains and tools small enough they could be used on watches or clocks.

"You must be Amy," he said and jumped down to the floor. "Carl told me you were on your way."

He held out his hand and Amy shook it. For someone who only came up to her chest, he had a surprisingly strong grip.

"Kenny here makes all the chains and pendants which protect our minds from intrusion by werewolves," Garrick said.

"Don't you dare make any comments along the lines of 'you should be working with gold'," Kenny said to Amy. He looked at her so fiercely, she took a step back."

"I wouldn't dream of it."

Then he broke out into a grin. "I'm just messing with you. I'm under four foot ten so legally I'm classified as a dwarf. I suffer from achondroplasia. All my family do. The way I see it, I can get upset about my lack of height, or I can make a joke about it. I know which I prefer."

Amy didn't know what to make of the man. He was rather attractive, despite his lack of height. His mousey hair almost reached his shoulders. He was clean shaven, so there was no facial hair to hide the scar down the side of his face.

Before she could think of anything to say, he held out a chain to her. The pendent looked almost identical to Garrick's. When she took it, he left his hand in the air, palm upward and curled his fingers in a 'come here' gesture.

"Come with me," he said. "I need to show you how to open it."

She glanced at Garrick, who nodded his head. "Go. You need to be alone with him when he demonstrates. That way, you two will be the only ones who know how to take the chain off you."

Somewhat reluctantly, she took the strange little man's hand and let him lead her into another room.

Plans

Warwick stared at Lia, the look on his face indicating that he didn't believe the words that were coming out of her mouth. Not that she could blame him. It wasn't that he thought she was a liar; he just didn't believe his technology could fail.

"What do you mean she didn't kill anyone? How could she stop herself? We gave her the means and ordered her to do it. She shouldn't have been able to resist."

Lia shrugged her shoulders. "I have no idea. Maybe she didn't resist. Maybe she's such a bad shot she accidentally missed. Who knows? Maybe it was just luck. Bad luck for us, good luck for them."

Warwick growled before dropping his head, refusing to meet Lia's eyes.

"I'm sorry I failed you."

He looked up again when she laughed. "My dear Warwick. You haven't failed. Your plan didn't succeed. My plan, however, did."

The look of confusion on his face made her laugh once more. "Killing the head of the local branch of the Agency, in fact killing anyone in the Agency, was only ever a 'nice to have'. My main goal was Garrick."

She could see that Warwick was still confused. "But I thought you wanted him dead."

"I do, but not yet. Take a seat. Let me explain how real leadership works."

He did as instructed. She wasn't surprised. It was, after all, an order and Warwick was good at following orders. At least for the time being. She knew he wanted to be more than just her second in command, but she had yet to ascertain if it was her position or her body he was after. Or maybe both.

She chose the seat across from him, so she could watch how he reacted to what she had to say.

"As an Agent, Garrick is a pain in the backside, a pain that needs to be removed, but not yet. As a man, he could be an asset to us."

"You'll never be able to turn him against the Agency," Warwick said.

Lia had to grit her teeth. She hated being interrupted, but it was the wrong time to reprimand him.

"I can't," she said, forcing herself to smile. "But Amy can."

She sat back, waiting for him to work out what she meant. It took him longer than it should have.

"You knew she liked him," he finally said. "And that he liked her. You knew that removing her self-control would force her to throw herself at him. That was your plan all along."

"Very good."

"But how did you know?"

Lia rolled her eyes. "Because I use my eyes to see things. The way they keep looking at each other makes it obvious. I can't believe you didn't notice."

"I haven't been watching them as closely as you have," Warwick muttered. It wasn't quite quietly enough for Lia not to hear, which meant he had intended her to.

Again Lia ignored his show of disrespect; she understood the reasons for the comment.

"So how does that help us?" Warwick asked.

"They're now an item, which means he trusts her."

"Which means he'll tell her things," Warwick said before Lia could finish what she was saying.

"Wrong," she snapped. "He'll tell her nothing. Agency business is Agency business and is never discussed with partners. You've interrogated enough Agents and their families. Haven't you figured that out by now?"

She huffed in frustration. While she appreciated that Warwick was a good second-in-command, she wished he would keep his mouth shut and listen sometimes.

"So what was the point?" he asked. He was beginning to sound like a petulant child.

"The point, dear Warwick, is that he will do anything he can to protect her. The more time they spend together, the more his mind will be on her instead of his job. He is a man, after all, and even the best of them think with parts of their anatomy other than their brain. He'll make a mistake and when he does, we will be there to take advantage."

"Can't we just make the half-breed bitch kill him the next time they are alone?" Warwick asked, reminding Lia that patience had never been a strong point for him. He was too prone to rushing in instead of planning, which was why he would never make a good leader.

"We can't make her do anything now that he has given her one of those god damn necklaces. You yourself told me it would block the implant if she had one. And before you ask, no we can't make her take it off."

"So we've accomplished nothing."

"Haven't you been listening? We've accomplished a lot. The game has only just begun and we have started to manoeuvre our pieces. We made the first move, which they countered. I'll give them a few weeks of peace before we make our next move, giving them chance to get closer to each other."

She smiled to herself. Garrick and Amy were playing into her hands and they had no idea they were doing so.

"In the meantime," she continued, "we should go on a recruitment drive. Organise a meeting for tomorrow night so we can discuss how to go about getting more to join our cause. I want to be ready for when the war really starts."

"War?" Warwick asked in surprise. "What war?"

"The war between us and the Agency, of course. So far there have been a few battles. Some we lost, some we won. But this is heading for a final showdown, a showdown the Agency doesn't even know is coming. Only one of us will survive and I can assure you it won't be them."

Tracker

Garrick was staring at his computer screen when Carl walked up to his desk.

"What are you studying so intently?" the older man asked as he lowered himself into the spare seat beside him.

"Amy's tracking data."

He turned his eyes away from the screen to see Carl raising his eyebrows at him.

"What tracking data?"

"The first time I met her, I may have put a tracker in that fitness device she always has on her wrist."

Carl's eyebrows remained where they were.

"May have? Does she know?"

"I didn't tell you," Garrick said. "Do you really think I would tell her?"

Carl shook his head. "She's going to be pissed when she finds out."

Garrick waved away his concern. "She'll be fine. Especially when I tell her we used it to track down the people who implanted that device in her."

Carl leaned forward and looked at the monitor. Garrick couldn't help smiling. Carl had no idea what he was looking at.

"Have we?" his boss eventually asked.

"Sort of. We know where she was taken and we know how long she was there for."

"How does that help? Surely the werewolves responsible won't still be there."

"Probably not, but I'm prepared to bet my salary that they will go back there sometime."

"Why?"

"Because Amy's been there before. A number of times."

Carl leaned back in his chair. Garrick could tell he was thinking through the implications of what that meant. He didn't speak, giving him the time he needed to come to the same conclusion Garrick himself had moments earlier.

"There's only two possible explanations," Carl said after a moment. "Either someone is taking her without her knowing or they have taken her against her will a number of times before and she's been lying to us about it."

"There is a third option," Garrick said. He didn't want to voice what he was thinking, but he knew he had to. "She could be going there willingly. This whole thing could be a set up."

Carl stared at Garrick so intensely it made him feel uncomfortable. It was almost as if he was trying to read his mind. Still, he refused to look away. Eventually Carl did.

"You don't believe that any more than I do."

Garrick nodded his head. "You're right, I don't. But I had to mention it. I don't believe for a minute Amy is anything other than what she is claiming. I'm prepared to bet my life that she didn't know werewolves exist, let alone that she is one. No. If she has been going to that location it has been against her will and without her knowledge."

"What do you plan to do?" Carl asked. Officially Garrick had to ask Carl's permission before he did anything, but both men knew Carl would agree to whatever Garrick asked.

"First, I'm going to take a look at what's there. Then I want to place a couple of Agents on surveillance duty. I want to know as soon as anyone else goes there."

"Fair enough," Carl said, "but you aren't going there alone." He held up his hand when Garrick started to protest. "This is not up for negotiation. You have no idea what's there. It could be an entire clan of rogue werewolves."

Garrick opened his mouth to remind Carl that he always worked alone, but thought better of it. Carl was right; the risk was just too great.

"Alright, I'll give my sister a call, see if she's free."

"She's not. She and her partner are on assignment."

Garrick was not happy, to say the least. He hated working with others; they always got in the way, but when he was forced to, his sister was his first, and only, choice.

142

Then Carl took him completely by surprise. "I will be coming with you." He emphasised the 'I'.

"You? When was the last time you were out in the field?"

Carl grinned. "Too long ago. It'll do me good. When do you want to leave?"

"How soon can you be ready?"

"Just let me get some equipment."

While his boss was in the armoury, Garrick entered the necessary details into his computer, officially logging his destination. If he didn't contact headquarters by the time he specified, an armed response unit would be sent to the address to investigate. They would arrive too late if he was dead, but if he was being held hostage they would rescue him.

There was no 'might' in the sentence. He had worked with one of the units for a while. They were good. Very good. When they went after a target, they always succeeded in the retrieval.

His hand hovered over the keyboard as his cursor flashed in the 'partner' field. Usually he left it blank and he wasn't sure if he should do so again. Would Carl want others to know he was out in the field?

"Screw it," he said to himself and entered Carl's name. If the man wanted to put himself in danger, Garrick wasn't going to keep it secret from those who might need to rescue them both. Retrieving two was a completely different mission to retrieving only one.

"Ready?" Carl asked from the doorway just as Garrick clicked on 'save'.

"Ready," Garrick confirmed. He grabbed his keys and gun from where they lay beside him on his desk and walked with Carl to the carpark.

"Are you sure you're up to this?" Garrick asked as he pulled out onto the main road. "You're getting on a bit, you know."

He took his eyes off the road long enough to see the older man glaring at him. He grinned. Carl may have been his boss, but he was also his friend and Garrick enjoyed teasing him. "Do you need a lesson on how to use your gun before we get to where we're going? I can pull over and give a demonstration if you like."

Carl growled at him, making him chuckle.

"So, you and Amy huh."

All trace of amusement immediately left Garrick's face. "We are not going to have this conversation."

Carl, too, turned serious. "Yes, we are. Have you actually thought it through?"

"What's there to think about?"

"You might be putting her in even more danger than she's already in."

"Or I might be reducing that danger by spending more time with her. If I'm in the house, it's less likely that she'll be taken."

"Speaking of which, do you have any theories as to what has been going on?"

Following his Sat Nav's instructions, Garrick signalled and turned onto a side road before answering. "Some. They may have been trying to get into her mind for a while and her human side was causing resistance."

"Wouldn't she remember that?"

"Not necessarily. They might have been able to make her forget, but not much else." The smile returned to Garrick's face. "We'll have to ask them when we get our hands on them."

"I noticed that she only seems to be at that specific location at night. Does that mean you're planning on staying at her place each night?"

Out of the corner of his eye, Garrick could see Carl's eyes sparkling. He was asking as a friend, not as his boss.

"Maybe. I don't know yet." Friend or not, he was not going to discuss his sex life with Carl.

Carl grunted. "I didn't realise it had gone that far. You've only officially been together for a couple of days."

"I'm not saying it has. She does have a spare room, you know."

"Like you're ever going to sleep there."

144

Garrick ignored the comment and concentrated on his driving. He was in unfamiliar territory and needed to rely on his Sat Nav.

A short while later, he turned his car off the road into an industrial estate. The warehouse that was his destination was large and looked like it had been abandoned for a while.

"Good place to hide out," Carl said as he stepped out of the car.

There were no other cars in the carpark, but that didn't mean there was nobody inside, so both men checked their guns before walking up to the building.

Despite the 'For Sale' and 'For Lease' signs, there was evidence that the building had recently been entered by a number of people. Garrick tried the door and found it unlocked.

Both men took out their guns and Carl nodded his head, giving Garrick the go ahead to open the door.

Despite it being a bright sunny day, the lack of windows on the ground floor made it dark inside. Garrick found a light switch but he wasn't holding out much hope that the electricity was still switched on.

"That's surprising," he said to Carl when the lights turned on.

The warehouse part of the building contained nothing but some rubbish that hadn't been cleared away when the previous tenants left, but the two men thoroughly investigated it before heading up the stairs to the offices.

The first one they checked was small, but the furniture was still inside. There was no sign of recent use, so they moved on. They found nothing of interest until they reached what they assumed was the main meeting room, or board room if the tenants had needed such a thing. There was evidence of recent occupation, but not much else.

The last room was small, containing a table and nothing else. Rope was tied around each leg and there was a stain which could have been blood at one end.

"Please tell me they didn't tie her to this table to implant the device in her," Carl said.

"We have no way of knowing. If that is what happened, I'm glad she doesn't remember anything."

"What do you want to do now?"

Garrick thought for a moment. "There's not much point in hanging around. Amy was brought here every few days, so maybe it's just a meeting place rather than anyone being here permanently."

He deliberately said 'brought here' instead of 'came here'. While it was a possibility that she did so willingly, he wouldn't allow himself to believe it was true.

"I'll assign a surveillance team to keep an eye on it round the clock for us," Carl said. "They'll be under strict instructions to observe only and inform you personally as soon as they see anything suspicious. Let's head back to headquarters. There's nothing more we can do here."

During the drive back, Garrick couldn't help wondering when he would get the call from the surveillance team, what they would have to report and how Amy was going to react when he told her he had bugged her.

Trap

Warwick glared at the car in front of him, which hadn't moved for at least ten minutes. He had no idea what was going on, but he could see nothing but cars, trucks and motorbikes in all directions. He was stuck in a traffic jam, in the middle lane, with no hope of going anywhere for the foreseeable future.

It was a warm evening and his air conditioning in his car had broken. He was sweating, but there was no way he was going to open the window to let in the car fumes.

He turned the radio on, flicked through the channels, found nothing worth listening to, and switched it off again in frustration. He was going to be late. Lia didn't like it when people were late. Bracing himself, he picked up his phone, put it on speaker and dialled her number.

"Warwick," her voice sounded from the metal object he was holding in his hand. "I was just about to call you. I'm stuck in traffic."

"Me too," he said. "Any idea what's going on?"

"A fatality, according to the local news. Some moron decided to walk in front of a fast moving car and we're the ones who have to pay the price. They've shut the road in both directions while they investigate. Some people are just selfish bastards. It happened between where I am stuck and the next exit, so I'm going to be here for a while."

"Which exit?"

She told him and he swore. "I'm just past the previous exit so I won't be going anywhere in a hurry. I'll phone Sean and let him know we'll both be late."

"Good," she said before she hung up.

He breathed a sigh of relief. At least she wouldn't be blaming him for not arriving on time.

He dialled Sean's number and drummed his hands on the steering wheel while waiting for him to answer.

147

"Sean here," a voice said. Warwick rolled his eyes. It was about time Sean learnt how to program people's numbers into his phone so he knew who was calling him.

"Sean, it's Warwick. I'm stuck in traffic so I'm going to be late."

Laughter came down the line. "Calling me because you're too scared to call the boss?"

"No," Warwick snapped. He didn't like being accused of being scared of Lia, even though it was, in some respects, true. "I've already spoken to Lia. She's stuck in the same traffic I am."

"Sorry," Sean said, though he didn't sound it. "That could explain why not many of us are here. Should we leave?"

Warwick shook his head before realising that the other man couldn't see him. "No. Wait for now. Lia will call with instructions if this doesn't clear up soon."

Warwick hung up before Sean could respond. He turned the radio back on and repeated the futile process of finding something worth listening to.

He thought back to his conversation with Lia about her plans for the half-breed. He failed to grasp the logic. Why wait? Why not act now? While he could understand the need to recruit more werewolves to their cause, he failed to see what good giving Amy and the Agent time to solidify their romance would do. Even if he did start to focus on her more, Warwick couldn't see it causing him to make a mistake, despite what Lia thought.

He liked Lia, he liked her a lot, and not just her body, but he sometimes couldn't help wondering if she was the wrong person to be in charge. And he didn't like taking orders from her. He would be more than happy to do so in the bedroom, given the chance, but that was it.

Was it time to think about taking over from her? He wasn't sure. On the one hand, he believed he could beat her if it came to a physical fight, after all, his wolf was larger and stronger than hers. On the other hand, he wasn't sure who would back him up and who would defend Lia. If he tried for a coup and failed, the chances were he would end up dead.

148

He was still pondering his options when, by some miracle, the car next to him started to move. He looked to the side and saw that the one the other side of him was also moving. Both were going backward. He glanced into his rear view mirror, but his line wasn't moving. Typical. It looked like cars were being told to reverse to the previous exit.

He could see a number of police about, directing the traffic, but as he still couldn't move, he decided to risk phoning Lia.

"Traffic's moving," he said as soon as she answered.

"What do you mean? I'm ahead of you and nobody near me is moving."

"I think they have blocked the road from the exit behind us and are getting us all to back up so we can use it."

"Okay. That means you'll be there before me. Make sure nobody leaves."

"Yes, Boss," he said and smiled to himself. It would give him the time he needed to speak to the others without Lia being around to overhear. He could feel them out about their feelings about her being in charge. He wouldn't, of course, talk about putting himself forward as her successor, but he could begin to gauge what sort of support he might get.

Eventually the car behind him moved and he followed it. Looking over his shoulder and occasionally looking in the mirrors, it didn't take him long to reach the exit. Then he was free and moving swiftly toward his destination. He had used the back roads often enough that he knew where he was going.

There were still several cars in the carpark when he arrived. Not as many as usual, but that was to be expected. Maybe the others would arrive before Lia, maybe they wouldn't. It wasn't his problem so he gave it no further thought.

Before exiting his vehicle, he looked at the others, trying to work out who was in the building and who was missing. There were a number he didn't recognise, but it didn't raise his suspicions.

It should have.

He strolled over to the warehouse, opened the door and walked in. As he began to climb the steps, his phone rang. He glanced at the caller ID and opted to answer it. Ignoring it was not an option.

"Lia," he said. "I've just arrived."

"Good. I can see cars behind me beginning to move so I should be on my way shortly."

"I'll let everyone know."

"Who's there?"

"Hold on. I'm just climbing the stairs."

Warwick reached the top and made his way to the meeting room they always used. He could hear talking, but didn't recognise the voice.

He opened the door and froze. A number of people he recognised as his fellow werewolves were sitting in chairs, their arms behind their backs, their hands in handcuffs. Handcuffs he recognised as those used by the Agency.

Several armed Agents were in the room, all with guns pointed at the werewolves, and a tall, muscular man stood at the front, talking to the room.

At least he had been until Warwick walked in. They stared at each other in silence for a moment, before Warwick reacted.

"Lia," he screamed out. "It's a trap."

He didn't get to say anything more before he felt something hit his head and everything went blank.

Truth

Garrick stared at the man who had just walked into the room, interrupting his speech. He yelled out a warning to whoever he was on the phone to. Before Garrick could say anything, one of the younger Agents hit him in the head with the butt of her gun, rendering him unconscious.

The man's phone fell from his hand, hitting the ground with the sound of plastic cracking. He hoped it wasn't broken; one of the tech guys might be able to use it to track down other rogue werewolves.

He hadn't expected his trap to ensnare anyone else and the man's arrival had taken him by surprise. Until that moment, everything had gone smoothly. He had received a call from one of the Agents assigned to stake out the warehouse, informing him that several cars had arrived and people were entering the building.

A quick chat with Carl later, he was driving to the location with a contingency of heavily armed Agents. Orders were to apprehend, not kill; orders which, so far, everyone had followed.

Taking the werewolves prisoner had been easy. Seeing the superior numbers, and how well armed they were, they had offered no resistance.

He was just in the middle of telling them what was going to happen to them when the new arrival walked into the room.

Garrick signalled to the young woman who had hit the man. "Take him to headquarters. Get a doctor to see him, just to ensure you haven't done any damage, but make sure he's secured to the bed and guarded at all times."

"Yes Sir," she said and immediately signalled to one of her fellow Agents to give her a hand lifting the inert body.

"Now where was I?" Garrick asked as soon as they were gone, looking around the room as he did so.

He wasn't expecting a response and didn't receive one. He looked from face to face. Nobody seated around the table would meet his eye. Their faces showed a mixture of defeat, terror and hate. One woman raised her head and glared at him, her gaze full of defiance. She was a striking woman and if he had met her before he got to know Amy and hadn't been on a mission, he would have been attracted to her. Other than her bright red hair.

"Who's in charge here?" he asked, expecting her to say that she was. Instead she looked to the open door, through which the man had been dragged.

"I guess he was," she said. "Seeing as Lia didn't bother to show up."

There was anger in her voice, though who it was directed at, he wasn't sure.

"Thank you," Garrick said. "And you are?"

"Someone who's not going to answer any more of your questions," she said, then turned her body so her back was to him.

"Fair enough," he said, then looked up at the Agents guarding the room. "Take them all back to headquarters. Put them in individual discussion rooms. Let's see what they are prepared to tell us when their buddies can't overhear."

He wasn't expecting any of them to talk and the plan was to convince them to join the program, to voluntarily take the serum, rather than interrogate them, but he was hoping someone would tell him something about who was responsible for what happened to Amy.

With two Agents to one werewolf, they were escorted out of the building and into the waiting vans, which had just arrived. Garrick called Carl to give him an update.

"We have nearly a dozen on their way to headquarters in the vans and one of the cars has an unconscious werewolf in it that may need medical treatment."

"What happened?" Carl asked. "Did he or she say something to piss you off?"

"Nothing to do with me," Garrick said. He wasn't upset by the accusation; Carl was just ribbing him. "Speak to one of your newest recruits. The short one with the high pitched voice."

"Did she overreact?"

"I wouldn't say so. To be honest, I'm not sure I wouldn't have done the same thing myself. He turned up after the others and immediately warned someone he was on the phone to. I think the Agent was just trying to stop him."

"Alright, I'll let it go if you think that's best. You were, after all, the one controlling the mission. Do you want to take care of the interviews yourself?"

"Not all of them," Garrick said. "Only the injured man and one of the women. She's rather striking, with dyed red hair. Blood red. You can't miss her."

"I'll make the arrangements," Carl told him. "See you soon."

Before leaving the room, Garrick picked up the man's phone, which was still lying where it had been dropped on the floor.

He switched it on, but it was locked. He needed to enter a pin, but he was confident the tech boys would be able to break into it.

Garrick drove directly to the building which housed the Agency's headquarters, arriving just ahead of the vans, despite leaving later than them.

He made his way directly to the infirmary, where he was told the male werewolf hadn't regained consciousness, but the doctors didn't think he had any injuries, other than perhaps a mild concussion.

Next he visited the tech lab, where he handed over the phone. "I want everything you can get me on the last person this phone called," he said. "And I want names and addresses for every other number in this phone, either in the contacts or the call register."

"You don't want much do you?" the young man with a stud in his nose said, but he was smiling as he said it.

"I know you'll give me everything you can, but I'm not expecting you to be able to do everything. I really want the woman the owner of this phone called though. I think he called her Lia, or something like that."

"Will do. I'll call as soon as I have something."

153

Garrick nodded his thanks before heading to the canteen to grab a quick snack. He wanted to give the female werewolf time to get settled into the room before he went to see her.

As soon as he had finished eating, he headed to Carl's office. The door was open and Carl signalled that he should enter as soon as he knocked.

"So far, everyone is refusing to talk. They aren't even giving us their names. Two are on the database, so we know who they are, another couple have police records so we've traced their details using their fingerprints. Your redhead is one of them. We have facial recognition going on the others, but I'm not holding out much hope."

"What's her name?" Garrick asked. "And she isn't 'my' redhead." He emphasised the 'my'.

Carl grinned at him. "Dawn Rayner. 27. Lives alone. Works at a local beauty parlour. Arrested for shoplifting a number of times when she was in her early teens."

Garrick raised his eyebrows. "I thought juvenile records were sealed."

"Not to us. Want to do this one alone or should I come along?"

"I think I may have more success on my own, but I'll call you if I need you."

Both men knew he wouldn't be making that call.

"She's been put in room 3.2. Good luck."

Garrick went to his office to retrieve his laptop before taking the lift to level 3 and heading to the room. He knocked on the door and walked in without waiting for permission. Two Agents stood guarding her. Both still had their guns drawn.

"I can take it from here, guys," Garrick said and held the door open so both of the men could leave.

The room he was in was pleasant enough. It contained a sofa and a couple of armchairs with a coffee table in between, sitting on top of a red and gold rug. Dawn had chosen the sofa so Garrick sat down on one of the chairs opposite her.

"Can I offer you a coffee or anything?" he asked as he placed his laptop on the table.

She looked at him. He could see the defiance in her, not just in her face, but in the way she held herself. She was alert, but was trying to give a false impression of being relaxed.

"This isn't what I was expecting," she said as she looked around the room, completely ignoring his question.

"This is for interviews, not interrogations," Garrick said. He leaned back in the chair and put his legs up on the coffee table. Dawn wasn't the only one who could fake being relaxed.

"Yet I'm still a prisoner," she said, holding her hands in front of her to show him the handcuffs.

"Tell me what I want to know and I'll take them off."

Dawn laughed. It wasn't the sarcastic type of laugh he was expecting. It was filled with genuine amusement.

"Do you really think I'm that stupid?" she asked. "My IQ is 140. What's yours?"

"I don't know. I've never been tested." He looked at her closely and wondered how he had failed to notice that her eyes were bright red, almost a perfect match for her hair. "What's with the contacts?" he asked.

"How do you know my eyes aren't really red?"

Garrick had had enough of the banter. He wanted answers. "Stop pissing about, Dawn. We both know werewolves don't have red eyes. Now, would you care to tell me why you are conspiring against the Agency?"

A shadow of fear crossed Dawn's face when he said her name, but she quickly hid it.

"How do you know who I am?" Her tone was challenging, playful even, but Garrick could tell she was faking it. She was worried that he knew her identity. Did she really think she couldn't be traced?

He leaned forward. "We know all about you, Dawn. How old you are. Where you live. What you do for a living. If you are so intelligent, why do you work in a beauty parlour? I can't imagine that taxes your brain much."

Dawn went pale. "How do you know all that?"

Garrick relaxed back again. "Why don't we play a game? You answer one of my questions, then I answer one of yours. As a show of faith, I'll start. We have access to your arrest records."

He didn't really tell her that as a show of faith. He wanted to rattle her. And the way she reacted suggested he had succeeded.

Her head swung around so she was looking at him. "But that's from when I was a kid."

He said nothing as he watched her watching him. Eventually she looked away. "What do you want to know?"

"Let's start with my previous question, shall we? Why are you conspiring against the Agency?"

She opened her mouth and Garrick was sure she was going to protest her innocence, but instead she closed it again. Her body sagged, but only a little. She may have been resigned to the inevitable, but she was far from defeated.

"I'm a werewolf. I like being in my wolf form. Why wouldn't I be against an Agency which is determined to stop all of us transforming?"

Garrick leaned forward again. "What are you talking about? We don't do anything to any werewolves to stop them transforming."

Dawn grunted. "Sure you don't. And I suppose you don't force my brethren to take annual injections either."

Garrick had no issue with telling her the truth. "We do, but it doesn't stop you transforming. Let me show you."

He switched on his laptop and positioned it so they could both see the screen.

"The first time we inject anyone with our serum, we request that they transform, just to make sure there were no unexpected complications."

He then went to a directory, selected a file at random and opened it up. He turned the screen so Dawn could see it fully and switched up the sound.

She watched a woman in a lab coat talking to a man, discussing how he felt after receiving his injection. He seemed upbeat and was happily taking part in the discussion. Dawn turned up the sound so she could hear better. The medical professional then asked the man if he wanted to try transforming.

He nodded his head and removed his shoes and socks before going behind a screen, which hid him from his shoulders to his knees. As Dawn watched, the man's shirt appeared on the top of the screen, followed by his trousers and underwear.

Her eyes widened as the man transformed.

"That's not possible," she said. "This must be staged. That man can't have had the injection you force on the likes of me."

"It's not staged," Garrick said calmly. "Choose any file you want. They will all show you the same thing."

Dawn did as instructed. Garrick watched her as she went through video after video after video. He could see her getting more and more frantic as she searched for a recording she could say was proof it was all fake.

Then she smiled. "I know who this is," she said as she opened another file. "She was one of us until she disappeared. Now I will see what really happened to her."

Garrick said nothing. He knew what Dawn was about to see.

The smile didn't leave her face as she heard the woman sullenly asking questions. It was obvious she had agreed to take the serum, rather than be imprisoned, but she wasn't happy about it.

Then she was asked if she wanted to change into her wolf form. Her reply was to ask what the point was as it was no longer possible. The doctor, or nurse, or whatever she was, stayed calm, gently explained that it was still possible, that nothing had been done to prevent it.

Reluctantly the werewolf went behind the screen and undressed.

"How the hell did you make this video?" Dawn yelled out when the woman turned into a wolf. When the woman turned back again, there were tears in her eyes. Based on how the rest of the discussion went, they were tears of joy.

Dawn pushed the laptop away from her and collapsed back into her seat.

"I don't understand," she finally said. "Why do you force these injections on us if they don't stop us transforming?"

Garrick felt like smiling, but didn't. Dawn was finally ready to listen to what he had to say.

"We don't force the injections on anyone. If you refuse to take it, we will have to keep you prisoner, but I can assure you our prisons are much nicer than you would expect. They are more like gated communities. The only difference is that you can't leave without an armed escort."

"Is that where my friend was taken?" Dawn gestured toward the laptop, indicating that she was talking about the woman in the video.

"No, she was allowed to leave. All she has to do is return once a year for a booster."

"So where is she?" Dawn's voice was quiet, as though all the fight had gone out of her.

"I have no idea. I presume she went home."

Dawn raised her head to look at Garrick. "Why did she lie to us?"

"Who?"

"Our so called leader. The only reason I agreed to join up was because I didn't see a choice. She told us if we registered with the Agency you would take away what we fundamentally are."

Garrick felt excitement running through him. She was finally going to tell him what he wanted to know. He managed to reign himself in.

"Maybe she didn't know. Maybe she thought she was telling the truth." He doubted it, but it was a possibility.

"So what does the injection do and why do we have to be locked up if we refuse to take it?"

"It takes away the urge to transform. It allows you to decide if and when you want to be a wolf. You may not realise this, but when your body makes you transform when you don't want to, most werewolves become violent, a danger to society. Our injection takes away that danger. You'll still be able to kill, but it will be a conscious choice if you do, not instinct."

Dawn nodded her head, though exactly why, Garrick wasn't sure. Maybe she was agreeing with what he was saying, or maybe she was indicating that she wanted to have the injection. He had no idea and didn't ask.

"Who is your leader?" he asked instead.

Dawn shook her head. "I can't tell you that, even if I wanted to. She went into our minds and forbade us from telling anyone."

Garrick wasn't surprised. It was a sensible thing to do if you had the power to do it.

"Describe her to me, then."

Again Dawn shook her head. "I can't do that either. Sorry."

She sounded like she genuinely was.

"I'm trying to find out who is responsible for what happened to a friend of mine. Someone in your group planted a device in her neck and sent her here to kill us all. Someone other than your leader must have been involved. So what can you tell me about that?"

A smile formed on Dawn's face once more. "I can tell you about the man you knocked unconscious. Not only is Warwick second in command, he is also the man who developed the implant."

Interrogation

Garrick sat on a chair next to the bed Warwick was strapped to. He looked him up and down, taking in his short, stocky frame, covered in faded jeans and a red and black checkered flannelette shirt.

He wondered what his profession might be, but didn't want to guess in case he insulted someone.

Based on his messy, slightly too long, black hair, Garrick assumed he was self-employed. Either that or he worked from home; he couldn't imagine an employer allowing him to look like that. While the look may work on younger men, it didn't on Warwick.

Garrick kicked the bed, hard enough to shake it.

"I know you're awake so you might as well stop pretending."

Warwick opened one eyelid, revealing a dull brown eye. Garrick could find nothing in the man's features that he thought a woman would find appealing, yet Dawn had insisted that he was a ladies man, at least he thought he was. Dawn didn't see it herself and nor did Garrick.

"I should be in hospital," he said.

"You've been examined by medical experts and there's nothing wrong with you, so why don't we have a little chat."

"I have nothing to say to you," Warwick said.

Garrick thought he didn't even have an attractive voice. Then again, who was he to judge what women would like. He'd have to speak to Amy about it, get her opinion on that sort of thing. Not that he was planning on forcing her to see Warwick. If he was, indeed, the man who had experimented on her, it might bring back bad memories, memories he would prefer she kept hidden from herself.

"Fine, Warwick, I'll do the talking."

Nothing had been found in any of the databases from the various law enforcement agencies around the world about Warwick, but Dawn had provided enough information for the analysts to find out almost everything about him. Everything except what he did for a living. After she had done so, she went with a member of the medical staff to find out more about the annual injections she could take if she registered and how they worked.

Garrick noticed that Warwick flinched when he said his name and decided to list all the facts he had written down about him, from his home address, to the car he drove, to the names of his parents, both deceased, and his still living sister.

Warwick showed no reaction to what Garrick was saying until he said Katherine's name.

"You stay away from Kathy," he yelled and tried to hit out at Garrick, but the handcuffs tying him to the bed prevented him from doing so.

"That depends on whether she's also a werewolf."

"You so much as look at her and I'll kill you."

Garrick made a show of looking him up and down. "And how do you propose to do that?"

Warwick growled.

"Let's make a deal shall we? You tell me what I want to know and I won't send a team of Agents to arrest your sister. After all, sometimes those sorts of missions don't go according to plan and the target ends up injured. Or worse."

Garrick had no intention of putting Katherine in any danger, but Dawn had said she was Warwick's Achilles heel and he planned on using that information to his advantage. He had already sent his sister and her partner to investigate whether Katherine was a werewolf or not. They were to observe only, not arrest.

"You bastard," Warwick spat at him.

Garrick shrugged. "I've been called worse."

"Lia was right about you. All you Agents are the same. No wonder so many of us refuse to enrol with your Agency. You're worse than the Gestapo."

Garrick raised an eyebrow. "I've never been compared to a Nazi before. Now who's Lia?"

"The person who is going to put an end to you and your fascist friends."

"Tell me about her."

Warwick sneered at him. "I won't tell you anything."

"Won't or can't?" Warwick didn't respond, so Garrick continued.

"So she doesn't trust you enough to let you know anything about her identity." Garrick was hoping that if he baited him, Warwick would let something slip. He didn't think he could, if this Lia person had the same control over him as she did over Dawn, but there was no harm in trying.

"Of course she does. I know everything about her. She just made sure I couldn't tell you."

"So she doesn't trust you to keep your mouth shut. She had to do something to you to make sure you couldn't betray her."

"Of course she trusts me," Warwick yelled out. "She let me perform the operation on the half-breed didn't she? She trusted that the implant I created would do what was needed without harming her."

Garrick knew he could get no more out of Warwick, but he had gotten more than he had been expecting. He had admitted to not only knowing about the implant, but inventing it. When Garrick was finished with him he would be handed over to the tech guys so he could tell them more about it, whether he wanted to or not.

At that moment, his phone rang. He saw who was calling and decided to answer it.

"Tab, what have you got to tell me?"

"We found Katherine. She's human."

"Thanks, Tab," Garrick said and hung up. He returned his attention to Warwick. "So, Kathy's human is she? How do you explain that?"

"I told you to keep away from her," Warwick growled.

Garrick gestured around the room with his arms. "I haven't left the room so how could I have gone anywhere near her? So does she know what you are?"

Warwick nodded. "She knows. She's the only one of my family who does. I was adopted as a baby. Well that's what my parents told me. I later found out I was stolen. I have no idea who my real family is. I killed the people who pretended to be my parents when I found out."

Garrick glanced down at the notes he had made about Warwick. His parent's deaths were put down to a wild animal attack so he may well have been telling the truth. There would be no point in investigating, though, as it happened too long ago. However, he could use it to blackmail Warwick into giving the tech guys all the information they needed about the implant. Something along the lines of 'Tell us what we need to know or we tell your sister what you did'. It would only work, of course, if Katherine didn't already know, and he was confident that she didn't.

It was a nice idea, but Garrick knew he wouldn't be able to go through with it. Thinking about doing something and actually doing it were two completely different things, in his mind, and he didn't have it in him to blackmail someone.

He knew people in the Agency who did though and he would pass the information on to them.

He decided to get things moving in a different direction. "Why have you never registered with the Agency?"

The question seemed to take Warwick by surprise. "Why would I?"

"Because of the benefits it gives you. Or are you another one of the followers of this Lia person who believes that the serum we provide will stop you transforming?"

Something told him that Warwick was already aware of the truth and it didn't take Warwick long to confirm it.

"I know exactly what your drug does. I just don't believe that humans have the right to restrict werewolves from being what they truly are."

"You mean killers."

"No, I mean werewolves. When and how we become wolves is part of our nature and nobody has the right to interfere."

Not in the mood for a philosophical argument, Garrick changed direction again. He took a phone out of his pocket and showed it to Warwick. The screen was broken, but the phone was still useable, as Garrick demonstrated by bringing up its list of stored contacts. Warwick went pale.

"Once I've finished with you, I'm going to be handing this phone over to a team of investigators who will trace every person you have stored in here and obtain details of everyone you have ever spoken to using this device."

He didn't see the need to inform Warwick that the investigation was already under way.

"You can't do that. It's a breach of privacy. It goes against my basic human rights." Warwick no longer sounded so sure of himself.

"Human rights?" Garrick raised an eyebrow. "You've made it clear you consider yourself a werewolf, not a human, so you have no human rights."

Garrick didn't believe what he was saying. Even after all his years in the Agency, or maybe because of them, he still viewed werewolves as people, people who deserved to be treated just the same as humans. As long as they registered with the Agency.

He scrolled through the list of contact names in the phone, stopping when he got to the one he wanted.

"Let's give Lia a call, shall we?" He pressed the dial button and held the phone up to his ear.

Warwick reached forward to grab it off him, but the handcuffs he was wearing prevented him from reaching it.

Garrick listened to the phone on the other end ring a number of times before it was answered.

"Which Agent am I speaking to?" a female voice asked.

If this was Lia, she certainly wasn't stupid. He put the phone on speaker. He wanted Warwick to hear everything she said.

"My name is Garrick. I've just been having a lovely chat with Warwick."

A rich laugh reached his ears. "Garrick. The one who's screwing the half-breed. Why am I not surprised? And why do I think that Warwick didn't find the chat 'lovely', as you put it."

"You're right. Why don't we meet and discuss my terms for handing him back to you?"

Again Lia laughed. "Now why would I want to do that? What possible reason could I have for exposing myself? He can't tell you anything important about me. Keep him. Do what you want with him. It's no loss to me."

Garrick was watching Warwick closely as Lia spoke. Hurt gave way to anger.

"You bitch. After everything I've done for you."

"Goodbye, Warwick." Lia's reply echoed around the room before the connection was cut-off.

Garrick was about to say something, but was interrupted by a knock at the door.

"Come in," Garrick called out and Carl walked in. He glanced at Warwick, but turned his attention to Garrick.

"All numbers in Warwick's phone have been traced, except one. The same goes to everyone else we arrested. All had their phones on them. It looks like everyone was using their registered numbers so we have addresses for everyone. We'll be sending Agents to see who are werewolves and who aren't and the werewolves will be rounded up."

Garrick looked at Warwick, who didn't seem to care about what Carl had just said.

"Carl, meet Warwick. There's a Kathy on his phone. She's already been checked out. She's innocent, a human. She knows about Warwick being a wolf, but that's no crime. Please make sure nobody else pays her a visit."

He wasn't expecting Warwick to thank him and he didn't. He hadn't said it for Warwick's benefit; he genuinely wanted someone who was obviously not flouting any of the Agency's laws to be left in peace.

"Which number couldn't you trace?" he asked.

"The same number was stored in most of the phones. Except for one person, who had dialled the number a few times and received calls from it, but didn't store it. He didn't store any numbers for some reason. Everyone else had it under the name of Lia. It turns out it's a burner phone so we can't trace it."

"This Lia person is definitely smart. She's the leader of this little gang of rebels. How are the other interviews going?"

Carl glanced at Warwick once more. Garrick saw the gesture and nodded his head, telling his boss it was okay to talk in front of him.

"Good. Most are co-operating. None of them are able to tell us anything about this Lia person. Some haven't even been able to say her name. Of those we arrested, all except two are interested in finding out more about what we actually do and how we help werewolves. I think they are all going to register with us."

Garrick nodded his head. If most of them had been lied to, like Dawn had been, then it was understandable that they wanted to know the truth.

"And the other two?"

Carl grimaced. "I have no idea why, but they were carrying poison and managed to take it before we could stop them. We hadn't even started asking them questions. We are going to inform their families that the deaths were as a result of accidental drug overdoses. It might be easier for them to handle than suicide."

"Why would they do that?"

Both men looked at Warwick.

"Don't ask me. I had no idea any of us were carrying poison. Maybe Lia programmed it into them, forced them to do it if ever they were captured, as a lesson to the rest of us. It looks like she's even more of a bitch than I first thought."

Carl returned his attention to Garrick. "Everyone has told us all they can, other than Warwick here, but it's not much. Lia was certainly thorough."

"What are you planning on doing with this guy?" Garrick indicated Warwick with his head. "He's the one who developed the implant."

"Is he now?" The sudden interest Carl felt was evident in his tone. "That all depends on how co-operative he is going to be."

Warwick grunted. "After what Lia just said about me, I'll tell you everything I can."

"The first thing I want to know," Garrick said, "is why put the device in Amy?"

"That should be obvious," Warwick said. "It can control anyone with werewolf blood in them, but if there's too much, they will be able to resist. Not enough and it will have no effect. Hence neither humans nor full werewolves could be used. Nor Agents."

It made sense and it was something Garrick should have thought of himself.

"How did it give her the power to move objects with her mind?"

Warwick leaned forward. "It did what?"

"You didn't know?"

Warwick shook his head. "I have no idea how that happened. It wasn't intentional." He leaned back again. "But I'm looking forward to working with your scientists to figure it out."

Garrick and Carl both smiled. The mission had gone better than either of them had expected. Now all they had to do was track down Lia and make sure she never did anything to hurt Amy ever again.

Disaster

Lia hung up her phone as soon as she heard Warwick call out the warning. Once she was out of the traffic jam, she turned left instead of right, heading back to her home instead of the warehouse.

She swore loudly to herself as she drove. She couldn't help wondering how many had been captured by the Agency and how many more would be tracked down. At least none of them would be able to tell them anything about her, other than her name.

She was glad that Warwick had had the sense to warn her. All he had said was that it was a trap, but she had no doubt that the Agency was behind it. After all, who else could it be?

She hit the steering wheel in frustration. She needed to increase the numbers in her resistance movement, not decrease them. 'If there was still a resistance movement, other than me,' she couldn't help thinking. Would the Agency get everyone? If so, it would be a complete disaster for her and the resistance.

Morbid thoughts and worse case scenarios filled her mind as she drove home, along with questions she couldn't answer. How had they found the warehouse? How had they known when the werewolves were going to meet? Had someone told them? Was there a traitor in their midst?

Lia shook her head. There couldn't be. She had read everyone's mind. Everyone was there for the right reasons; none of them was a spy.

But she had only done so when they first joined. Was it possible someone had been persuaded to switch sides?

There was no way to find out the answers for the time being, so as soon as she entered her house, she slipped off her shoes, walked into the kitchen and put the kettle on.

As she waited for the kettle to boil, a different line of thought entered her mind. How did she know anyone had been captured? She only had Warwick's warning to go by. Had he faked it all? Had he wanted to have the meeting without her so he could try to take control? He was ambitious, but was he clever enough to go to those sorts of lengths?

She didn't think so, but she couldn't be certain.

She took her phone out and looked at it. If she called Warwick, would he answer? If he didn't, would it be because he had been captured by the Agency or because he was avoiding her calls?

She could try using her other phone, the one he didn't know about, but that would mean he would then have her number and if he didn't answer, she still wouldn't know why.

She sighed and put the phone away. It was pointless doing anything for a while.

She drank her tea while reading a book before going for a shower. It helped to relax her body, but not her mind. She hated not knowing what was happening. She was the sort of person who was always in control of a situation.

She was tempted to phone one of the others, but if her suspicions about Warwick were true, would it make her look weak, would it be playing into his hands?

She switched the TV on, but wasn't really watching it; her mind was on other things. She kept staring at her phone on the coffee table, but it still made her jump when it rang.

She picked it up and looked at who was calling her. Warwick. Should she answer? If she didn't, she wouldn't find out what was going on. It was possible he had escaped and wanted to give her an update. It was equally possible that he was calling to say he had replaced her. He wouldn't live long if that was the case.

Then again, he could be in custody and the Agency had use of his phone.

She let it ring, finally answering it just before it went to voicemail.

"Which Agent am I speaking to?" she asked, praying she had read the situation right.

She recognised the voice on the other end.

"My name is Garrick. I've just been having a lovely chat with Warwick."

169

She forced herself to laugh, even though she was worried. Warwick hadn't been setting her up and was now in the hands of the Agency, along with who knew how many other members of her resistance group.

She forced herself to sound unconcerned. "Garrick. The one who's screwing the half-breed. Why am I not surprised? And why do I think that Warwick didn't find the chat 'lovely', as you put it."

"You're right. Why don't we meet and discuss my terms for handing him back to you?"

Again Lia laughed. This time it was genuine. Did he really think she was that stupid? "Now why would I want to do that? What possible reason could I have for exposing myself? He can't tell you anything important about me. Keep him. Do what you want with him. It's no loss to me."

The last part was only partially a lie. He had been a good second in command, most of the time, but now that the Agency had their hands on him, he would be of no use to her ever again, even if he did, somehow, manage to escape.

It never occurred to her that Garrick would have allowed Warwick to listen in on their conversation, so it took her by surprise when she heard him yell out.

"You bitch. After everything I've done for you."

Knowing that the Agency were probably trying to trace the call, she said, "Goodbye, Warwick," then hung up.

She didn't regret what she had said, but she did wish that Warwick hadn't heard it. She felt no ill will toward him and hearing those words must have hurt. She fully expected the Agency to kill him for what he did to Amy and those weren't the last words she would have wanted him to hear from her.

"Damn," she said and threw the phone onto the sofa. She hadn't wanted to believe that Warwick had betrayed her and was trying to take over the team, but it would have been better than the alternative; the alternative which turned out to be true.

She ran her fingers through her hair in frustration. Now what was she going to do? She would have to start from scratch, build up a whole new team. That would take time, time she didn't have.

She wasn't worried about being found; none of the people she dealt with would be able to provide the Agency with any useful information, she had seen to that, and she was confident that they were all too scared of her to even attempt to contact her if they had decided to register with the Agency. Making two of them kill themselves would have made sure of that. If, however, anyone did, she would have to deal with them.

It was possible, of course, that those who hadn't made it to the warehouse had no idea what was going on, but the Agency would probably be able to find them through the others.

She picked up her phone again. She really did not want to make the call, but she knew she had to. She may be in charge of the local branch of the resistance, but she still had to report to the werewolf who was in charge of co-ordinating the efforts country-wide and he, in turn, had to report to the worldwide council. Lia didn't like it, but in reality she was just a small cog in the wheel.

She scrolled through her list of contacts, found the one she wanted and hit the button. She could hear it ringing on the other end when she held it closer to her ear.

It rang for what seemed like ages before it was finally answered. Lia had been too nervous to count the number of rings. While she was powerful, in regard to strength, speed and the ability to make other werewolves do her bidding, the man she was about to speak to was by far superior to her in every way.

"Lia," a deep voice said. "How nice to hear from you."

Derek sounded like he meant it, but as soon as Lia gave him her news, she doubted he would be so friendly.

"Derek, I have a problem."

She almost said 'we', but stopped herself in time. This was her problem to deal with and Derek would not take too kindly to her suggesting that wasn't the case.

"Go on," he said. She could hear the faint sound of ice-cubes hitting the edge of a glass and could picture him swirling the amber liquid around as he spoke. He always drank a glass or two of whisky in the evenings and the time was late enough for him to be doing so already, though only just.

She told him everything she knew. Or, to be more precise, everything she didn't yet know, but was determined to find out. He didn't interrupt with questions until she had finished speaking. When he did, he didn't sound angry.

"Alright. What do you plan on doing?"

"Well, first I am going to find out exactly how the Agency knew when and where we were meeting. If I discover we had a traitor, that person is going to wish they were dead. Secondly, I am going to be paying a personal visit to every member of my team to find out who has given up their freedom and signed on with the Agency. Then I'm going to make them regret it."

"That's not a good idea," Derek told her. "While I won't tell you not to contact or visit anyone who may have been compromised, I will advise you not to. The Agency may have Agents keeping an eye on them and you don't want to risk exposing yourself. I assume you took all necessary precautions with all members."

"Of course." She, herself, had undergone the same mental invasion from Derek so she would be unable to provide the Agency with any information about him, should she ever get captured.

"Good. I appreciate you calling me. I can't imagine it was easy. Don't worry about recruiting at the moment. I have some things coming up soon that, should all go according to plan, may mean that I can send you some people to help out. For now, just keep your eyes and ears open and let me know as soon as you find out more about what happened."

"Thanks, Derek, I will."

When Lia hung up the phone, she was feeling a lot better than she had been before making the call. Surprisingly, Derek wasn't blaming her for what had happened, but that could change once she had more information. For the time being, she would follow his instructions and do nothing, other than investigate.

Deciding it was too early to go to bed, Lia poured herself a glass of wine, switched the TV channel to something more interesting and lost herself in a murder mystery.

Confession

Garrick was nervous when he rang the doorbell. He was there to tell Amy that he had been tracking her and he had no idea how she was going to react.

"Hey honey," he said as soon as she opened the door. The first time he had called her that, it felt so right it had become a habit. She didn't seem to mind.

"Hey yourself." She reached up to put her arms around his neck and he leaned down to kiss her. He intended it to be just a soft welcoming kiss on the lips, but when she opened her mouth, he couldn't resist slipping his tongue inside.

He put his arms around her waist and pulled her tighter against him, deepening the kiss as he did so. Not usually one who liked public displays of passion, with Amy he didn't seem to care who saw them.

"I take it you missed me," she said when she broke away.

"Is it that obvious?" Garrick asked as he smiled at her. He had been in relationships before, but never had he wanted to spend so much time with his chosen partner, never before had he been annoyed that work had to take priority. All his other women had been distractions that could easily be put aside, nothing more. As a result, none of them had lasted very long. This relationship was going to be different. Not only did he want this one to last, he could feel it was going to. As long as she was still speaking to him after his confession.

"Let's go inside," he said. "There's something we need to talk about."

"This sounds serious." After she had closed the door, she took his hand and led him down the corridor. "Coffee?"

"I'd love one."

The moment he entered the kitchen, he heard something entering the house via the dog flap and went down on one knee so Ainin could reach him without having to jump up.

The dog bounded up to him with such enthusiasm he almost knocked him over.

"Hello, boy," he said. He ran one hand down his back and used the other to rub his ear, something the dog seemed to really enjoy. "Have you been looking after Amy for me?"

"Of course he has. He's a great guard dog. Never lets anyone in he doesn't know, do you boy?"

Amy made kissing noises toward the canine, who barked his reply.

"Other than me, you mean," Garrick said as he stood up.

"That's not his fault. He could smell the werewolf blood you injected into yourself. It confused him, remember."

"And there was me thinking it was just my charm."

Amy laughed lightly. "That may have had something to do with it. Now what do you want to talk to me about?"

"Let's go into the lounge. I have some good news and some bad news."

Taking their coffees with them, they left the kitchen, accompanied by Ainin. Once in the lounge, he jumped onto his favourite part of the sofa, turned around a couple of times and curled up in a ball. Though he closed his eyes, he was only pretending to be asleep; every few seconds one eye would open slightly. He was acting as though he was relaxed, but, like a good Agent, he was alert and ready to act.

Garrick couldn't help smiling to himself. He was comparing a damn mutt to a fully trained Agent. Then again, given some of the Agents he had been forced to work with, he would have preferred to have Ainin as a partner.

There was room on the sofa between Amy and the dog, just, but as much as Garrick wanted to cuddle up with her, he needed to keep some distance between them while he filled her in on all that had happened.

Seating himself in the only armchair in the room, he proceeded to tell her everything, from rounding up the werewolves, to the interviews and the final outcomes. Other than mentioning how he had tracked them down, he held nothing back.

175

Throughout the entire dialogue, Amy said nothing. She didn't react when he mentioned Warwick's name, nor Lia's. She didn't interrupt with questions as she waited patiently for him to finish.

"So the man who operated on me has been found," she stated in an emotionless voice. "And he can no longer hurt me?"

As much as Garrick wanted to assure her that was the case, he opted for honesty instead.

"I can't guarantee it, but I believe he is no longer a threat and Carl agrees with me."

Amy nodded before looking away.

Garrick leaned forward and took hold of her hand, waiting until she turned her head back to him before speaking.

"If I thought he had any intention of hurting you again, I would lock him up for the rest of his life."

"I know," she said. Then she looked away again. "It's just that I feel nothing. I thought I would feel relief or anger that he's not being sufficiently punished for violating my body, but I don't."

Garrick squeezed her hand. "Maybe it's because he's not the one behind it all. It's Lia we need to catch. Does the name ring a bell?"

"No. Nor does Warwick. Do you have a picture of him?"

Garrick took his phone out of his pocket and scrolled down to the picture he had taken before leaving headquarters. He held it out so Amy could see it and her eyes widened.

"I know this man," she said. "Or at least I feel I have seen him before. I can't tell you where or when though."

Garrick quickly put his phone away. There was a risk that seeing Warwick would trigger memories that he was glad Amy still had sealed away somewhere inside her head.

"So, how are you planning on tracking down this Lia person?" Amy asked. Her voice was soft, perfectly matching how small and vulnerable she looked at that moment, despite her height. Garrick longed to take her in his arms and tell her he would never let anything happen to her ever again, but he had yet to tell her the most important piece of information.

"At the moment we have no idea, but we're working on it. Don't you want to know how we found the other werewolves?"

176

Amy shrugged. "Does it matter?"

"Yes, actually. It matters a lot."

Garrick braced himself and took a deep breath, before admitting what he had done.

"I've been tracking you."

Garrick didn't really know how he was expecting Amy to react, but immediate acceptance was definitely bottom of the list of possibilities.

"I guess that makes sense."

Garrick gaped at her. He couldn't believe what he was hearing. "You're not mad at me?" he finally managed to ask.

Amy looked genuinely confused. "Why would I be mad at you? I'm an anomaly, a half-breed, something that shouldn't exist. Of course you would want to keep an eye on me. Until recently, you probably didn't trust me. Hell, there are probably a large number of Agents who still don't trust me."

Garrick opened his mouth to speak, but Amy held out her hand to stop him. "Don't argue. In their position I wouldn't trust me either."

Garrick was wise enough to stay silent.

"How long have you been tracking me?" she asked. "Come to think of it, how have you been doing it?"

She sounded curious rather than accusatory and Garrick hoped his ears weren't deceiving him. He released her hand and pointed to her wrist.

"I put a tracker in your fitness device the first time I met you."

She lifted her arm so she could see it clearer. "Smart."

Garrick shook his head. "I expected you to be mad, not impressed."

Amy took his hand in hers. "I like that I can surprise you. But there's one thing I'm still curious about. If you knew I was going to that warehouse, why didn't you investigate sooner?"

Garrick felt something he didn't feel very often: embarrassment, with a touch of guilt. Amy was right; he had a tracker on her so why hadn't he been actively monitoring her? He could have prevented her being operated on.

"To be honest, I forgot about it. I got so caught up in getting to know you, it slipped my mind. It wasn't until we discovered the implant in you that I remembered. It's the first and only time I have looked at the data."

He prayed she believed him. It was the truth and he didn't want her to think he had been secretly spying on her.

He looked up to see her smiling at him. "You really are an idiot. Now come here and kiss me."

He did as instructed. "I quite like you bossing me around," he told her, then kissed her again.

They began to get a little carried away and Amy's head ended up on Ainin when she laid back so Garrick could climb on top of her. The growl they received told them that, while the dog didn't usually mind what the two of them did, he did when it affected him, and there was no way he was going to be moving.

"Maybe we should take this upstairs," Amy suggested.

"I'd love to, but I have to get back to work. Can I come back later?"

"Only if you bring Chinese with you. And a bottle of wine."

"I'll see what I can do." He kissed her once more before getting up. He hated to leave her, but he really did have work to do. Carl had given him a couple of werewolves who had failed to re-register to track down and he had already spent too much time with Amy.

Ainin gave him a meaningful look. If he was going to be bringing food later, it had better include a bone. "I'll see what I can do for you as well, boy," he said as he ruffled the fur on the top of his head.

Amy showed him to the door, where he reluctantly kissed her goodbye.

"Why haven't you asked me to remove the tracker?" he asked.

"I kind of like you being able to trace where I am. If something else happens to me, I now know you will come and rescue me."

"Always," he said and kissed her cheek.

The rest of the day went slowly. He easily found the two werewolves he had been sent to hunt down, only to find that they were dead; they had died in a car crash on their way to re-register, hit by a drunk driver.

The knowledge left a bitter taste in his mouth. He hadn't known them personally, but he still hated the fact that two people had died needlessly.

Later that evening, he phoned Amy to find out what she wanted to eat. He hadn't been seeing her long enough to know what her favourite dishes were and even if he had, he would still ask. He would never presume; he would always let her choose.

A trip to the takeaway, bottle shop and supermarket later, he was standing on her doorstep, food and wine in hand.

When Amy opened the door, his eyes widened in appreciation. She had dressed up for the evening. The little black dress she had chosen was hugging her body in all the right places. He could picture himself peeling it off her, tantalisingly slowly.

"You look great," he said.

She had tied her hair back and was wearing contact lenses. He missed the glasses, but appreciated seeing a different look on her. She wasn't wearing any makeup and he loved the way her pale skin contrasted with the darkness of her hair and her bright hazel eyes, whose thick lashes drew his own eyes to them.

'Great,' he thought to himself. 'That's an understatement', but it was too late to take it back.

"Thank you," she said as she took the bottle from him.

The evening flew by. The food was good and the wine went well with it. Ainin left them in peace as he ate his bone outside, but that didn't stop him coming into the house and offering to help clean the plates when he heard Amy in the kitchen.

Garrick had no expectations. Things with Amy were progressing slowly and he didn't want to rush. He would be staying the night, as he had had a few glasses of wine, but whether it was in the spare room or not, only time would tell. He didn't want to be separated from her, but it was her decision.

Garrick was looking through Amy's CD collection when she returned to the lounge, a second bottle of wine in her hand.

"Your taste is pretty varied," he said, not the least embarrassed that he had been caught going through her things. "I never had you down as a rap fan."

"I'm not," she replied as she filled both of their glasses. "I like the odd song, but that's as far as it goes. I bought those albums because I liked one of their hits, only to discover the rest of the songs are crap."

Garrick laughed. He loved the way she didn't beat around the bush. "I'm with you there. I could probably say the same about my music collection."

He returned to the sofa and held his arm out, inviting Amy to cuddle up with him.

They stayed in that position for a long while, talking about anything and everything. Soon talking changed to touching and it wasn't long before Garrick had to pull away.

"If we don't slow down, I'm not sure I'm going to be able to stop."

"Then don't."

Amy got off the sofa and held her hand out to him.

"Come on," she said. "Let's go to bed."

Threat

Amy lay in bed, listening to the sound of her shower running. It had been a great night. She and Garrick hadn't gone all the way, but they had done everything but that. When she closed her eyes, she could still feel the touch of his hands on her skin.

She hadn't gotten much sleep, but she felt more refreshed than she had in a long time.

She was debating whether to get up and make breakfast when the bathroom door opened and Garrick walked in wearing just a towel. She knew exactly what that piece of cloth was hiding and memories of having her hands on his flesh filled her mind, making her wet between the legs.

"What would you like for breakfast?" she forced herself to say, even though food was the last thing on her mind.

He climbed onto the bed and kissed her. "How about you?"

She giggled, which was unlike her. "I'm not edible."

He kissed her again. "You were last night."

He moved onto her neck and she couldn't hold back a contented sigh.

"I like that sound," he said then ran his tongue along her collar bone, making her shiver in excitement.

"We don't have plans for today, do we?" she asked.

Garrick pulled away from her. "Unfortunately, yes."

"If I hide all your clothes, then we'll have to stay here."

Usually she wouldn't dream of saying something like that, but Garrick brought out something in her no other man had been able to. She hadn't known him that long and they had only been together for a few weeks, but she was comfortable around him. She felt she could be herself without being judged or criticised. She wanted things to work out with Garrick and he had given her no reason to think they wouldn't.

"Tempting," he said, "but I promised Lawrence we would visit. He's been hassling me for a few weeks. The implant seemed to access the wolf in you and he wants to see if it opened up the door."

It sounded like Amy was nothing more to either of them than an experiment, but she knew that wasn't the case. Lawrence only wanted to help her; help her become all she could be.

"He also wants to make sure it hasn't triggered something which will make me transform against my will," she guessed.

"Something like that."

Garrick stood up and removed the towel. She really wished he hadn't. Seeing his naked body made her own start to ache in places she had never ached before. She had been sexually involved with other men, but none had made her feel the way Garrick did. Why she hadn't let things go all the way during the night, she had no idea. He was willing, more than willing, but something told her it was too soon. The fact he didn't try to change her mind made her love him all the more.

She sat up. Where had that thought come from?

As she watched him get dressed, she realised that it was true. She really did love him. In her book, it was way too soon in their relationship for her to have such strong feelings, but it looked like she would be needing to toss the book out of the window.

Her musings were interrupted by his voice. "Are you alright?"

She shook her head, as though trying to dislodge her thoughts. "Sure," she said. "Just thinking about something."

"From the intense look on your face, I really hope it was me. Now what can I make you for breakfast? I make a mean boiled egg."

"That sounds perfect. Give me a minute and I'll get up and help you."

"Oh no you don't. You are staying right here. Now get back under those covers before you get cold."

"Yes Sir," she said, with just a trace of sarcasm.

Garrick left the room, but wasn't gone long before returning with a mug of tea. Ainin trailed behind and jumped up on the bed as soon as she had placed the hot beverage on the bedside table. It had only taken two accidents for him to learn to stay away while she was holding a steaming cup.

"He's trying to tell me he wants breakfast, but I'm not sure what you give him."

"Two cups of biscuits. His bowl's in the pantry. If you sneak in an extra half a cup, he'll love you even more than he already does."

"I don't think that's possible," Garrick said with a grin. "Given the choice, I think the furball would prefer to come with me to my place than stay here with you. He absolutely adores me."

As if he understood what Garrick was saying, Ainin turned his back on him, curled up next to Amy and laid his head in her lap.

"You were saying?" she said.

"Damn dog," Garrick grumbled. Then he raised his voice a little. "It's up to you boy. You can stay here or you can come with me and get fed."

"That's bribery."

"And?" Garrick indicted toward the open bedroom door with his head. "Come on boy."

Ainin looked at Amy, then at Garrick. His eyes went back to Amy, his face saying, 'I would prefer to stay with you, but he has food', then he jumped off the bed and ran out of the room.

"I can tell you're male," Amy called after him. "Always thinking with your stomach."

Garrick left her alone and soon returned with a couple of boiled eggs in eggcups and a few slices of toast, cut into soldiers. He instructed Amy to sit up straight and placed the tray on her lap.

He then undressed and got back into bed beside her.

After sharing the breakfast, in more intimate ways than Amy could tell her mother, Amy got dressed while Garrick stacked the dishwasher. For someone so job-focused, he was surprisingly domesticated.

"Are you sure you don't mind going to see Lawrence?" Garrick asked when Amy finally made it into the kitchen.

"No, it's fine. I like Lawrence and Rosemary." She purposely didn't mention Nadia. If Garrick noticed, he didn't comment.

"We'll have to go to my place first, so I can get changed."

Amy looked him up and down. His clothes did seem a bit rumpled, which was hardly surprising seeing as they had been dumped on the floor and left there all night.

"You may be right."

Ainin insisted on going along, so they took Amy's car. It was the first time Amy had visited Garrick's house and she was impressed. It wasn't the bachelor pad she had been expecting.

The small, one storey house was neat and tidy. It was tastefully decorated and everything seemed to fit. It lacked personal items, like family photos, but Amy could understand why. If a rogue werewolf managed to find where Garrick lived and broke in, Garrick wouldn't want pictures of his family members on display.

Even the games console and his collection of first person shooters were hidden in a drawer so they couldn't be seen.

The kitchen was spotless.

"How do you keep this place so clean?" Amy couldn't help asking.

"That's easy. I don't spend that much time here. I often eat at headquarters and sometimes even sleep there. And I have a cleaner who comes in once a week."

"You'll have to see if she can do my place as well. She does a great job."

"Yes, he does." Garrick emphasised the 'he' and Amy blushed. It was normal to assume that a cleaner was a woman, but it was incorrect to do so.

Ainin raced around the house, checking out every room before giving his seal of approval by going into the back garden and peeing on a plant.

Amy asked if Garrick needed any help getting changed. Both knew it would be a mistake; the chances were they wouldn't make it out of the bedroom for hours.

Instead, Amy was left to wander around the house while Garrick changed his clothes. Only then was she permitted entry into his bedroom.

Once again, she was surprised. It didn't look like a man's bedroom. The quilt cover and matching pillowcases were a tasteful shade of grey, as were the walls. The blinds were pulled up, allowing Amy a great view of the garden. The sun shining through the window lit up the room, making it feel warm and welcoming.

"I have a confession to make," Garrick said as she stared out of the window. "It was Tab who decorated this place. She did everything, including buying the bed. I have no idea why she chose such a big one, but it's certainly comfortable."

"Maybe she thought you were into orgies," Amy teased. "She has good taste."

Garrick took her into his arms. "She likes you, so she must have," he said, then kissed the top of her nose. "We should get going. Where's that mutt of yours?"

"Watering your plants."

Garrick shook his head and took hold of Amy's hand. "Come on."

Once they were in the car, Garrick was about to put it into gear and pull away when Amy stopped him.

"Aren't you forgetting something?"

She opened the glove box and took out the blindfold she had worn every time she had been to Lawrence and Rosemary's house.

Garrick smiled at her. "I think I can trust you, don't you? Lawrence would agree."

"It's not about trust, it's about safety. We can't know for sure that I won't be taken again or that they won't find some way of getting into my mind."

"You're wearing your chain aren't you?"

"Of course, but it's still not worth the risk. I would feel happier not knowing where we are going."

"Alright." Garrick didn't sound happy about it, but in this situation, his happiness wasn't high on Amy's priority list. Lawrence and his family were doing a lot for the werewolf community and their safety had to come first.

185

Amy insisted that the blindfold remain in place until they had arrived at the house. They received a warm welcome from Lawrence and Rosemary, though they seemed more excited to see Ainin than they did either Amy or Garrick.

There was no sign of Nadia, much to Amy's relief.

They were escorted to the back yard, where they were offered cold drinks, then Lawrence took Garrick away to discuss business, promising not to keep him long.

Rosemary took the opportunity to ask Amy about her relationship with Garrick. She was pleased they had become a couple and wanted to know all the details, but Amy refused to say anything.

Hearing movement behind them, both ladies turned around, expecting to see Lawrence and the man in question approaching, but instead Amy's eyes met Nadia's. Her face fell.

"Nadia, how nice to see you," Rosemary said as she stood up to greet her daughter. "I wasn't expecting you home so soon."

"It was boring so I left early," Nadia said then kissed her mother on the cheek.

"Let me get you a drink."

Amy was not happy about being left alone with Nadia, but there was nothing she could do about it. Nadia dropped into the seat her mother had just vacated and turned to Amy.

"Who the hell do you think you are?" she said. It came out as a growl. "You come in here, make yourself at home. You're nothing but a filthy half-breed who doesn't deserve to associate with the likes of us."

Amy opened her mouth to protest, but the words stuck in her throat. The look Nadia was giving her was filled with pure hate.

Nadia hadn't finished. "Garrick is mine, not yours and if you don't end things with him soon, I am going to kill you."

Confrontation

Amy glared at Nadia. She didn't feel frightened. Instead she felt angry. All she wanted to do was wipe the smug smile off her face. She heard someone snarling and it took her a moment to realise it was her.

Nadia's face dropped. She no longer looked so sure of herself. She went pale and stood up, putting more distance between them. When Amy stood and moved closer, Nadia backed away.

Amy had no idea what was frightening her, but something was.

The sound of someone approaching caught her attention and she swung her head around. Rosemary was walking toward them, carrying a glass filled with orange liquid. The moment their eyes met, Rosemary stopped moving and dropped the glass, which bounced on the soft grass, spilling its contents everywhere.

"Lawrence," she called out loudly. It wasn't quite a scream, but it was close.

She then began moving, very slowly, closer. "It's okay, Amy," she said softly. "Everything's going to be okay."

Amy frowned in confusion. Why was Rosemary acting as though she was scared of her? Or was she scared for her?

When she was close enough to Nadia to speak without shouting, she said, "I have no idea what you did, but I suggest you get out of here. Now."

She stepped in front of her daughter, who was trying to protest her innocence.

"Just go," Rosemary snapped. "You can tell me your lies later." She never took her eyes off Amy as she spoke and looked like she was ready to run.

Nadia huffed, but slowly backed away. It was almost as if she didn't want to turn her back on Amy, as though keeping her in sight while she retreated was essential. Amy felt this sudden overwhelming desire to laugh, but managed to stop herself from doing so.

Lawrence came running down the path from the house, Garrick a few steps behind him. Both men skidded to a halt beside Rosemary. It was Lawrence who found his voice first.

"May I come closer?" he asked.

Amy had no idea why he was asking. "Of course," she tried to say, but all that came out was a snarl. Instead she nodded her head.

She didn't move as Lawrence stepped closer. Garrick also took a step forward, but Lawrence looked at him and shook his head.

Once he was close enough, Lawrence took hold of her hands. Amy did nothing to stop him.

"Look at me," he said gently.

Amy did so and could see his face was filled with worry.

"Take a deep breath," he told her. "Slowly in and slowly out." Amy obeyed and was told to repeat the procedure a few times.

The tightness in Lawrence's face relaxed and he almost managed a smile. "How are you feeling?" he asked.

"Confused," she said, relieved that she was able to form the words.

"I'm not surprised. Come and sit down."

He escorted her back to her chair and beckoned the other two to join them.

"What happened?" Amy asked. The way everyone was looking at her was making her nervous.

"That's what we are hoping you can tell us, honey." Garrick sounded tense, but he wasn't showing it. He had taken hold of one of her hands and was rubbing it gently.

"I don't know. Why is everyone looking like they fear me?"

"Your eyes changed colour. They turned yellow, like a wolf's. It's a sign that you were about to transform."

"I was what?" Amy hoped she had misheard.

"I'm not saying you were," Garrick quickly said. "You just looked like you were."

"But I don't know how to transform."

"We know," Lawrence said soothingly. "That's why we were so worried. Transforming without knowing what you are doing is dangerous for yourself and others around you. So what happened to make you want to turn into a wolf?"

"Nothing," Amy said. "I didn't want to turn into a wolf."

"Part of you wanted to and the way your eyes were lit up, I think you wanted to attack someone."

Amy couldn't speak. She had been angry at Nadia for the way she had threatened her, but she hadn't wanted to cause her physical harm.

"Nadia must have said something to her," Rosemary said. "Amy was fine when I left the two of them alone."

"I'd like to know what," Garrick said. "That was a rather extreme reaction."

"I don't want to talk about it," Amy said hastily. She couldn't tell them what Nadia had said; they would never believe her.

"That's okay," Garrick said before Rosemary or Lawrence could speak. "You don't have to if you don't want to."

A look passed between the two men. Amy had no idea what it meant, but it stopped Lawrence from speaking.

"Would I have attacked someone? Have I become dangerous?"

"I don't think so," Lawrence said. "You just needed a moment to get yourself under control. Now it's happened once, you know what it feels like and you can take steps to calm yourself down."

Amy realised she was shaking. Garrick moved his chair close and put his arm around her.

"It's okay. No harm was done."

"I don't think it's a good idea to put her through any tests today," Rosemary said and Lawrence nodded his head in agreement. "I'll put the kettle on. Maybe a cup of sweet tea will help her relax."

Amy hated sweet tea, but didn't have the heart to say so. Rosemary meant well and she appreciated her kindness.

"I hear you've been busy tracking down the rogue werewolves who implanted that device in Amy," Lawrence said to Garrick.

Amy knew he was just trying to take her mind off what had happened by talking about something else and she was grateful to him.

Garrick told him everything, though Amy suspected that he knew most of the details already. When he talked about the suicides, Amy interrupted with a question.

"Is it really possible for a werewolf to control someone to make them kill themselves?"

It was Lawrence who answered. "Yes, if the person is strong enough and the mind they are trying to manipulate is weak enough. Think of it like hypnotism, only much more powerful."

"So you're saying that Lia implanted into their minds the need to kill themselves if they were captured and questioned and there was nothing they could do to stop themselves doing it?"

"Something like that. It's actually a bit more complicated, but that's the general gist."

Amy shivered. "I'm never going to take my necklace off if it will prevent that happening to me. The Agency will have to cut it from my cold dead body if they ever want it back."

Garrick chuckled and Lawrence smiled.

"What's so funny?" Rosemary asked as she approached with a tray.

"Nothing important, my dear," Lawrence said and stood up to take the tray from his wife and place it on the table.

As well as four cups and the teapot, Amy noticed the tray contained a jug of milk and a bowl of sugar cubes. That meant the tea hadn't been poured yet so Amy would be able to have hers without either of the additives.

"Is there any limit to what Lia can make someone do?" she asked.

"I don't know. She's powerful, but until I meet her, I have no idea just how powerful." Lawrence almost sounded as if he was looking forward to it.

"Can you do it?" Amy asked. "Can you make someone do something they don't want to?"

"Unfortunately, yes. Every chain that is created has to be tested before it can be given to the designated owner. Agents volunteer to be the guinea pigs and I'm the one who tries to break into their minds."

"They must trust you very much."

"Far from it," Garrick said, giving Lawrence a sideways grin. "We just trust that Kenny makes them properly."

The comment made Rosemary laugh and a smile crept onto Amy's face.

The four of them stayed chatting about other things non-werewolf related for a while. Amy liked the two werewolves. They made her feel at home, part of the family. It was just a shame that Nadia lived at home still. Amy had no idea where she had gone and didn't feel the need to ask; she was just glad that she was no longer nearby.

Every now and then she caught Garrick looking at her, checking she was okay. He must have been desperate to ask what caused her episode, but he didn't bring it up.

"We should be going," he said as the sun was reaching its zenith. "I promised Amy I would take her to lunch. Now where has Ainin got to?"

He must have heard his name because Ainin materialised, bounding toward them from the far end of the garden.

"He has great hearing," Garrick said as he held out his hand to Amy and helped her rise.

Garrick grabbed the tray from the table and Amy picked up a few glasses which there hadn't been room for, and they made their way to the kitchen.

Nadia was in there. Garrick quickly glanced at Amy before entering the room.

"Just leave them on the side," Nadia said. "I'll stack the dishwasher."

"I need to use the bathroom before we go," Amy said and almost ran down the corridor. Seeing Nadia had made her edgy.

Not nervous, but angry once more and she needed to get away from her.

She took care of her business and returned to the kitchen. The door was open so she could see inside and clearly hear the conversation going on. Both Nadia and Garrick had their backs to her so did not know she was listening in.

"What did you say to upset Amy?" Garrick asked.

"Nothing. How can you blame me?"

"Because I know you."

Nadia huffed. "I only told her the truth, that's all. That's she's just a half-breed who doesn't deserve to associate with the likes of us."

Garrick shook his head. "I never took you for a snob, Nadia. It's an ugly characteristic that's unbecoming on you. But that wouldn't be enough to get her angry. What else did you say?"

"I just pointed out that she wasn't good enough for you, that you deserve better."

Garrick turned so he was looking at Nadia. Amy held her breath, wondering what he was going to say.

"Not good enough?" She could hear how incredulous he was. "Who are you to judge who is and isn't good enough for me? You hardly know Amy. If you bothered to take the time to find out who she really is you would find out she is far too good for the likes of me. I'm lucky to have her."

Amy's eyes widened as Nadia got closer to Garrick and put her arms around his neck.

"But we both know I'm the one you want. You would be so much happier with me. You love me just like I love you. Why don't you just admit it?"

Garrick took hold of Nadia's wrists and pulled her arms away from him. "Nadia, you're right, I do love you."

Tears filled Amy's eyes. She wanted to run and hide, but she couldn't get her legs to move. She couldn't tear her eyes away as Garrick continued.

"I love you like a sister. You mean a great deal to me, but that's all you will ever be. I hope things work out with Amy, but if they don't, it won't be you I move on to. I have never felt that way about you and I never will. I'm sorry if my words hurt you, but I have never done anything to make you think otherwise."

"You're lying," Nadia said. "You're just using Amy to get me jealous."

Garrick shook his head. How he was staying so calm, Amy had no idea.

"I'm falling in love with Amy. Now you can either be happy for me, or you can stay out of our lives. Right now, I don't care which."

He turned his back on Nadia and walked away. The minute he saw Amy, he stopped.

"How much of that did you hear?"

"Enough," she said. Tears were flowing down her face, but they were tears of joy. He was falling in love with her! "I love you, too."

Garrick walked up to her and gently wiped the tears from her face with his hand. Then his kissed her delicately on the lips.

"Come on. Let's get out of here. I want to show you just how much I want you and this time I won't take no for an answer."

Amy knew he didn't mean that literally and couldn't keep the smile from her face. "Trust me. I won't be saying no."

Devastation

Lia threw her phone down in frustration. It had been nearly two months since she told Derek about what happened to her group and still he was telling her to do nothing.

At least she had been able to ascertain that there hadn't been a traitor among them. It had never occurred to her that Garrick would put a tracker on Amy. She was seething when she found out. If she had known, she would never have taken her to the warehouse. She would have to be more careful from now on.

Derek was still talking about something big he had planned, but was refusing to give her any details. It was annoying. How was she supposed to make plans? All she could do was watch Amy. Garrick seemed to spend so much time there now that he had practically moved in. It was more or less impossible to get her alone, had she a reason to do so.

And she missed Warwick. This was unexpected. She wanted to call him and discuss what Derek could be up to. It wasn't that she missed the man, he was just someone to talk to. Now she had nobody.

She was well aware that he wasn't physically dead, but he was dead to her. He'd told the Agency everything he could about the implant, the resistance, his fellow werewolves. She was glad that she had prevented even him revealing anything important. It had caused a huge argument at the time and she wasn't sure she had done the right thing. Now she was.

Not that she blamed him. After what he had heard her say, it wasn't a surprise that he turned against her. She would have done the same herself, had it been to anyone other than the Agency. She hated them with a passion which just kept growing.

She'd begun to amuse herself by plotting what she would do to the head of the Agency when she got her hands on him. She knew who he was. Carl Weston. He had a lot to atone for. But nothing compared to those werewolves who betrayed their own kind by providing blood to the Agency. Lawrence, Rosemary and

Nadia. She had no idea where they lived, but eventually she would track them down and when she did... She didn't even need to finish the thought for it to make her smile.

Then she would move on to every werewolf that worked for every branch of the Agency. Once they were disposed of, the blood supply would run dry, turning Agents into ordinary men and women, making them easy pickings.

She'd often spoken of her plans to Warwick and he had said she was insane. Maybe she was, a little. She preferred to think she was just ambitious.

But all that would have to wait. For now she could do nothing. With nothing else to do, she decided to go to bed. Maybe the morning would bring news, but she wasn't holding her breath.

For once, she was right; the following day, she received a call from Derek. It was the first time he had called her; usually it was the other way around. And he had news. Big news. Whatever he had planned would be happening the next day and it would be global. He still refused to provide details, but promised he would call her as soon as the mission had been accomplished. That night Lia went to bed full of excitement and was, for once, looking forward to the morning.

-------------------------∞-------------------------

Garrick was lying on the sofa, watching TV. Amy was cuddled up next to him, her back pressed against his front. His arm was around her, pulling her close. He felt comfortable and content. Though he wasn't particularly interested in the show she was watching, he was happy to lay there with her in his arms. The drama would soon be finished and then they would head up to the bedroom.

His phone vibrated in his pocket and he apologised to Amy as he moved so he could retrieve it. Seeing it was Carl calling him, he almost ignored him. But his boss had been doing his best lately not to disturb him on evenings he was with Amy, so it was probably important.

"Hi, Carl," he said. He was looking at Amy as he spoke and saw her roll her eyes. He grinned at her.

The smile dropped from his face when Carl spoke. He had never heard him sound so stressed.

"I need you to come into headquarters. Immediately. You might want to bring Amy with you. All Agents are being called in."

The phone went dead before he could agree.

His concern must have shown on his face because Amy asked him what was wrong. She even paused the TV show so she could give him her full attention.

"I don't know," he admitted. "Everyone has been called in. Carl even suggested I bring you along."

"That doesn't sound good," Amy said and switched off the television. "Just let me get changed and I'll be ready to go."

While Amy was gone, Garrick went to the kitchen, making sure Ainin had plenty of food and water. He had no idea what they would be walking into, or how long they would be gone, so the dog would have to be left behind.

Then he checked his gun. He always carried it with him, just in case. He hoped he wouldn't need to use it, but something bad had obviously happened. If it was nothing too serious, Carl would have given him some details.

"Ready?" Amy asked as she entered the kitchen. She was dressed in black jeans and a white top with blue flowers on it. Garrick recognised it as one of her favourites. He didn't like it, but she did, so he kept his opinion to himself.

She had chosen to wear her low-heeled black boots. A good choice, given that they had no idea what they would be facing when they arrived at headquarters.

Garrick nodded in reply to her question and took her hand in his as he passed her on his way out of the room.

She grabbed her handbag and keys when they reached the front door and called out a goodbye to Ainin, who barked in reply.

"You're worried," Amy stated as Garrick drove. He had hardly spoken since getting into the car.

"Yes, I am," he said. "Carl has never called in all Agents before. And he has always given me information when passing on an instruction. Not that this was an instruction. It was an order."

"Why does he want me there?"

"I have no idea. And that's what's concerning me most."

They didn't speak again until they reached headquarters. They got there sooner than Amy had been expecting. Garrick was usually a careful driver, making sure he obeyed all road rules, but tonight he broke the speed limit and drove through a few red lights.

Other than Mack, who was standing guard, the reception room was eerily empty.

"Garrick. Amy. Any idea what's going on? I've never seen so many Agents gather here at the same time."

"I was hoping you could tell me," Garrick said. Mack shrugged. He obviously had no better idea than Garrick had.

Garrick used his ID to open the security doors and led Amy to the lifts. Unsure where to go, he selected the floor Carl's office was on.

The corridor was deserted, as was the office.

"Where is everyone?" Amy asked.

"I have no idea."

They were making their way back to the lifts when Carl's voice sounded over the loudspeaker.

"Would all personnel please make their way to the canteen."

"That makes sense," Garrick said. "It's the only room big enough for all of us."

The canteen was crowded by the time they got there. Garrick spotted his sister waving at him and manoeuvred them over to her. She had Tom with her.

"Any idea what the emergency is, Tab?"

His sister shook her head. "All I know is that Carl has called in everyone, not just the Agents. I was expressly told to bring Tom with me."

"It's good to see you Tom," Amy said. Over the past couple of months, she and Garrick had spent quite a bit of time with the

197

couple and she was now close to both Tabitha and her fiancé. He had popped the question a few weeks ago and, of course, Tabitha had said yes.

Garrick could see that Tom was worried. He was holding Tabitha's hand and kept squeezing it.

A hand fell on Garrick's shoulder and he looked around. Lawrence was standing behind him.

"It looks like Carl's called in everyone," he said. "I don't know why, but it can't be for anything good."

"Where's Rosemary?" Tabitha asked.

"The other end of the room, with Nadia. We didn't think it was a good idea to bring her over here." He glanced at Amy as he spoke.

"I appreciate that," Garrick said. He hadn't seen Nadia since she had made a move on him. She had called him a few times, but each time he hung up without answering. Her text messages and emails had been read, but not responded to. Until she stopped trying to change his mind about Amy, he wanted nothing more to do with her.

Silence descended and all eyes turned toward Carl, who had just walked in. Garrick had never seen him look so defeated. He seemed to have aged ten years since he had seen him only a few hours ago.

Carl cleared his throat to get everyone's attention before speaking loud enough for everyone in the room to hear.

"Thank you all for coming. I wish I hadn't had to call you all in. There are two reasons you are here. The first is so you can hear the news I have to deliver firsthand. I don't want any false rumours going round. The second is to make sure you are all alive."

Murmuring filled the room and the gathered crowd were looking at each other. Carl waited for the noise to die down.

"Reports have been coming in from all over the globe. There has been a massive werewolf uprising. Agency headquarters have been attacked in numerous cities around the world. Liverpool, Calais, Munich, San Francisco, Manila, Perth, to name but a few.

198

Nearly every country has reported violence and more reports are coming in."

There were gasps and Garrick thought he heard someone crying. It was worse than he could possibly have expected, but Carl hadn't finished speaking.

"Every branch of the Agency which has been attacked has been decimated. Everyone in the buildings were killed, human and werewolf, Agent and other personnel. We have lost a few branch heads. The names of the dead are being collated and will be shared, but it may take a few days to complete."

Questions were called out, but Carl ignored them. He waved his hands in a downward motion, silently calling for quiet.

"The good news is that all data is still secure. Names and addresses of Agency werewolves are still protected. So far it looks like every branch had time to enact priority one protocol, notifying High Command and changing their passwords. As you all know, none of our systems can be accessed without the right ID and password. All data is wiped if the wrong information is entered more than twice or if a hack is detected. No location is reporting a breach."

"What about those who weren't at their headquarters when they were attacked?" someone called out.

Carl wiped his hand down his face. He seemed worn out. Garrick didn't envy him. He couldn't imagine how hard it must be to give such grave news.

"We believe, in most cases, no warning was able to be given so Agents and other staff turned up as they usually would. All were executed. It seems that eventually the werewolves left the buildings they had taken over. All reports coming in now are from Agency workers who have shown up to find bodies everywhere."

"What are our orders?" a female voice asked. Garrick looked over to see who it was. He recognised her as an Agent, but didn't know her name. He felt proud of her. She was acting like a true Agent. Instead of reeling from the horror of what she had been told, she wanted to know what she could do to help.

"For now, nothing. We have people monitoring for more reports and they're setting up a list of attacked bases and the status of each. We will be taking a role call and anyone not accounted for will need to be found. We'll be sending out Agents in groups of no less than four. Until you hear otherwise, unless you are on assignment, you are not to leave these premises. High Command will be in contact. Every branch not affected by these attacks will be asked to send Agents to those that are and I will be looking for volunteers."

Hands immediately shot up.

"Thank you. But until we know what is needed and where, all I can do is take names. My assistant will be collecting a list of volunteers and their speciality, so if you would like to form an orderly queue at the table at the back of the room, it would be much appreciated."

He had hardly finished speaking before people were moving. Agents, scientists, admin personnel, even some of the cooks, all were volunteering to go to other branches and offer whatever assistance they could.

Carl made his way over to Garrick. He nodded at Amy. "I'm glad you were able to be here. We have no idea where the next attack will be and I'd rather know you are safe."

"What do you want us to do?' Tabitha asked.

"As soon as we know we're not next on the werewolves list of targets, I want you two," he pointed to Tabitha and Garrick, "to go out and find out anything you can. You both have good werewolf contacts. I know I said groups of no less than four, but Garrick won't appreciate being saddled with others so I'm making an exception."

He then turned to Lawrence. "I want you and your family to stay here. At least for the time being. Nobody knows where you live, other than myself, Garrick, Tom and Tab, but I'd rather not take any chances."

"I understand," he replied. Then he turned to Amy. "Amy, my dear, would you care to join Rosemary and myself in the library? I think Garrick is going to be busy for a while. Don't worry, I'll make sure Nadia keeps away."

He held out his hand and Amy took it. "In that case, I would love to."

She gave Garrick a quick kiss on the cheek and let Lawrence lead her away. Carl went with them.

"Is she okay?" Tom asked.

Garrick shook his head. "No. This news has been a shock to her, but she'll pretend she's fine until she's alone with Lawrence and Rosemary. They'll look after her."

He was watching her retreating back as he spoke. Then he turned to Tom. "Sorry, Tom, but I am going to have to drag your fiancée away."

"Where are we going?" Tabitha asked.

"You heard the boss. We're needed out on the streets, checking in on our contacts."

"I thought we were ordered to wait until we had been given the all clear."

"You weren't planning on obeying that order were you?"

He turned and walked away. Tabitha shook her head in resignation, kissed Tom goodbye and ran after him.

Aftermath

"I don't get it," Tabitha said as Garrick pulled away from the kerb. "We've spoken to every werewolf we can think of. Even those we know have contact with rogue wolves, but won't admit it. Nobody knew this was coming."

"Maybe only those in the cities which were attacked were told."

Tabitha shrugged. "Maybe. Where are we going now? Back to headquarters?"

"Not yet," her brother said. "We have one more stop to make first. Warwick has been most forthcoming since Lia turned her back on him. It's a long shot, but you never know, he may know something."

"Even if he does, will he be able to tell us?"

Garrick shrugged. "There's only one way to find out."

It didn't take them long to reach Warwick's apartment. Garrick had visited him there a few times since his capture and he was beginning to like the guy. He had been a great help, telling the Agency scientists everything he could about the implant he had invented.

Warwick was walking down the path when Garrick pulled up. He nodded his head when he spotted the two Agents, but he didn't smile.

"I was just coming to see you," he said as soon as they were out of the car. "Are the rumours true?"

"That depends on what you've heard."

"Let's go up and grab some coffee or something. I have a feeling this is going to take a while."

Warwick led them into his apartment building and they opted to take the stairs up the two flights to his floor.

His apartment was small, but fully functional. Garrick had been surprised at how clean it was the first time he went there. And the fact that the kitchen was not only well stocked with healthy food, but the number of semi-professional cooking items suggested Warwick was something of an accomplished chef. He lived alone, so it couldn't have been a girlfriend or boyfriend.

The smell that hit them when they entered made Garrick's mouth water. A fruit flan was cooling on the side and he couldn't help hoping he would be offered a slice.

Noticing where his eyes were, Warwick disappointed him by saying it wouldn't be ready for a while.

Warwick put the kettle on and told his guests to take a seat. The apartment was open plan, so he was able to talk to them from the kitchen. He told them everything he had heard.

Warwick knew a lot of details and, while most of it was either untrue or exaggerated, there was enough truth in it to make both Garrick and Tabitha concerned with how quickly the information had spread. It was almost as if someone was intentionally spreading the news.

Garrick then told Warwick what the Agency knew. Only half of the cities Warwick had been informed of had actually been attacked, at least that was the latest information Garrick and Tabitha had received. They were both well aware that more locations could have been added to the list since their last update.

"Did you know something like this was being planned?" Garrick asked.

Warwick shook his head. "Nothing was ever mentioned in front of me. I know Lia reported to someone who headed up the resistance in this country and he, in turn, reported to the global leader, but I wasn't even told his name. Nobody was."

He laughed cynically. "Resistance. I can't believe I'm still calling us that. What were we resisting?" He shook his head at his own disbelief.

It was a rhetorical question so neither Garrick nor Tabitha answered him.

Garrick stood up. "Thanks for the coffee. And the chat. If you hear anything that might be of interest, please let us know."

Warwick and Tabitha also stood. "Of course," he said. "Have you had any luck tracking down Lia?"

"Absolutely none. Have you heard from her at all?"

Warwick shook his head. "I'm not expecting to. Not unless she decides to kill me, which is unlikely. Too much effort. I'm not important enough to her, as she made abundantly clear."

Garrick could hear the bitterness that Warwick was still feeling. Not that he blamed him.

The two men shook hands. Then Garrick and Tabitha left.

"Are you sure you trust him?" Tabitha asked once they were in the car.

"I wouldn't use the word trust, but I have no reason to believe he's lying to us. We captured him so he is now on our radar. Lia wouldn't be stupid enough to keep in contact. She's good at keeping her identity secret. She's wouldn't risk being found out by visiting him or arranging to meet him somewhere just in case we are watching him or have his phone bugged. As he said, he's not important enough. She used him to make that implant and after that failed to achieve its purpose, she had no further use for him."

Garrick didn't like the way his sister was looking at him.

"How do you know it didn't achieve its purpose? How can you be sure what the purpose was?"

"Warwick told us."

"And you believe him?" Before Garrick could say anything, Tabitha continued. "How can you be certain he knew what the plan was? Or maybe Lia is preventing him from talking about the real motive?"

Garrick said nothing. Tabitha was right; he couldn't be certain. But what was the point in worrying about it? There was no way for them to find out. Amy had been sent to headquarters to kill as many people as possible. What other purpose could there possibly be? There was only one he could think of.

"Are you saying Amy is a spy?"

"Of course not," Tabitha said immediately. "I trust her as much as you do. I like her. I think she's good for you. I don't believe she would ever do anything to hurt you."

"So what are you suggesting?"

"I'm not suggesting anything. I'm just pointing out that you can't possibly know as much as you think you do."

The rest of the journey back to headquarters was made in silence. Garrick didn't like the fact that Tabitha was right.

Mack was still on duty when they entered the building.

"Don't they ever give you time off?" Tabitha asked, smiling at him.

"My shift finished an hour ago, but I volunteered to stay here. All Agents have reported in, but there are a couple of scientists, one analyst and one of the guys from admin who are yet to be accounted for. Agents are being sent out to look for them and guards requested to accompany them."

"No surprise there," Garrick said. "All of your guys put duty first. I don't think any of your team know the meaning of work/life balance."

Mack raised his eyebrows at him. "And you do?"

Tabitha patted Garrick's cheek. "He does now he has Amy."

Garrick pushed her hand away and growled at her, making her laugh. Even Mack chuckled. The comment and his reaction weren't particularly funny, but given what had happened, you had to find amusement where you could.

They said farewell to Mack and went through the security door.

"Go and see Tom," Garrick said. "He's sure to be worried about you. I'll report to Carl."

Tabitha didn't argue.

When she got out of the lift, she didn't say goodbye or look behind her as she made her way down the corridor. Garrick watched her with a trace of amusement. She wasn't running, as that wouldn't be dignified, but she was walking at a much faster pace than normal.

He liked Tom, a lot, and was pleased that he was going to become part of the family. Tom was good for his sister and treated her well. He made her happy and that was all that really mattered to Garrick.

The lift announced he had reached the floor Carl's office was on and the doors opened. It always annoyed him when the lift spoke. It was unnecessary. He was more than capable of reading the display which told him what floor he was on. He didn't like the superior tone of the voice recording. It was almost as if the machine was giving him orders.

Of course, he hadn't mentioned this to anyone, just in case they thought he was going mad.

He found a tired looking Carl in his office. He looked up when Garrick knocked on the open door and beckoned him in.

"Please tell me you have some good news."

Garrick shook his head. "Unfortunately not. Nobody has heard anything."

"Anything they will admit to, you mean."

Garrick shook his head once more. "No. I mean nobody knew this was coming. Most didn't even know it had happened. Rumours are flying around the werewolf community, but not many believe them. And not all of it is true. Unless more cities have fallen. How's Buenos Aires, for example?"

He didn't like the look that crossed Carl's face.

"Gone."

Garrick was shocked. "What do you mean 'gone'?"

"It was completely wiped out. Every Agent and all support staff. Everyone. Only the wolves who supplied their blood are safe. They weren't there when it was attacked. Nobody could contact the base so Lawrence phoned his counterpart and asked if she was prepared to investigate. He advised against it, but had to ask anyway. She ignored him and said she would go."

"What did she find?" Garrick asked, though he wasn't sure he wanted to know.

"Bodies. Everywhere. They had been torn to pieces. She immediately called High Command. They sent her a list of all staff, with photos. Retired Agents in the vicinity were called in and between them they managed to identify every body. The only ones not among the dead are a couple who are honeymooning in the Caribbean and a small number who are on vacation."

"Jesus," Garrick said. "They must have stayed there for hours, waiting for each shift to arrive. Do you think they knew the pattern and the times of the change-overs?"

206

Carl shrugged, though it looked like the movement took a lot of effort.

"How many other cities have been hit?' Garrick asked.

"Since you left, other than Argentina, only South Africa and Sweden have reported casualties. Sweden had two locations attacked. Berlin was also hit, but they got the warning from Munich so were prepared and managed to prevent the wolves getting into any secure areas."

"I didn't realise the resistance was so well co-ordinated. Or so widely spread."

"None of us did. High Command is in shock."

"They're not the only ones," Garrick muttered. He couldn't imagine there was anyone working for the Agency who wasn't.

He studied Carl closely. He didn't look well. His skin was pale and there were bags under his eyes.

"Have you managed to get any sleep?" he asked. He and Tabitha had been gone for several hours and he was exhausted. He couldn't imagine how Carl was feeling.

"I've been busy."

"You'll do nobody any good if you collapse. Go and grab a bed in one of the rooms for a few hours. I'm sure someone can cover for you."

"You should try to get some rest as well. Amy is still with Lawrence and Rosemary in the library. Last I looked, she was asleep in one of the chairs, though how she managed to get comfortable enough to drop off I have no idea. Take her home. It should be safe enough."

"Yes Sir."

Carl shook his head at the younger man's insolence.

Before obeying the instructions, Garrick made sure Carl was in bed and that someone who had already managed to grab a few hours sleep was in his office, with strict instructions to only disturb him if absolutely necessary.

Amy was still sleeping when Garrick entered the library. Lawrence and Rosemary were both still awake. There was no sign of Nadia.

"How is she?" Garrick asked.

"Shocked. Stressed. Scared. Confused. As you can imagine, this wasn't something she was expecting to happen."

"It wasn't something any of us were expecting."

"No, but we have been in this business for a long time. This world is all new to her. She must be wondering exactly what she has gotten herself into."

Garrick took a seat. "It's not as if she had a choice. She can't change what she is. Having said that, if there was a way to get her out of this, I would."

"I know. And so does she. What I think she needs right now is for you to take her home and take her mind off it."

Garrick tried to smile, but failed. He was exhausted, but that didn't mean he planned on going straight to sleep.

"That is exactly what I plan on doing."

Liverpool

Garrick looked down at Amy, who was sleeping in the bed next to him. Her hair was all over the pillow and she was making quiet noises as she dreamed. He hoped she was dreaming about him, but he had no way of knowing.

He had successfully taken both of their minds off what had happened and he had slept well, for a few hours, until the sound of his phone vibrating woke him.

It was a text from Carl, informing him that the affected cities had all requested assistance. A few key Agents and other workers were being asked to deploy. They were being asked, not ordered, and could say no. Garrick was one of them. Liverpool had lost all its most senior Agents and they needed someone who could quickly take control.

He had yet to give a response.

A few months ago, he would have immediately said yes, but now, as he looked down at Amy, he wasn't sure if he could leave her.

He gently ran his hand down her cheek and she stirred in her sleep.

"Hello, beautiful," he said when her eyes fluttered open.

"What time is it?" she asked as she stretched.

"A little after nine."

She sat up in a panic. "I have to go to work."

"It's okay," he said, soothingly. "It's Saturday."

He didn't blame her for not remembering. It had been a long night; they hadn't gotten in until after four in the morning and she had only just woken up. Her brain hadn't had time to kick into gear.

She sighed as she lay back down. It was a contented sigh, one he hoped to hear more often. "I suppose we had better get up." Then she smiled. "Unless you have something better in mind?"

As much as he wanted to say yes, he had something he needed to talk to her about.

"We need to talk." To his own ears, the words sounded harsh.

"Okay," she said and pulled herself up so she was leaning against the headboard. Garrick moved the quilt up so it was covering her once more.

"I have been asked to go to Liverpool, to help them until they can get new Agents permanently based there."

"How long will you be gone?"

The question took him by surprise. He had been expecting an argument. He didn't think she would beg him not to go, but he was prepared for a heated discussion. Her outright acceptance wasn't one of the scenarios which had played out in his mind.

"Wait a minute. I haven't said I'm going yet."

"Of course you're going. How can you not? They need you there right now."

"But what about you?"

"I'll be fine. I have a feeling Carl will have other Agents keeping an eye on me and Lawrence anticipated you would be called away and has already said I can stay with them if ever I feel vulnerable."

Garrick grunted. While he appreciated the kind offer, he couldn't see how it would work, not while Nadia lived there.

Amy placed her hand on his cheek. "I'll be fine."

"You'd better be," he said, then leaned forward to kiss her.

He pulled back when a thought struck him.

"Come with me."

Amy laughed. "You know I can't. I have work. And study. And it's not as if you're going on a sight-seeing tour. What would I do all day, or night, while you are working?"

"I'll think of something."

She placed her other hand on his other cheek so she was cradling his head.

"You know I love you, but it just wouldn't work. It's not as if we won't be able to speak each day over Skype or Facebook Messenger or something. And it won't be forever."

"It will be for a few months." He should have been persuading Amy that he needed to go; instead he found himself trying to convince her, and himself, that he shouldn't.

"And they will be the longest few months of my life." She kissed his lips. "Now go and tell Carl you have made your decision."

"Yes, Ma'am."

Garrick turned so he could reach his phone on the bedside table, then changed his mind. This was something he should do in person. He turned his attention back to Amy.

"Now what were you saying about doing something more fun than getting out of bed?"

It was quite a few hours later that Garrick walked into Carl's office carrying a hold-all.

"What's that?" he asked.

He looked like he hadn't slept, though Garrick had been told he'd had a few hours. Stubble covered his usually clean shaven jaw and his moustache needed a trim. His clothes were crumpled as though he had slept in them, which, Garrick thought, he probably had.

"I took a detour on the way here to your place. Your wife insisted I bring you some clean clothes."

Carl held out his hand for the bag. "She looks after me too well. I don't deserve her."

"She also put in a can of deodorant." Garrick theatrically sniffed at his boss. "And from the smell of you, you need to use it."

"If you've just come here to insult me, you can get out of my office right now."

Garrick stepped back, grinning. "Actually, I've come to let you know I'll go to Liverpool. When do you need me to depart?"

"As soon as possible. Go see the travel section and they'll make all the arrangements for you."

Garrick nodded his confirmation and headed up two floors to the admin department. He didn't visit 'travel' often and didn't know anyone who worked there.

Usually there was only one or two people in that part of the building, but today it was teeming with workers, all busy booking flights and accommodation for the Agents and peripheral staff who would be flying out to the stricken cities.

He walked up to the nearest desk and took the seat in front of it. The woman on the other side didn't even look up as she said, "Just give me a moment."

Garrick watched her tapping on her keyboard, her eyes never leaving her screen. She was wearing headphones, though whether she was on the phone or listening to music, Garrick didn't know.

"That's all booked for you," she said and Garrick almost asked how she knew where he was going, then he realised she wasn't speaking to him.

"My pleasure," she said. She took the headphones off her head and turned her attention to Garrick. She didn't bother to introduce herself. "Where and when?"

Garrick didn't take offence at the lack of courtesy. She wasn't being rude; she was just busy.

"Liverpool, as soon as possible."

Her eyes were on her screen once more as she started typing.

"Just you?" she asked.

"Yes."

"I can get you on a 7 pm flight tonight to London then you have the choice of taking a connecting flight or the train. I recommend the latter. It will save you hanging around at the airport for a few hours and you will get there sooner."

"Fine by me," Garrick said. He wasn't a snob as far as public transport was concerned and he was looking forward to catching the tube, as his British counterparts referred to their underground system.

"Will the Titanic hotel be alright, or would you prefer the Radisson? The Titanic has better reviews, but no pool."

"The Radisson will do." He'd stayed in the Radisson the last time he visited Sydney and he found it adequate. He assumed the one located in the UK would be much the same.

"All booked for you, Mister Barton. Details have been sent to your phone and email address. Is your passport up to date or do I need to arrange one for you?"

"No, it's fine thanks. How do you know who I am? I don't think we've met before, have we?"

For the first time since he had sat down opposite her, she seemed to actually look at him and give him her full attention.

"Everybody knows who you are Mister Barton. Now is there anything else I can help you with?"

"Please, call me Garrick. I think that's everything. Thank you."

He stood up, but the woman spoke to him again before he could leave.

"It you need local currency, go and see Sally over there, last desk on the left."

"Will do," Garrick said. "Thanks for all your help."

"My pleasure. If you'll excuse me." She didn't wait for an answer before putting her headphones back on and speaking into the microphone.

"I guess I'm dismissed," he said to himself, too quietly for her to hear.

Sally turned out to be just as efficient as whoever had booked his travel and accommodation. He wished he had gotten her name. He felt he had been rude in not doing so, but she had seemed too busy to be bothered with such a trivial question.

He told Sally where he was going and she went to one of the draws in her desk and withdrew a few bundles of notes. She counted half a dozen and handed them over.

"They're mixed bundles of tens, twenties and fifties. You'll also want this." She handed over a plastic card.

"What's this?" he asked as he picked it up and inspected it.

"An Oyster card. You'll need it for the train and underground."

"Thanks," he said and placed it in his pocket, along with the money.

He stood up and turned to walk away, but turned back when Sally loudly cleared her throat. She was pushing a piece of paper toward him and tapping part of it with a long fingernail. It was painted bright red, he couldn't help but notice. He wondered, momentarily, if her nails were real.

"Sign here. Get receipts for everything if you don't want it deducted from your wages."

"I will," Garrick said. He couldn't help smiling as he signed his name where she was indicating.

"Enjoy your trip Mister Barton."

"I'm sure I will," he said, though something told him he was lying.

Separation

Garrick had been in the UK for over a month and he had had enough. The people were nice enough and he enjoyed the sightseeing, what little he had been able to do. But the weather was getting him down. And he missed Amy. He knew he was going to, but not as much as he was. Their nightly video calls were no longer enough for him. He wanted to do more than see her. He wanted to hold her, kiss her, make love to her.

He'd had plenty of offers since arriving in Liverpool, but he had turned every single one down. He hadn't even gone out for a drink or lunch with anyone.

And then there was the accent. He was just getting used to it when support arrived from Glasgow and Northern Ireland. While the Scots and the Irish were all great people and an immense help to him as he tried to get the Liverpool branch back on its feet, they all liked to drink and wouldn't take no for an answer whenever he was invited to join them. They didn't become too rowdy or unpleasant to be around, but by the end of the evening he couldn't understand anything they were saying.

He was feeling down when he called Amy and even seeing her face didn't cheer him up. It was her birthday, her first one since they had become a couple, and he couldn't be there with her.

She had plans to go out with friends and Lawrence and Rosemary had invited her over at the weekend, so it wasn't as if she would be lonely or missing out on celebrating, but that didn't help.

He was close to telling Carl that he had had enough and was going home, but he was still needed where he was and would be for at least another month, maybe two.

He hated not being able to wish Amy a happy birthday in person. He had arranged with his sister to buy her a present, but it felt like a meaningless gesture as he couldn't give it to her himself.

Amy assured him that she was fine, but to his eyes, she looked tired. He didn't ask if she was sleeping properly as she would say she was even if it wasn't true.

Work and her studies were keeping her busy and several Agents dropped by to visit regularly, to make sure she was alright, even Carl.

"I miss you," he said, thinking it was a huge understatement.

"I miss you too," she said. "So does Ainin." As if on cue, the dog barked his agreement. "When are you coming back?"

He wished he could give her an answer, but he couldn't. Instead he told her about his trip to London the previous weekend, describing how he became the typical tourist. She seemed to find his commentary amusing, or maybe she was just being polite.

All too soon they had to end the call, as both had places they needed to be.

As he closed his computer, Garrick sighed. He wasn't sure how he was going to survive the rest of the week, let alone the next month or two.

------------------------∞------------------------

"I am not going to blindfold you," Tabitha said. "That is absolutely ridiculous."

Amy stared at her and refused to get into the car. Her arms were folded and she had no intention of moving unless her terms were complied with.

"Then I'm not going," she said. She could be stubborn when she wanted to, as Garrick had found out. "Please give my apologies to Rosemary and Lawrence."

Tabitha huffed. "No wonder Garrick complains about you," she muttered, intentionally loud enough for Amy to hear. "Do I really want to know what you and Garrick do with this?" she asked, holding out the blindfold Amy had given her.

"Not what you think," Amy replied, though the look on Tabitha's face suggested she didn't believe her.

216

Only once the blindfold was in place did Amy get into the car. Tabitha was driving Amy's car. Ainin was already secured in the back seat and was watching them both with an amused look on his face.

"It really isn't necessary you know," Tabitha said as she put the car into gear.

"Yes, it is. It's not worth taking any risks. Rosemary and Lawrence have been good to me. I don't want to risk their safety. The same applies to you. Why do you think I always refuse to come to your house?"

"I figured it was because Garrick let you know how messy it is."

Amy laughed. "He has warned me about that."

The journey didn't take as long as normal and Amy couldn't help wondering how many road rules Tabitha broke. She just hoped none had been caught on camera as it was Amy who would receive the fine.

There was no sign of Nadia when they arrived. Tabitha had promised that she wouldn't be there; it had been the only way she had managed to persuade Amy to spend the day there.

Amy had no proof that the threatening emails she had been receiving had come from Nadia, but she had her suspicions. She hadn't mentioned them to anyone as they were easy to ignore. They always came from the same email address, which she had now sent to go directly into the 'junk' folder and they got deleted without being read.

The phone calls, however, were another matter. If they continued, she would tell Carl. She didn't want to upset Lawrence and Rosemary by saying someone kept phoning her then not saying anything until she hung up and she thought it was their daughter. Nadia was also Tabitha's best friend so she couldn't confide in her. Telling Garrick was completely out of the question; he would catch the next plane home.

Rosemary had cooked a fantastic lunch and baked a birthday cake. It was a lemon drizzle cake and Amy had never tasted one with so much flavour. She wasn't a huge chocolate fan, but she greatly appreciated citrus.

Tom couldn't join them, as he was working, but he would be dropping by later.

Amy didn't ask where Nadia was or when she would be home. She was enjoying herself and didn't want to spoil her mood by thinking about the woman.

Since Garrick had flown to England, Lawrence had visited her a few times, working with her on her werewolf powers, none of which she was able to willingly tap into, despite numerous attempts.

Today, however, was about celebrating her birthday, so no mention of her werewolf side was made. Her mother still didn't know. Amy saw no need to tell her. She visited her as regularly as she used to before she found out the truth about her father and Garrick had gone with her a few times, but what Garrick really did for a living was kept a closely guarded secret.

Mary, her mother, seemed quite taken with Garrick and made a great deal of fuss over him whenever he visited. Amy didn't blame her. Not only was he attractive, with a great body, but he could also be very charismatic when he wanted to.

"You should go and visit him," Rosemary said as the two women stacked the dishwasher while Lawrence washed up the things that were too big to go in. Tabitha had been placed in charge of making coffee.

"You know I can't do that. I have work and my studies."

"Haven't your studies finished for the term?" Lawrence asked.

Amy hadn't realised he had been keeping that close an eye on her.

"Yes, but I have a dissertation I need to work on."

"I'm sure that can be done just as easily in England as it can here," Rosemary said.

"Maybe, but what about work?"

"I'm sure they'll let you take a week or so off. Even on this short notice."

"I don't know." Amy genuinely had no idea if what Rosemary was saying was true or not.

"Ask them. When was the last time you took a holiday?"

Amy tried to answer, but she couldn't remember when she had taken anything more than a couple of days off. Her manager had been bugging her about the amount of leave days she had accumulated.

"Give your boss a call."

"I can't. It's Saturday."

"So? He calls you on the weekends sometimes."

"Only about important work matters."

"So?"

Amy tried to argue more, but soon gave up. Rosemary was quite a force to be reckoned with when she set her mind on something. Reluctantly she dialled her boss's number. He had no problem with her calling him outside of work hours and was more than happy to approve her taking a week off, starting the following weekend, on the condition that she finished the two things she was working on.

"Any more excuses?" Rosemary asked, with a twinkle in her eye and a smile on her face.

"I guess not. I suppose I'll have to go to a travel agency on Monday in my lunch hour. Though getting a flight at such short notice will be a problem. At a decent price, anyway."

Lawrence was drying his hands on a towel, having finished washing up the things that didn't fit in the dishwasher. "Come with me," he said and led her to his office.

He moved the spare seat from in front of his desk and positioned it next to his before indicating that Amy should sit. He switched on his computer and logged on to his favourite flight booking website. It didn't take long for him to find a flight leaving the following Saturday at a reasonable price and the return one a week later.

Before Amy knew what was happening, her flights had been booked and paid for. Amy tried to insist on using her own credit card, but Lawrence said he had an account so it would be too difficult to change the payment details. Amy knew he was lying, but also knew he wouldn't let her pay him back no matter how hard she tried. Instead of arguing, she just thanked him.

"This way," he said, "I can guarantee you'll go."

"Everything sorted?" Tabitha asked when they walked into the lounge to find the two women drinking coffee. Two extra steaming mugs were on the table.

"Yes. Flights have been booked and paid for, so she can't back out now. She just needs to sort out some local currency, but she can do that at the airport."

"Garrick is going to be so excited when you tell him," Rosemary said as Amy sat down on the sofa and picked up her drink.

"I'm not going to tell him," she said. She blew on her mug and placed it back down. It was too hot to drink. "I don't want to get his hopes up just in case something goes wrong."

Tabitha burst out laughing. "I would give almost anything to see his face when you show up at his hotel." Then she turned serious. "What are you doing tomorrow?"

"Nothing that can't be postponed. Why?"

"Because you and me are going to go shopping. You're gonna need some new lingerie for the trip."

Amy groaned, wishing she had said she was going to be busy.

Visit

Nadia couldn't keep the smile off her face as she walked away from her father's study. Her date had not gone well and she couldn't get away from him soon enough. She had hoped to sneak into the house unnoticed and head up to her room, but couldn't resist eavesdropping when she heard her father talking to Amy in his study.

She had heard everything. Not just that Amy was planning on visiting Garrick, but the date and time of her flight as well. She didn't know how she was going to use the information, she just knew that she would.

She hid from sight when her father and her rival left the room and headed to the lounge. She postponed going to her bedroom so she could listen in again, just in case anything interesting was said.

She wasn't disappointed. The fact that Amy wasn't going to let Garrick know she would be visiting was information that Nadia could use.

She practically ran up the stairs, reaching her room just as the doorbell rang. It was probably only Tom so she paid it no heed. She made sure her bedroom door was securely shut behind her. She didn't want anyone walking in unannounced and catching what she was doing.

She logged her computer onto the internet and headed straight to the same website her father had used. It didn't take her long to find the flight Amy was on and note down its estimated landing time. Next she checked train times in London and calculated when Amy was due to arrive at Garrick's hotel. Of course, she could actually get there hours later, but at least Nadia had a starting time.

Then she booked her own flight. She would leave on the Friday to ensure she got there first. She booked herself into a hotel in London for just one night. After all, she didn't want to meet Garrick too early. No, she had to ensure she was in his room when the half-breed arrived.

With everything organised, all she could do was wait.

A few hours later, she heard Tom, Tabitha and Amy leave, a farewell bark informing her that Ainin had also been visiting. She missed the dog. He was the only canine to allow her anywhere near him; all others would back away, growling.

She waited patiently for another hour before descending the stairs and letting her parents know she was home. They asked about her date and she lied and said it went okay. As if a date could ever go okay if it wasn't with Garrick. What was she thinking even trying?

They never mentioned Amy or her upcoming trip to the UK. Nadia wasn't surprised. They never talked about Amy to her. Or Garrick. The only reason she knew he had gone to England was because she had overheard Tabitha discussing it with Tom. Nobody knew she knew and she planned on leaving it that way. Finding out which hotel he was staying at had been easy; she just started a conversation with one of the travel girls and made sure it came up.

Of course, she didn't mention Garrick by name. She just showed an interest in those sent to Liverpool in general and the young girl informed her that everyone was staying at the same hotel.

Now all she could do was wait. It was going to be a long few days. To pass the time, she thought about what she could tell people to explain her going away. She needed a reason and a destination, not just for her parents, but for Tabitha as well. While she loved Tabitha like a sister, her being related to Garrick sometimes caused problems.

Eventually she decided to just say that she was going on holiday. After all, it had been a while since she had gone away. The last time had been when she and Tabitha had gone to Papua New Guinea to walk the Kokoda trail and that had been over a year ago.

Everyone she spoke to believed her story, but Tabitha was surprised by how sudden it was. To allay her suspicions, she secretly admitted to her friend that she was missing seeing Garrick, who was still rejecting all her attempts to contact him, and thought a last minute break might do her good.

Tabitha bought it. While she was an intelligent woman, she did have this habit of always seeing the best in people

At last, Friday arrived. She had been so excited about her trip that she had packed the day before. Her father offered to drive her to the airport, but she decided to catch a taxi. She was worried that he would want to wait with her until she caught her flight and he would know she wasn't really going to South America like she had said.

At the airport, she purchased some pound notes and looked at the money in disgust. It didn't look or feel real. It could have been Monopoly money as far as she was concerned, if not for it having the queen's head on it.

She placed it all in her purse, eager to get it out of her hands. She hoped she was going to be able to use her credit card most of the time, instead of cash. Once she met up with Garrick, he would insist on paying for everything; that was just the way he was.

She went to her gate, took out a book and lost herself in it until it was almost time to board. A quick trip to the bathroom and a double check that she had her boarding pass later, she was ready to join the queue.

The flight was tedious. She was unable to sleep, so was irritable when she arrived. She headed straight to her hotel and crashed for a few hours.

When she woke she decided to go sightseeing. She had never been to England before and had always wanted to see some of its most famous places.

She took an open top bus tour and instantly regretted it. There was a chill in the air and the coat she had on wasn't thick enough. As a result, she was grumpy again when she returned to her hotel.

She didn't feel like braving the streets of London, looking for somewhere to eat, so ordered room service and ate it while watching TV.

The next morning she logged on to Heathrow airport's website to check the estimated arrival time of Amy's flight. There was no delay, so she didn't need to adjust her plans. She caught the tube to Euston followed by a direct train to Liverpool, arriving later than expected due to delays, but still within plenty of time.

She caught a taxi to the hotel Garrick was staying at and charmed the young man on reception into giving her his room number. Initially he had insisted on phoning through to the room, but Nadia managed to persuade him she was his girlfriend and wanted to surprise him.

She was about to knock on his door when a thought occurred to her. What if he wasn't in? She hadn't thought to ask the man on reception if he had seen him leave.

Pushing the thought aside, she knocked on the door. Almost immediately it was answered and the sight of Garrick made her heart skip a beat.

His hair had grown a little longer than he normally wore it, but she liked it. She wanted to run her fingers through it as he kissed her neck. If she played her cards right, she would shortly be doing just that.

"Nadia," he said in surprise. "What are you doing here?" He didn't sound happy to see her, but she was sure that would change once he got over his shock. He would be grateful she travelled half way around the world to see him.

"I came to see you of course. May I come in?"

She wasn't happy that he was blocking the door with his body. She shouldn't have had to ask to enter.

"Why?"

Nadia didn't understand the question. Why did he think she wanted to enter his room? She could hardly stay outside.

"We can't talk out in the corridor."

He didn't move out of the way. "I meant, why did you come to see me?"

"Don't you think we should discuss this inside?"

She looked meaningfully down the corridor, but there was nobody in sight.

224

"No, I don't. Why did you come here?"

Nadia was confused. Hadn't she already answered that question? "I wanted to see you."

"Well I don't want to see you."

She wasn't sure what shocked her more, the words or the anger with which they were delivered.

"I've come a long way to see you and sort out our issues."

"You shouldn't have bothered."

"The least you can do is hear me out."

"Why? Have you got anything to say that's worth listening to? Are you going to apologise for your behaviour?"

Of course she wasn't going to apologise. As far as she was concerned, she had nothing to apologise for. But that didn't stop her saying, "Maybe. Let me in and you'll find out."

It didn't work. He crossed his arms, making himself even more of an unmovable barrier.

Nadia had had enough of his attitude. He should have been overjoyed to see her; he should have been grateful for the effort she had made.

"It's been a long day, Garrick," she snapped at him. "The flight was terrible. I couldn't sleep at all. And I'm suffering from jet-lag. If you still don't want to speak to me after I have come all this way, fine. Continue acting like a spoilt child. See if I care. You could at least let me shower before kicking me back to the airport."

She could tell he was conflicted. He was sometimes too nice for his own good.

"Alright," he eventually said. "You can shower and change clothes, then I want you gone."

Grinning, she picked up her suitcase and walked into his room.

It was adequate, but far from luxurious. If she had been forced to spend more than a few days in another country, she would have demanded something much higher class.

It contained a large bed, desk, TV, wardrobe, a door which she assumed led to a bathroom, and not much else. From the look of things, it didn't even have a balcony.

"Bathroom's there," he said, pointing to the closed door. "Don't be long. I want you gone as soon as possible."

He didn't wait for her to react before heading to the desk and sitting down. He began typing on his laptop as though he had already dismissed her from his thoughts.

Nadia was seething. This was not going as she had expected. She checked her watch. She would need to make the shower last a while if she wanted to still be there when Amy arrived.

Taking as long as she could, she washed her hair using the hotel supplied shampoo. She wasn't impressed with it. She would need to use a hot oil treatment when she got home if she had to put up with using it for long.

She expected Garrick to knock on the door and tell her to hurry up, but he didn't. Maybe he had forgotten she was there.

She finally switched off the water and stepped out of the shower. She wrapped one towel around her body and used the other to tie up her hair. She was about to leave the bathroom when she heard a knock on the door.

"Now what?" Garrick said loud enough for her to hear through the closed bathroom door. His mood obviously hadn't improved.

There was no way for Nadia to know if it was Amy at the door, but she had to assume it was.

Her timing was perfect. She left the bathroom dressed in just a towel as Garrick opened the door. Her eyes met Amy's and she couldn't keep the smile off her face. There was no way the half-breed would believe she had only just arrived or that Garrick didn't want her to stay. Their relationship was as good as over and she would make sure she was around to comfort him. He was going to be hers at last. There was nobody now to get in her way.

Heartbreak

Garrick couldn't believe his eyes. Amy was standing in front of him. His Amy. Joy flowed through him. He wanted to pull her into his arms and never let go. But the look on her face stopped him.

She wasn't looking at him; she was staring behind him. He turned around and saw Nadia wearing nothing but a towel and a smug smile.

He turned back to Amy, but before he could explain, she turned and ran.

"Amy, no," he shouted down the corridor. "This isn't what it looks like."

He ran after her, but she must have tapped into her werewolf speed because she reached the lift before he could catch her.

The doors opened as he grabbed her arm. She turned around and pushed him away with such force he was thrown down the corridor. By the time he recovered, the lift doors had closed.

He frantically pushed the button as though pressing it multiple times would call it back to him before it deposited Amy on the ground floor. He tried calling her, but there was no answer.

When the lift returned, it was empty. He had expected it to be, but he was still disappointed. He had no idea where Amy was going. If she wasn't in reception by the time he got there, he didn't know where to start looking.

He pushed the button for the ground floor several times and swore when the doors didn't immediately close.

As soon as they opened once more, he ran out and scoured the lobby, raking his eyes over everyone, then instantly dismissing them.

There was no sign of Amy.

He ran to the reception desk.

"Did you see where the woman went?" he asked. "Tall, slim, a little on the pale side. Long dark brown hair."

"Someone matching that description just ran out the door. She seemed upset."

"Which direction did she go in?" He prayed she hadn't caught a taxi. If she had, he had no hope of finding her.

"Left, I think."

"Thank you," Garrick said and was running toward the exit before he had finished speaking.

As soon as he was out of the building, he scanned both left and right, just in case. He couldn't see her. He took his phone out of his pocket and called her, but it went straight to voicemail.

"Shit," he said loudly, then gave an apologetic smile to a couple of ladies who were walking by.

He went left, hoping the receptionist was correct. There weren't many people about and he spotted one that could be Amy, but her hair was hanging lose and Amy's had been tied back in a ponytail.

"Shit," he said again. There were a few side streets she could have taken and a bus was just pulling away in the distance. He had no way of knowing if she was on it.

For the first time in his life, he felt helpless. He looked around him desperately, but to no avail.

Feeling dejected, he saw no other option than to go back to his room and hope she turned up.

His door was still open when he made it back and Amy's suitcase was sitting outside. He grabbed it and dumped it on the bed, pushing past Nadia to get to it. She still wasn't dressed.

When he turned to face her, it took all of his self-control to keep his temper in check.

"You complete and utter bitch. You planned this, didn't you?"

"Garrick, what on Earth are you talking about? How could I possibly know Amy was coming here?"

He might have believed her, had she not been smiling. Not only did she know that Amy was flying to England, she knew exactly when; he was sure of it. That was why she had wanted to take a shower. And why it had taken so long. She had to exit the bathroom at just the right moment.

Of course, he could be wrong, but he didn't think so.

He had never felt such rage before.

"Get dressed and get out."

"But Garrick, where will I go?"

"You can go to hell for all I care," he shouted at her.

She flinched and retreated into the bathroom, taking her suitcase with her.

Garrick was pacing the room when she emerged once more, fully clothed. She had chosen jeans that hugged her body, emphasising her long, shapely, legs. The top she wore was so tight it left nothing to the imagination. He wasn't impressed. And he didn't like the way she was smiling at him. It was almost as if she found the situation amusing.

"Let's talk. Amy's gone and probably won't be coming back. Let me make you feel better."

He did nothing as she walked up to him. The moment she placed her hand on his arm, he grabbed it and twisted it around. He knew he wasn't hurting her as werewolves had high pain thresholds, but part of him wished he was.

"If you ever lay a hand on me again, I will kill you." It wasn't a threat; he meant it.

She looked genuinely confused. "But we're meant to be together. Now that you no longer have Amy, there's nothing stopping us."

Garrick pushed Nadia away from him. "We were never meant to be together. I could never feel anything for you other than friendship and right now, I don't even feel that. Get out Nadia, before I do or say something we'll both regret."

Tears filled her eyes. He had no idea if they were genuine or not and he didn't care.

"You can't mean that."

Garrick didn't bother to answer. Instead he picked up her suitcase, went up to the door, opened it and threw it out. He held the door open for her. "Don't make me do the same to you."

With her werewolf strength, it was unlikely he would win if it came down to a fight, but he didn't think she would refuse. He felt a small sense of satisfaction when she left. Slamming the door after her was immensely pleasurable.

He went to the bed and collapsed down onto it. He had no idea what he was going to do.

He tried to call Amy again, but it still didn't ring and all he heard was her voice telling him to leave a message.

Then he phoned Tabitha. He had no idea what time it was for her but she wouldn't mind, given the circumstances.

He told her everything that had happened and his suspicions. Tabitha didn't get a chance to get a word in until he had finished.

"Amy booked her flight at Lawrence and Rosemary's place so it's possible Nadia overheard," Tabitha said when she was finally allowed to speak. "I didn't think she was home, but it's possible she was. It's the only explanation. Neither Lawrence nor Rosemary would have told her anything."

"You don't think her being here when Amy arrived was coincidence then?"

"Of course not. She's been pining after you for years. You've just been too dumb to notice. I knew she hated you and Amy being together, but I never thought she would go this far. I would have warned you if I thought she was going to cause trouble."

While Garrick appreciated what his sister was saying, it didn't help him find Amy.

"What do I do now? Amy could be anywhere."

"Is she still wearing that thing you put her tracker in?"

Garrick felt like a complete idiot. He was sure she was. He had noticed it on her wrist as she dropped her suitcase when she saw Nadia and he didn't think she would have removed it.

"Yes, she is. I can't believe I didn't think of that."

"Well, while I was given brains and beauty, you missed out on both, brother dearest."

"Thanks, Tab, I love you too," he said sarcastically.

While he spoke he placed his phone on the bed and hit the speaker button, freeing up his hands to grab this laptop and enter his password.

He logged onto the Agency's secure server and opened the software which would tell him exactly where Amy was, if he was lucky.

A map of Liverpool appeared on the screen with a blue dot in a park. It wasn't moving which meant she hadn't caught a bus or taxi to the train station, at least not yet.

Unless, of course, she had remembered about the tracker and had thrown it away, but he refused to let himself believe that.

"She's not far away," he told Tabitha as soon as he found the hotel he was in on the map.

"Then go get her," Tabitha said. "Good luck."

"Thanks," Garrick said, then hung up. He logged off and switched off his computer before grabbing his room key card and putting it in his wallet. He practically ran from the room, silently praying that Amy wouldn't move before he got to her.

It took all of his willpower not to swear at the lift when it didn't arrive immediately and when it finally did, he pushed the button for the lobby so hard he was lucky he didn't break it.

The lift stopped twice on the way down to let others on, much to his annoyance. He pushed his way to the front, not caring if he was being rude, so he could make a fast getaway as soon as the doors opened.

He had memorised the route to the park he hoped Amy was still in and broke into a steady jog as soon as he exited the hotel. Even so, it took him a good fifteen minutes to reach the entrance. Then all he had to do was work out where she was. The park was bigger than he had been expecting and he had no idea where to start.

He stopped everyone he saw, asking if they had seen her. Nobody had. Eventually an elderly couple, out walking their Cavalier King Charles, said there was someone matching her description on a bench further up the path they were on. The reason they remembered her was because she was crying and they had asked her if she was okay.

Knowing it must be Amy they were talking about, Garrick thanked them and headed in the direction they had indicated.

As soon as he saw her, he stopped. He had no idea how to approach her. He didn't want her running off again and if she used her werewolf speed again, he had no hope of catching up with her.

He approached her slowly. Her head was in her hands and she didn't look up. If she was aware of his presence, she gave no indication.

She was seated at one end of the bench, so he sat on the other end, keeping as much distance between them as he could.

She still didn't react, so he gave her a moment to acknowledge that he was there, even if it was to tell him to go away and leave her alone.

She remained silent and didn't take her head out of her hands. He could see her body shaking as she silently cried. The sight broke his heart, not just because she was so upset, but because it was his fault.

"I swear to God, I didn't know she was coming. When she arrived I told her to leave. She asked to take a shower first as it had been a long flight. I stupidly relented. That's all there is to it. I swear on my life. Nothing is going on between us. It never has and it never will."

He purposely didn't say Nadia's name. The way he felt about her, he wasn't sure he would be able to say it without snarling.

"Why should I believe you?"

Her voice was filled with so much pain he couldn't bear it. He didn't realise he had moved until he felt her in his arms. Hoping she wouldn't push him away, he said, "Because I don't think I can go on if you don't."

His words didn't stop her tears; they had the opposite effect. Her crying became vocal and her shaking increased.

He held her tighter. "Stop crying, honey. Please stop crying. I'll do anything to make things right. Anything. I'll leave the UK immediately. I'll stop seeing Lawrence and Rosemary. I'll even quit the Agency if that's what it takes. Just tell me what I have to do and I'll do it."

They weren't just words; he meant everything he said.

Amy didn't respond; she just continued to cry. He held her until her shaking stopped and she went quiet.

"I hate her," she said, her voice trembling.

"Right now, so do I."

"I never want to see her again."

"That makes two of us."

He relaxed his hold on her so he could look at her. Her head was buried in his chest so he placed his hand under her chin and gently lifted it. He used a finger to wipe away her tears, but others soon replaced them.

"What can I do?" he asked.

She just shook her head before placing it on his chest once more.

"Where is she?"

"I don't know and I don't care. I kicked her out of my room. If she knows what's good for her, she won't be coming back."

"How can you be certain?"

"I can't, but if she's stupid enough to show her face, I'll let you kick the shit out of her. How does that sound?"

"Right now, that sounds pretty good."

He kissed the top of her head. "Please, will you come back to the hotel with me. I'll change room if you want."

He felt her nod her head and he breathed a sigh of relief. They had a long way to go before things would be good between them again, but he would do everything he could to make sure he set things right.

Lewis

In the end, Garrick changed hotels, not just the room. It took some convincing, and a phone call to Tabitha, but eventually Amy agreed to stay in the UK for the week as she had originally planned.

Tabitha told Nadia's parents what had happened and they both agreed that she must have known about Amy's visit. They promised to deal with her as soon as she returned and offered their sincerest apologies to Amy, not that she blamed them in any way.

Once she had accepted the fact that it had all been a set-up and that Garrick was completely innocent, Amy began to relax. He showered her with affection and, despite what had happened, she was glad she made the trip.

Somehow Garrick managed to wrangle a couple of days off so he could spend time with her and show her the sights. When he did have to work, he took her with him. Everyone had heard a lot about her and were delighted to meet her.

Tabitha called one evening to inform them that Nadia had turned up and was claiming that Garrick, not realising that Amy would be visiting, had invited her to join him in Liverpool. Nobody believed her.

Time flew by and all too soon it was time for Garrick and Amy to say goodbye again. They'd grown even closer during their week together and neither of them were looking forward to being apart again.

"I've been thinking," Garrick said on their last night together. They were curled up in bed, recovering from an energetic love-making session. "When I return home, we should think about moving in together."

Amy pulled herself out of his arms so she could look at him. "You're serious," she said in surprise when she saw how he was looking at her.

"Of course I'm serious."

Amy didn't know what to say. It wasn't something she had given any thought to. They hadn't been together long enough to take such a big step, had they?

Garrick must have sensed her uncertainty. "Give it some thought, that's all I'm asking. Discuss it with Ainin. I'm sure he'll agree. After all, he does adore me."

Amy burst out laughing.

"What?" Garrick asked, his alleged confusion so obviously fake he could have won a worst actor Oscar. "Are you telling me he doesn't?"

"That depends on whether you have a bone for him or not. I'm pretty sure the number you bribe him with will decrease if you saw him every day."

"I promise that won't happen."

Amy opened her mouth to respond, but he placed his finger on her lips, silencing her.

"Let's not talk about it right now. When you're back home, think about it and let me know your decision when I get back."

"Alright," Amy said.

"Good," Garrick said, "because right now we've got more important things to do than talk about our living arrangements."

"Like what?"

The way he kissed her was all the answer she needed.

Morning arrived far too soon and Garrick treated Amy to a full English breakfast ordered from room service. They stayed in bed as they shared their food, feeding each other and stealing food from each other's plates.

Reluctantly Amy packed and Garrick went to London with her on the train, staying with her in the airport until she boarded her plane.

The return journey was nothing like the outbound one. Her trip to the UK had been exciting. She was going somewhere she had never been before. And she was going to see Garrick. Now she was leaving him behind. She missed Ainin and wanted to see him again, but that didn't ease the pain of having to say goodbye to Garrick.

Tabitha picked her up from the airport and drove her straight to her home, where she had dropped the dog off on the way to the airport. She had taken good care of him while Amy had been away and having him live with her had made her consider getting her own pet.

Ainin rushed to her the moment she entered the house, covering her in wet sloppy kisses. It took her a while to calm him down enough for her to make it into the kitchen to make coffee.

She was tired and wanted to go to bed, but she would be better off forcing herself to stay awake for a while longer and get back into a standard sleeping pattern.

She invited Tabitha to join her and conversation turned to Nadia and the fact she had moved out of home. She didn't like the fact that nobody believed her version of events and decided to rent her own apartment. Not even her parents knew where.

Amy couldn't keep the smile off her face. It meant she would be able to visit the werewolves without the fear of running into her.

She did feel a little sorry for her, though. She believed that Nadia genuinely loved Garrick and she couldn't imagine what it would be like to feel like that and not have your feelings reciprocated.

As soon as the coffees were finished and Tabitha ran out of gossip, she left to allow Amy to get some rest.

Unable to relax, Amy put the washing on and then went grocery shopping. She felt as though someone was watching her, but every time she turned around, there was nobody there.

Putting it down to jetlag, she forced it from her mind and concentrated on what she would eat for the next few days and what treats she should buy Ainin.

Later that day, she cooked herself salmon salad and ate it while watching a crime show she liked. A quick call to Garrick later, she tucked herself up in bed and was soon fast asleep.

--------------------------∞--------------------------

236

Lia looked at her phone. She had no idea who the missed call was from and wasn't sure if she should call back. Whoever it was had left no voicemail.

It had been three days since Amy had returned and she had found out some interesting information, but she wasn't sure how to use it, seeing as she no longer had a team and Derek had failed to send anyone to her. She debated whether to call him and let him know what she had discovered, but decided not to. She would wait until he bothered to contact her.

Throwing caution to the wind, she selected the number which had called her and hit 'call'.

It rang twice before a male voice answered. It was deep and pleasant to listen to.

"Lia. Thank you for calling me back. My name is Lewis. Derek sent me."

Lia smiled. At last, Derek was doing as he had promised; though he could have called her to let her know to expect one of his associates.

"We should meet," Lia said, hoping he looked as good as his voice sounded.

"Agreed." He named a time and a place. It was a large woodland with paths which were good for walking or running. She had never been there herself, but had heard good reports about it. It was quiet so they wouldn't be disturbed by many people, especially as early in the morning as he wanted to meet.

She agreed and set her alarm. She would have to get up earlier than normal if she was to get there on time. Part of her was nervous, but the rest of her was excited. What had Lewis been sent to do? What part was she to play?

It took her ages to get to sleep that night and as a result, she was groggy when her alarm woke her. A quick shower fixed that and she was ready to face the day by the time she left her house.

Dressed in running gear, she drove to the designated wood and began to walk. Lewis had provided directions, but she still checked the map of trails before heading off.

As she rounded a bend, she found him where he promised he would be, sitting on top of a large bolder, drinking from a water bottle.

At least she hoped it was him. He was absolutely gorgeous. From his square, masculine jawline and dark hair that looked so soft she wanted to run her hands through it, to his deep green eyes which seemed to bore into her, right down to her soul, he was stunning.

As she approached, she raked her eyes over his body and liked what she saw. Dressed in a tight fitting t-shirt, which did nothing to hide his well-defined muscles, and a pair of running shorts, he looked like a professional athlete in training.

"Lia," he said when she got close enough for him to address her without shouting, though how he knew it was her, she had no idea.

The sun, having risen an hour earlier, was beating down, making her sweat. At least she thought it was the sun; it could just as easily have been the man sitting in front of her.

She looked around at the trees. She wasn't overly fond of being in the middle of nature, which was strange for a wolf, but he had certainly chosen a good spot to meet.

"Do you come here often?" she asked.

"Every time I'm in town."

His voice sounded even nicer in person. She wanted to ask him where he was from, but stopped herself. The man was here on a mission, nothing more, and she shouldn't let herself get distracted.

"Let's walk and talk," he said and stood up. He rose gracefully, like a dancer, but she couldn't image him in ballet tights, prancing around a stage.

"What do you want to know?" she asked. He set a fast pace, but nothing she couldn't handle.

"Nothing. I've been told everything I need to know about you. I've been here a few days, checking out the local headquarters of the Agency and I've followed Amy around."

The comment surprised Lia. "Really? I would have thought I would have noticed you."

"I'm good at what I do," he said. "Very good."

"And what do you do, exactly?"

"Whatever needs to be done. So, Amy went away recently. Anything I should know about?"

Lia told him everything she knew about Amy's trip; the reason for it and what happened as soon as she arrived in the UK. Lewis seemed particularly interested in that part of it.

"So this Nadia person is a bit of a trouble-maker, is she?"

Lia shrugged. "Not exactly. It's just that she wants Garrick and will do anything to get him."

"Anything? Now that is interesting. And I bet she's feeling rather pissed off with him and Amy right now."

Lia said nothing. He was looking into the distance, voicing his thoughts out loud instead of asking anything of her.

He brought his attention back to her. "Where can I find her?"

"Nobody knows, not even her parents. She moved out of the family home not long after she got back."

"Then we have a job to do. We have to find her. Not only where she lives, but where she works, if she does work. What she does for fun and where. Are there any routines she always follows, that sort of thing?"

"She works at the Agency," she said.

"Good. Then you should be able to follow her home."

Finally Lia had something useful to do. It wasn't going to be easy, but she had a strange feeling it was going to be a lot of fun.

Date

Nadia was running late. She had promised her boss she would start work early, but she was in desperate need of a coffee first. Her favourite café was almost on her way, so she could justify the slight detour. She had pre-ordered her drink via their app, so it would be ready and waiting for her as soon as she arrived.

She didn't notice the man as she entered the building and walked straight into him, spilling his drink down his clean white shirt.

"I am so sorry," she said as she checked that none of the liquid had hit her. She didn't have time to go home and change.

Breathing a sigh of relief, she looked up into the greenest eyes she had ever seen. They were captivating.

Forcing herself to step back so she could get a proper look at the man she had just accosted, she saw a stunningly attractive man, in his late twenties, early thirties, she guessed. He was breathtaking.

"My fault," he said as he pointlessly tried to brush the stain off his shirt with his hand. "I should have been watching where I was going."

She could clearly see his red aura, identifying him as an unregistered werewolf. She should report him, but there was something about him that made her not want to. He made no comment about her also being red.

"Please, let me buy you another."

"There's no need. Honestly." He held out his hand. "I'm Lewis."

"Nadia," she said as she shook it.

"Pretty name for a beautiful lady." Then he grimaced. "That sounded a little cheesy, didn't it."

She smiled as she nodded. "A little."

She almost swore when the young man behind the counter called her name, letting her know her drink was ready. She visited the café most mornings, even before she moved out of her parent's house, so Gary recognised her as soon as she walked in.

Her need for a caffeine fix was suddenly the last thing on her mind. She wanted to stay and talk to this handsome stranger, but she didn't have the time.

"Are you sure I can't get you a replacement?"

Lewis looked even nicer when he smiled. She found her eyes drifting to his left hand, looking for a wedding ring. His hand was ring free.

"If you really want to make it up to me," Lewis said, "you can let me buy you a proper drink. Tonight perhaps?"

"I don't usually go out with strange men."

"A sensible precaution. And I agree I am a little strange, though how you know that already is beyond me."

Nadia laughed. This man was charming as well as attractive.

"Won't you make an exception?" he asked.

She took her mobile phone out of her bag. "Give me your number and I'll think about it."

She entered in the digits he reeled off and then put her phone away again, exchanging it for her purse. She took out her credit card as she walked up to the counter, Lewis following behind.

"I'll pay for this man's order as well," she said, as soon as he had asked for a replacement drink. "Apparently he thought it was a good idea to wear his first one."

Gary smiled at her as he entered the details in and then told her the total. She swiped her credit card, before putting it back into her purse, which found its way into her bag once more.

"I'll see you tomorrow, Gary. Goodbye, Lewis. It was nice running into you. Literally."

"I look forward to hearing from you," he said.

"I haven't agreed to call you."

"You will."

She turned her back on him and walked away, unable to keep the smile from her face. He certainly had confidence.

Ever since her failed attempt to win Garrick from Amy, she had been feeling lost and lonely and more than a little angry. One conversation with this man and she had forgotten all of those feelings. Maybe she would give him a call.

She walked the rest of the way to work, arguing with herself. She hadn't lied about not dating strangers, but it was nothing to do with her safety. As a werewolf, she was more than capable of looking after herself. It was more a case of wanting to know a little about someone before she wasted her time on them.

She was considering making an exception in Lewis's case. Maybe she could get to know him over a glass of wine instead of over the phone.

However, she reminded herself, he was a wolf and may be just as strong and fast as she was, maybe even more so. Did she really want to be alone with someone who might be able to overpower her before she found out more about him?

She spent the rest of the day trying to concentrate on work, but her mind kept drifting to Lewis. She couldn't get his eyes out of her head. Numerous times she reached for her phone, intending to give him a call, but each time she quickly put it down again.

Normally she would call Tabitha for advice, but she was still mad at her best friend for not taking her side. Garrick may be her brother, but wasn't the girl code supposed to outweigh blood?

It reached 4 o'clock and she decided to give up for the day. She'd started early so she was entitled to leave early. She looked at her phone one more time and thought 'to hell with it'. She sent Lewis a quick text and then packed up her stuff and went home.

She had arranged to meet him at eight, so had plenty of time to bathe and eat dinner. She found herself debating what to wear. She wanted something that made her look good, but not too good. She didn't want to give him the wrong impression. If it was the wrong impression. She wasn't quite sure.

Opting for smart trousers and a blouse which wasn't too revealing, she matched them with high heeled ankle boots. Before leaving her apartment, she gave herself one last look in the full length mirror.

She had chosen a bar which she could walk to and that she knew well. She would feel comfortable there if she had to sit alone while waiting for Lewis to arrive. It never occurred to her that he might stand her up.

She went straight to the bar and ordered her usual. Once she had her glass of dry white wine in her hand, she looked around the room and was pleased to spot Lewis in the corner, waiting for her.

"I was supposed to buy that," he said as she took a seat at his table.

"You can buy the next one."

As it turned out, he bought the next two. The evening went well and she found she hadn't laughed so much in a long time. He was good company and kept her entertained. He was happy to talk about himself, when asked, but seemed more interested in her, what she liked, what she hated, and he asked her opinion on many things.

The fact that she worked for the Agency came up and he was curious about her reasons. She explained them to him, and even tried to persuade him he should give the injections a try, but he refused, saying he liked his freedom too much. Being registered meant the Agency would know where he lived and he didn't like the idea of that. He never asked why she wasn't registered, though her aura would have told him that she wasn't.

It was late by the time they left the bar, but she declined his invitation to walk her home. She never spent the night with a man after a first date, but she was tempted to this time. It was better if they parted where they were, rather than trying to do so on her doorstep. If she invited him in for coffee, it was doubtful he would leave before morning.

She did, however, agree to let him take her to dinner the following Saturday night.

The rest of the week dragged by and the weekend took ages to arrive. Nadia had long ago concluded that, despite proof to the contrary, time didn't pass at a standard pace and that it sometimes went quicker and at other times slower.

Saturday night finally arrived and this time she chose a tight-fitting red dress with matching high-heeled sandals. She looked great, even if she did say so herself. She transferred all of her essentials from her usual handbag to a black clutch which went well with her outfit, then waited for Lewis to pick her up.

He arrived on time, driving a black Ferrari.

"Impressive," she said as she climbed in. "But it should be red."

"Sorry, this is the only one the hire company had."

She laughed lightly.

The restaurant Lewis chose was excellent. It wasn't Michelin starred, but it was warm and cosy and the food was delicious. After the meal, they took a stroll by the river, hand in hand.

"I really want to see you again," Lewis said when they made it back to his car. "Are you free tomorrow?"

Nadia desperately wanted to say yes, but forced herself not to. It was too soon. She wanted to slow things down. She liked this man, she liked him a lot.

"I'm busy tomorrow. How about Tuesday evening?"

"How about Monday?" he countered.

She relented. "Alright. Monday. You can pick me up at seven."

He drove her home, parking outside her house and walking her to her door so he could kiss her goodbye. What started out as a friendly kiss on the lips soon developed into something much more. When Nadia finally managed to remove her arms from around his neck and step away from him, it took all of her will power not to invite him inside.

"I'll see you Monday," he said and winked at her. She watched him walk back to his car. Even from behind, his body was an impressive sight.

Once he had driven away, Nadia closed the door and leaned back against it. The kiss had been amazing. She couldn't wait for Monday night so she could kiss him again.

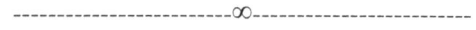

Lewis drove away from Nadia with a smile on his face. Things were going well. His task was to seduce her and then persuade her to betray the Agency. He had to admit, it was one of the more pleasant tasks he had been given. He enjoyed being with her much more than he thought he would.

He drove to the house he was renting and swapped cars. He needed to see Lia and having a Ferrari parked outside her house would draw unwanted attention.

It wasn't too late, so he doubted she would be in bed, but he phoned ahead, just in case. She seemed pleased to see him and offered him a beer as soon as he entered her home.

He told her about his evening and how things were progressing. Nadia was being open and, he assumed, honest with him. The Agency came up, but she never mentioned that she provided blood for them, only that she worked there. He could understand her keeping that to herself. After all, she had only known him a few days.

Garrick had also come up. Lewis was an expert in directing conversations to the topics he wished to discuss without the other participants realising what he was doing. He didn't ask directly about Garrick, as he wasn't supposed to know about him. He merely asked what it was like working so closely with Agents. Nadia had brought up Garrick on her own. Or so she thought.

"There's a lot of resentment there," Lewis said. "Not only against Amy and Garrick, but also his sister. And her parents. With the right nudge, I'm confident we can get her on our side. We will finally have our first spy in the Agency."

"How far are you willing to go to make sure of that?" Lia asked, then took a swig from her bottle of beer.

Lewis gave her a smile which was designed to make her legs go weak. He'd seen the way she looked at him. He was prepared to put money on the fact she was glad she was sitting down.

"However far I have to."

Lia leaned closer to him. "In that case, maybe you should get in some practice."

He moved closer to her, making her believe he was going to kiss her. Just before their lips touched, he patted her cheek. "I don't mix business with pleasure."

He could almost feel her fury wash over him. He could have just politely turned her down, but where would have been the fun in that?

"I've got to go," he said as he stood up. He drained the last of his beer and placed the empty bottle on the table.

Lia didn't see him to the door.

Sunday he spent doing things he enjoyed, not thinking about Lia or Nadia or his date. He put everything from his mind as he relaxed. He was entitled to a day off, especially as he was going to get such good results the following evening.

Monday arrived and he picked Nadia up at the exact time he had said he would. He didn't like arriving anywhere early as he had worked out that women didn't like to be interrupted while they were getting ready. Arriving late was something he would never do, if it could be avoided.

The welcoming kiss she gave him told him he already had her eating out of the palm of his hand.

"Where are we going?" she asked as soon as she was in the car.

"You'll see when we get there."

If his lack of details bothered her, she didn't show it.

"Black Olive," she said as he pulled into the carpark. "I've heard about this place, but never been. It gets great reviews."

"That's one of the reasons I chose it."

The other reason was that it had private booths so they could talk without anyone easily overhearing. He waited until the plates from their main course had been taken away and they had ordered dessert before 'confessing' to her.

From across the table, he took hold of her hands with his. "There's something I need to tell you."

He purposely set the tone of his voice. She would believe he was going to tell her something he rarely trusted others with.

"I work with the resistance."

She didn't react. She didn't pull away or squeeze his hands. For the first time since he met her, he couldn't read her.

"Go on," she said. She sounded like she wanted to know more, but wasn't sure if she should.

"I'm trusting that you won't pass on anything I tell you to the Agency." Experience had taught him that one little word, 'trust', seemed to have a dramatic effect on women, for some reason. It seemed it worked on Nadia as well. This time, she did squeeze his hands.

He told her why he joined and what they hoped to achieve. Of course, he didn't tell her the truth. He enjoyed killing Agents and wanted to live in a world in which werewolves were the superior race and humans were nothing more than slaves, not where they lived openly as equals.

He did his best to persuade her to join him without mentioning that he wanted her to betray the Agency; that would come later.

Just as he thought she was going to agree, she pulled her hands away and leaned back in her seat.

"I'm sorry, Lewis. I agree with what the Agency does. They help werewolves. They don't persecute them, like you are making out. I could never agree with your beliefs. I will never join the resistance." She sounded as though she was disappointed in him, as though he had let her down somehow.

Anger surged through him. He had been so sure he had her right where he wanted her. How could he have been so wrong?

He forced his anger down. He could let it show, but that wouldn't frighten her as much as he wanted to. Instead his kept his voice cold and steady.

"In that case, my dear, I am going to have to make sure you can't tell anyone anything about me. What my name is. What I look like. That I'm unregistered. That I'm a member of the resistance. I can't risk you telling anyone anything."

"You can't get into my mind," Nadia said and tapped her necklace. "This will stop you."

"I'm not planning on getting into your mind."

He casually picked up his wine glass and took a mouthful of the dark red liquid.

Was she scared? He hoped so. She certainly looked like she was.

He placed his glass back on the table and looked her in the eyes.

"Tonight, my dearest Nadia, I'm going to kill you."

Murder

Lewis smiled at Nadia. It felt good to see her shiver. He didn't want to kill her, but he couldn't risk her telling anyone about him. The fact he didn't want to do it didn't mean he wouldn't enjoy it. Now all he had to do was decide how. And where.

"Don't even think about calling for help," he told her. "Not unless you want me to slaughter half the people in here."

It wasn't an idle threat. He was confident he could do it.

"So, are you working with Lia?" Nadia asked.

The question took him by surprise. He had been expecting her to beg for her life, to tell him she would do anything he wanted her to if he promised not to harm her.

Then again, she had always come across as a confident woman. Maybe the question shouldn't have surprised him. Seeing as she was going to die within the hour, he saw no harm in answering her.

"Yes, I am."

"Tell me about her."

Alarm bells started to ring. Her life was in danger. Why would she want to know about Lia? Had he misread the situation? No, of course he hadn't. He knew women and how their minds worked. He knew how to push their buttons and Nadia was no exception. She was just stalling, nothing more, hoping to delay her execution. For a moment he wondered how she even knew about Lia, until he remembered that she worked for the Agency.

"What do you want to know?"

"What does she look like? What's her last name? Where does she live?"

It felt like he was being interrogated. These weren't the sort of questions a woman facing her own death should be asking.

He looked around, but nothing appeared to be out of place. All he could see were diners enjoying their meals and the waiters serving them. She couldn't have set him up. He had booked the restaurant and hadn't told her where they were going. She hadn't been in contact with anyone since they arrived. She hadn't even gone to the bathroom to make a surreptitious phone call. He was just being paranoid.

"I can't tell you any of those things. She got in my head. I'm physically incapable of telling you anything about her." He didn't see any harm in telling her as she probably already knew that Lia had done it to others.

He'd heard a rumour that Lia made some of her team kill themselves if they got captured by the Agency. He had thought there was no truth to the claim, but now he had met her, he wasn't so sure.

He wasn't telling Nadia the complete truth. Lia hadn't even tried to get into his head and he was confident he would have been able to stop her if she had made the attempt. It was Derek who had planted in his brain the block on speaking about anything to do with Lia.

Nadia played with her glass, swirling the wine around in it before taking another sip. When she placed it back on the table, Lewis refilled it. After all, it would be her last evening alive, so she might as well enjoy it.

"So she's stronger than you are."

Lewis almost spilled the wine.

"I didn't say that," he snarled.

Nadia ignored his comment. "If she's stronger than you, what makes you so sure I'm not? Are you really sure you can kill me?"

Nadia was beginning to worry him. She shouldn't be acting like this. Her confidence should be gone, or at least waning.

"Trust me. You're no match for me." He gave her a cocky smile.

All she did was shrug her shoulders and say, "We'll see."

Dessert arrived and was eaten in silence. He watched her slowly consume her slice of chocolate mud cake, one small mouthful at a time, taking her time as if she didn't have a care in the world.

He hardly tasted his piece of apple pie with ice-cream. When the waiter returned and enquired whether they wanted coffee, Nadia placed her order before he had a chance to say no.

"For someone who's about to die, you don't seem especially concerned," he said once the waiter had departed.

"That's because I'm not. I know you're not going to be able to kill me. You might try, but you won't succeed."

Lewis changed the subject. He talked about his plans for the future, a future where the Agency didn't exist. He no longer cared what Nadia thought of him. If she didn't like what he was saying, too bad.

They discussed his opinions like any normal couple would. Lewis found it all a little surreal.

Coffee arrived and was consumed. Then it was time to go. There would be no more delay. Nadia made no objections when he asked for the bill and quickly paid it. She didn't even say she was going to 'powder her nose'.

He escorted her to his car and opened the door for her, but she didn't get in.

"I think," she said quietly, "that there may be one or two people who want to have a nice chat with you."

His jaw dropped as she removed an earpiece from her ear. She then undid the thin silk jacket she was wearing and removed a microphone. Not only had someone been in contact with her, but they had also been listening to everything he had said. All of the things he didn't mind telling her because she wasn't going to be in a position to pass it on to anyone, they had been hearing it all. That was why she mentioned the name of the restaurant when they arrived and why she seemed to be prolonging the evening. It wasn't because she wanted to delay her death. It was because she wanted to give the Agency time to get into position.

He'd messed up big time. He was going to be in a lot of trouble when Derek found out, and find out he would. How could he have misjudged Nadia so badly? He'd been so sure she was infatuated with him.

Almost as if she could read his mind, she said, "Experience has taught me that when something seems too good to be true, it usually is. And you, my dear, were definitely too good to be true."

He'd never hit a woman before, but right then he desperately wanted to. The mocking way she said 'my dear' was infuriating. He'd killed plenty of women before, but never with his bare hands. He had never hit any of them. He was seriously considering making an exception to his rule and giving Nadia what she deserved. He lifted his arm up, his fist clenched threateningly.

She leaned over and whispered in his ear. "I wouldn't do that if I were you. Look around."

He did as instructed and wished he hadn't. He was surrounded by Agents. All had their guns drawn and pointed at him. He did a quick mental calculation and decided he'd be able to kill some of them, but not all. It was unlikely he wasn't going to end up in custody or a body bag.

"If I'm going down," he said, "I'm taking you with me."

He tried to grab her, but she moved out of his way quicker than he thought possible.

"I don't think so," she said, then ran off. He'd never seen a woman move so fast in high heels.

"I'll get you, you bitch," he shouted after her.

"Put your hands in the air," one of the Agents called out. "We don't want to hurt you."

"Yeah, right," he shouted back. He looked around him, noting where each Agent was standing, the distance between them, how far it was to the exit, looking for any weak spot.

He could make it into his car before they shot him, but he didn't stand a chance of driving away. They would shoot out his tyres, his windscreen, his side window, anything they could hit. Including him.

Nadia was standing next to a butch looking woman, talking to her, and Lewis couldn't help wondering if they were friends. Or maybe more than friends. Was that why she had managed to fool him? Did she bat for the other side, as the saying goes?

He shook his head. No. She was definitely attracted to him. Her eyes were filled with hunger whenever they looked at him. It was something he had done which had made her suspicious of him. This situation was his own fault.

The two women weren't looking at him. He could use that to his advantage. With their attention on each other, he had a chance of escaping.

The sound of ripping cloth filled the carpark as he transformed. Hearing the noise, Nadia and the other woman turned toward him. He was racing at them so fast he was a blur. The Agent pulled her gun, but she was too late; he was already leaping for Nadia's throat. She didn't even have time to scream.

But the Agent was faster than he had been expecting, jumping in the way just as his jaws closed. Instead of his intended target, his teeth were around the Agent's throat. Without a second thought, he ripped it out. The taste of her blood as it flowed into his mouth was exquisite. He heard a rasping breath. He hadn't killed her outright, but he doubted she would live for long.

He didn't stick around to find out. He ran into the dark, putting as much distance between him and the Agents as he could. Bullets flew around him, but none hit their intended target.

He momentarily thought about the car he was abandoning. He had hired it under a false name so it was unlikely it would be traced to him and he had used a stolen credit card.

The last thing he heard before he was too far away was Nadia screaming out a name. Tabitha.

Funeral

Garrick was not happy when the ringing of his phone woke him. He glanced at the clock and swore. He picked up his phone, noted who was calling him and answered.

"Why the hell are you phoning me at 2 in the morning Lawrence?" he said through gritted teeth.

"I'm sorry but this couldn't wait. I wish there was an easy way for me to say this, but there isn't. Tabitha's dead."

He felt like he had been punched in the stomach. He couldn't have heard right. His sister couldn't be dead.

"What happened?" he forced himself to ask.

He didn't want Lawrence to tell him. Hearing the words would make it real. But he had to know.

"A mission to take in a rogue wolf went wrong. He tried to attack Nadia but Tab stepped in the way. I'm so sorry, Garrick."

"Nadia? Why in God's name was Nadia there?"

"It's a long story. She started dating this guy and something seemed off, so she spoke to Tab about it and Tab got her to wear a wire on their next date."

"What the hell were they thinking?" Garrick said, his teeth clenched once more. He was forcing himself not to yell. After all, it wasn't Lawrence's fault. "Taking on a rogue, just the two of them."

"Try to stay calm," Lawrence said. "They didn't. Tab did the right thing. There were ten Agents in total, plus Nadia. It should have been easy."

"So what went wrong?"

"He was fast, very fast. One second he was a human, the next he was a wolf and had his jaws around Tab's neck. Some of the Agents swear they never even saw him move."

Garrick didn't believe what he was hearing. The Agents had to be lying. They had messed up and were just looking for an excuse.

"Who was there?" he asked. He wanted to speak to them personally, to get the truth out of them.

"They were all experienced Agents, Garrick. Carl has already interviewed each one. I've even questioned them myself. They aren't covering anything up, I promise you."

"I still want to speak to them."

"You'll get your chance. Carl's busy organising you a flight home. Pack your bags. He'll have sent you details by the time you get to the airport."

Garrick took a deep breath. He needed to calm down. Staying angry wasn't going to accomplish anything.

"Alright."

"Garrick, one more thing. Nobody's told Amy yet. We weren't sure if you wanted to or not."

That was one phone call Garrick wasn't looking forward to, but Lawrence was right; he did want to be the one to give her the news.

As soon as he was off the phone, he took a shower to wake himself up before he packed his bags. He was purposely postponing making the call, but eventually he had no more excuses.

It was so good to hear her voice. She sounded excited to be speaking to him unexpectedly. That would soon change. He purposely didn't make it a video call; he couldn't bear to see her face when he said the words he was dreading saying.

"You'd better sit down," he said. Tears filled his eyes and he was sure she could hear them in his voice.

"What's wrong?" she asked.

"There's been an accident. An operation went wrong. Tab's dead."

A tear rolled down his cheek, but he didn't notice it.

"I am so, so sorry. I can't even begin to imagine how you are feeling. What can I do to help?"

'Typical Amy,' he thought to himself. 'Thinking of me rather than herself.' He could hear her quietly crying.

255

"Nothing, honey. I'm coming home. I'll be with you as soon as I can. Then I'm going to need you to hold me and never let go."

"How's Tom?" she asked.

A feeling of guilt passed through him. He hadn't even given a thought to Tabitha's fiancé.

"I don't know. I haven't spoken to him. It was Lawrence who called me."

"Has anyone told Nadia? She'll be devastated."

Garrick couldn't believe Amy was concerned about a woman she hated, but that was one of the reasons he loved her; everybody mattered to her, not just those she liked.

"She knows. She was there."

"She saw it?" Amy sounded horrified. "That's awful. I wouldn't wish that on my worst enemy."

"Me neither," Garrick found himself saying.

His phone made a noise, telling him someone had sent him a text.

"I'm sorry, honey, but I've gotta go. I think I've just been sent my flight details. I'll pass them on to you. I love you."

"I love you too," she said before he disconnected.

He was right; the text was from Carl, informing him that his flight details had been emailed to him. He quickly opened his email account and found the information. He then phoned a taxi, as it was too early to catch a train, and went to check out of the hotel. By the time he had finished the paperwork, the taxi was waiting for him.

"What time's your flight, love?" the driver asked as he climbed into the passenger seat of the taxi.

He told her and she glanced at the time on her dashboard. She raised her eyebrows. "Let's hope we don't hit traffic," was all she said.

Garrick kept glancing at the speedometer once they hit the motorway. He was at the wrong angle to get an accurate reading, but he was sure she was breaking the speed limits.

She got him there in plenty of time and he gave her a huge tip.

As soon as his suitcase was checked in, he went to the gate and forwarded his flight details to Amy. He didn't expect her to meet him at the airport, but he wanted her to know when to expect him.

Then he phoned Carl, to thank him for getting everything organised so quickly. His boss passed on his sympathies and told him he had given the other nine Agents involved a leave of absence and was forcing them to speak with a councillor. The same applied to Nadia, who had agreed to move back in with her parents, for her own protection. Lewis threatened to kill her and nobody wanted to take the risk that he wasn't going to try.

All the anger Garrick felt toward Nadia faded away. He knew how she felt about Tabitha and that she was probably blaming herself for what had happened. He hoped she did speak with the councillor; it would do her a lot of good.

"Have you spoken with Tom?" he asked.

"Yes. I was the one who broke the news to him. Let's just say he's not taking it very well."

"I'll give him a call."

As soon as he ended his call with Carl, he tried Tom, but there was no answer. A short while later, he called back. Tom was staying with a friend; he couldn't cope being in the home he shared with Tabitha. Garrick could understand that. He let Tom know he was heading home and made him promise to call him if there was anything he could do.

The flight was long and tiresome. Garrick didn't even allow himself to have any alcohol to help him sleep; he wanted to be fully functional when he landed.

He was tired and irritable by the time his plane touched down and it took ages to retrieve his bags and get through immigration. His mood instantly improved when his eyes fell on Amy. She was standing next to Carl, waiting for him to arrive.

Ignoring all protocol, she didn't wait for him to exit into the arrivals lounge. She ran up to him and threw her arms around him. Out of the corner of his eye, he saw Carl show a security guard his badge so that she wouldn't get arrested.

"I've missed you so much," he whispered in her ear.

"I'm so glad you're back. I just wish it was under different circumstances."

"Me too, honey. Me too."

When they approached Carl, he took Garrick's trolley from him, allowing him to walk with his arm around Amy. The funeral had already been organised and he quickly provided details. Garrick had a couple of days to settle back in and prepare himself for a ceremony he never thought he would be attending. He had always believed he would die before his sister, even going as far as giving her the details of where he wanted his ashes scattered.

Carl took him to his place to pick up clean clothes and then drove them both to Amy's house. She'd asked him to stay with her, at least for a few days, and he had agreed.

Ainin was pleased to see him, even though he didn't have a bone for him, and covered him in saliva as he licked everywhere he could reach before Garrick stopped him.

The following day, Garrick went to visit Tom. He'd never seen anyone look so cut up. He was pale and there were bags under his eyes, which were still red from crying.

"Has he slept at all?" Garrick asked Paul, the friend who Tom was staying with, when Tom went to the kitchen to put the kettle on.

"Only when I forced him to take a sleeping tablet. He's talking about selling his place and moving away. He says he won't go back there and has asked me to go and collect some things for him."

"I'll do it," Garrick said. "I have to pack up Tab's things anyway. I can't imagine Tom wanting to. I'll put everything in storage so he can decide what he wants to do with it when he's in a better place emotionally."

Garrick didn't stay long as his presence seemed to be upsetting Tom, rather than helping him. With Amy's help, he packed a bag for Tom and boxed up all of Tabitha's things. He hired a storage unit and placed everything inside. Later he gave Paul the key and Tom's bags.

The day of the funeral arrived and Garrick felt numb. Part of him didn't want to go. How could he say goodbye to his little sister, especially in front of so many people? Almost everyone from his branch of the Agency wanted to attend. None of his family were religious, so the ceremony wasn't being held in a church. The crematorium didn't have enough space for everyone who was there, so speakers had been set up for those who would have to remain outside. Thankfully the weather was warm and no rain was predicted.

Garrick was standing outside, waiting for the hearse to deliver the coffin containing Tabitha's body. Amy was waiting inside for him, along with his parents. They had arrived the night before so Garrick had been able to perform introductions. Amy and his mother had formed an instant bond and were comforting each other. His dad, predictably, was hiding his emotions.

Lawrence stood with Garrick, as did Tom and Carl and two of Tom's cousins. The six of them would carry the coffin in.

Rosemary was with Nadia and young Emily. Garrick hadn't gone to speak to them, but he would later.

The hearse finally arrived and the men got into position. Garrick found the coffin surprisingly light and almost asked for it to be opened so he could check his sister's body was really inside.

Silence fell as they entered the crematorium. Garrick kept his eyes forward; he couldn't bear to see any of the mourners. Once the coffin had been set in the correct place, he went to join Amy and his parents. Amy moved across so he could sit between her and his mother and he took hold of their hands. He glanced across at his father and saw that he, too, was holding his mother's hand.

The service wasn't the tedious affair he had been expecting. It was well run and the man in charge talked about life and the happiness Tabitha had filled the world with instead of dwelling on death. A number of people spoke, telling entertaining stories about Tabitha, including Nadia. Tears ran down her cheeks the whole time.

Tom didn't do a speech. He barely made it to the service. He had asked Garrick to deliver the eulogy and he had reluctantly agreed. He'd spent a long time writing it, with Amy's help, and he was satisfied that it said all he wanted it to.

All too soon it was his turn to speak. He had to force himself to stand. He could feel everyone's eyes on him as he took his place and began to orate. A tear fell down his face as he reached the end. He brushed it away before returning to Amy and his parents.

Finally it was all over and there was nothing more to do other than watch the coffin slide from view and the curtain close. Tabitha's ashes would be given to Tom eventually, but, at Tom's request, Garrick would keep them safe until he was in a better emotional state.

Carl had hired a hall for everyone to retreat to and caterers laid on sandwiches and other nibbles as well as cups of tea and coffee. Stronger drinks were available for those who wished to partake.

Garrick mingled until he couldn't stand receiving people's sympathies any longer. Amy stayed by his side and noticed him glancing across at Lawrence and his family.

"Go and speak to her," she said. "She's grieving too. And I'm probably the last person she wants to talk to."

Garrick nodded. He let go of Amy's hand and walked over to them. Emily saw him approaching and ran up to him. He dropped to one knee so she could wrap her arms around his neck. He carried her over to her adopted family.

"How are you?" he asked Nadia. It was the first time he had spoken to her since he kicked her out of his hotel room.

"Not good," she said. "I can't imagine you're doing any better."

"Not really."

"I'm sorry Garrick. If I'd never—"

He stopped her before she could finish the sentence. "None of this is your fault. I've read the report. You did what you could to help bring in a rogue werewolf. You put yourself at risk to get information about the resistance. Stop blaming yourself. It isn't justified."

"Thank you," she said. She held out her hand to place it on his arm, but withdrew it before making contact.

"Can I have a quick word?" Lawrence asked and Garrick handed Emily over to Nadia.

"She's scared," Lawrence said as soon as they were out of hearing. "She's worried that this Lewis person is going to find her and make good on his promise to kill her."

"Tell her not to worry. I'll take care of it."

"What are you going to do?"

"I'm going to find that son of a bitch and when I do, I'm going to kill him."

Revenge

Lewis went to his rental and packed his bag. He needed to get out of there, fast. It was unlikely the Agency would find it as he had rented it under an assumed name, and not the one he used on the hire car, but it wasn't worth taking any chances.

Using yet another fake driving licence and stolen credit card, he booked himself into a hotel room for the night. He would need to get another car in the morning. But first, he needed to call Derek and let him know what had happened. He was not going to be happy.

Derek was surprisingly calm when Lewis finished telling him the full story. He agreed that what Lewis had done was logical. It had worked in the past and there was no way for Lewis to know he was being played by Nadia.

"Do you want me to head home?" Lewis asked, secretly hoping he would say yes.

"Not yet. I think you can still be of help to Lia. Nadia has probably already provided the Agency with your description so dye your hair and stop shaving. And do not, I repeat, do not go after Nadia. She will be well guarded. You can have your revenge when we are in a position to take down the Agency once and for all."

"Understood," Lewis said then hung up.

His next call was to Lia. She was probably going to gloat about his failure. He was quite pleased when it went straight to voicemail. He wasn't so happy when she called him back at just past midnight. He had just fallen asleep and the ringing of his phone jerked him awake.

Surprisingly, Lia didn't seem happy that he had failed. The death of the Agent pleased her, but she had been hoping that he would succeed with Nadia and asked what the next move was and how she could help.

He thanked her and said he would call her back in the morning, after he had gotten his head together. He had no idea what he was going to do, but he didn't want to admit that to Lia.

He slept badly. Every time he closed his eyes he could see Nadia's face. Derek had told him to stay away from her, but he wasn't sure he would be able to. He was going to kill her for setting him up. He didn't know how, he just knew that he would. And soon.

He rose early, ate breakfast in his room and headed out, walking to the local shopping centre, which he discovered had two hairdressers and a barber. He could, of course, get a bleaching kit and dye his hair himself, but he cared about his appearance and wanted it to be done professionally.

The first hairdresser was fully booked for the rest of the week. The second however, after a bit of sweet talking and a sob story about being dumped by his cheating girlfriend, said they could fit him in the following day for a dye, cut and blow dry. If he was changing his hair colour, he might as well change the style as well.

He ran his hand over his chin. He usually shaved each morning and he found the stubble irritating. He hated the thought of growing a beard, but he would look stupid with just a moustache.

His next stop was to a real-estate agency where he made appointments to view a number of vacant fully furnished houses later in the day. Next he had to get himself another hire car, before his appearance no longer matched that on the fake driving licence.

By the end of the day he had something to drive and somewhere to live. Both were lower class than his previous hires. He also had a new set of clothes, bought from a cheap retail shop. For a while he would be wearing those instead of his designer suits. By the end of the week, nobody would recognise him.

He didn't contact Lia, despite his promise. He had nothing to say to her. Once he knew what he was going to do and how she could help, then he could give her a call.

It took him two days to decide that Nadia was still his way into the Agency. The fact he couldn't get the idea of revenge out of his mind was only part of it.

He tried to call Lia, but there was no answer so he left her a voicemail, outlining his plan. He neglected to mention that Derek had told him to keep away from Nadia. A short while later, she called him back.

"Are you insane?" Lia said as soon as he answered. "She's probably going to be closely guarded."

"That's the point. I'm hoping she will have Agents keeping an eye on her twenty-four seven. What better way to find out the identities of Agents, where they live, who their families are?"

"I'm impressed," Lia told him. "It's not something I would have thought of. Watch the watchers."

"Precisely. All I need to know now is where she is. She's moved out of her place."

"She moved back in with her parents."

Lewis smiled. This was almost too easy. "What's their address?"

"I don't know."

"What do you mean you don't know? Well, find out."

"I can't. And trust me, I've tried. It's a closely guarded secret."

"Damn. Never mind. I'll find her. She's a creature of habit. I can't imagine she's avoiding all of her favourite places. I'll be in touch if I need anything."

When he hung up, he tapped his phone against his chin, a habit he had when he was thinking. He would have to leave it a few days, until his beard had begun to grow, then he would stake out the coffee shop where he first met her. They knew her well there and he couldn't imagine she would find somewhere else. Nadia was one of those women who didn't like to compromise and once she had found a coffee she liked, it would take a lot to make her go somewhere else.

In the end it took a week before she turned up. It took him that long to work out she was still going there, just at a different time to her usual. Some days she was early, others she was late.

He had been tempted to ask the staff about her, but he was worried they would tell her and he didn't want her tipped off.

He spent another week watching her, seeing who was keeping an eye on her, but he failed to spot anyone. If someone was, they were as good as he was. He also failed to find out where she lived. He observed her going to the Agency headquarters each day, but never saw her leave. Frustration was beginning to set in. He was tempted to just kill her the next chance he got, but he was a professional and that would achieve nothing. He would just have to wait.

A few days later, there was a knock on his door. Assuming it was a salesman or someone touting their religion, he ignored it, but the caller didn't go away. The knocking became more insistent.

Grumbling to himself, he opened the door. When he saw who stood on his doorstep, a feeling of dread filled him. He was in serious trouble.

---------------------------∞-------------------------

Lewis wasn't the only one getting frustrated. Garrick had spent almost every minute of his spare time trying to track down Lewis, but to no avail. The man seemed to have disappeared. Nobody matching his description could be found anywhere. It would have been helpful if Nadia had taken a photo of him, but he could hardly blame her for not thinking of it.

His car and the place he had been renting were thoroughly searched, but both had been hired under assumed names and he had left nothing behind which would give any indication as to his real identity or where he would go next.

It was possible, of course, that he had left the city, or even the country, but Garrick didn't think so. From what Nadia had said about him, he was sure he would stick around, to make Nadia pay for setting him up if for nothing else.

Life at the Agency continued as normal. Tom handed in his resignation; he couldn't bear to be in the building as it was too full of memories of Tabitha.

Garrick stayed in touch with him and was aware that he was spending all of his time searching for Lewis. They shared what little information they had and made sure they weren't both covering the same ground.

A few weeks after the funeral, Garrick got a call from Nadia. It was the first time she had called him since that day, so he took the call.

"Garrick, I think someone is watching me. I haven't seen them, but I can feel it. I know that sounds strange, but I'm scared. Has someone from the Agency organised Agents to keep a watch over me?"

It had been discussed, but it was decided it would be a waste of resources. They would be better off concentrating on finding Lewis. Nadia herself had also insisted that that was the best course of action, but that didn't mean her wishes had been adhered to.

"No. When and where?" He didn't accuse her of being paranoid; it was highly likely she was being watched.

She gave him the name and location of the café where she got her coffee and let him know what time she would be going there the next day. He wasn't happy that she was still visiting the place, even though she had to drive there rather than walk, but he approved of the fact that she never went at the same time two days in a row.

"I'll investigate. Thanks for letting me know."

He smiled when he hung up. It was Lewis, it had to be. Finally he would get his hands on him.

He arrived at the location a lot earlier than Nadia, but he didn't enter the café. Instead he went to the building opposite and climbed onto the roof. From there, he had a good view of the café and the road it was on.

He took out his binoculars and viewed the road, looking at all the parked cars and noting down their licence plate numbers.

Nadia arrived and entered the café. A short time later she exited, coffee in hand, and got back into her car. One car pulled away and appeared to be following her, but it could just be coincidence.

266

As soon as he got back to headquarters, he ran the licence plate and discovered it was a hire car. He visited the firm and obtained a copy of the man's driver's licence. It didn't match the man he had seen driving the car, in regard to hair colour and facial hair, but that didn't mean it wasn't the same man. He showed it to Nadia and she confirmed it looked like Lewis. There was no hiding his eyes.

Garrick didn't want to take any chances, so he watched for two more days. Both days, Nadia was followed by the same man in the same car. Investigations uncovered that he had rented a house under the same name, so Garrick decided to pay him a visit.

Before doing so, he called Tom, letting him know where he was going and when. Tom arranged to meet him there.

It was dark outside when Tom's car pulled up behind Garrick's. The men got out and met between the cars.

"Stay here until I am certain it's Lewis inside and I have him under control."

"Alright," Tom said, though he didn't sound happy about it.

Garrick checked his guns and made sure his handcuffs were readily available before he made his way to the front door.

There was no answer when he knocked, so Garrick knocked again, louder and more persistent. He was about to knock for a third time, when the door opened.

The man standing in front of him looked exactly how Nadia had described him, if you changed the hair colour and removed the facial hair. The look of shock on his face told Garrick this was the man he was looking for.

He took advantage of the man's surprise and had him in handcuffs before he had time to react.

"You and me are going to have a little chat," he said and pushed him backward into the house. He followed after him and closed the door behind him. He would let Tom in once he had Lewis tied up and was one hundred percent certain he had the right man.

---------------------------∞---------------------------

Tom watched Garrick enter the house then returned to his car. He had an old high school buddy who was a member of a militia group. The man owed him a favour and he had called it in.

He opened the boot of his car and removed an RPG launcher. He inserted the grenade, as he had been instructed, and pointed it toward the house.

He didn't care that Garrick was inside; all that mattered was that he had the man who killed Tabitha right where he wanted him.

Giving no thought to Garrick, he aimed his weapon and fired. A sense of euphoria flowed through him as he watched it hit his target. The explosion was satisfyingly loud.

He didn't stick around to witness the destruction. He needed to get away before anyone saw him. Stashing the weapon back in his car, he jumped into the driver's seat.

"That was for you, Tab," he said as he sped away.

Amnesia

Lewis groaned as he sat up. "What the hell hit me?" he asked as he looked around. "Oh, I guess it was the house."

Rubble lay all around him. He shook his head to clear it and wished he hadn't as pain shot through him. He tried to stand, which wasn't easy with his hands tied behind his back.

He heard movement behind him and turned around to find Garrick staring at him.

"You're awake, I see," Garrick said. There seemed to be no hostility in his voice.

"What the hell happened?" Lewis asked. Garrick had just started to interrogate him when there was an explosion and it felt like the entire house was collapsing.

"I don't know."

Lewis looked at Garrick sharply. Something was wrong. He sounded unsure of himself. From what he had heard from both Lia and Nadia, that was something that never happened. He was always in control, of himself and the situation, even when things weren't going as planned.

"Where are we?" Garrick asked.

The question confused Lewis. Why would Garrick be asking where they were? He had turned up on his doorstep so he must know their location. Lewis decided to humour him.

"My house. At least the house I was renting."

Garrick looked around him at the mess. The amount of dust in the air suggested that whatever had destroyed the room they were in, happened not too long ago. "Something tells me you're not going to get your deposit back."

Then Garrick frowned at him. "Who are you? Come to think of it, who am I? And what are we doing here?"

Lewis couldn't believe what he was hearing. Was Garrick winding him up? But what would be the point of pretending he had lost his memory?

"We need to get out of here before the authorities show up," he said, wondering how Garrick would react. "Can you get these off me?"

Garrick did so, then stared at the handcuffs in wonder. "How did I know how to do that?" There was a trick to releasing the cuffs and he had done it instinctively.

"I'll explain later," Lewis said as he rubbed his wrists.

He left the destroyed room and climbed over bricks and broken pieces of wood and other things and made his way to the back of the house. By some miracle, his bedroom was still intact, so he quickly packed his things into a bag and grabbed his wallet and car keys.

"Let's go," he said to Garrick, who just looked at him, refusing to move.

"How do I know I can trust you?" he asked.

"Right now, you don't have a choice. You can either come with me or you can stay here and wait for the Agency to arrive. It's up to you, but I'm leaving."

"What Agency?"

Lewis couldn't believe his luck. Garrick really had lost his memory. The roof collapsing on them must have hit him in the head. They were lucky they were still alive. Lewis didn't believe in God, but if loss of memory was the only thing either of them suffered, then someone was looking out for them.

"I'll explain once we're safe. Now are you coming or not?"

Lewis drove to a local park. It was dark so it was unlikely that anyone would be about to disturb them. As he drove, he pondered what to do. He would need to get a hotel room for a few nights. And a change of clothes for Garrick. And he would need to ditch the car. He had no idea if Garrick had passed on any information about him to anyone else, but he didn't want to take the risk.

Once he had himself and Garrick out of sight, he would put his mind to how to make the most of the situation. Nobody had ever been able to get an Agent to betray the Agency before, but Garrick didn't know he was an Agent.

His phone was in his pocket. Somehow it had survived the explosion. He would have to give Lia a call, and Derek, to let them know what had happened.

He led Garrick over to a bench and asked if he had his phone on him. Garrick checked his pockets and withdrew a mobile. Lewis took it from him, dropped it on the ground and stamped on it.

"They can trace it," he explained. In reality he didn't want Garrick making or receiving any calls which might jog his memory.

"Are you now going to explain who 'they' are?" Garrick asked as he sat down. If he cared that his phone had just been destroyed, he didn't show it.

Lewis sat next to him. "I will, but I don't think you are going to believe me."

"Try me."

"I'm a werewolf. So are you. There is an Agency who hunts us down. I was captured and you rescued me, which was why I was in handcuffs. I have no idea how they found us or what happened to the house."

Garrick was looking at him as though he was insane.

"We're both werewolves?"

Lewis shrugged. "I told you you wouldn't believe me."

"Of course I don't believe you. No sane person would."

"You want proof? Come for a run with me."

Lewis was aware that, like all Agents, Garrick injected himself with a serum made from werewolf blood, which gave them enhanced speed. He wouldn't be as fast as Lewis himself was, but he hoped it would be enough to convince Garrick that he wasn't human.

Lewis took off, going much slower than he could, but faster than a human. Garrick stared at his retreating body, shook his head and took off after him. Lewis allowed him to catch up before increasing his speed. He didn't slow until they had done a full lap of the park and had returned to the bench. Neither were out of breath.

"Now do you believe me?" he asked.

"Maybe. So what else do I need to know?"

Lewis debated how much to reveal. In the end, he decided to tell him nearly everything, other than the fact he was on the Agency's side, not the werewolves'.

"I'm Lewis," he said. "We've been friends for years, which is why you risked your life to rescue me."

"And I am?"

"Tony. Tony Barrett." There was no way he was going to let Garrick know his real name; it might bring back his memory. "You're my second in command. I'm the leader of the local resistance movement, which is why I was targeted."

"So it was you they were trying to kill, not me?"

"They were trying to kill both of us."

He then went on to explain everything he knew about the Agency. The fact they forced werewolves to register with them and take regular injections, which prevented them from turning into a wolf, and killed them if they didn't. How they could recognise an unregistered werewolf by their aura.

"So you're saying that the red glow I can see surrounding you is your aura and it's only red because the Agency haven't injected you with their serum?" Lewis nodded. "So I glow red as well?"

Again Lewis nodded. It didn't matter that he was lying as Garrick wouldn't find out. It was impossible to see your own aura. "But only werewolves or Agents can see it. And before you ask, no it doesn't show up in a mirror so you can't check."

"What else can you tell me about myself?"

Lewis decided to stick to the truth, almost. "Your parents are still alive but don't live nearby. You had a sister, who you were close to."

"Had?"

"The Agency killed her."

Lewis waited for that news to register with Garrick, then continued. "No wife or kids. You've been with the resistance too long to risk settling down. You didn't want to put a partner in danger."

"Where do I live?"

272

"The other side of town," Lewis said, "but you can't go there. Agents are probably watching it, hoping to catch one of us, assuming they know we're not dead."

Garrick didn't question what he was being told. Lewis wasn't sure he believed him, but he was showing no obvious sign of doubt.

"So what do we do now?" he asked.

"First, we have to ditch my car. It can be traced to me. I'll acquire another one in the morning. We need to get off the streets. There are people I can call, but not until the morning."

"Hold on a minute," Garrick said. "Something isn't right here. If I've lost my memory because I got hit in the head, why don't I have a concussion? Shouldn't I have some symptoms? Pain in the head? Dizzy spells? Blurred vision?"

"It's the werewolf blood in you. It made you heal quickly."

Lewis had no idea if he was right or not, but it sounded plausible.

"Other than my memory it seems," Garrick said.

Lewis grabbed his bag from the car and then the two men began to walk. Lewis used the Sat Nav on his phone to find the nearest hotel and booked a room with twin beds using his own credit card; he had run out of fake or stolen ones. He would need to get hold of more. It was a risk, but not much of one. He hadn't told anybody his last name so the chances of him being found were low.

He woke early the next morning and went out to buy breakfast. Garrick was awake by the time he returned, still dressed in his ripped and dirty clothes. He was playing with the pendant on the chain around his neck. Lewis knew what it was. He wondered whether he could persuade Garrick to remove it, giving him full access to his mind, but decided not to try. It might cause him to become suspicious and that was the last thing that Lewis wanted.

After they had eaten, Lewis said he would go out and buy Garrick some clothes. He didn't think it was a good idea for Garrick to go outside looking the way he did. Garrick looked down at himself and was forced to agree.

"Stay here," Lewis said. "Any idea what size you are?"

"Hold on," Garrick said and went into the bathroom. Lewis could only assume he was checking the labels in his clothes. He called the details out through the closed door and Lewis noted them down.

"I'll be back soon," Lewis said loudly enough for his voice to travel through the door. "Don't go anywhere."

Leaving Garrick alone might be a mistake, but it was a risk he had to take. The man had no memory of who he was, so as far as he was concerned, Lewis was telling him the truth. At least, he had been given no reason, so far, to doubt him. But that didn't mean he wouldn't get his memory back while Lewis was away and if he did, Lewis had no idea what Garrick would do.

Despite his misgivings, Lewis left the hotel room. It didn't take him long to find a shop that was open and had jeans and t-shirts in Garrick's size. Almost as an afterthought, he also purchased socks and underwear. He hadn't asked him what type he preferred, but something told him Garrick wasn't fussy.

Next he purchased toiletries for himself and Garrick. The bathroom in his rented house had been severely damaged so he hadn't ventured into it. His mouth tasted like a warthog's backside, not that he knew what one tasted like, and he needed to brush his teeth and use mouthwash.

While he was out, he took the opportunity to phone both Lia and Derek. Lia wanted him to kill Garrick, but Derek thought he was doing the right thing by trying to get him on their side.

When he returned to the hotel room, Garrick was sitting on one of the beds, watching TV, wearing just a towel. His wet hair indicated that he had taken a shower.

Lewis wasn't into men, but he couldn't help noticing how perfectly sculptured Garrick's body was. While women appreciated Lewis's body, he could imagine them liking Garrick's more and he couldn't help feeling a little jealous. Then his eyes fell on the bruising covering the entire left side of Garrick's body. The fact that he had escaped the house with no broken bones was nothing short of a miracle.

Lewis himself ached all over, but didn't think his body looked as battered as Garrick's did, but then again, he hadn't looked at himself in a mirror.

He threw the bags onto the bed Garrick was on, all except for the one containing the toiletries.

"I'm going for a shower. Get dressed."

"And then what are we going to do?" Garrick asked.

Lewis had started toward the bathroom, but stopped and turned to look at back at Garrick.

"Then we are going to work out how to get our revenge on the Agency."

Questions

While Lewis was shopping for clothes for him, Garrick showered and then sat on the bed, thinking. Something didn't feel right. He had listened to everything that Lewis had said and while he couldn't detect any lies, he was sure he wasn't telling the full truth.

He thought about his t-shirt, which he had thrown in the bin because it had blood on it, blood from the gash in his head. What had really caused the house to explode? If he had stuck around and investigated, he might have been able to figure it out, but Lewis had whisked him away so quickly there hadn't been time to take a proper look.

Even if he had, would he have known what to look for? What was his background? Was he an expert in that area? He had no way of knowing.

Then there were the handcuffs. If the Agency had placed them on Lewis, then how did he know how to remove them? And why hadn't he done so earlier?

He glanced across at the jacket he had placed on the only chair in the room. Something told him it was important to him, so despite the fact that it had definitely seen better days, he couldn't bring himself to throw it away.

When he had woken up in the house that Lewis claimed to have been renting, he had found a gun near his hand and had instinctively picked it up and put it in his jacket pocket.

If it was his gun and he and Lewis had been alone in the house, why was it near his hand?

He had another one down the back of his trousers and a third in a jacket pocket, along with lots of ammo. He also found a knife in the inside of his jacket and another down one boot, so he had been heavily armed. While this fitted in well with the story of him rescuing Lewis from the Agency, it could also indicate many other things.

How did he even know this mysterious Agency existed? He only had Lewis's word for that.

There was something about Lewis that had him on edge. He was a little too smooth. He gave Garrick the impression he was only telling him what he wanted him to know. He was taking advantage of his loss of memory and Garrick had no idea why.

Then there was the fact that Lewis had destroyed his phone. While the excuse that it could be being tracked was plausible, if Lewis had been in the hands of the Agency, wasn't it more likely that his phone would be tracked? Yet Garrick had seen that he still had it on him. Was there something on his own phone that Lewis didn't want him to see?

Other questions tumbled through his mind, but went unanswered. Did he really have a sister that was killed by this mysterious Agency? Him having a sister somehow felt right and something inside him told him she was dead, but how? Was it natural causes? Was it an accident? Or was it actually murder, as Lewis had said? And if so, who was responsible?

His mind drifted back to when he had first woken up with no memory. If he had just rescued Lewis, why would they have gone back to his house? It made no sense. Unless there had been something there they needed to collect. But if that was the case, why hadn't Lewis mentioned it?

Too many things didn't add up. Too much of what he had been told just didn't feel right.

He played with the chain around his neck. That was something else that felt important and he wanted to know why. Had someone special given it to him? Did it symbolise something? It was one of the many things he was desperate to know but he didn't trust that Lewis would tell him the truth if he asked him.

The other thing that was troubling him was his name. Surely it should have felt familiar or a memory should have been triggered as soon as he heard it, but it felt like a stranger's. He practiced saying it a few times.

"Hi, I'm Tony. Tony Barrett. Tony's the name. Mister Barrett, but you can call me Tony."

He shook his head. The words didn't feel right in his mouth.

Needing something to do, he went to the bathroom, picked his ruined t-shirt out of the bin and ripped a piece off it, one that had no blood on it. He then returned to the bed and proceeded to strip down and clean his guns. It came to him so naturally he must have done it many times before.

He wondered where he had learned. Had he been in the military? Had he served his country? Had he gone to war? Did they let werewolves serve in the armed forces? Was he even a werewolf?

That was the biggest elephant in the room. He couldn't get his head around the fact that werewolves were real. Allegedly. And he was one.

How could he be a mythical creature that wasn't supposed to exist? He had to admit that he was able to run faster than a human should have been able to, but there had to be a different explanation. Maybe he had been experimented on. Maybe the Agency did exist, but instead of hunting down and killing werewolves they were trying to create elite humans and he and Lewis had been their unwilling victims.

But why would Lewis lie? If he was trying to cover something up, why make up something that was clearly impossible? It just didn't make sense.

Garrick was feeling frustrated. He hated not knowing who he was. He had no idea about his past. Had he had his heart broken? Had he broken someone else's heart as well? Or instead? Had he broken the law? Had he killed someone? Was he wanted by the police as well as the Agency?

He wanted to go out, but he no longer had any clothes he could wear and where would he go even if he did? All he could do was wait for Lewis to come back and hope that he really was the friend he claimed to be.

Eventually Lewis returned and handed him some bags, which he assumed contained clothes. While Lewis showered, Garrick got dressed. The clothes were a reasonable fit and were non-descript enough that he wouldn't catch anyone's attention.

"What was my sister's name?" he asked as soon as Lewis exited the bathroom, drying his hair with a towel.

"Tabitha." There was no hesitation. If Lewis was lying, he was good at it. It wasn't the sort of name that would spring to mind when confronted with a question you didn't know the answer to.

He pulled his chain from under his t-shirt. "What's this? Why do I wear it?"

Lewis shrugged. "I have no idea. You were wearing it when I first met you. I've never seen you without it. You've never told me anything about it and I've never asked."

It was a reasonable answer, one he couldn't argue against. He tried something different.

"Why should I believe we are both werewolves? It's not a plausible explanation for our speed."

Lewis threw his towel on the floor. "I was wondering how long it would be before you asked me to prove it."

Garrick's eyes went wide as he started to undress.

"What the hell do you think you are doing?"

"Proving it to you. I don't want to ruin my clothes so I have to take them off first."

Garrick watched Lewis undress, revealing a well-maintained body. The sight didn't turn him on, so he obviously wasn't gay or bisexual, but he didn't feel the need to turn around either. He must have seen naked men before, enough for it not to bother him.

Once he was naked, Lewis began to transform. His jaw elongated, his ears grew and became pointed, fur began sprouting all over his body. Garrick was neither fascinated nor repulsed. He felt like he had seen this happen before, many times.

Well that was one question answered. He no longer doubted that Lewis was exactly what he claimed to be.

He waited patiently for Lewis to become human again and put his clothes back on.

"I guess you're a werewolf," he said as though it was the most natural sentence in the world. For him, it probably was. "So can I do that?"

"You used to be able to. I assume you still can. If you can remember how. Care to give it a try?"

Garrick shook his head. "Not right now. Does it hurt?"

"No. It's just a natural change in your body. Kind of like your cock elongating when you get excited."

Garrick grinned. He couldn't help himself. "Trust me, that's nothing like what happens when my body gets excited."

Lewis chuckled.

"Come on. Let's get out of here. We need to get ourselves another car and makes some plans."

Garrick still had a nagging doubt that something wasn't right, but he couldn't put his finger on exactly what it was. He temporarily put it from his mind. He would think about it more later, next time he was alone.

He picked up his jacket, put it on and followed Lewis out of the room.

Amy looked at her phone, wondering whether she should make the call or not. Garrick was probably just on a mission and couldn't take her calls or call her back. She was worrying over nothing.

But he had promised to call her as soon as he had finished work for the night, no matter how late it was, and he had never broken a promise before. And now it was morning.

If Tabitha had still been alive, she wouldn't think twice about calling her, but she wasn't.

Could she really call Lawrence or Carl? They would just think she was being a needy girlfriend, checking up on her man. After all, that's what she was being, wasn't it?

But she was worried about him. She just needed to know that he was safe.

Taking a deep breath, she dialled Carl's number. It rang four times before he answered and after each one she almost hung up. Part of her was praying that he wouldn't answer, that he wouldn't find out that she was panicking just because Garrick hadn't called her and wasn't answering his phone.

"Hi, Amy, this is a nice surprise. What's up?"

He didn't sound like he was angry at being disturbed.

"I know I'm probably being paranoid or overanxious, but I can't get hold of Garrick. He promised to call me last night and didn't. His phone keeps going to voicemail."

She braced herself for him to laugh at her, but he didn't.

"That doesn't sound like him. I can understand why you called me. Let me check the logs."

She could hear him tapping on a keyboard. A few moments later he was back on the line.

"It looks like he had a lead on Lewis he wanted to check out. He entered all of the information; car make and model as well as the registration and the address he went to. But he never checked back in. He always logs on to provide an update or calls in. Let me give him a call. If I don't get an answer, I'll send a team to the address he was going to. Don't worry. I'm sure he's fine. I'll call you back as soon as I know anything."

"Thank you," Amy forced herself to say before hanging up. 'Don't worry', Carl had said. How was she supposed to not worry? It wasn't just her he hadn't contacted, it was also the Agency, something he had never done before, according to Carl. Something must have happened to him.

She could feel panic welling up inside her. She needed to do something to take her mind off it all, so she took Ainin for a walk. It didn't help. While it occupied her body, her mind was still free to think and she couldn't stop imagining all of the things that could have happened. She pictured Garrick lying in a ditch, barely alive. Or by the side of a road. Or in a morgue, dead.

By the time she got home again, she was feeling even worse. Carl sent a text to say he was leading a team who would try to track Garrick down. This was both good news and bad. Carl hadn't been able to contact him, which meant it wasn't just her calls he wasn't answering. However, it indicated that something was really wrong. She couldn't help wishing he had answered Carl's call and told him he never wanted to see her again. It would hurt, a lot, but it would have meant he was alive.

It was a Saturday, so she didn't have work as a distraction. She tried to study, but failed abysmally. Half an hour after opening her book, she had read the opening paragraph of the chapter four times and still hadn't taken in what it said.

She slammed the book closed in frustration. Ainin whined. He was worried about her.

"I'm sorry, boy," she said as she rubbed his ear. "I don't mean to worry you. I just wish Garrick was here."

She jumped when her doorbell rang. She ran to answer it. Maybe it was Garrick, but he now had his own key, so why wouldn't he use it? Maybe it was Carl with good news. Garrick had been found and was injured, but okay.

She froze. Maybe it was Carl with bad news. Maybe they had found a body.

She stared at the door, unable to find the courage to answer it. When the doorbell rang again, Ainin barked, telling her to get on with it.

With a shaking hand, she opened the door.

But it wasn't Carl standing on her doorstep, nor Garrick. It was Nadia.

Search

Carl quickly put a team of Agents together to go to Garrick's last known destination, with himself as the lead. It wasn't that he didn't trust anyone else to find him, it was just that he felt a personal connection to Garrick which made his safety his responsibility.

He made sure everyone was adequately armed before giving the command to head out. They were taking two cars, both Agency cars that had bulletproof glass.

As soon as they approached the address Garrick had left, Carl spotted Garrick's car and instructed the driver to pull up behind it. It was parked close to a house which was partially destroyed. A quick check of house numbers told him it was the one Garrick had logged that he was going to. It was surrounded by crime scene tape, indicating that law enforcement had been and gone.

A sense of dread settled in the bottom of Carl's stomach as he took out his phone and called a contact he had in the local police department.

A feeling of relief flowed through him when he was told that no bodies had been found. Given the situation, he received permission for his team to enter the premises, at their own risk. He was given no assurance around how safe it was.

He made another quick call, to an Agent who had experience in explosions and finding their causes, and she agreed to meet them at the scene as soon as she could.

He told the assembled team all he knew and said they would wait for Sally Haynes to arrive. Most of those present had worked with her in the past and knew she would be able to tell them what had happened. More importantly, she would let them know what parts of the partially destroyed building were safe for them to enter.

While waiting, Carl decided to gain entry into Garrick's car, in case he had left anything inside which would indicate where he had gone.

It was locked, so he had one of the Agents open it for him. The Agent in question had been a car thief in her youth and had been given the choice between going to jail or joining the Agency. Carl thought she made the right decision.

The Agent had the car unlocked in seconds, making Carl wonder how secure any car really was. He checked the glove box first and found Garrick's wallet. The gun he usually kept there was gone and there was no sign of his phone. Carl checked the car thoroughly but could find no evidence that anyone else had been in the car or anything to show where Garrick had gone or why he had left the car behind.

There was also no sign of blood, indicating that Garrick hadn't been ambushed before leaving the car.

Carl looked at the remains of the house again and prayed that Garrick hadn't been inside when it collapsed.

Sally arrived sooner than Carl had been expecting and she whistled when she saw the state the house was in.

She was a tiny woman, with short blonde hair, cropped into a bob. Despite her diminutive stature, she wasn't timid and was used to issuing orders.

Carl was technically her boss, but that didn't stop her ordering him to keep his distance while she investigated. She showed no fear as she calmly walked up to the broken structure and climbed over rubble to enter the premises.

She wasn't gone long and had a frown on her face when she walked back to Carl.

"It's safe enough for others to enter, as long as they're careful."

Carl nodded and the rest of the team set off.

"What happened?" Carl asked.

"If this had been in a war zone, I would have said it was hit by a small missile or a rocket propelled grenade, but here?" She shrugged her shoulders. "However, I would still put my money on that's what it was."

Carl thanked her before telling her to go home. After all, it was her day off.

By the time he entered the ruins, Agents had explored most of the remains of the house. The bathroom had toiletries in it, indicating someone had been living there when it was attacked, but the bedroom contained no personal items.

Blood was found in the lounge and a sample had been taken for analysis and DNA comparison.

"Anything useful?" he asked the Agent who was giving him the report. "Anything to tell us if Garrick or Lewis were here or where they might have gone?"

The Agent shook his head. "Nothing. But we'll keep looking."

Carl didn't thank him. He was just doing his job, after all. He took the blood sample and said he would take it to headquarters.

He drove a little too fast on his way back and went straight to the lab, telling the first scientist he saw that he had to stop whatever he was doing and get onto DNA testing the blood sample he handed over.

"Compare it to Garrick Barton's DNA and also test for werewolf genes," he snapped.

Then he took a deep breath. Realising how terse he was being, he apologised and explained the situation. The young man said he completely understood and would get the results to him as quickly as he could.

He went to his office, opened up an app on his computer and typed in Garrick's mobile number. If it was switched on, he would be able to find out where it was. The screen told him the program was unable to find a signal.

He wasn't disappointed. It had been a long shot anyway. If the phone had been switched on, it wouldn't have kept going straight to voicemail. The phone could be switched off, out of power or broken. Any of those situations would result in the program not working.

He closed down the app and opened another one. Most Agent's didn't know it, but all of their phones contained trackers, which would work even if the phone was out of action. Garrick was aware of this and knew how to disable it, but Carl hoped he hadn't done so.

285

It took a while, but eventually a map appeared on his screen with a flashing red dot. Garrick was in a park; at least his phone was.

Carl made a quick call to one of the Agents who were still at Lewis's house, asking for two of them to meet him at the park. They arrived before he did and had already called in the licence plates of the few cars which were in the car park.

"The phone was about five hundred meters from the carpark in that direction," he said, pointing with his finger. The three of them headed out, checking the ground and surroundings as they went, moving slowly enough to not miss anything.

They passed a couple of waste bins, both of which were checked before they headed toward a bench. On the ground was the remains of a phone. It was smashed beyond repair, but Carl recognised it as the make that Garrick used.

"Search the immediate area," he instructed and pulled the back off the phone as soon as they could no longer see what he was doing. Inside he found what he was looking for. There was no question that he was holding the remains of an Agent's phone.

"Where are you, Garrick?" he said to himself.

He heard ringing and looked over. One of the Agents was walking toward him as he spoke into his phone, hanging up just before he reached him.

"One of the cars in the carpark was hired by someone with the same name given to the real estate agent who rented out the house."

"So Garrick made it to the house, then came here with Lewis," Carl said. "The question is, who was holding who prisoner?"

It was a rhetorical question and the Agent had the good sense not to try to answer.

Carl's phone rang and he grabbed it. Seeing it was from a number within headquarters, he said, "What have you got to report?"

"I'm sorry sir, but the DNA is a match to Agent Barton's."

Carl swore loudly. He then apologised and thanked the young man for getting the results so quickly.

He ended the call and dialled another number. This was one phone call he wished he didn't have to make.

-------------------------∞-------------------------

Amy stared at Nadia. She was too shocked to speak. She had no idea what Nadia was doing there, but she was the last person she wanted to see.

"Please can I come in?" Nadia asked. She seemed nervous, but could well be faking it.

"No," Amy said and tried to shut the door, but Nadia put her foot in the way.

"Please. I'm not here to cause trouble. I'm here to apologise."

Too stressed to argue, Amy stood aside and allowed Nadia to enter.

"The kitchen's at the end of the hall," she said then shut the door. Somewhat reluctantly, she followed Nadia down the hallway.

Without asking if Nadia wanted anything to drink, Amy put the kettle on.

"What do you want Nadia? Now really isn't a good time."

"I know Garrick's missing. That's part of the reason I'm here. The last few weeks have made me realise what a complete and utter bitch I have been. I owe you an apology. Even though she's no longer here, I can still hear Tab telling me to do it before it's too late. We never know what is going to happen and I know if I don't do this, I'll regret it for the rest of my life."

Amy said nothing. She didn't know what to say. If Nadia was up to something, she had no idea what it was.

Nadia took a deep breath before continuing. "I had no right to try to come between you and Garrick. I have been in love with him for a long time and thought it was just a matter of time before we got together. Then you came along and stole him from me."

Amy opened her mouth, but Nadia held up her hand.

287

"There's no need for you to say it. I know that's not what happened. He was never mine for you to steal. I guess I was delusional, thinking that if I got you out of the picture, he would be mine. I reacted badly. I'm just giving you an explanation, not an excuse. There's no excuse for what I did."

Still Amy remained silent. The kettle switched itself off and she made two cups of tea. She had no idea if Nadia even drank tea and didn't care. The other woman made no complaint when she added milk but no sugar to one of the mugs and passed it to her.

"I don't expect you to forgive me; I wouldn't if I was in your shoes. I just had to come over to let you know how sorry I am and that you don't have anything to worry about from me. I now know that no matter what I do, Garrick could never love me the way he loves you and I have to move on."

"Why now?" While Amy could almost believe what Nadia was saying, she couldn't understand why she chose that moment to see her. She knew that Garrick was missing and that Amy would be worried sick. Did she think Amy was more likely to forgive her while she was so vulnerable?

"I can't even begin to imagine what you are going through right now and I couldn't bear the thought of you going through it alone."

She sounded so sincere that Amy found herself believing her.

"Take your drink through to the lounge. I'll find some biscuits to go with it."

The two women sat and talked for a few hours, getting to know each other. Nadia said she wished they had done that in the first place and blamed herself completely for not allowing that to happen. They found they had a lot in common and, under different circumstances, might have been friends.

When Amy's phone rang and she saw it was Carl, she tensed up.

"It might be good news," Nadia said.

Amy answered it and, with Carl's permission, put it on speaker so Nadia could hear what Carl had to say.

"We've found Garrick's car at a house that the person he suspected was Lewis was renting. The house was partially destroyed when we got there. There's evidence that he was inside."

"What evidence?" Nadia asked as she reached over and took Amy's hand in hers.

Both women heard Carl hesitate before saying, "His blood was found inside the house."

Amy began to hyperventilate.

"It doesn't mean anything," Nadia said. "There are a lot of reasons why he may have been bleeding. He may be fine, other than a slight cut."

"We found his phone in a nearby park," Carl continued. "Smashed. There is also evidence that he was there with Lewis."

"Where is he?" Amy asked. "What's happened to him?"

"We don't know."

Amy burst into tears.

Nadia took her in her arms and started rocking her. "They'll find him. I promise you, they're going to find him. He's okay. They'll get him back to you."

Nadia kept her arms around Amy, holding her and saying soothing words until she eventually stopped crying.

Two days later, late in the evening, Carl got a call from one of his Agents.

"We think we've tracked down Lewis."

The words were music to his ears. He had tasked every Agent to finding either Lewis or Garrick, but nobody had been able to find anything.

"Are you certain?"

"No, but we've been checking with every hotel in the area and the desk clerk at this one recognised the description of both Garrick and Lewis. And it looks like Lewis may have checked in under his own name."

It was almost too good to be true. But Carl wouldn't let himself get his hopes up. He had been to visit Amy the previous evening and she was in a terrible state. Nadia had moved in with her, just to make sure she ate something and got some sleep.

"Give me the details. I'll get a team together."

He wouldn't ask for volunteers as he was sure everyone wanted to be involved. Instead he chose the most seasoned Agents, those who could remain cool under any circumstance. He had no idea what they were going to find and wasn't going to take any chances that one of them would shoot before they found out what was going on.

"One other thing," the man on the other end of the phone said. "The clerk said that Garrick wasn't being held prisoner. He said they seemed like good friends."

"Let's not jump to any conclusions," Carl said. "Either Garrick is playing a part or Lewis is making him remain with him somehow."

As he said the words, he knew he would have to give the order to treat Garrick as a threat.

"Understood," the Agent said and hung up.

The entire journey to the hotel, Carl was tense. Garrick was friends with most of those he had chosen to bring him in and he wasn't sure how they would react if they were forced to shoot him. On top of that, Garrick was a formidable opponent who could probably take out a number of Agents single-handedly. If he was now the enemy, it was a dangerous situation Carl was leading the Agents into.

As soon as he arrived, he showed the woman in reception his credentials and she provided him with a key to the room Lewis and Garrick were staying in. She also confirmed she thought both men were in there.

Carl thanked her before making his way to the room, stopping outside the door and waiting for all of his Agents to be in position before opening the door.

He handed the key to the woman on his right, placed himself in front of the door, drew his gun and nodded his head. She swiped the card and pulled down on the handle. Carl then kicked the door open.

Without taking time to observe the scene, he rushed in. A man was sitting on the bed and jumped to his feet as Carl approached and aimed his gun at him. There was no sign of Garrick.

"Put your weapon down," Carl instructed.

"You're from the Agency, I presume," the man said in a loud voice. He looked enough like the description he had been given that Carl was confident that he was confronting Lewis.

He heard the other Agents come in behind him. Two remained outside, guarding the door. They had instructions to shoot anyone who came through, even if it was Garrick.

Carl ignored the comment. "Lewis, you are under arrest for the murder of Tabitha Barton."

Lewis smiled. For someone who was surrounded by guns, all aimed directly at him, he didn't seem concerned.

"I don't think so," he said calmly then called out, "Tony."

He was transforming before he finished speaking. Carl was shocked by how fast he was. One second he was looking at a human, the next a wolf was launching itself at him. He almost didn't react in time. But he had planned for this scenario. He dropped to the ground and the Agent behind him shot the wolf in the chest once, twice, three times. At that distance, he couldn't miss.

The wolf went down, landing in a heap on the floor. As blood trickled from his mouth, he took one last breath and went still.

At the same moment, the bathroom door crashed open and a man emerged, gun drawn. The door hit one Agent and another went down as bullets started flying.

Carl stood up, swung around and fired four rounds into Garrick's unprotected back.

Reunion

Carl looked at Garrick through the monitor as he struggled against the straps which were holding his arms and legs in place. Not knowing what he was going to face, Carl had taken a tranquilizer gun with him and had pumped Garrick full of enough sedative to knock him out before he could get away.

Garrick had managed to shoot two Agents, but both were wearing body armour so suffered no more than bruising and sore muscles.

Carl sighed. It could have gone a lot worse.

As soon as Garrick had come round, he had questioned him. Garrick held nothing back. He said his name was Tony Barrett, he was a member of the resistance and was a werewolf. He also said he knew that the Agency had killed his sister and as soon as he managed to free himself, he would get his revenge.

Carl didn't know what was wrong with him. He showed no sign of recognising him, or where he was. The only other people Carl had allowed into the room were Lawrence and Nadia, neither of whom Garrick paid any attention to.

Both were now in his office, watching Garrick struggle.

"Opinions," he said. "What did that bastard Lewis do to him and how?"

"If you ask me, I don't think Lewis did anything, other than take advantage of the situation," Lawrence said. "Garrick is still wearing his chain, so he couldn't have gotten into his head. He also has signs of a recent headwound and we all know he was in the house when it collapsed. Maybe this is nothing more than lost memories and lies."

"You mean Lewis discovered that Garrick lost his memory, so he has no idea who and what he is, and somehow Lewis convinced him they are friends?" Nadia asked.

"Something like that."

"Then let's find out," Carl said.

Leaving the other two to watch from his office, Carl returned to the medical suite in which Garrick was tied up.

From his prone position, Garrick lifted his head and glared at him, but remained silent as Carl entered the room and took a seat beside the bed to which Garrick was strapped.

"Let me run a scenario by you," he said. "You wake up in a partially demolished room with no idea who you are or how you got there."

A look passed across Garrick's face and was quickly gone, but not before Carl saw it. Lawrence had been right, but Garrick wasn't prepared to admit it.

"Let me continue. Lewis, if that's his real name, told you all about yourself. What did he tell you about the Agency?"

"The truth. That you hunt down and murder werewolves. That you killed my sister."

"Actually it was Lewis that killed Tabitha, but I don't expect you to believe that. So tell me, what did he do to convince you that he was telling the truth about you? I'm sure you must have had your doubts."

"He showed me how fast he was, how fast I am. There's no way in hell I'm human."

"I can assure you you are," Carl said. "But you're an Agent and like all Agents, you inject yourself with a serum made from werewolf blood. It makes you stronger, faster, improves all of your senses, as I'm sure you've seen."

Garrick just grunted. He was listening to what Carl was saying, but not believing any of it.

"But again, why should you believe me? And I know you well enough to know that, even without your memories, you wouldn't just accept what you were being told. What did he do to finally remove your doubts?"

"He turned into a wolf."

Carl nodded his head. "I can see why that would work. So he has you convinced that you are who he said you are and that we are the enemy. What can I do to change your mind?"

Garrick tried to raise his arms once more. "Releasing me would be a good start."

293

Carl laughed. "We both know that's not going to happen."

"Then this conversation is going nowhere. Why don't you just piss off and leave me alone or get my execution over and done with."

"We're not going to execute you. That's not what the Agency is about."

"You killed Lewis in cold blood. What was that if not an execution?"

The accusation angered Carl and he leaned forward. "Self-defence. He turned into a wolf and was going for my throat."

He took a deep breath to calm himself down. "Damn it, Garrick. Why won't you even try to consider that we may be telling the truth, that everything you were told were lies?"

Garrick looked at him coldly. "My name is Tony."

Carl sighed. He was getting nowhere. As he left the room, he could feel Garrick's eyes boring into his back. The man he considered a friend, more than a friend, hated him and he had no idea how to fix the situation.

He returned to his office and collapsed into his chair. He ran his fingers through his hair in frustration. "Any ideas?"

"Send Amy in," Nadia said.

Carl sat up straight. "No way. She's having a hard enough time coping as it is. Knowing that he has no memory of her might be the final straw. I know you don't like her, but that's just beyond cruel."

"She's tougher than you think," Nadia said. "I've been by her side since Garrick first went missing. We've called a truce. I'd even go as far as to say that we are becoming friends. I'm not suggesting this to hurt her. I really think it may help. If anyone is going to trigger his memory, it's going to be her."

Carl listened to what she was saying. It made sense, but he didn't like the thought of putting Amy alone in the room with Garrick, even if he was tightly secured. He might break loose and Amy would never be able to defend herself. Putting Agents in with them would defeat the purpose.

"All you can do is ask," Lawrence said.

Reluctantly, Carl called her and explained the situation. He had already told her that Garrick had been found alive, but he hadn't told her about his memory loss. He just said that something was wrong with him that they had to fix, assuring her that it wasn't life threatening.

She agreed to his request instantly, as he knew she would, and promised to head straight over. The fact that Garrick wouldn't recognise her didn't seem to bother her.

"Take me to him," were her first words as soon as she was escorted to Carl's office.

"Are you really sure about this?" he asked. "He won't know you. He'll think you're the enemy. He may even try to hurt you."

Amy didn't hesitate. "I'm sure."

"I'll take her down," Nadia said.

Carl and Lawrence watched the screen, waiting for the door to open. Finally it did and Amy walked in. The door closed behind her.

Trepidation filled him as he watched her turn around and lock the door.

Garrick was filled with confusion. The man who called himself Carl was either a great actor or he really did know him as Garrick, an Agent who worked under him. The only other two people who had been in to see him had also been convincing.

Yet if he was, indeed, an Agent, then that would mean he was a killer, that he hunted down and killed innocent people, just because they were werewolves, and he didn't think he was capable of doing that.

On the other hand, could he trust what Lewis had told him? This Carl person had said that wasn't what the Agency did. But then again, he had no reason to believe him.

And what about his sister? Both men had confirmed that she was dead, but they blamed each other.

He couldn't reconcile anything in his mind. Lewis had convinced him that he was telling the truth by turning into a werewolf, but Carl had an equally plausible counter story for everything he had been told.

And why was he still alive? Why hadn't the Agency killed him yet? What did they want from him?

But if Lewis had been lying, what had he been hoping to gain?

Questions swam around his mind, with no hope of being answered. All Garrick knew for certain was that he was being held prisoner and had to escape.

He lifted his head when the door opened once more, but it wasn't Carl this time. A tall thin woman walked in, too thin in his opinion. And she was a little too pale for him to find attractive. Her long dark hair was tied back behind her head and her rimless glasses distracted him from paying too much attention to her hazel eyes and long eyelashes.

He was mildly surprised when she locked the door behind her.

"Are you insane?" he heard Carl's voice echo around the room, presumably from a PA system. Did that mean that there were also microphones and cameras? "What do you think you are doing?"

"Making sure you don't interfere," she said, looking up at an object in the far corner of the room he hadn't noticed before.

"What are you supposed to be?" he asked as she looked him up and down. "A shrink?"

She ignored the question and continued to study him. He began to feel a little uncomfortable. It was almost as if she was mentally undressing him.

"Wow. I never thought I would enjoy seeing you tied up. You are usually so in control it's kind of a turn on seeing you so helpless."

Garrick was speechless. If she was there to interrogate him, she had a funny way of going about it.

She climbed onto the bed, straddling him. She unzipped his jacket and removed his knife from his inside pocket and placed it on the table next to them.

"How did you know that was there?" he asked. Nobody else had thought to look for it, not even Carl.

"I've undressed you many times. Though you don't usually have your jacket done up."

She could have been lying. He could have been searched while he was unconscious. But if that was the case, why would they let him keep the weapon? To make him believe that she knew him? Perhaps.

She placed her hands on his t-shirt and moved it up to his neck, exposing his bare chest.

Part of him felt a little disappointed when her eyes didn't widen in appreciation, but the disappointment soon fled when she put her hands on him. Her touch was soft and delicate and immensely pleasurable. When she placed her lips near his navel and began to trail kisses up his body, he almost moaned. When she reached his throat, she nibbled his neck before moving on to his earlobe, which she sucked.

"I see you haven't forgotten how much you enjoy this," she whispered into his ear.

His body wanted her and his mouth longed for her to kiss him, but instead she moved away and climbed off the bed. If she had been sent to tease him into submission, she was going to fail, but that didn't mean his body wasn't responding to her manipulations.

She went to his feet and removed his boots, taking the knife he had concealed down one and placing it on the table beside its mate. He looked at them out of the corner of his eye. If his hands were free, grabbing one and holding it against her throat until he was released would be easy. Leaving them there was a mistake she might regret making.

His socks were also removed before she climbed onto him once more. Starting just below his scrunched up t-shirt, she made her way down his body with her tongue, stopping when she reached the top of his jeans. She undid the button and lowered the zip before continuing down a little further.

Then she sat up and removed her cardigan and threw it, landing it on the camera, completely covering it.

"How can we protect you if we can't see what's going on?" Carl's voice sounded out. "Stop what you are doing and get out of there now, Amy."

To Garrick's ears, he sounded scared rather than angry. Garrick glanced down at his arms, which were secured to the bed. What did Carl think he would be able to do?

Amy ignored the voice and she pulled down his jeans. He lifted his hips a little to assist her. She tugged them down as far as she could before the straps on his legs got in the way.

"Behave," she said as she climbed off the bed once more and untied one strap at a time and pulled his jeans from his body.

Curious as to how far she was willing to go before she revealed her true agenda, he didn't move his legs.

She stood next to the bed and trailed her hands down his body, stopping at the waist band of his underwear. His body clearly showed her it wanted her to go lower.

She then looked at him. "All you have to do is say no."

Saying no was the last thing on his mind. She had him close to begging her to free him from the confines of his clothing and put her mouth on him. He was feeling excited, not violated.

She waited a moment for him to object. When he didn't, she removed his underwear.

Then her hand was where he wanted it to be. He laid his head down and revelled in the sensations flowing through him.

All too soon she withdrew and he raised his head once more so he could see her pull up her dress and remove her underwear.

As she slowly lowered herself onto him, he gasped. He had been expecting her to stop a long time before this moment. He knew that Carl was still listening in and would be able to work out what was going on, but he didn't care. All he cared about was how good this woman was making him feel.

He wanted more, much more. He wanted his hands on her. He wanted to feel his lips on hers.

"Untie me," he said. He wasn't sure if he had actually spoken out loud.

Carl's voice saying, "Amy, don't you dare," told him he had.

Amy leaned forward and released first one arm, then the other. It would have been easy to reach for a knife; she wouldn't have been able to stop him, but instead he sat up and pulled off first his jacket, then his t-shirt, dropping them on the floor. Then he put his hand behind her head and pulled her to him. He removed her glasses and placed them beside his knives. He then let her hair loose. As he ran his fingers through it, he kissed her deeply. She kissed him back as though she was as hungry for him as he was for her.

They were both gasping as they pulled apart.

He unzipped the back of her dress, took hold of the hem and when she lifted her arms, pulled it over her head. It landed beside the bed and was quickly followed by her bra. If she cared that her clothes were just being thrown on the floor, she didn't show it.

As she slowly moved up and down on him, his hands and mouth were all over her, savouring the taste of her. Being with her felt so right, so natural. What he was feeling was more than just physical and he found himself wishing he could remember her.

He still wanted more, so he placed his arms around her and shuffled as far to the side as he could. Then he rolled her over so he was on top.

As he made love to her, he kept kissing her. He couldn't get enough of her. She ran her fingernails down his back, making him cry out in pleasure. Her voice soon joined his as her hands found his buttocks and encouraged him to go deeper.

When it was over, they both collapsed onto the bed, worn out and sweating. He rolled over to look at her and gently ran his hand down her face. How could he have not found her attractive when she walked in? She was the most beautiful woman he had ever seen.

They said nothing, they just held each other. She settled down against his chest and he stroked her hair. Soon her breathing slowed and he knew she was asleep. Still he held her. He didn't want to let her go.

Eventually he slid off the bed and found a blanket to cover her naked body. He put on his clothes and then uncovered the camera. He wanted whoever was watching to see that he hadn't hurt her. He had no idea why it mattered to him, but it did.

He sat on a nearby counter and watched her breathe. He had no idea who she was or what she was to him. All he knew was that he felt this overwhelming desire to protect her.

How long he watched her for, he didn't know, but he eventually came to a decision. He slid off the counter and unlocked the door. He then moved to the centre of the room, held his arms out to show he wasn't armed and looked up at the camera.

"Come and get me. I'm prepared to listen to what you have to say."

Truth

To say Carl was angry was an understatement. First Amy locked the door, preventing them from rescuing her, should the need arise. Then she revealed that Garrick still had weapons on him. He was going to have a few words with the Agents who were supposed to have searched him. Then Amy blocked the camera and from the sounds coming from his computer, he could understand why.

He didn't know if she had released Garrick's restraints when he asked her to, but something told him that she had. If Garrick hurt her in any way, Carl would never be able to forgive himself. Neither would Garrick, when he eventually got his memory back. He should never have allowed her in that room.

"Stop pacing," Nadia snapped at him. "I'm just as worried as you are. If I thought she was going to be that stupid, I would never have suggested we let her see him."

"He won't hurt her," Lawrence said.

Carl glared at him. "You don't know that."

"I know Garrick and even without his memory, he won't be able to do anything to her. He's just not that sort of man."

"I wish I knew what was going on in there."

After a few cries, which were definitely not the sounds made by someone in pain, all had gone quiet.

"Can we move the camera to try and dislodge her clothing which is blocking it?" Nadia asked, but Carl shook his head.

"It's in a fixed position. We can't move it remotely."

"There's movement," Lawrence said and pointed at the screen, which clearly showed Garrick stepping away from the camera, Amy's cardigan in his hand. Amy was on the bed. Though she had her back to them and was covered up, they could clearly see her chest moving in and out as she breathed.

"She appears to be sleeping," Nadia said with relief.

"Now what's he doing?" Lawrence asked as Garrick sat on the counter, his eyes on Amy.

"Watching her," Carl said. "And thinking. I'd bet my life that he's no longer sure that Lewis told him the truth."

"Are you going to talk to him?"

Carl shook his head. "Not yet. Firstly, I don't know how he will react if I wake Amy. Secondly, he needs time to process everything."

"What do you think he is going to do?" Nadia asked.

Carl shrugged. "I guess we will have to wait and see."

Garrick made them wait a long time. Not once did his eyes move to his knives on the table. They never left Amy.

Once it was clear that nothing was happening, Carl, Lawrence and Nadia took turns watching the screen. Lawrence went to make coffee for them all and was just walking back into the room when Nadia announced that Garrick was moving.

They watched him unlock the door. Carl was tempted to order the guards he had stationed outside to go in and put Garrick in handcuffs, but he held off giving the order.

Garrick then demonstrated he wasn't armed, looked at the camera and announced that he was ready to talk.

"You heard the man," Carl said. "Let's go and talk to him."

Carl was nervous as he walked down the corridor. While Garrick was appearing to be reasonable, it could be a trap. If given the chance, he could easily overpower a number of Agents and Carl still had Amy's welfare to think about, despite the fact that Garrick hadn't hurt her and showed no sign that he would.

They arrived at the door and Carl called out before opening it. Garrick was back on the counter, looking at Amy once more. She was still sleeping.

"Who is she?" Garrick asked as Carl walked into the room.

"I'll tell you all about Amy later. First let's get you to one of our meeting rooms."

"An interrogation room, you mean."

"No. We're not going to interrogate you. There's nothing we want from you."

The look Garrick gave him told Carl he didn't believe him, but he slid off the counter anyway. He looked at Amy once more.

"Will someone stay with her? I don't want her to be alone when she wakes up."

"I'll stay," Nadia said.

Carl held up some handcuffs. "Do I need to use these?"

Garrick shook his head and then turned around and placed his arms behind his back, positioning himself so Carl would easily put them on him if he wished to.

"Come on," Carl said and put the cuffs back into his pocket.

Garrick followed Carl out of the room and Lawrence and two armed guards fell into step behind them.

"That's not necessary, you know," Garrick said and Carl ordered them to stand down. He figured Garrick would be able to overpower them anyway and he didn't want him able to get his hands on any weapons. His own gun was hidden from view, as was Lawrence's.

He led Garrick to one of their more comfortable meeting rooms and told him to take a seat on one of sofas. Garrick sat down, but he didn't seem relaxed.

Between them, Carl and Lawrence told him everything about Amy, who and what she was, how they met, how she had been controlled, temporarily, by werewolves to attack the Agency. They left nothing out, not even how Nadia tried to come between them.

Garrick's eyes filled with concern. "Is she safe with her?"

"Yes. They've worked out their differences."

"I wish I could remember her."

"You will," Lawrence said, but Carl wasn't so sure. The memory loss might be permanent. He hoped not, but it was a possibility.

They then told Garrick about himself, including how Tabitha had died.

"Are you telling me that I have been living with her killer for the last few days?" His voice was so cold, it made Carl shiver.

"Unfortunately yes."

"And an Agent killed him?" Carl nodded. "I don't suppose you know a way of bringing him back to life so I can kill him again, do you?"

Carl couldn't help smiling. "I wish there was a way. Believe me, I wish there was."

"All that matters is that Lewis is dead," Lawrence said. "Now does anything we told you ring a bell?"

Both men had been hoping that the information would trigger something, but Garrick just shook his head.

They went on to tell him about the Agency and his job as an Agent. They showed him videos of his chats with some rogue werewolves and of him willingly being given the serum made from werewolf blood.

He said it removed his doubt about who was telling the truth, but did nothing to help him remember.

"Maybe a tour of the base," Carl suggested and the three men went to every room on every level. Many people greeted Garrick and said they were glad he was back, but he recognised none of them.

They returned to the meeting room and Garrick sat with his head in his hands. Carl could understand how frustrated he must be feeling.

"Is there anything else we can try? Can your medical experts give me electric shock therapy or something?"

"Nothing that will work."

Garrick banged his fist against the arm of the sofa. "There must be something."

"There is," Lawrence said. "But it's risky."

Carl immediately knew what Lawrence was going to suggest.

"No. It's too dangerous."

"Surely that's my decision to make," Garrick said. "Tell me."

Lawrence looked at Carl, seeking permission. Carl couldn't help thinking he should have done that before saying anything, but he nodded his head anyway. Garrick was right; it was his decision to make.

"One thing we didn't tell you is that werewolves can enter each other's minds. Not only can they read their thoughts and their memories, but they can also force them to do things against their will. When we captured some of Lia's gang—"

Garrick interrupted before Lawrence could finish his sentence. "Who's Lia?"

The two men quickly filled him in. He then said Lawrence could continue.

"It seems like Lia had implanted an order in the minds of some of her followers to kill themselves if they were ever captured by us. The rest she prevented from telling us anything about herself. We know nothing, what she looks like, where she lives, what her full name is. Nothing."

Garrick quickly put two and two together. "So because I have werewolf blood in me, werewolves can get into my head. Isn't that kind of risky?"

"It would be if it wasn't for the chain you wear."

Lawrence took his out from below his shirt and showed it to Garrick. Garrick did the same, checking that they were identical. "Go on."

"This keeps werewolves out. We can explain how later. Take yours off and I can reach your mind."

Garrick, who had been leaning forward, relaxed back, though the tension didn't leave his body.

"You want to go into my head and try to trigger my memory internally."

"Something like that."

"You'll be able to see all of my memories?"

"Yes."

Garrick raised his eyebrows. "That's a lot to think about. What are the dangers?"

"If I trigger in the wrong way, your brain might overload and completely shut down."

Garrick said nothing. Neither did Carl or Lawrence. They gave him the time he needed to process what he had been told. It wasn't going to be an easy decision to make. If he was in Garrick's position, Carl didn't think he would even contemplate it. In his opinion, the risks were far too great and there was no guarantee that it would work. Given the choice between permanent memory loss and potential brain damage, for Carl the choice was easy.

Garrick's lack of reaction suggested it wasn't so easy for him.

"Have you done this before?" Garrick finally asked Lawrence.

"No, but I know someone who has. Twice. Once was successful. The other time, not so much. But if you are going to do this, I recommend you let me try. We've been close friends for years, ever since my son brought home his new army buddy. I already know a lot of what is in your head. Also, I am already privy to most, if not all of the Agency secrets which might be revealed."

Garrick then turned to Carl. "Would you do it?"

Carl didn't hesitate. "No. Definitely not."

He then asked Lawrence the same question. Lawrence took longer to reply, eventually saying, "Probably not."

Carl's phone chose that moment to ring and he told whoever was on the other end of the line where they were. A few moments later, Nadia walked in, closely followed by Amy.

Carl was watching Garrick closely. He saw his eyes widen and his pupils slightly dilate. He might not remember her, but she still had the same effect on him. Garrick held out his hand and she went to him. He took hold of her hand and guided her to sit beside him.

Amy looked into his eyes and a trace of sadness filled her face before she had chance to hide it.

"No joy I take it."

"No," Garrick said. "But Lawrence has a suggestion, something which is dangerous but we should consider giving it a try."

"We?"

Garrick smiled at her. "I have the distinct feeling this is something I should run by you before making a decision."

Lawrence then filled her in on his suggestion. He didn't try to gloss over the dangers, nor the fact that it might not work.

"What do you think?" Garrick asked when he had finished.

"This isn't something I know anything about," Amy said. "And it's not my mind we are talking about. I'll support you whatever decision you make."

Garrick looked at each person in turn before his eyes fell on Lawrence. He couldn't believe what he was about to say. So much could go wrong, but he had to try.

"Let's do this."

Recall

Garrick and Lawrence were alone in the room; the others were watching from Carl's office. Lawrence had said he didn't want any distractions and sent them away.

Garrick was nervous, but he was doing his best not to show it. He glanced up at the camera in the corner of the room to assure himself that Amy was watching.

"Are you ready?" Lawrence asked him.

Of course he wasn't ready. How could anyone be ready to have their mind entered and manipulated?

He nodded his head, worried that if he spoke his voice would shake.

"Then take your chain off." As soon as he said the words, Lawrence looked up at the camera. "We may have a problem. What if he can't undo it?"

"We'll give Kenny a call," Carl's voice said.

"Who's Kenny?" Garrick asked.

"The man who makes all of the chains and pendants this branch of the Agency wear. Other than the wearer, he's the only one who knows how to undo them."

"Interesting," Garrick said then pulled his chain from under his t-shirt and took the pendant in his hand. Instinct took over and a few small manipulations caused the pendant to open and the chain to undo. He placed it on the table almost reluctantly. For some reason he couldn't explain, he didn't want to let it go.

"I understand how you feel," Lawrence said as he smiled at him. "An Agent is never without his chain. Neither am I."

"Let's get this over and done with. What do you want me to do?"

"Nothing. Just relax. I'll do everything."

'Relax!' Garrick thought to himself. How was he supposed to relax? Just removing his chain made him tense.

He took a couple of deep breaths, forcing the tension from his taut muscles.

"Will this hurt?" he asked.

"I have no idea."

That wasn't the answer he was hoping for, but it was too late to change his mind now; his pride wouldn't let him.

Lawrence asked him if he was ready and he nodded his head. He wasn't, but he was never going to be.

Lawrence then placed his hands on either side of Garrick's head and told him to look into his eyes. As he did so, they changed colour, going from green to a bright red. Garrick found them fascinating. He could see different shades, which moved and interacted with each other.

He felt something trying to reach his mind. It was like tickling but without the actual sensation. He instinctively tried to block it.

"Relax," Lawrence said. "Let me in. I can force my way in but I'd rather not if I don't have to."

Garrick tried to do as he had been asked, but found he couldn't. He willed himself to drop the mental barrier that he didn't even realise he had put in place, but was unable to do so.

"I guess we do this the hard way, then," Lawrence said.

Garrick felt something pushing against his mind, forcing its way in. It was so swift and sudden, even if he did know how to stop it, he wouldn't have been able to. He cried out in shock. It wasn't painful, but the sensation was far from pleasant.

Then everything went numb. He couldn't feel any connection to his body. He tried to move his arm, but failed. He tried to move his eyes away from Lawrence's, but they were held in place. Then his vision started to blur and he could no longer focus on anything.

"Breathe, Garrick."

Garrick didn't know he was holding his breath until Lawrence spoke. He slowly forced the air out of his lungs before allowing them to fill up again.

Other than the sound of his own breathing, the room was silent. If Lawrence was breathing, Garrick couldn't tell. Images formed in his mind, unbidden. He was in the room with Carl and Lawrence, being told the truth about himself. Then he was on the bed with Amy, making love to her. Next he was in the hotel room, talking with Lewis. He relived every conversation, every action. All of the lies he had been told he was forced to rehear, only this time they sounded different, less convincing.

He watched Lewis turning into a wolf. Then he was running beside him, going at speeds no human should have been able to accomplish.

He was living his life in reverse and he assumed Lawrence was seeing all of it.

Next he was in Lewis's house, waking up with rubble all around him and over him. A jolt of agony shot through his head and he cried out, in surprise more than pain.

Then everything went black.

"I've gone back as far as the house collapsing," Lawrence said. "I think I managed to reach the point when he received the head trauma but I've hit a barrier."

Garrick wasn't sure if he was talking to him or those who were listening in.

"Can you break through?" he heard Carl say, his voice sounding oddly robotic as it came through the PA system.

"I can try, but it's risky. I may cause permanent damage."

"Do it," Garrick said. He hadn't agreed to this just to give up at the first hurdle.

Something hit him. It felt like he was being hit repeatedly by a hammer, but on the inside of his skull, not the outside. He wanted to close his eyes, to shut it out, but whatever hold Lawrence had on him wouldn't let him.

As the hammering increased, so did the pain. His body began to shake as he tried to deal with it. Sharp spikes kept slamming into his brain, continuously, over and over, always in the same spot. He felt like his mind was going to explode. Finally he could take no more and let out the scream he had been holding back.

It made no difference. The onslaught continued. He screamed over and over, no longer aware of anything other than the continual jolts of agony.

He thought he heard Amy crying out, begging Lawrence to stop, but he couldn't be sure it was real.

Just as he thought he was going to pass out, something broke. Whatever had been keeping Lawrence out, shattered, sending out shock waves all through his head.

"Take it easy," he clearly heard Lawrence say. "Breathe in and out, slowly and deeply. Get your body back under control."

The shaking eased as he concentrated on regulating his breathing. He found he was able to move once more, except for his eyes. They remained locked on Lawrence's. He wondered how the other man managed to keep them open for so long without blinking.

"I've broken through the barrier," Lawrence said. "I just hope I haven't done any physical damage."

Garrick tried to remember past the building collapse, but found he was still unable to do so. He could feel panic rising up inside him. Had he been through all of this for nothing?

"Why can't I remember anything?"

"It's okay," Lawrence said calmly. "Whatever was holding your memories prisoner is gone, but they are still in hiding. I'm going to have to coax them out. Are you ready?"

Garrick nodded.

He felt a sensation inside his head again, but this time it was probing, gently touching instead of forcing its way in.

An image formed in his mind of a woman's face looking down at him. She was making cooing noises. He could feel his fingers gripping one of hers, but it felt enormous. Then it struck him; he was a baby. This woman must have been his mother, but he didn't recognise her.

More images swarmed in. A man with a full beard and friendly eyes, dressed in workman's clothes. His father?

Next he was looking down at a baby in a crib. Something told him this was his sister.

Moments from his childhood played out for him as he slowly aged. He knew now that the two people he had seen were indeed his parents. He knew their names. He knew who Tabitha was. He heard his family calling him Garrick and he knew, beyond a shadow of a doubt, that that was who he was. He wasn't Tony. He was Garrick and always had been.

He saw school friends and could recall each of their names. Girlfriends came and went. His first sexual experience wasn't anything to write home about, but he improved over time.

He relived his time in the army, seeing fighting and things he wished he could permanently forget. He became friends with Lawrence's son and then attended his funeral. Lawrence recruited him into the Agency and he witnessed again his first werewolf transformation.

Memories flooded through him. Too many, all at once. And with them came his feelings, his emotions. He went from happiness, to anger, sadness, frustration. They went from one to the other so quickly he couldn't keep up.

He had no idea when Lawrence sat back, but he was no longer sitting in front of him, he could no longer feel his hands on his head.

Still the memories came, consuming him, making him relive them. His breathing became fast and shallow. He wasn't sure he could cope with much more. The onslaught of images and emotions was unbearable. He felt like screaming again, but fought against it. He closed his eyes, not wishing Lawrence to see in them what he couldn't hide.

Then Amy appeared, on the bus, the first time he saw her. Everything slowed down, allowing him to re-experience the moment, not that he had realised at the time that it even was a moment.

Every feature of her face was stored in his memory in minute detail. He didn't know, until he relived it, that he had taken such an interest in her.

He skipped forward to being in her house, making friends with
Ainin. He watched her try to run away, feeling again the amusement he had felt then at such a futile attempt to escape.

The days skipped by, going from one encounter with her to the next. He smiled at her stubbornness, her refusal to believe she was part-werewolf. The way she came on to him when she had the implant in her and his body responded as it had then. He felt once more the realisation that he cared for her, that he wanted her.

He was no longer feeling overwhelmed. Instead he relished every memory as it returned, feeling once again what it was like to kiss her for the first time, to feel his lips against hers, to touch her, to hold her.

Then they were in the UK and she was running away, running from him and Nadia. He felt a surge of anger before helplessness consumed him. Then he found her and the joy returned.

Just as he was enjoying his memories, he got the phone call about Tabitha. Once more he carried her coffin and vowed he would kill Lewis.

Well, Lewis was now dead. Not by his hand, but that didn't really matter.

When he opened his eyes once more, Lawrence was looking at him, a questioning look on his face.

He looked up at the camera in the corner of the room and smiled.

"I know who I am."

Revelation

Two weeks after Garrick had his memories restored, Lia was getting frustrated. She had informed Derek of Lewis's demise and had been told to await instructions.

She was still waiting.

She longed to recruit, to rebuild her division of the resistance, but she had been told not to. She felt useless. She was a great asset, but wasn't being allowed to accomplish anything.

And on top of that, Amy and Garrick were getting closer and closer. It was making her sick. It wasn't that she wanted Garrick, after all he was an Agent, but she felt it was wrong that a mere half-breed should be so happy.

Her phone was sitting on the table and she heard it vibrate, indicating she had received a text message.

She almost ignored it. She wasn't in the mood for dealing with anyone, not even Derek. She was fed up with being at his beck and call with nothing to show for it.

In the end curiosity got the better of her and she read it. She was so surprised by the content, she sat up straight and had to re-read it.

It was from Derek. He was in town and wanted, no demanded, to meet. It was as good a time as any so she called him and arranged a place. It was a park, somewhere where it wouldn't seem odd for people to be, but at that time of the evening offered relative privacy.

He was waiting for her when she got there, and he was not alone. More than two dozen men and women were with him.

It wasn't the first time she had met him, but her memories of him had been wiped. However, there was no mistaking which one he was. He was sitting alone on a bench while the others were keeping a respectful distance.

He was nothing like she had been expecting. His deep voice had her picturing a tall, attractive, fit and lean man of about mid-to-late thirties. The man she was looking at was short, for a male, and could do with losing some weight. He must have been at least fifty, judging by his greying hair.

And he was not an attractive man. His big nose dominated his face and his eyebrows were so bushy they made his eyes almost invisible at first glance. You had to look twice before you noticed them.

"Lia," he said as she approached, standing up to greet her. "It's good to see you again."

The glow of the streetlamp gave his skin and the whites of his eyes a yellow tinge, making him look like he was suffering from jaundice.

She shook his hand and took a seat next to him when he sat down and indicated that she should do so.

"I'm sorry to have left you in the dark for so long, but I was busy making plans for around the country and around the world. It wasn't an easy thing to pull off, attacking so many Agency bases at once, and since then, we have been working on a second wave of attacks."

"Which is why you're here," Lia said. She had made a statement, not posed a question, but Derek still nodded his head. "You're going to attack here."

Again Derek nodded. "Not just here. We are primed to hit locations all over the world. Many more than last time."

"Why? What good will it do? All that happened last time was a number of Agents were killed. Every base you attacked is up and running again and all probably now have extra security."

Derek smiled at her. "Because this time, we are going to get into their computer systems. Gain access to one and we can gain access to all. We can find out the names and addresses of every werewolf across the globe who is helping the Agency by supplying them with blood. We know that in some parts of the world, the Agency isn't as ethical as they claim to be. We have been aware for a long time that in certain countries werewolves are being held prisoner and their blood forcefully extracted. We want to know where they are being held and rescue them."

The conviction and enthusiasm in his voice was contagious, but Lia still had her doubts. They had failed to gain access to the computer system in any location they attacked last time, so what made him think this time would be any different? The resistance had discovered that as soon as any base was attacked, it was Agency policy to set a program running that changed all passwords to one known by only one or two people. Even if they did manage to capture someone alive and torture them enough to login in, they wouldn't be able to, unless it was one of those entrusted people and they would never let themselves be captured alive.

Lia almost asked how Derek planned on accomplishing his mission, but stopped herself before the words formed. He wasn't going to tell her. Especially not out in the open where the others could overhear. She very much doubted any of those present knew full details.

"When do we attack?" she asked instead.

"That, my dear, is down to you. There is one or two small things I need you to do for me first."

He looked around him at the assembled gathering. "Ladies and gentlemen, I would like to introduce you to Lia. Not only is she going to get us inside the Agency's headquarters here, but also into their computer systems."

A smile formed on Lia's face. She knew exactly what he was planning on doing and she couldn't wait to do her part.

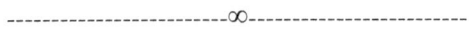

Garrick's phone rang, but he ignored it. He was in the middle of making plans with Carl. There had been an influx of rogue werewolves. Too many Agents were spotting them, but these new arrivals were skillful and experienced in evading capture. Something was brewing, but they had no idea what or when or where.

"From now on, no Agent goes out alone. That includes you," Carl said. Garrick rolled his eyes.

"I mean it," Carl continued. "After what happened in other cities, we can't afford to take any risks."

"You think they're planning an attack then."

"Of course they are planning an attack, but will it be an all-out assault, or will they decide to pick off individual Agents?"

Garrick's phone rang again and he glanced at it. Seeing that it was Amy, he answered.

"I'm really sorry to bother you, but I've had a fall while taking Ainin for a walk. A man who saw me claims to be a doctor and thinks I may have broken my wrist and is recommending I go to hospital and get an x-ray."

"Where are you?" Garrick asked. "I'll be there as soon as I can."

Amy told him she wasn't far from home and would meet him there.

"This can wait," Carl said, having overheard what Amy had said. "Go. I'll get back to trying to locate Tom."

Garrick had remembered that Tom had met him at Lewis's house and wanted to speak to him about what had happened, but nobody could find him. He had disappeared and locating him had become the Agency's number one priority. Garrick wasn't the only one concerned for Tom's safety.

Garrick drove fast. Amy wasn't seriously injured, but a broken bone could still be painful and you never knew when complications could set in.

By the time he arrived, she had wrapped her wrist in a bandage. She winced when he unwrapped it. It was badly swollen. He had seen a few injured wrists before and although it didn't feel like it was broken, it was a good idea to get it checked out.

He wanted to take her to the medics at headquarters, but they didn't have x-ray equipment, so he drove her to the nearest hospital and had Carl make a few calls so she was seen quickly. The doctor who examined her sent her for x-rays, telling Garrick to go to the waiting room.

Unable to settle, he paced the room. He was getting angry glares from others who were waiting and forced himself to take a seat.

When Amy returned, she was crying. He took her in his arms. "What's wrong?"

"My chain's gone," she managed to say through her sobbing. "The one you gave me."

He didn't need to be told which one she was talking about. He had only ever given her one chain and that had been at headquarters. If she wasn't wearing it, it meant she was vulnerable to werewolves. Given the number of rogue wolves who had been spotted, it wasn't a good time to be unprotected.

"I had to remove all jewellery for the x-ray and when I got my things back, everything was there except the chain and pendant."

"It's alright," he said as he held her tight. "We'll go straight to headquarters and get you another one."

He pulled away from her and dried her tears with his hand. As he walked her to his car, he asked about her wrist. She informed him that it wasn't broken so she just needed to keep it strapped up and try not to use it for a few days.

By the time they reached their destination, Amy had calmed down.

Mack was on duty and greeted them both.

"Does he live here?" Amy asked as they took the lift down to the floor they wanted. "Or does he just have no social life?"

Garrick chuckled. "It's just coincidence he's always here when you are. He's a happily married man. He married his partner as soon as gay marriage became legal. They have two young children via a surrogate."

"Oh." Garrick chuckled again when Amy blushed.

When they got to Kenny's workroom, there was a sign on the door saying he was out to lunch.

"I guess we come back later," Garrick said and led Amy back to the lift. "Are you hungry?" Amy shook her head. "Let's wait in my office then. I'm sure he won't be long."

Amy had just taken a seat behind Garrick's desk when an alarm went off.

"What's that?" she asked.

Garrick thought about lying to her, but decided to tell her the truth. "We're under attack."

Amy didn't have chance to respond. Carl ran into the room.

"There are werewolves in the building."

He wasn't panicking. Given the situation, it would have been understandable if he was, but he was his usual calm self.

Garrick asked Amy to move out of the way before he switched on his computer. He brought up the images from the security cameras in main reception.

He counted nearly two dozen intruders. Some were in wolf form. Those that weren't were heavily armed. Bodies lay everywhere. He could see Mack lying on the floor. His throat had been ripped open. Amy was looking over his shoulder at the carnage.

"Jesus," she said.

Three pairs of eyes watched as a werewolf took Mack's ID badge and tried to open the door which led to the lifts.

Garrick looked at Carl. "Have you run the program to change all passwords and disable everyone's access to the system and the security doors and lifts?"

Carl nodded. "As soon as the alarm sounded and I saw what was going on. You and me are the only ones who can get in now."

"Good." He then looked Carl up and down. He didn't appear to be armed. "Go grab your gun. I'll meet you by the lifts."

Carl ran off and Garrick locked the screen on his computer before looking at Amy. "Stay here. Lock the door behind me."

She was trembling. "I'm not wearing a necklace. If a werewolf finds me they'll be able to read my mind and control me."

Garrick pulled out his chain and took hold of the pendant. He released the chain and placed it around Amy's neck and did it up again.

"I have a spare in my locker. I'll grab it on my way to the top floor."

"I don't think so."

Garrick backed away in horror as Amy's face changed. It didn't metamorphosise like when a werewolf changed form. Her hair, nose, eyes, ears, everything was still the same, but the look on her face was one he had never seen before and one he never thought he would, not on Amy, anyway. It made her look like a completely different person. Even her voice sounded different.

"Hello, Garrick," she said. "It's nice to finally meet you. You've been looking for me for a long time."

"Who are you?" Garrick asked. He was beyond confused. Amy, the woman he loved, was standing in front of him, but she wasn't Amy, she was someone else.

Laughter filled the room. It was almost manic. It wasn't the sort of laugh he would have expected to come from Amy's body.

"Haven't you worked it out by now? I'm Lia."

Armageddon

Garrick couldn't breathe. The werewolf he had been searching for for months was standing in front of him and she was Amy? His brain couldn't work out what was happening.

Then he realised that he had given her his pendant and that he was unprotected. A feeling of dread settled in his stomach. And Lia knew he and Carl were the only two with the password for the computer systems.

He looked into her eyes and shivered before looking away. Lia was inhabiting Amy's body. There was no sign of Amy there at all.

Lia tapped him on the cheek. "Now be a good boy and open the door so my friends can join us."

He shook his head. If the werewolves got into the complex, they would slaughter everyone. He wouldn't do it. No matter what Lia threatened, he wouldn't do it.

She grabbed hold of his face with both hands and forced him to look at her. He tried to put up mental barriers, but Lia cut through them as though they were paper. Without his pendant, there was nothing he could do to prevent her forcing her way into his mind.

He struggled to pull away from her, but she was too strong for him. He had fought werewolves before and sometimes he won, sometimes he lost, but Lia made them seem like wimps. There was nothing he could do. She had control of him and he had no way of escaping. His only hope was that Carl or another Agent would find them and kill him.

"You will do everything I say," Lia said.

He felt the command sink into him and take control of him. It would always be there, in the back of his mind, ready to activate whenever Lia opened her mouth. At least until the serum he regularly took wore off.

He drew his gun and put it to his head, but she called out, "Stop," before he could shoot. His hand froze, his finger on the trigger. Sweat poured from his forehead as he fought for control of himself. He tried, desperately, to tense his finger, to pull back that little piece of metal which could put an end to his life, but he tried in vain.

Lia was watching him in amusement. "Put the gun away and log on to your computer."

He obeyed. He didn't have a choice.

He felt like screaming as he sat down in front of his laptop and entered his password to reopen the view from the cameras.

Lia sat on the table next to him and stroked his hair as if he was her pet. It made him feel sick and he knocked her hand away, making her laugh once more.

"Now open the door."

He opened the correct screen and clicked on the button which would remotely open the door to the lifts. The werewolves may be in the building, but they wouldn't be able to get to any of the floors, not unless they forced their way into the fire stairs. The lifts were locked down.

Lia must have known this because she then ordered him to release them. He watched as invaders entered the lifts and selected every floor.

Carl ran into the room and Garrick knew what he would see: Amy sitting on the desk beside him, both watching the screen. He would have no idea it was Lia.

"How the hell did they get through the security door?" he yelled. He hadn't figured out that it was Garrick who had opened it. "Are they in the lifts now?"

Garrick turned to him, doing nothing to hide the horror he was feeling, both for what he was being forced to do and for what he knew was going to happen next.

"Run," he shouted but Carl just stared at him, not understanding the warning. Garrick wanted to get his friend out of harm's way, despite knowing that it was already too late.

All he could do was watch as Carl's eyes fell on Amy and he went pale. She was grinning manically.

"Kill him," she purred and Garrick pulled his gun and shot Carl in the head.

Before his body hit the floor, Garrick dropped his gun and ran over to him. He wanted to tell him he was sorry, but Carl was already dead. Tears filled his eyes as he took his lifeless body into his arms.

"Enough," Lia snapped. "You can grieve later. Right now I want you to find some information for me. I want the name and address of every werewolf who is working with the Agency. Then I want the details of every Agent worldwide, every scientist, every admin person. Hell, I even want to know where I can find the tea lady, if you have one. And then I want to know who your leaders are."

If Garrick did as she asked, it was going to be mass murder. Every employee of the Agency would be hunted down. But Lia hadn't finished.

"And then I want to know the location of every single one of your prisons. Worldwide."

It would be the end of the Agency. The end of werewolves being able to control when they changed. Humans would become nothing more than prey.

Garrick had never felt despair before, but now it consumed him. It was going to be Armageddon and he began praying that he wouldn't be around to see it. He hoped against hope that Lia would kill him as soon as he had given her what she wanted, but something told him he wouldn't be that lucky.

He didn't even try to not obey her; it would do no good. When he had found the files she wanted, he moved away from the computer. Why the Agency kept all personnel information in a place accessible from any location instead of putting in security walls between countries, he had no idea, but it was going to be their downfall.

Screams could be heard coming down the corridor. Lia's friends had reached the floor they were on.

He watched helplessly as Lia inserted a memory key and opened a file on it. It contained email addresses, which she then used to create an email. She couldn't find a way to download the employee files, so she just cut and pasted the details. The names and addresses of every person and werewolf who worked for the

Agency were soon winging their way around the world. Every major city would soon see an uprising, the likes of which the world had never witnessed before.

And it was all his fault. If he hadn't given Amy his chain and pendant, none of this would be happening. Amy? Lia? Was there a difference? How had she fooled him so completely?

A man Garrick had never seen before sauntered into the room. His gun was drawn, pointed at Garrick and he hoped he would pull the trigger.

"It looks like your plan worked," Lia said when she saw who had arrived. "I have sent all of the information you asked for to all email addresses. It's just a matter of time before the rest of the resistance destroys the Agency."

Then she looked at Garrick. "Garrick, meet Derek, my boss and the mastermind behind this attack. Derek, meet Garrick. Don't worry, he's completely under my control."

"He doesn't seem very happy about it," Derek said, then laughed. He walked up to Lia and kissed the top of her head. "I knew you could do it." He gestured toward Garrick with his head. "Does he know?"

"Not yet."

"Then take him to one of the interrogation rooms they claim aren't interrogation rooms. I'm sure he's dying to know everything. I can take care of things here."

"Can I keep him?" Lia asked. The question made Garrick's blood go cold.

"You can do anything you want with him now that he's given us access to everything we need."

"Thank you," Lia said sweetly, then ordered Garrick to follow her.

She led him to a meeting room and took a seat on the sofa, telling Garrick to do the same. He put as much distance between them as he could.

"If it makes you feel any better, Amy doesn't know I exist."

Joy filled him, which was strange, given the situation. Amy, his Amy, the woman he loved, wasn't part of what was going on.

"Explain." Garrick wanted to speak to Lia as little as possible, but he was desperate to know the truth.

Lia leaned back and put her feet up on the table. "Get yourself comfortable. This is going to be a long story."

Garrick ignored her.

Lia shrugged. "Suit yourself. I supposed you could say that Amy and I are two personalities who inhabit the same body. I think the term is split personality disorder. I know all about Amy and witness everything she does. And God how I hate her. Even though she doesn't know I exist, she keeps getting in my way, doing things like insisting on wearing a blindfold whenever she went to visit Lawrence and his family. It hasn't done much good though, has it? Soon they will all be dead, even that brat they adopted. Unless, of course, we think we can undo the brainwashing she has been subjected to."

Garrick reacted without thinking, going for her throat, but she stopped him before he could lay a finger on her.

"Now that wasn't very nice. You will not try to harm me in any way, ever again."

Garrick growled. Her instruction might have stopped him acting, but it wouldn't stop him imagining cutting her throat. But it was Amy's throat as well. He was suddenly glad that Lia had stopped him. Maybe Amy was still alive.

"Now, where was I? Oh yes. I have lived in Amy's body from the very beginning, though I couldn't take control of it until she reached adulthood. Have you any idea what it's been like, being trapped inside a body but not being able to communicate or control the body? It was torture and I had to suffer it for years."

Garrick didn't feel sorry for her. Nothing she told him could make him feel anything for her other than contempt.

"I had to watch as Amy enjoyed herself, doing things I hated, being with people I detested, eating food I couldn't stand. I cannot begin to describe the joy I felt when I was finally able to take control. I soon learned that Amy had no memory of what happened while I had control of her body. I could do anything I wanted and she would never know. I may have human blood in me, but I've always known that I'm a werewolf. I may, technically, only be half-werewolf, but I have the heart of a true werewolf and have always considered myself as one. Unlike Amy. I met with others of my kind and learned how to fight and how to perfect my skills."

"That explains why bruises kept appearing on her body that she couldn't explain," Garrick said. "She thought she was just clumsy."

"I know what she thought," Lia snapped. "Better than you do. But this isn't about her. This is about me."

"Then by all means, continue," Garrick said, not even attempting to hide his sarcasm.

Lia glared at him. "You will learn to show me more respect." Garrick grunted. "I hate Amy. I always have. She's so weak and pathetic, not even knowing what she is. Then you came along and changed all of that. But did she embrace her werewolf side? No, of course she didn't. Christ, when she was attacked by a man on a bus, I had to take over before she got hurt."

Garrick was a little unnerved to hear that Lia could take over Amy's body whenever she chose to. Did that mean he had sometimes been making love to Lia without knowing? The thought made him feel sick. He vowed never to ask the question just in case he didn't like the answer.

Lia had finished ranting. "Didn't you ever wonder why she was so compliant when you took her hostage at her house or why she agreed to going to see her mother? That was because of me. I was making her stay calm and agree to your demands. I didn't want the idiot doing something which would get us both killed. It was also me that intensified the lust she was feeling for you when she had the implant." She smiled, but it wasn't the sort of smile Garrick was used to seeing on that face. "It feels so good to finally be in control permanently."

Garrick's eyes widened in shock. Did that mean Lia was never going to let Amy out again? What did that mean for Amy? Did she no longer exist?

Lia leaned over and patted him on the cheek. "Don't worry. If you're a good boy, I may let her out occasionally for you to play with."

Garrick pushed her hand away. "Don't touch me. Don't ever touch me." He could barely control his rage.

Lia laughed. "But Garrick, dear, I thought you liked this body having its hands on you."

He wanted to kill her so badly it almost hurt. To try and take his mind off it, he changed the subject. "How did you manage to keep yourself hidden from me? How did you keep in contact with your fellow conspirators without me finding out? Come to think of it, how did you stop Amy finding out? Surely finding strange text messages or calls from her phone to people she doesn't know would start to raise questions."

"It wasn't easy. The more time you spent with Amy, the more frustrating it became. I have a spare phone that Amy never found. It was always on silent when I was Amy instead of me. When Amy was in control, people would leave messages and I would call them back when I took over once more."

"Did Ainin know the difference?" Garrick believed the dog had a lot of intelligence and surely must have seen when Lia was controlling Amy's body.

"He knew. He could sense me somehow and kept away."

"Smart dog," Garrick said. He was fearful for the animal. What would Lia do to him now that she was the one in charge? Werewolves were notorious for hating other animals, especially dogs.

As if she could read his mind, Lia said, "I think I'll keep him around. He's never tried to attack me so I think I will do him the same courtesy."

Garrick released a breath he didn't realise he had been holding.

"Why did you put that implant in Amy? Why not just take over her body when you were here?"

"Because you would have known it wasn't her. You knew the moment I took over her body that something was wrong."

Garrick couldn't argue with that. Lia was right; she was in Amy's body, but somehow still managed to look nothing like her.

"I couldn't figure out how you found us afterward. I thought we had a traitor. Imagine my surprise when I found out about the tracker you put on her. It was smart. Now do you have anything else you want to talk about right now?" Lia asked.

"If I never have to speak to you again, I will die a happy man." Lia might have control of him, but if she thought he was going to play nice with her without her forcing him to, she was going to be deeply disappointed.

She seemed to find his attitude amusing. "Be nice to me and I'll let you spend more time with Amy."

"I would rather you killed me now."

If he had been hoping to annoy her, it didn't work. She smiled as she said, "Your punishment for your belligerence is to tell Amy what has happened."

Then her face changed. It softened and Garrick knew he was looking at Amy, not Lia.

She frowned and looked around her. "How did I get here?"

"You were knocked unconscious. The werewolves have taken over."

He then told her everything. Well, nearly everything. He explained that Lia had arrived and took control of him, making him give her access. He admitted to being forced to kill Carl. Amy was crying by the time he finished. The only thing he didn't mention was that she was Lia. It was information she didn't need to know. He took her in his arms.

"So what happens to us? Why are we still alive?"

He kissed the top of her head. "They are keeping me alive because they think I may still be of some use. They will keep you alive, as extra assurance that I will co-operate. Not that I have a choice seeing as they can get in my head."

"I am so, so sorry," Amy said as she sobbed. "This is all my fault. If I hadn't lost my necklace, none of this would have been possible."

He pulled her tighter to him. "Hush. It's not your fault at all. I think they stole your necklace. They may even have caused your injury somehow, forcing you to get an x-ray and remove it."

He had no doubt that he was telling the truth. All it would have taken was for Lia to take control of Amy's body, just long enough to cause her to fall.

As he held her tight, his thoughts drifted to Lawrence, Rosemary and Nadia. He hoped that Carl had thought to send them a warning, but he had no way of knowing. He wanted to call, them, to tell them to run for their lives, but Lia wouldn't let him. If he tried, she would take over Amy's body and order him to stop, so he didn't even make the attempt. He wouldn't even be able to send them a text. If they were at their own property instead of the Agency house, they might be safe, as the address wasn't recorded anywhere, but how long would it be before Lia forced him to reveal the location? They were as good as dead and there was nothing he could do to stop it.

He wanted to cry, but not in front of Amy.

He kissed her head once more. "It's going to be alright. Somehow we will get free."

As he said the words, he knew that he was lying. Until the serum wore off, he was going to be Lia's plaything. There was no-one coming to rescue them and they would never be free. Nothing would be alright ever again.

From Trudie:

I hope that you enjoyed this book. Please help others have the same opportunity by leaving a review on your favourite platform.